ROTTEN
ENGLISH

Rotten English

A LITERARY ANTHOLOGY

Dohra Ahmad

 W. W. Norton & Company   New York • London

Copyright © 2007 by Dohra Ahmad

For information about permission to reproduce selections from this book, write to permissions, W. W. Norton & Company, Inc., 500 Fifth Avenue, New York, NY 10110

Manufacturing by LSC Harrisonburg
Book design by Dana Sloan
Production manager: Anna Oler

Library of Congress Cataloging-in-Publication Data

Ahmad, Dohra.
    Rotten English : a literary anthology / Dohra Ahmad.
        p. cm.
    Includes bibliographical references.
    ISBN 978-0-393-32960-5 (pbk.)
1. English literature. 2. English-speaking countries—Literary collections. 3. Dialect literature, English. I. Title.
    PR1109.A44 2007
    820.8—dc22

                                                        2007005013

W. W. Norton & Company. Inc.
500 Fifth Avenue, New York, N.Y. 10110
www.wwnorton.com

W. W. Norton & Company Ltd.
15 Carlisle Street, London W1D 3BS

10 9 8 7

To Eliya Sage and Melina Rose

whose languages will always delight me

CONTENTS

SECTION THREE
"I Wanna Say I Am Somebody": Selections from Vernacular Novels

ROTTEN ENGLISH

INTRODUCTION
"THIS IS MA TROOTH"

ONE DAY as I was compiling material for this anthology, I sat in a train station in Jamaica, Queens, reading Paul Keens-Douglas's poem "Wukhand," when an older man sitting next to me began to chuckle. "That's just how we talk back home," he said, pointing at the page. "I never saw it written down before." This collection consists of two and a half centuries of writing that had never been written down before, of authors codifying previously untranscribed speech patterns. Keens-Douglas's poem opens boldly in the voice of a Trinidadian day laborer addressing a potential employer with the plea "Sah, gimme a wuk nah. / Ah looking ole but ah strong." Other selections capture the speech of convicts and child soldiers, bluesmen and housemaids, from Mississippi to Scotland to India. But more than that, *Rotten English* consists of literary works of extraordinary originality, power, and beauty. The poem that amused my train-platform neighbor employs a spectacular range of literary techniques, weaving in direct address, personification, biblical reference, and a good deal of humor. Like Keens-Douglas, all of the other authors included here forge vernacular language into poems, short stories, and novels that captivate readers with their artistry.

What would once have been pejoratively termed "dialect literature" has recently and decisively come into its own. Half of the novels that won the Man Booker Prize over the past twelve

years are in a non-standard English: the British Common-
wealth's most prestigious literary award honors passages like
"It ain't like your regular sort of day" (the opening line of
Graham Swift's *Last Orders*) and "What kind of fucken life is
this?" (the persistent refrain of DBC Pierre's *Vernon God Little*).
The reading public has been just as approving, eagerly devour-
ing works like Alice Walker's *The Color Purple* and Junot Díaz's
Drown. Many vernacular novels, Walker's as well as Roddy
Doyle's *The Commitments*, Irvine Welsh's *Trainspotting*, and Alan
Duff's *Once Were Warriors*, have become acclaimed movies. This
success is by no means limited to fiction; vernacular poetry has
flourished in venues like the Nuyorican Poets Café and HBO's
Def Poetry Jam. The aim of this collection is to represent that literary florescence, along with the earlier works that anticipated
and enabled it. *Rotten English* celebrates the stunningly unan-
ticipated ways in which English has changed as it grew into a
global language.

Before outlining its history, I should explain what I mean
by "vernacular literature" in the first place. What the writers
included here have in common is their choice of composing
in linguistic codes that are primarily spoken rather than written, and also ones that have generally been perceived as having a lower status than Standard English. Those primarily
spoken languages have as many labels as variants: among others, non-standard, dialect, demotic, slang, pidgin, creole, and
patois. Such designations are slippery and politically loaded:
"vernacular," for example, originally referred to the language
of a house slave, but sounds to the modern ear more neutral
than the often derogatory "dialect." I prefer "vernacular" not
only because of that neutrality, but even more so for the wonderful way in which it exemplifies the duality of the phenomenon it describes: from an openly debased slave language, to

a mode associated with avant-garde experimentation and literary prowess. Other writers use different terms. Kamau Brathwaite, the West Indian poet represented here in both the poetry and essay sections, coined "nation language" for the explicit purpose of replacing "dialect." If dialect is the language spoken by caricatures, Brathwaite writes, nation language on the contrary is "an English which is like a howl, or a shout or a machine-gun or the wind or a wave." It is organic, dynamic, confrontational. As far as what to call it, my own favorite formulation comes from the martyred Nigerian writer and environmental activist Ken Saro-Wiwa, whose compelling and heartbreaking *Sozaboy: A Novel in Rotten English* provides the title of this collection. In his introductory note, Saro-Wiwa tells us of his goal to create a hybrid language that "throbs vibrantly enough and communicates effectively"; *Sozaboy*, along with vernacular literature more generally, far surpasses those criteria.

All of the writers in this volume compose in languages that throb vibrantly and communicate more than effectively. They each challenge the hierarchy implied by "dialect" versus "language" or "standard" versus "non-standard," insisting that the codes they practice be recognized for their strength, coherence, and communicative capacity. What we term Standard English, their work reminds us, is after all only one dialect among many—the one that happened to be spoken by the groups of people responsible for compiling dictionaries and assembling grammar manuals. As James Baldwin points out in the essay included here, language functions as "a political instrument, means, and proof of power," and only politics separates a language from a dialect. But whatever the label used, vernacular literature is something we immediately recognize when we see it. It may be easier to define by what it is not: it is not what we learned in school and, as my neighbor in the train station perceived, not something that generally appears in writing. In fact, the term "vernacular literature" is something of an oxymoron, for the very definition of "vernacular" is a native or local language, in specific contrast to a literary one. The works included here derive much of their power—as well as their complexity—from this inherent, and inherently exciting, paradox.

Vernacular authors of our own time are not the first to revolt against an established literary language. Though we experience their works as innovative and fresh, they follow a literary lineage that dates back centuries. When Chaucer wrote his *Canterbury Tales* in Middle English instead of French, when Dante composed in Italian instead of Latin, they too offended prevailing literary sensibilities by using a primarily oral language. These literary revolts then became consolidated into standard forms, so much so that we now take their language completely for granted. Linguists and literary scholars may disagree over how much credit to bestow upon individuals like Chaucer, or Shakespeare after him; but what is clear is that the combination of gifted and popular vernacular writers with print technology promoted the local lingo of one city— London—to an early version of what we now recognize as Standard English. (The Jamaican poet Louise Bennett makes this point brilliantly in her poem "Bans O'Killing," reminding an apocryphal Standard English–enamored listener that "Dah language weh yuh proud o'/ We yuh honour and respeck, / Po' Mass Charlie! Yuh noh know sey / Dat it spring from dialect!")

It is that particular local dialect that British imperialism then exported around the world over the next three hundred years. This volume owes its wide reach to the span of England's empire—and more specifically to the empire's policy of imposing English on its subjects as a language of commerce, education, and governance. In his notorious 1835 "Minute on Indian Education," Thomas Macaulay deemed all Indian languages unfit to convey Western science, and recommended that an intermediary class, "Indian in blood and colour, but English in taste," be trained to disperse Western knowledge to its benighted country folk. That policy was at once a smashing success in reaching its goals—by some estimates a billion people around the world now speak English—and an utter failure in realizing its ultimate objective. For even as the sun never set on the British Empire, it shone as well on increasingly multiplying varieties of the Queen's tongue. Never could Macaulay have anticipated the diversity and richness of what he would undoubtedly have considered "corrupt" versions of English. Over time the formerly colonized people of Africa, Asia, the Caribbean, and the Pacific permanently transformed what Chinua Achebe identifies as "the world language which history has forced down our throats."

The empire dispersed mutating Englishes around the world in three overlapping ways. In settler colonies like the United States, Canada, South Africa, and Australia, the settlers' languages naturally developed in their own directions, as languages always will. In trading colonies like India and Nigeria, pidgins (hybrid jargons that nobody used as a native language) evolved into creoles (naturalized offsprings of pidgins). And across the Caribbean and southern United States, a new West African English emerged as captives arrived on slave plantations, their native languages banned. This was a new mode of communication, born in servitude and incorporating centuries of oral tradition. As M. NourbeSe Philip writes in her innovative poem "Discourse on the Logic of Language," English is the enforced "father tongue" that replaces a lost mother tongue. "I must therefore be tongue dumb," Philip continues, though the beauty of her own writing belies that verdict. It is due to this long and deep legacy of linguistic oppression—and the linguistic subversion it in turn engendered—that writers of the African diasporas appear here more than any other group.

During the eighteenth and nineteenth centuries, two diametrically opposed forces affected the language of English literature. On the one hand, Samuel Johnson and Noah Webster poured their energy into regularizing the fluid and hybrid English language. On the other hand, a whole variety of other Englishes—all that escaped the regularizing impulse—found expression in regional and dialect literatures. Robert Burns wrote in what many saw as a dying variant, Scottish English, thus preserving it in its most euphonious incarnation. In the United States, Mark Twain, Finley Peter Dunne, Paul Laurence Dunbar, Charles Chesnutt, and Joel Chandler Harris recorded the Southern, Irish American, and African American varieties of the American language. George Bernard Shaw (in *Pygmalion*) and Rudyard Kipling (in his *Barrack-Room Ballads* and other Cockney poetry) explored the ways in which speech marked difference in not only race and region, but also class.

The highly self-conscious literary project of Modernism placed the vernacular mode in a still more central position. In their quest for immediacy and vibrancy, Modernist writers of the early twentieth century—James Joyce, William Faulkner, Gertrude Stein, Langston Hughes, and others—held orality as a high virtue. Gertrude Stein, in her experimental work *Three Lives*, attempted to channel German immigrant and African American voices. Langston Hughes incorporated a blues idiom into his highly crafted poems. Zora Neale Hurston put her anthropological training to use both as she collected folklore from rural Florida and as she invented the unforgettable characters of *Their Eyes Were Watching God.* James Joyce's stream of consciousness broke decisively with conventions of Standard English. For many of these writers the act of molding oral expression into literature had an implicitly political aim, notwithstanding Richard Wright's view that the product pandered to a condescending white audience. In the case of Hughes, like Twain and Burns before him, the political content was often explicit: tracking his work over several decades, we can see a decisive shift from "I's gwine to quit my frownin' / And put ma troubles on the shelf" in 1925, to "Lies written down for white folks / Ain't for us a-tall: / *Liberty and Justice*— / Huh!—*For All?*" in 1951.

It was during the anticolonial struggles of the twentieth century that the latent political potential of vernacular literature fully emerged. The "New Englishes" now began to serve a variety of liberatory purposes. If colonialism and its assorted intellectual paraphernalia used English to enforce a deep-seated racial hierarchy, new versions of that same language now disassembled that hierarchy. Shakespeare's Caliban—a recurring figure in the writing of this period—tells his master Prospero that "you taught me language, and my profit on't / Is, I know how to curse." Yet these writers extracted other profits, using the imposed language for more than a howl of protest. As Wole Soyinka writes, anticolonial nationalists adapted the "enslaving medium" of English into an "insurgent weapon." Since politics and culture operate symbiotically, vernacular literature was at once a cause and a result of political decolonization. By the end of the process, in the words of the Barbadian novelist and cultural critic George Lamming, "English is no longer the exclusive language of the men who live in England. That stopped a long time ago." Within the United States as well, writers like Ralph Ellison, Amiri Baraka, and Piri

Thomas used vernacular voices at once to communicate and to bolster the battles for civil rights.

In her poem "Colonization in Reverse," Louise Bennett characterizes this process as "tunabout." Just as her own vernacular writing turns classical poetry on its head, enfranchisement by formerly colonized people can "turn history upside dung." Her diagnosis brings us into the contemporary period, in which non-standard English literature has flourished and proliferated. For even while decolonization resulted in at least nominally independent states, it also brought about the movement of bodies from the global South to the cities of the North. Those many exoduses produced first new vernaculars, and then new vernacular literatures. Bennett, along with Sam Selvon and Linton Kwesi Johnson, writes the lives and language of West Indians in London; Parv Bancil and Gautam Malkani of South Asians in London; M. NourbeSe Philip of West Indians in Toronto; Rohinton Mistry of South Asians in Toronto; Junot Díaz of Dominicans in New York and New Jersey; Oonya Kempadoo of East Indians in the Caribbean; and Shani Mootoo and Sasenarine Persaud of the Indo-Caribbeans who then went on to Canada. Their fiction and poetry demonstrate how immigration has further reversed the top-down process by which culture was imposed during the colonial period: now—in Bennett's words again—the former colonial subjects have come to inhabit and alter "de seat a de Empire."

The model of immigration conveyed here is not one-way but far more complex. Junot Díaz reminds us that the homeland is never fully left behind: every summer "Santo Domingo slaps the diaspora engine into reverse, yanks back as many of its expelled children as it can." We also witness the impact of internal migration. Rohinton Mistry's depiction of a Goan nanny's lonely life in Bombay resonates with the same isolation and linguistic domination we might associate exclusively with international transplantation. Even her name, Jacqueline, mutates into "Jaakaylee" until she begins to identify herself by the bastardized version. Hughes encapsulates the tragedy of internal migration with the four simple lines "When I was home de / Sunshine seemed like gold. / Since I come up North de / Whole damn world's turned cold." Gloria Anzaldúa, adding to the complexity, celebrates the borderland regions for which the term "immigration" is meaningless.

If English itself was always a hybrid language, we now have hybrids of hybrids. Sasenarine Persaud elaborates on Brathwaite's Afro-Caribbean "nation language" to better represent his own Indo-Guyanese experience. Junot Díaz describes two Dominican kids in a Japanese mall in New Jersey as "the only gaijin in the whole joint." In *The Commitments* Roddy Doyle has his recurrent hero Jimmy Rabbitte declare, "The Irish are the niggers of Europe, lads. . . . An' Dubliners are the niggers of Ireland. . . . An' the northside Dubliners are the niggers o' Dublin.—Say it loud, I'm black an' I'm proud." Here we can perceive a global colored consciousness, at once unified and divided by language. Resistance to standardization, as it should, comes in myriad forms.

It is during these most recent decades, roughly from the 1980s to the present, that the gender politics of vernacular literature has begun to shift. With its often shocking and almost never decorous content, vernacular writing had historically been something of a "bad-boy" undertaking; during the anticolonial period it mirrored decolonization at large in being disproportionately male. However, the more recent work of Anzaldúa as well as Alice Walker, Sapphire, M. NourbeSe Philip, and others show how effective this type of writing can be for embodying and addressing explicitly feminist concerns. In

Walker's *The Color Purple,* Celie writes herself out from under an abusive stepfather and domineering husband. Sapphire takes up Walker's mantle in chronicling how literacy enables Precious Jones to survive incest. And as Roddy Doyle's *The Snapper* demonstrates, a male writer too can delve into a beautifully realized female point of view that exposes the many hypocrisies of patriarchy.

I should point out that the vernacular renaissance captured in this volume has by no means been exclusive to English. Hu Shih inaugurated a new literary tradition by breaking with classical Chinese. Latin America has changed the sound of Spanish. Russian writers continue to experiment with "mat," a filthy slang that some legislators have attempted to ban. Faiza Guene, with *Kiffe Kiffe Demain,* is only the most recent of the many writers of North African and Caribbean descent who have offered analogous challenges to academy French. None of these parallel movements in other languages appear in this volume because of my emphasis on the artistic contributions of the writers who have transformed English in particular.

Indeed, my main objective in compiling these works together is to show how they function in terms of artistic technique. None of these are manifestos, which argue for acceptance without offering solid examples of their artistry. Nor are they mere transcriptions of existing speech codes, as reviewers too often describe them. On the contrary, their apparent directness and accessibility is deceptive. The label of "authentic," usually intended as highest praise for a piece of vernacular writing, is a red herring. It can lead us to confuse an author with her or his characters, and thus to overlook the creative process involved. Among the possible models of artistic creation—from invention (generally perceived as an active process), to channeling (generally perceived as passive), to transcription (even more passive)—critics often mistakenly characterize vernacular writing as either of the latter. There are of course multiple cases to the contrary. Writers like Rohinton Mistry, a Canadian Indian man who writes here as a Goan woman, and Sam Selvon, an Indo-Trinidadian who assembles a whole range of Afro-Caribbean characters, present the most obvious challenges to a demeaning ethnographical reading. Further, every one of these authors is a master of code-switching. Their works negotiate among various modes of communication; many, like Paul Laurence Dunbar and Claude McKay among others, composed other works in more formal registers; and they themselves have had to negotiate the Standard English–dominated worlds of publishing and publicity. Each has, to a greater or lesser degree, functioned as part of Macaulay's intermediary class—though by no means toward the end Macaulay conceived.

Far more significant than whether "anyone actually speaks that way"—i.e., the false notion of authenticity as the highest literary goal—is what the authors *do* with the artistic construct that is vernacular language. These pieces offer much more than a simple recording; they are works of art, not of reportage. It is for this reason that I have grouped the selections by genre, in order to give readers a sense of the special concerns and techniques particular to writers of vernacular poetry, short fiction, and novels. (Playwrights like Wole Soyinka, Suzan-Lori Parks, Parv Bancil, and Earl Lovelace have also crafted excellent vernacular drama; I have omitted their work for fear that too little of their plays' spirit would survive in printed and excerpted form, but have listed specific plays in the Suggestions for Further Reading.) As I explain in the brief introductions to each section, many of the poets are concerned with music, short story writers with the tall tale, and novelists with autobiography and historical revisionism. However, there are also several overarching themes and techniques common to nearly all of the writers included here. Despite the extraordinary diversity of geography, chronology, and biography, they all exhibit an anti-institutional stance, a wicked sense of humor, a deep engagement with history, and a constant preoccupation with language.

Perhaps more than any single other characteristic, this literature is anti-institutional by nature. These authors write in direct opposition to all socially accepted institutions, whether school, church, various forms of the welfare state, or Standard English itself, on its own and as the arm of these other often repressive institutions. The voices of their characters emerge against and despite those institutions. For Peter Carey's Ned Kelly, confrontation with the Australian police contours his reality for as long as he can remember: "My 1st memory is of Mother breaking eggs into a bowl and crying that Jimmy Quinn my 15 yr. old uncle were arrested by the traps. . . . I were 3 yr. old." Similarly, it is the sudden appearance of "somebody in brown uniform with cap like pilot, and wearing boots like dimdim and black belt" that jars John Kasaipwalova's short story "Betel Nut Is Bad Magic for Airplanes" into action. It makes sense that vernacular literature, hounded by authority figures, would inherently mistrust anyone in a uniform. Thus when the scathing eye of these narrators falls upon them, army and convent suffer the same fate as police. As the wide-eyed ingenue Ann puts it in Frances Molloy's *No Mate for the Magpie*, all she learns during an ill-fated convent stint is that "if ye didn't turn yer back on iverybody in the worl', ye didn't stan' a snowball's chance in hell of iver gettin' inte heaven." Vernacular undermines doctrine as nothing else could.

Molloy, along with others in the collection, turns an equally satirical gaze upon schools. These writers approach education with intense skepticism, dramatizing both its overt failures and the potential loss of culture and identity it entails. In Sapphire's punchy summary, Precious Jones tells us that "I always did like school, jus' seem school never did like me." But even succeeding in school has its shortcomings. "I often wish now that I'd fayled," confesses Patricia Grace's narrator Whetu, a Maori scholarship student. "It seems we get put through this machine so that we can come out well-educated and so we can get interesting jobs. I think it's supposed to make us better than some other people—like our mothers and fathers for example, and some of our friends. And somehow it's supposed to make us happier and more FULFILLED. Well I dunno." Here Whetu unknowingly reflects on the legacy of Macaulay: to be educated, in a colonial context, necessitates distance from one's own culture and community. For the Kenyan writer Ngũgĩ wa Thiong'o, that legacy provides enough of a reason not to use English. Illustrating his point that "language was the most important vehicle through which [colonial] power fascinated and held the soul prisoner," Ngũgĩ tells of the humiliation and physical abuse that would face any Kenyan schoolchild in the 1950s who made the mistake of speaking Gikuyu at school. For Ngũgĩ, the colonial legacy thoroughly taints English. Many others in this collection share his experience, transposed to Jamaica, Ireland, or Harlem; yet the ways in which their own writing changes English provide sufficient redemption.

With their clear anti-institutional stance, these works eschew inclusion in a literary canon. Mutabaruka speaks for many authors when he declares that "dis poem will not be amongst great literary works / will not be recited by poetry enthusiasts / will not be quoted by politicians / nor men of religion." This also means that, despite free use of classical techniques like metaphor, personification, alliteration, and many others, there is nearly no overt allusion to previous literary works. Instead of claiming a lineage, each piece of writing appears as created anew. The impulse is to appear direct, unmediated, and unliterary. Where we do find moments of literary allusion, or intertextuality—Sapphire, for example, openly acknowledges her debt to Langston Hughes and Alice Walker—they establish an alternative canon. Ultimately we have a new group of texts that speak directly to one another, constituting a strong literary tradition.

This literary tradition disdains propriety. The harsh realities depicted in some of the pieces—rape, incest, drug abuse, war, genocide—are depicted in frank, unapologetic, often disturbing terms. Sapphire opens *Push* with the arresting lines, "I was left back when I was twelve because I had a baby for my fahver." Drugged by his captors, Uzodinma Iweala's child-combatant narrator proclaims, "I am liking the sound of knife chopping KPWUDA KPWUDA on her head and how the blood is just splashing on my hand and my face and my feets." It would surprise no regular reader of Irvine Welsh when a hapless character must field from his girlfriend's lover the question, "Ever fucked it up the erse?" That harsh material is often mediated, and sometimes magnified, by the blackest possible humor. These works are imbued with humor that is sharp, witty, wry: comedy, here, always goes hand in hand with tragedy. Even the lightest among these works follow the title of Langston Hughes's 1952 book *Laughing to Keep from Crying;* others both laugh and cry in the same breath.

Much of the "difficult" material in this volume arises from specific historical episodes. With its links to colonialism, slavery, nationalism, decolonization, and immigration, vernacular literature brings the historical record to life. Ken Saro-Wiwa's

Sozaboy lives through and narrates Nigeria's horrific Biafran Civil War of 1967–70; Molloy's Ann experiences firsthand Northern Ireland's "Troubles." Other works take it upon themselves to narrate unsung, unacknowledged histories. Mutabaruka's "Dis Poem," for example, opens with the Middle Passage, announcing that "dis poem / shall speak of the wretched sea / that washed ships to these shores." Ironically, the literary works at once rely upon, mourn, and also provide redemption for the traumatic events they depict.

Each one of these works is acutely attuned to issues of language and power; each has a clear purpose of reclaiming and valorizing codes that had thus far been presented (even, frequently, by their own speakers) as substandard. These writers salvage painful histories through linguistic invention that is almost aggressive in its spirit of playfulness. They seize and modify what M. NourbeSe Philip calls "good-english-bad-english english, Queenglish and Kinglish—the anguish that is english in colonial societies." Puns, neologisms, musicality, orality, all function as weapons against cultural domination; all provide ways of making an imposed language one's own. If one finds, as Selvon's West Indian immigrants do, that "it ain't have no word in the English dictionary" for an important concept, then in response "OUR PEOPLE make it up," thus at once changing a language and asserting a community. In many instances here, the power of language is such that names and other words can often rob characters of their identities, as when Saro-Wiwa's Mene becomes "Sozaboy," or soldier boy. But in just as many other cases, characters use language strategically in order to take control over their circumstances. We frequently see how words that wound can be reclaimed: "faggot," for example, in the case of R. Zamora Linmark's Edgar; or "nigger" for Junot Díaz and Roddy Doyle.

Despite its pretense of directness and immediacy, therefore, the medium is never transparent. All these writers choose very carefully and deliberately to write in a non-standard language, and many accordingly insert reflections on that choice. Patricia Grace shows how Whetu causes "a bit of a stir" with his condescending white teacher: "I say 'yous' instead of 'you' (pl.). It always sends her PURPLE." In Grace's portrayal Whetu knows the rules, can recite them by heart, but can also choose to break them. He may have learned them, but he has not internalized them. This is only one of the many self-referential moments throughout this collection that cohere around the themes of colonial domination and the importance of telling one's story despite and against that domination. Other of the self-referential comments point, in various ways, to the difficulty and the fragility of the vernacular project. As the authors included here demonstrate, vernacular literature is in some ways an impossible undertaking. It can only approximate, and never fully reproduce, the force and flow of the oral expression on which it relies. Paul Laurence Dunbar's poem "When Malindy Sings" speaks to that critical problem. Dunbar writes that it may appear "easy 'nough fu' folks to hollah, / Lookin' at de lines an' dots"—in other words, to read out written language. On the other hand, however, "when hit comes to raal right singin', / 'T ain't no easy thing to do." Dunbar begs the question of whether his own poetry constitutes "raal right singin'" or just hollering. Whether these lines serve as a metaphor for the limitations of what he does, or an indirect praise for his own art, is left to the reader to determine.

The authors also exhibit a fear that even if vernacular literature can successfully reproduce the qualities of oral expression, it will ultimately doom itself through publication.

Since its power arises in part from its oral and underground qualities, the logic goes, the act of becoming written literature will inevitably sap that power. One of the aspects of vernacular literature that makes its composition such a challenging endeavor is that authors must construct their own sets of rules for how to write it. They thus create new fixed codes as they transcribe, just as Shakespeare, Dante, and Hu Shih contributed so heavily to consolidating a written vernacular English, Italian, and Chinese, respectively, that had previously been primarily oral forms. This is of course a critical process in the growth and evolution of any language. However, in codifying vernacular codes, authors legitimize them and thus rob them of some of their anti-institutional force. We might call this the irony of arrival. Mutabaruka's poem, for example, has now irrevocably appeared "amongst great literary works," and is itself recognized as one. This is a central paradox of vernacular and other avant-garde literatures: their authors do in fact want readers, both to make a living and to ensure the vitality of their work. Further, when they find those readers, they foster new literacies and ultimately generate a new literary canon. But in creating those readerships and those new canons, they fundamentally change their relationship to concepts like authority and the "establishment." As Mutabaruka himself sums up the problem, "revolutionary poets / 'ave become entertainers."

Without overestimating my own contribution in gathering these works together under a single cover, anthologization can represent a significant step in the often unsavory direction of canonization. After all, for literary works that owe their very existence to their underground positioning, institutional approval is double-edged. By definition vernaculars are no longer vernacular once they are written; their whole identity rests precisely in not being literary. The selections here are quite alive to those deep ironies of the vernacular mode. Each attests to the living and organic nature of language, even to the point of showing how it can escape the control of its own creator. As vernaculars mutate into universal lingos, there will always be new vernacular codes with which to craft more vibrant and dynamic literature.

SECTION ONE • "RAAL RIGHT SINGIN'" • VERNACULAR POETRY

SECTION ONE • "RAAL RIGHT SINGIN'" • VERNACULAR POETRY • SECTION ONE • "RAAL RIGHT SINGIN'" • VERNACULAR POETRY • SECTION ONE • "RAAL RIGHT SINGIN'" • VERNACULAR POETRY • SECTION ONE • "RAAL RIGHT SINGIN'" • VERNACULAR POETRY • SECTION ONE • "RAAL RIGHT SINGIN'" • VERNACULAR POETRY • SECTION ONE • "RAAL RIGHT SINGIN'" •

SECTION ONE

"RAAL RIGHT SINGIN'"

VERNACULAR POETRY

THIS SECTION demonstrates the continuity and diversity of vernacular poetry over two centuries. Robert Burns's poems introduce two crucial connections: the link between music and vernacular poetry, and the association of vernacular poetry and nationalism. Like Jamaica's Louise Bennett and Barbados's Kamau Brathwaite nearly two hundred years later, Burns wrote to preserve and celebrate a way of speaking that was, to him, synonymous with a marginalized people. His Scottish tongue was akin to the "nation language" Brathwaite would analyze and employ beginning in the 1960s. And as American poet Paul Laurence Dunbar would do at the turn of the twentieth century, Burns took on the roles of folklorist and ethnomusicologist as often as that of poet, compiling the existing lyrics he feared would otherwise disappear. Indeed, vernacular poetry has always been intertwined with music, from Scottish airs (in the case of Burns), to spirituals (Dunbar), calypso (Brathwaite, Paul Keens-Douglas, and M. NourbeSe Philip), reggae (Linton Kwesi Johnson and Mutabaruka), blues (Langston Hughes, Amiri Baraka, and Brathwaite again), jazz (Sonia Sanchez), salsa (Tato Laviera), and most recently hip-hop (Stacy-Ann Chin, Saul Williams, and many others).

Appropriately, the music these poets incorporate is hybrid and adaptable. In Hughes's poem "Po' Boy Blues," for example, the set form of the blues receives new content as it makes a painful migration north. Essential to vernacular poetry, hybrid musical genres enliven vernacular fiction as well: calypso meets country-western in Earl Lovelace's short story "Joebell and America," while Patricia Grace's "Letters from Whetu" showcases a new Maori/English beachside rock and roll.

Finally, these selections highlight the oral quality of vernacular poetry. As Brathwaite discusses in his study *History of the Voice* (excerpted in this volume), these poems are intended to be read aloud to a rapt and receptive crowd. Though carefully crafted, they often appear improvised. Like jazz musicians, the poets work hard in order for their compositions to appear effortless and immediate. Their poems both spring from and regenerate an oral tradition, while enlarging and modifying that tradition through their life as published works.

BORN IN 1919 IN KINGSTON, Louise Bennett was one of Jamaica's most beloved poets. Early in her impressive career, Kamau Brathwaite writes, "her instincts were that she should use the language of her people," and as a result she found enthusiastic crowds but no publishers. Despite those initial difficulties, by the time of her death in 2006 "Miss Lou" was recognized across her island as a national treasure for her poetry, folklore, and performance. In "Colonization in Reverse" as in many of her poems, her topic is "tunabout," or the unexpected ways in which colonialism and immigration have altered a culture that had seen itself as superior and eternal. More threatening even than World War II, Bennett suggests, is the "colonizin in reverse" that her poetry celebrates and enacts. "Bans O'Killing" highlights the history of English as a hybrid and initially nonstandard language itself: to avoid hypocrisy, any opponent of creole poetry would also need to disavow the work of such canonical standbys as Chaucer, Shakespeare, and Burns.

COLONIZATION IN REVERSE

(1966)

Wat a joyful news, Miss Mattie,
I feel like me heart gwine burs
Jamaica people colonizin
Englan in reverse.

By de hundred, by de tousan
From country and from town,
By de ship-load, by de plane load
Jamaica is Englan boun.

Dem a pour out a Jamaica,
Everybody future plan
Is fe get a big-time job
An settle in de mother lan.

What an islan! What a people!
Man an woman, old an young
Jus a pack dem bag an baggage
An turn history upside dung!

Some people doan like travel,
But fe show dem loyalty
Dem all a open up cheap-fare-
To-Englan agency.

An week by week dem shippin off
Dem countryman like fire,
Fe immigrate an populate
De seat a de Empire.

Oonoo see how life is funny,
Oonoo see da tunabout?
Jamaica live fe box bread
Out a English people mout.

For wen dem ketch a Englan,
An start play dem different role,
Some will settle down to work
An some will settle fe de dole.

Jane says de dole is not too bad
Because dey payin she
Two pounds a week fe seek a job
Dat suit her dignity.

Me say Jane will never fine work
At de rate how she dah look,
For all day she stay pon Aunt Fan couch
An read love-story book.

Wat a devilment a Englan!
Dem face war an brave de worse,
But me wonderin how dem gwine stan
Colonizin in reverse.

BANS O'KILLING

(1944)

So yuh a de man, me hear bout!
Ah yuh dem sey dah-teck
Whole heap o'English oat sey dat
Yuh gwine kill dialect!

Meck me get it straigth Mass Charlie
For me noh quite undastan,
Yuh gwine kill all English dialect
Or jus Jamaica one?

Ef yuh dah-equal up wid English
Language, den wha meck
Yuh gwine go feel inferior, wen
It come to dialect?

Ef yuh kean sing "Linstead Market"
An "Wata come a me y'eye",
Yuh wi haffi tap sing "Auld lang syne"
An "Comin thru de rye".

Dah language weh yuh proud o',
Weh yuh honour and respeck,
Po' Mass Charlie! Yuh noh know sey
Dat it spring from dialect!

Dat dem start fe try tun language,
From de fourteen century,
Five hundred years gawn an dem got
More dialect dan we!

Yuh wi haffe kill de Lancashire
De Yorkshire, de Cockney
De broad Scotch an de Irish brogue
Before yuh start kill me!

Yuh wi haffee get de Oxford book
O' English verse, an tear
Out Chaucer, Burns, Lady Grizelle
An plenty o' Shakespeare!

Wen yuh done kill "wit" and "humour"
Wen yuh kill "Variety"
Yuh will haffe fine a way fe kill
Originality!

An mine how yuh dah-read dem English
Book deh pon yuh shelf
For ef yuh drop a "h" yuh mighta
Haffe kill yuhself.

THE UNOFFICIAL DEAN of West Indian vernacular poetry, Kamau Brathwaite has a strong presence across the islands due in large part to his commitment to rendering the rhythms of calypso in his much-admired poetry. Born in Bridgetown, Barbados, in 1930, Brathwaite has also lived in England, Ghana, Jamaica, and the United States. "Wings of a Dove," taken from his 1967 collection *Rights of Passage*, brings to life what linguists call "code-switching" as it ranges confidently between an omniscient Standard English narrator and the chanting oracle "Brother Man the Rasta man." Like Oonya Kempadoo's *Tide Running*—as well as a great deal of other Caribbean literature—the poem represents the dubious benefits of tourism. Here, planes and cruise ships land, "full o' silk dem / full o' food dem . . . full o' flash dem / full o' cash dem," only to meet an apocalyptic fate.

WINGS OF A DOVE

(1967)

1

Brother Man the Rasta
man, beard full of lichens
brain full of lice
watched the mice
come up through the floor-
boards of his down-
town, shanty-town kitchen,
and smiled. Blessed are the poor
in health, he mumbled,
that they should inherit this
wealth. Blessed are the meek
hearted, he grumbled,
for theirs is this stealth.

Brother Man the Rasta
man, hair full of lichens
head hot as ice
watched the mice
walk into his poor
hole, reached for his peace
and the pipe of his ganja
and smiled how the mice
eyes, hot pumice

pieces, glowed into his room
like ruby, like rhinestone
and suddenly startled like
diamond.

And I
Rastafar-I
in Babylon's boom
town, crazed by the moon
and the peace of this chalice, I
prophet and singer, scourge
of the gutter, guardian
Trench Town, the Dungle and Young's
Town, rise and walk through the now silent
streets of affliction, hawk's eyes
hard with fear, with
affection, and hear my people
cry, my people
shout:

Down down
white
man, con
man, brown
man, down
down full
man, frown-
ing fat
man, that
white black
man that
lives in
the town.

Rise rise
locks-
man, Solo-
man wise
man, rise
rise rise
leh we
laugh
dem, mock
dem, stop
dem, kill
dem an' go
back back
to the black
man lan'
back back
to Af-
rica.

2

Them doan mean it, yuh know,
them cahn help it
but them clean-face browns in
Babylon town is who I most fear

an' who fears most I.
Watch de vulture dem a-flyin', hear de crow a-dem crow
see what them money a-buy?

Caw caw caw caw.
Ol' crow, ol' crow, cruel ol'
ol' crow, that's all them got
to show.

Crow fly flip flop
hip hop
pun de ground; na
feet feel firm

pun de firm stones; na
good pickney born
from de flesh
o' dem bones;

naw naw naw naw.

3

So beat dem drums
dem, spread

dem wings dem,
watch dem fly

dem, soar dem
high dem,

clear in the glory of the Lord.

Watch dem ship dem
come to town dem

full o' silk dem
full o' food dem

an' dem 'plane dem
come to groun' dem

full o' flash dem
full o' cash dem

silk dem food dem
shoe dem wine dem

that dem drink dem
an' consume dem

praisin' the glory of the Lord.

So beat dem burn
dem, learn

dem that dem
got dem nothin'

but dem
bright bright baubles

that will burst dem
when the flame dem

from on high dem
raze an' roar dem

an' de poor dem
rise an' rage dem

in de glory of the Lord.

ROBERT BURNS

ROBERT BURNS is widely considered Scotland's national bard. Born in Alloway, Ayrshire, in 1759, Burns worked at various points as a farm laborer, flax-dresser, customs officer, poet, and what would now be called ethnomusicologist. He had planned to travel to Jamaica to take a job as a bookkeeper until the unexpected success of his 1786 collection *Poems, Chiefly in the Scottish Dialect,* which he had published to finance the trip. Burns died in 1796, leaving behind a considerable influence on Romantic poetry and an inestimable one on Scottish nationalism. From out of his formidable oeuvre I have included three fairly representative poems, one very well known and the other two less so. "Auld Lang Syne" testifies to the almost invisible ubiquity of the vernacular tradition: the ballad is so familiar that it generally escapes notice as an exemplar of Scottish dialect poetry. Both "Highland Mary" and "Bonnie Lesley" comment on the continuity among quasi-colonial situations even over a span of centuries. In much the same way that the anticolonial poetry of W. B. Yeats, Rabindranath Tagore, and others would do later, "Highland Mary" uses a romanticized female to represent a threatened land. Within the poem's nostalgic verses, the departed Mary merges with the landscape for which she is named. Lesley has left for different reasons: in a witty precursor to the "brain drain" problem familiar from recent decades, Scotland loses its loveliest girl when she "gaed o'er the Border . . . / To spread her conquests farther."

AULD LANG SYNE

(1786)

Should auld acquaintance be forgot,
And never brought to mind?
Should auld acquaintance be forgot,
And auld lang syne!

For auld lang syne, my dear,
For auld lang syne.
We'll tak a cup o' kindness yet,
For auld lang syne.

And surely ye'll be your pint stowp!
And surely I'll be mine!
And we'll tak a cup o'kindness yet,
For auld lang syne.

For auld lang syne, my dear,
For auld lang syne.
We'll tak a cup o' kindness yet,
For auld lang syne.

We twa hae run about the braes,
And pou'd the gowans fine;
But we've wander'd mony a weary fit,
Sin' auld lang syne.

For auld lang syne, my dear,
For auld lang syne.
We'll tak a cup o' kindness yet,
For auld lang syne.

We twa hae paidl'd in the burn,
Frae morning sun till dine;
But seas between us braid hae roar'd
Sin' auld lang syne.

For auld lang syne, my dear,
For auld lang syne.
We'll tak a cup o' kindness yet,
For auld lang syne.

And there's a hand, my trusty fere!
And gie's a hand o' thine!
And we'll tak a right gude-willie waught,
For auld lang syne.

For auld lang syne, my dear,
For auld lang syne.
We'll tak a cup o' kindness yet,
For auld lang syne.

HIGHLAND MARY

(1792)

Ye banks and braes and streams around
The castle o' Montgomery,
Green be your woods and fair your flowers,
Your waters never drumlie!
There simmer first unfauld her robes,
And there the langest tarry;
For there I took the last fareweel
O' my sweet Highland Mary.

How sweetly bloom'd the gay green birk,
How rich the hawthorn's blossom,
As underneath their fragrant shade
I clasp'd her to my bosom!
The golden hours on angel wings
Flew o'er me and my dearie;
For dear to me as light and life
Was my sweet Highland Mary.

Wi' mony a vow and lock'd embrace,
Our parting was fu' tender;
And pledging aft to meet again,
We tore oursels asunder;
But, oh! fell Death's untimely frost,
That nipt my flower sae early!

Now green's the sod, and cauld's the clay,
That wraps my Highland Mary!

O pale, pale now, those rosy lips,
I aft hae kiss'd sae fondly!
And clos'd for aye the sparkling glance
That dwelt on me sae kindly!
And mouldering now in silent dust
That heart that lo'ed me dearly!
But still within my bosom's core
Shall live my Highland Mary.

BONNIE LESLEY

(1792)

O saw ye bonnie Lesley
As she gaed o'er the Border?
She's gane, like Alexander,
To spread her conquests farther.

To see her is to love her,
And love but her for ever;
For Nature made her what she is,
And ne'er made sic anither!

Thou art a queen, fair Lesley,
Thy subjects, we before thee;
Thou art divine, fair Lesley,
The hearts o' men adore thee.

The Deil he could na scaith thee,
Or aught that wad belang thee;
He'd look into thy bonnie face,
And say, "I canna wrang thee!"

The Powers aboon will tent thee;
Misfortune sha' na steer thee;
Thou'rt like themselves sae lovely,
That ill they'll ne'er let near thee.

Return again, fair Lesley,
Return to Caledonie!
That we may brag we hae a lass
There's nane again sae bonnie.

PAUL LAURENCE DUNBAR

THE TURN-OF-THE-CENTURY American poet Paul Laurence Dunbar was born in Dayton, Ohio, in 1872. He began writing poetry at age six, first published it at age twenty, and achieved nationwide fame when his first two collections were reprinted in 1896 as *Lyrics of a Lowly Life.* He went on to write short stories, novels, and a play. Before his death in 1906 he suffered from depression and tuberculosis. "A Negro Love Song" conveys the theme of duplicity central to much vernacular literature. The reassurance "'Cose I do" that ends the deceptively simple poem can be taken as sincere or sly; only the tone of delivery, unavailable to readers, can determine its intent. "When Malindy Sings" cleverly undermines the vernacular endeavor by introducing the troubling notion that the written word will never achieve the power of its spoken counterpart. "Easy 'nough fu' folks to hollah, / Lookin' at de lines an' dots," Dunbar's narrator says pejoratively, contrasting written music with the "natural" beauty of Malindy's untrained voice. Here Dunbar implies that even his own poetry contains only a shade of the full expression found in music, song, and speech.

A NEGRO LOVE SONG

(1895)

Seen my lady home las' night,
   Jump back, honey, jump back.
Hel' huh han' an' sque'z it tight,
   Jump back, honey, jump back.
Hyeahd huh sigh a little sigh,
Seen a light gleam f'om huh eye,
An' a smile go flittin' by—
   Jump back, honey, jump back.

Hyeahd de win' blow thoo de pine,
   Jump back, honey, jump back,
Mockin'-bird was singin' fine,
   Jump back, honey, jump back.
An' my hea't was beatin' so,
When I reached my lady's do',
Dat I couldn't ba' to go—
   Jump back, honey, jump back.

Put my ahm aroun' huh wais',
   Jump back, honey, jump back.
Raised huh lips an' took a tase,
   Jump back, honey, jump back.
Love me, honey, love me true?
Love me well ez I love you?
An' she answe'd, "'Cose I do"—
   Jump back, honey, jump back.

WHEN MALINDY SINGS

(1896)

G'way an' quit dat noise, Miss Lucy—
　　Put dat music book away;
What's de use to keep on tryin'?
　　Ef you practise twell you're gray,
You cain't sta't no notes a-flyin'
　　Lak de ones dat rants and rings
F'om de kitchen to de big woods
　　When Malindy sings.

You ain't got de nachel o'gans
　　Fu' to make de soun' come right,
You ain't got de tu'ns an' twistin's
　　Fu' to make it sweet an' light.
Tell you one thing now, Miss Lucy,
　　An' I 'm tellin' you fu' true,
When hit comes to raal right singin',
　　'T ain't no easy thing to do.

Easy 'nough fu' folks to hollah,
　　Lookin' at de lines an' dots,
When dey ain't no one kin sence it,
　　An' de chune comes in, in spots;
But fu' real malojous music,
　　Dat jes' strikes yo' hea't and clings,
Jes' you stan' an' listen wif me
　　When Malindy sings.

Ain't you nevah hyeahd Malindy?
    Blessed soul, tek up de cross!
Look hyeah, ain't you jokin', honey?
    Well, you don't know whut you los'.
Y' ought to hyeah dat gal a-wa'blin',
    Robins, la'ks, an' all dem things,
Heish dey moufs an' hides dey face.
    When Malindy sings.

Fiddlin' man jes' stop his fiddlin',
    Lay his fiddle on de she'f;
Mockin'-bird quit tryin' to whistle,
    'Cause he jes' so shamed hisse'f.
Folks a-playin' on de banjo
    Draps dey fingahs on de strings—
Bless yo' soul—fu'gits to move 'em,
    When Malindy sings.

She jes' spreads huh mouf and hollahs,
    "Come to Jesus," twell you hyeah
Sinnahs' tremblin' steps and voices,
    Timid-lak a-drawin' neah;
Den she tu'ns to "Rock of Ages,"
    Simply to de cross she clings,
An' you fin' yo' teahs a-drappin'
    When Malindy sings.

Who dat says dat humble praises
    Wif de Master nevah counts?
Heish yo' mouf, I hyeah dat music,
    Ez hit rises up an' mounts—
Floatin' by de hills an' valleys,
    Way above dis buryin' sod,

Ez hit makes its way in glory
   To de very gates of God!

Oh, hit's sweetah dan de music
   Of an edicated band;
An' hit's dearah dan de battle's
   Song o' triumph in de lan'.
It seems holier dan evenin'
   When de solemn chu'ch bell rings,
Ez I sit an' ca'mly listen
   While Malindy sings.

Towsah, stop dat ba'kin', hyeah me!
   Mandy, mek dat chile keep still;
Don't you hyeah de echoes callin'
   F'om de valley to de hill?
Let me listen, I can hyeah it,
   Th'oo de bresh of angel's wings,
Sof' an' sweet, "Swing Low,
   Sweet Chariot,"
Ez Malindy sings.

LANGSTON HUGHES

LANGSTON HUGHES was America's foremost blues poet, and remains the most familiar name from the Harlem Renaissance. Born in 1902 in Joplin, Missouri, he grew up there and in Kansas, Illinois, Mexico, and Ohio, where he began to write poetry during high school. He moved to New York in 1921, and while writing also worked as a busboy, research assistant, and sailor. In addition to poetry, he wrote fiction, essays, plays, operas, children's books, and two autobiographies. Hughes died in 1967. In the quiet and contemplative "Mother to Son," a thoroughly believable mother encourages her child to continue the struggle she has begun for him. "Po' Boy Blues" channels a blues idiom, transforming the Mississippi Delta form by using it to describe the new and brutal experience of Northern migration.

MOTHER TO SON

(1922)

Well, son, I'll tell you:
Life for me ain't been no crystal stair.
It's had tacks in it,
And splinters,
And boards all torn up,
And places with no carpet on the floor—
Bare.
But all the time
I'se been a-climbin' on,
And reachin' landin's,
And turnin' corners,
And sometimes goin', in the dark
Where there ain't been no light.

So boy, don't you turn back.
Don't you set down on the steps
'Cause you finds it's kinder hard.
Don't you fall now—
For I'se still goin', honey,
I'se still climbin'
And life for me ain't been no crystal stair.

PO' BOY BLUES

(1927)

When I was home de
Sunshine seemed like gold.
Since I come up North de
Whole damn world's turned cold.

I was a good boy,
Never done no wrong.
Yes, I was a good boy,
Never done no wrong,
But this world is weary
An' de road is hard an' long.

I fell in love with
A gal I thought was kind.
Fell in love with
A gal I thought was kind.
She made me lose ma money
An' almost lose ma mind.

Weary, weary,
Weary early in de morn.
Weary, weary,
Early, early in de morn.
I's so weary
I wish I'd never been born.

LINTON KWESI JOHNSON has been championing dub poetry, the fortuitous marriage of reggae and verse, since the dual release in 1975 of *Dread Beat An' Blood* as both a poetry collection and an album. Born in 1952 in Chapelton, Jamaica, Johnson moved to London in 1963, studied at the University of London, joined the Black Panthers, and founded the poetry and drumming collective Rasta Love. Since then he has fostered dub through his multiple roles as radio journalist, poet-in-residence for the Borough of Lambeth, and record producer. Unlike Bennett's wry commentary on how Jamaican immigrants have changed the face of England, Johnson's seminal poem "Inglan Is a Bitch" offers only the bleakest portrayal of London's reception to its new arrivals. His immigrant speaker finds neither peace nor livelihood, even though "mi dhu day wok an' mi dhu nite wok / mi dhu clean wok an' mi dhu dutty wok."

INGLAN IS A BITCH

(1980)

w'en mi jus' come to Landan toun
mi use to work pan di andahgroun
but workin' pan di andahgroun
y'u don't get fi know your way around

Inglan is a bitch
dere's no escapin it
Inglan is a bitch
dere's no runnin' whey fram it

mi get a lickle jab in a bih 'otell
an' awftah a while, mi woz doin' quite well
dem staat mi aaf as a dish-washah
but w'en mi tek a stack, mi noh tun clack-watchah

Inglan is a bitch
dere's no escapin it
Inglan is a bitch
no baddah try fi hide fram it

w'en dem gi' you di lickle wage packit
fus dem rab it wid dem big tax rackit
y'u haffi struggle fi mek en's meet
an' w'en y'u goh a y'u bed y'u jus' can't sleep

Inglan is a bitch
dere's no escapin it
Inglan is a bitch
a noh lie mi a tell, a true

mi use to work dig ditch w'en it cowl noh bitch
mi did strang like a mule, but bwoy, mi did fool
den awftah a while mi jus' stap dhu ovahtime
den awftah a while mi jus' phu dung mi tool

Inglan is a bitch
dere's no escapin it
Inglan is a bitch
y'u haffi know how fi survive in it

well mi dhu day wok an' mi dhu nite wok
mi dhu clean wok an' mi dhu dutty wok
dem seh dat black man is very lazy
but if y'u si how mi wok y'u woulda sey mi crazy

Inglan is a bitch
dere's no escapin it
Inglan is a bitch
y'u bettah face up to it

dem a have a lickle facktri up inna Brackly
inna disya facktri all dem dhu is pack crackry
fi di laas fifteen years dem get mi laybah
now awftah fifteen years mi fall out a fayvah

Inglan is a bitch
dere's no escapin it

Inglan is a bitch
dere's no runnin' whey fram it

mi know dem have work, work in abundant
yet still, dem mek mi redundant
now, at fifty-five mi gettin' quite ol'
yet still, dem sen' mi fi goh draw dole

Inglan is a bitch
dere's no escapin it
Inglan is a bitch
is whey wi a goh dhu 'bout it?

PAUL KEENS-DOUGLAS

BORN IN SAN JUAN, Trinidad, in 1942, Paul Keens-Douglas has
since participated in practically every aspect of Caribbean cultural production. He has lived in Granada, Jamaica, and
Canada; his many occupations include poet, radio and television producer, educator, community organizer, and calypson-
ian. In addition to his own prize-winning poetry, Keens-Douglas
is best known for the innovative Carnival Talk Tent, which has
made storytelling as much a part of Trinidad's Carnival as
music and dance. With "Wukhand," Keens-Douglas humor-
ously explores a theme that consumes many poets, namely that
of poetry as labor. Like Seamus Heaney's "Digging,"
"Wukhand" expresses that theme through the image of a
hand. Here the speaker's hand, like poetry, has "ah past, ah
present an ah future"; it is productive and also romantic. The
speaker, a day laborer seeking employment, initially presents
his hand as "tough like mangrove root," but finally admits that
"me dam hand near fallin off." For the laborer as for the poet,
it is essential to make the job look easy. Part of the effort that
goes into vernacular poetry, "Wukhand" reminds us, involves
the erasure of that very effort.

WUKHAND

(1976)

Sah, gimme a wuk nah.
Ah lookin ole but ah strong.
Never mind ah skinny sah,
Ah could work like ah beas.
Ask anybody, ask dem suh:
Clean yard, shine car, cut grass,
Ah tekkin anyting sah.
You see dis hand sah, it like stone
Never mind it lookin marga.
Dis hand could pelt cutlass
Like Sampson pelt de ass jaw,
Dis hand clear brush from Toco to Town,
When tree see me dey does bawl;
If dey could ah run, is ah straight case,
Cause I is de man with de Lightnin in me hand.
Me blade does flash in de sun
Like fish gainst river stone,
An when ah finish, is me one standin
An all bush lay down, quiet quiet.
Yes sah, dis hand is a wukkin hand.
Yu lookin at me sah,
With me pants foot roll up,
An me mareno lookin holy, holy,
Never mind dat sah; look sah, look me hand
Tough like mangrove root,

Hard like iron cable.
Dis is ah hand sah, a real hand, a wukkin hand,
Ah hand with ah past, ah present an ah future.
Dis hand chuck banana, sah,
Cut dem, draw dem, an stack dem,
Under sun, under moon, an in de dark,
An when de back cry out, an foot say stop,
Dis hand still goin like ah champ,
Ah stroke to de left, an ah stroke to de right.

Dat was me, de man with de iron hand.
Dont judge me by me size sah,
Ah lookin' small, ah know dat,
But me hand sah, watch it.
Dis hand have character,
Dis hand throw net like was feather,
An when dis hand pull back sah,
Was fish in any weather.
Ah catch dem, cut dem, clean dem
Ah couldn't afford to eat dem.
Yes sah, dis is ah hand sah.
When dis hand was ah boy sah,
It throw stone, pelt rock,
Wash in river, an cook on fire.
It get cut, bruise, bounce, burn an break.
Dis hand sah, grow up strong.
It help police pull hose
When man house start burnin down,
It tired pullin car out ah ditch,
It break fight under plenty strain,
But is ah wukkin hand sah.
An dis hand sah, have touch,

Crack ah egg, pick ah flower,
Caress ah woman, ahhhh, sah
As gentle as de mornin sun
Growin fierce, but not destroyin
Beautiful sah, beautiful.
An dis hand have speed sah,
Yes speed.
See dis hand sah, pull ace suh,
From any part ah de pack,
An so it pullin ace, is so it wukkin hard.
But dis hand is ah honest hand sah.
Dis hand pick up two hundred dolla
Lying dey in open street,
An dis hand send it straight to de station.
Yes sah, dis hand make headline,
De paper call me de 'honest hand'.
Wha yu say sah?
Yu eh have no wuk?
Yu makin joke sah.
How yu mean yu eh have wuk?
Ah rich lookin fella like yu,
Stand up in front yu big house,
An dress up as if weddin yu goin to.
Ah know is joke yu jokin sah,
But dis hand could take ah joke.
What sah? dis is not yu house?
Yu jus stan up here waitin on taxi?
But look me crosses with dis niggerman,
Ah stan up here only wastin me time with he,
Ah poor man like me, with arthritis,
Me dam hand near fallin off,
An he can't even sponsor ah cup ah coffee.

Only posing up in front de people place.
Ah have a good mind to arrest yu.
Look man, move out ah me sight yu hear?
Before ah leggo de hand on yu.
Well, yes.

RUDYARD KIPLING

RUDYARD KIPLING was one of the most distinguished English writers of the nineteenth century. Born Joseph Rudyard Kipling in Bombay, India, in 1865, he was sent to England at age six. In 1882, after attending the United Services College, he moved back to India and began to write short fiction. Despite his considerable achievements in fiction and poetry, he may remain best known for the children's stories collected in *The Jungle Book.* He won the Nobel Prize in 1907, later turned down both knighthood and the position of poet laureate, and died in 1936. "Tommy," which appeared in his 1892 collection *The Barrack-Room Ballads,* addresses the hypocrisy of civilians glorifying the military while mistreating individual soldiers. When risking his life at war, the speaker is a revered "Mister Atkins"; at leisure, he diminishes to a reviled "Tommy." The Widow, here, is Queen Victoria, whom Kipling pillories in "The Widow at Windsor."

TOMMY

(1892)

I went into a public-'ouse to get a pint o' beer,
The publican 'e up an' sez, "We serve no red-coats
    here."
The girls be'ind the bar they laughed an' giggled
    fit to die,
I outs into the street again an' to myself sez I:
    O it's Tommy this, an' Tommy that, an'
        "Tommy, go away";
    But it's "Thank you, Mister Atkins", when the
        band begins to play,—
    The band begins to play, my boys, the band
        begins to play,
    O it's "Thank you, Mister Atkins", when the
        band begins to play.

I went into a theatre as sober as could be,
They gave a drunk civilian room, but 'adn't none
    for me;
They sent me to the gallery or round the music-
    'alls,
But when it comes to fightin', Lord! they'll shove
    me in the stalls!
    For it's Tommy this, an' Tommy that, an'
        "Tommy, wait outside";

But it's "Special train for Atkins" when the
    trooper's on the tide,—
The troopship's on the tide, my boys, the
    troopship's on the tide,
O it's "Special train for Atkins" when the
    trooper's on the tide.

Yes, makin' mock o' uniforms that guard you
    while you sleep
Is cheaper than them uniforms, an' they're
    starvation cheap;
An' hustlin' drunken soldiers when they're goin'
    large a bit
Is five times better business than paradin' in full kit.
Then it's Tommy this, an' Tommy that, an'
    "Tommy, 'ow's yer soul?"
But it's "Thin red line of 'eroes" when the
    drums begin to roll,—
The drums begin to roll, my boys, the drums
    begin to roll,
O it's "Thin red line of 'eroes" when the drums
    begin to roll.

We aren't no thin red 'eroes, nor we aren't no
    blackguards too,
But single men in barracks, most remarkable like
    you;
An' if sometimes our conduck isn't all your fancy
    paints,
Why, single men in barracks don't grow into
    plaster saints;

While it's Tommy this, an' Tommy that, an'
    "Tommy, fall be'ind",
But it's "Please to walk in front, sir", when
    there's trouble in the wind,—
There's trouble in the wind, my boys, there's
    trouble in the wind,
    O it's "Please to walk in front, sir", when
        there's trouble in the wind.

You talk o' better food for us, an' schools, an'
    fires, an' all:
We'll wait for extry rations if you treat us rational.
Don't mess about the cook-room slops, but prove
    it to our face
The Widow's Uniform is not the soldier-man's
    disgrace.
For it's Tommy this, an' Tommy that, an'
    "Chuck him out, the brute!"
But it's "Saviour of 'is country" when the guns
    begin to shoot;
An' it's Tommy this, an' Tommy that, an'
    anything you please;
An' Tommy ain't a bloomin' fool—you bet
    that Tommy sees!

THE RADICAL SCOTTISH POET and essayist Tom Leonard was born in 1944 in Glasgow. After attending the University of Glasgow, he published his first collection, *Six Glasgow Poems,* in 1969. His collected works, *Intimate Voices,* won the Scottish Book of the Year Award in 1984—and was banned from Central Region school libraries that same year. In this poem, informally known as "The 6 O'Clock News," Leonard differentiates between a BBC announcer and "wanna yoo scruff." As Jolisa Gracewood explains, the poem operates as a kind of "funhouse mirror" in which the speaker exposes the alleged "neutrality" of Standard English by mimicking it in a Glasgow vernacular.

UNRELATED INCIDENTS—NO. 3

(1984)

this is thi
six a clock
news thi
man said n
thi reason
a talk wia
BBC accent
iz coz yi
widny wahnt
mi ti talk
aboot thi
trooth wia
voice lik
wanna yoo
scruff. if
a toktaboot
thi trooth
lik wanna yoo
scruff yi
widny thingk
it wuz troo.
jist wanna yoo
scruff tokn.
thirza right
way ti spell

ana right way
to tok it. this
is me tokn yir
right way a
spellin. this
is ma trooth.
yooz doant no
thi trooth
yirsellz cawz
yi canny talk
right. this is
the six a clock
nyooz. belt up.

MARY McCABE

THE WRITER and political activist Mary McCabe was born in 1950 in Glasgow, Scotland. Working in English, Scots, Gaelic, and German, she has published fiction, nonfiction, and poetry as well as radio plays and a children's book. In this brief and lilting poem, McCabe portrays the Scottish language as a natural feature that is just as intrinsic and welcome as any topography. As McCabe writes in the bilingual (or, more accurately, bidialectical) notes to her poem, she returned from her first trip abroad to find that "it wis the Scots voices that telt me ah cuid never lowp the kintra"—or, in her own translation, "it was that first sound of spoken Scots that told me, despite my love of travel, I could never emigrate."

COMIN BACK OWER THE BORDER

(2004)

Comin back ower the Border
The first ye ken ye're hame
It isna jist the biggins
The brick gien wey tae stane

It's nae the kintra roon aboot
Craggies, cleughs an corries
Stanes keeking through the shilpit yird
Less caurs an bikes an lorries

It's nae the pastels o the North
The weather-gleam i the lift
The snell gurlie teeth o the wind
The smirr in the mochie drift

It's "wee this" "see thon" "Och, gonnae"
The "O" sae straucht an lang
The "R" rollin richly roon the braes
The speak on the rise o a sang

CLAUDE McKAY'S life and work transcend borders and genres. Born Festus Claudius McKay in Sunnyville, Clarendon, Jamaica, in 1890, he worked as a police officer until 1912, when he published two poetry collections and left for the United States. There he studied at the Tuskegee Institute and Kansas State University, and later became politically active as a socialist. His best-known work, *Home to Harlem*, appeared in 1928. By the time of his death in 1948, McKay had lived in England, the Soviet Union, and Morocco, and had written several novels, journalistic pieces, poetry collections, and two autobiographies. In this early poem McKay offers a commentary on the invisibility of so much labor, including that of poetry.

QUASHIE TO BUCCRA

(1912)

You tas'e petater an' you say it sweet,
But you no know how hard we wuk fe it;
You want a basketful fe quattiewut,
'Cause you no know how 'tiff de bush fe cut.

De cowitch under which we hab fe 'toop,
De shamar lyin' t'ick like pumpkin soup,
Is killin' somet'ing for a naygur man;
Much less de cutlass workin' in we han'.

De sun hot like when fire ketch a town;
Shade-tree look temptin', yet we caan' lie down,
Aldough we wouldn' eben ef we could,
Causen we job must finish soon an' good.

De bush cut done, de bank dem we deh dig,
But dem caan' 'tan' sake o' we naybor pig;
For so we moul' it up he root it do'n,
An' we caan' 'peak sake o' we naybor tongue.

Aldough de vine is little, it can bear;
It wantin' not'in' but a little care:
You see petater tear up groun', you run,
You laughin', sir, you must be t'ink a fun.

De fiel' pretty? It couldn't less 'an dat,
We wuk de bes', an' de lan' is fat;
We dig de row dem eben in a line,
An' keep it clean—den so it *mus'* look fine.

You tas'e petater an' you say it sweet,
But you no know how hard we wuk fe it;
Yet still de hardship always melt away
Wheneber it come roun' to reapin' day.

MUTABARUKA

ALONG WITH Linton Kwesi Johnson, Mutabaruka is one of the central figures in dub poetry. Born Allan Hope in 1952 in Kingston, Jamaica, he attended a technical school, converted to Rastafarianism while working at the Jamaica Telephone Company, left Kingston for the rural parish of St. James, and began publishing poems in the 1970s, first as Allan Mutabaruka and then under the single name by which he is now known. "Dis Poem" is Mutabaruka's best-known composition. The spoken-word masterpiece, sometimes contentious, sometimes elegiac, sometimes self-mocking, compresses several centuries of African and African-diaspora history into a few pages. Beginning with the Middle Passage, Mutabaruka goes on to invoke figures of resistance from his own generation, finally folding the reader into the activist community his poem creates.

DIS POEM

(1992)

dis poem
shall speak of the wretched sea
that washed ships to these shores
of mothers crying for their young
swallowed up by the sea
dis poem shall say nothin new
dis poem shall speak of time
time unlimited
time undefined
dis poem shall call names
names like
lumumba
kenyatta
nkrumah
hannibal
akenaton
malcolm
garvey
haile selassie
dis poem is vex
about apartheid
racism
fascism
the klu klux klan
riots in brixton

atlanta
jim jones
dis poem is revoltin against
first world
second world
third world
division
manmade decision
dis poem is like all the rest
dis poem will not be amongst great literary works
will not be recited by poetry enthusiasts
will not be quoted by politicians
nor men of religion
dis poem is knives . . . bombs . . . guns . . .
blazing for freedom
yes dis poem is a drum
ashanti
mau mau
ibo
yoruba
niahbingi warriors
uhuru . . . uhuru
namibia uhuru
uhuru
soweto
uhuru
afrika!
dis poem will not change things
dis poem needs to be changed
dis poem is the rebirth of a people arising . . .
    awaking . . . overstanding
. . . dis poem speak

is speakin . . . has spoken
dis poem shall continue
even when poets have stopped writing
dis poem shall survive . . . u . . . me . . .
it shall linger in history
in your mind
in time . . .
forever
dis poem is time
only time will tell
dis poem is still not written
dis poem has no poet
dis poem is just a part of the story his-story . . .
     her-story . . . our-story
the story still untold
dis poem is now ringing . . . . talking
irritatin
making u want to stop it
but dis poem will not stop
dis poem is long
cannot be short
dis poem cannot be tamed
cannot be blamed
the story is still not told about dis poem
dis poem is old
new
dis poem is copied from
the bible
your prayer book
the new york times
readers digest
the c.i.a. files

the k.g.b. files
dis poem is no secret
dis poem shall be called
boring
stupid
senseless
dis poem is watchin u
tryin' to make sense from dis poem
dis poem is messin up your brains
makin u want to stop listenin to dis poem
but you shall not stop listenin to dis poem
u need to know what will be said next in dis poem
dis poem shall disappoint u because . . .
dis poem is to be continue
   in your mind . . .
   in your mind . . .
   in your mind . . .

BORN IN TOBAGO in 1947, M. NourbeSe Philip studied economics at the University of the West Indies and politics and law at the University of Western Ontario. After practicing law in Toronto for seven years, she decided in 1983 to write poetry full-time. Since then she has also published novels, short stories, plays, essays, and children's books. While the vast majority of vernacular writers demonstrate their anti-institutional bent by eschewing overt intertextuality (except toward nonliterary "texts" like calypso, rap, and television), Philip goes against that prevailing anti-institutional grain by recasting the story of Demeter and Persephone in a Caribbean milieu. In this opening poem to the song cycle "And Over Every Land and Sea," the Greek goddess of agriculture appears as a biological mother in search of her adopted child, spirited off not to Hades but to chilly Canada. As in her essay "The Absence of Writing or How I Almost Became a Spy," included in Section Four, Philip exhibits a concern with lineage, inheritance, and how both can be broken.

QUESTIONS! QUESTIONS!

(1993)

Where she, where she, where she
be, where she gone?
Where high and low meet I search,
find can't, way down the island's way
I gone—south:
day-time and night-time living with she,
down by the just-down-the-way sea
she friending fish and crab with alone,
in the bay-blue morning she does wake
with kiskeedee and crow-cock—
skin green like lime, hair indigo-blue,
eyes hot like sunshine-time;
grief gone mad with crazy—so them say.
Before the questions too late,
before I forget how they stay,
crazy or no crazy I must find she.

NTOZAKE SHANGE is an innovative artist whose work unites poetry, theater, and dance. She was born Paulette Williams in Trenton, New Jersey, in 1948, grew up there and in St. Louis, Missouri, and attended Barnard College. She then moved to California, where she earned a graduate degree, taught college courses, and began to compose poetry. In the early 1970s she took on the names Ntozake, meaning "she who comes with her own things," and Shange, meaning "she who walks like a lion," and started collaborating with the dancer and choreographer Paula Moss on the experimental work that would eventually become *for colored girls who have considered suicide/when the rainbow is enuf.* First produced in 1975, *for colored girls* is what Shange calls a choreopoem, a full-length performance consisting of actors reciting poetic monologues. The seven women who perform *for colored girls* exhibit a wide range of voices that serve to, in Shange's words, "deslaveryize" the English language. Shange has also written essays, novels, children's books, and several other plays. This excerpt from *for colored girls* offers an eloquent comment on the condition of "bein . . . colored . . . in this modern world."

NO MORE LOVE POEMS #1

(1975)

ever since i realized there waz someone callt
a colored girl an evil woman a bitch or a nag
i been tryin not to be that & leave bitterness
in somebody else's cup/ come to somebody to
    love me
without deep & nasty smellin scald from lye or
    bein
left screamin in a street fulla lunatics/ whisperin
slut bitch bitch niggah/ get outta here wit alla
    that/
i didn't have any of that for you/ i brought you
    what joy
i found & i found joy/ honest fingers round my
    face/ with
dead musicians on 78's from cuba/ or live musi-
    cians on five
dollar lp's from chicago/ where i have never
    been/ & i love
willie colon & arsenio rodriguez/ especially cuz i
    can make
the music loud enuf/ so there is no me but
    dance/ & when
i can dance like that/ there's nothin cd hurt me/
    but

i get tired & i haveta come offa the floor & then
   there's
that woman who hurt you/ who you left/ three or
   four times/
& just went back/ after you put my heart in the
   bottom of
yr shoe/ you just walked back to where you hurt/
   & i didnt
have nothin/ so i went to where somebody had
   somethin for me/
but he waznt you/ & i waz on the way back from
   her house
in the bottom of yr shoe/ so this is not a love
   poem/ cuz there
are only memorial albums available/ & even
   charlie mingus
wanted desperately to be a pimp/ & i wont be
   able to see eddie
palmieri for months/ so this is a requium for
   myself/ cuz i
have died in a real way/ not wid aqua coffins &
   du-wop cadillacs/
i used to joke abt when i waz messin round/ but a
   real dead
lovin is here for you now/ cuz i dont know any-
   more/ how
to avoid my own face wet wit my tears/ cuz i had
   convinced
myself colored girls had no right to sorrow/ & i
   lived

& loved that way & kept sorrow on the curb/
   allegedly
for you/ but i know i did it for myself/
i cdnt stand it
i cdnt stand bein sorry & colored at the same time
it's so redundant in the modern world

SECTION TWO · "SO LIKE I SAY . . ."

VERNACULAR SHORT STORIES

SECTION TWO · "SO LIKE I SAY ." VERNACULAR SHORT STORIES · SECTION TWO · "SO LIKE I SAY . . ." · VERNACULAR SHORT STORIES · SECTION TWO · "SO LIKE I SAY " . VERNACULAR SHORT STORIES

SECTION TWO · "SO LIKE I SAY " VERNACULAR SHORT STORIES SECTION TWO · "SO LIKE I SAY " · VERNACULAR SHORT STORIES · SECTION TWO · "SO LIKE I SAY " VERNACULAR SHORT STORIES · SECTION TWO · "SO LIKE I SAY . . ." · VERNACULAR

T HESE SHORT STORIES from India, New Zealand, Papua New Guinea, Scotland, Trinidad, and the United States have in common an informal voice that charms and cajoles its readers. Vernacular short fiction has always embraced the theme of the hustle. Even as we take in tales of how a bashful narrator has been hustled, we often have a sense that we too are being taken in. The earliest story in this section is Mark Twain's famous yarn "The Celebrated Jumping Frog of Calaveras County." Twain's mantle has been assumed by such wry storytellers as Charles Chesnutt in his Reconstruction-era *Conjure Woman* collection and Earl Lovelace in his humorous account of 1970s Trinidad. Chesnutt's recurrent protagonist Julius McAdoo strategically employs seemingly innocent plantation tales in order to serve his own unspoken ends. In Lovelace's story, "Joebell believe the whole world is a hustle" and operates accordingly.

The Scottish writer Irvine Welsh adds yet another layer of complexity by using short fiction as an opportunity for self-parody. In "Granny's Old Junk," the elements Welsh employs so successfully in his other fiction appear in a most unexpected place. Welsh's self-parody both reminds us of how vernacular literature has become institutionalized and also leads us to wonder whether we are the ones who are being duped. We should have such suspicions in relation to other vernacular genres as well: Paul Keens-Douglas's poem "Wukhand," Jonathan Safran Foer's novel *Everything is Illuminated,* and Sam Selvon's novel *The Housing Lark* come most readily to mind. But short stories, rooted as so many of them are in the "tall tale," are especially entertaining and bedeviling.

CHARLES CHESNUTT

CHARLES CHESNUTT was born in 1858 in Cleveland, Ohio. After the American Civil War he moved with his family to Fayetteville, North Carolina, where his parents had been "free persons of color" before the war. He worked as a teacher and school administrator in the Carolinas, returned to Cleveland in 1884 to practice law, and also began writing short stories. In 1899 he published *The Conjure Woman and Other Conjure Tales,* a collection of linked frame tales featuring the ex-slave Julius McAdoo. By the time of his death in 1932, Chesnutt had also written several novels and a biography of Frederick Douglass. Throughout *The Conjure Woman,* Chesnutt demonstrates how local lore can be employed strategically. The collection is narrated by a wealthy white Northerner named John who has recently arrived in rural North Carolina with his neurasthenic wife, Annie. In hiring Julius as their coachman, they also acquire a local informant and a master storyteller. As in Twain's "True Story," the narrator does not possess all the knowledge that we ultimately do: in this case, John characterizes Julius's tales as "revealing the Oriental cast of the negro's imagination," but we readers come to know better. The story with which Julius entertains John and Annie serves at once to symbolize slavery's profound assault on the integrity of its victims' bodies and also to carry out Julius's own postbellum agenda.

PO' SANDY

(1899)

On the northeast corner of my vineyard in central North Carolina, and fronting on the Lumberton plank-road, there stood a small frame house, of the simplest construction. It was built of pine lumber, and contained but one room, to which one window gave light and one door admission. Its weatherbeaten sides revealed a virgin innocence of paint. Against one end of the house, and occupying half its width, there stood a huge brick chimney: the crumbling mortar had left large cracks between the bricks; the bricks themselves had begun to scale off in large flakes, leaving the chimney sprinkled with unsightly blotches. These evidences of decay were but partially concealed by a creeping vine, which extended its slender branches hither and thither in an ambitious but futile attempt to cover the whole chimney. The wooden shutter, which had once protected the unglazed window, had fallen from its hinges, and lay rotting in the rank grass and jimson-weeds beneath. This building, I learned when I bought the place, had been used as a schoolhouse for several years prior to the breaking out of the war, since which time it had remained unoccupied, save when some stray cow or vagrant hog had sought shelter within its walls from the chill rains and nipping winds of winter.

One day my wife requested me to build her a new kitchen.

The house erected by us, when we first came to live upon the vineyard, contained a very conveniently arranged kitchen; but for some occult reason my wife wanted a kitchen in the back yard, apart from the dwelling-house, after the usual Southern fashion. Of course I had to build it.

To save expense, I decided to tear down the old school-house, and use the lumber, which was in a good state of preservation, in the construction of the new kitchen. Before demolishing the old house, however, I made an estimate of the amount of material contained in it, and found that I would have to buy several hundred feet of lumber additional, in order to build the new kitchen according to my wife's plan.

One morning old Julius McAdoo, our colored coachman, harnessed the gray mare to the rockaway, and drove my wife and me over to the sawmill from which I meant to order the new lumber. We drove down the long lane which led from our house to the plank-road; following the plank-road for about a mile, we turned into a road running through the forest and across the swamp to the sawmill beyond. Our carriage jolted over the half-rotted corduroy road which traversed the swamp, and then climbed the long hill leading to the sawmill. When we reached the mill, the foreman had gone over to a neighboring farmhouse, probably to smoke or gossip, and we were compelled to await his return before we could transact our business. We remained seated in the carriage, a few rods from the mill, and watched the leisurely movements of the mill-hands. We had not waited long before a huge pine log was placed in position, the machinery of the mill was set in motion, and the circular saw began to eat its way through the log, with a loud whir which resounded throughout the vicinity of the mill. The sound rose and fell in a sort of rhythmic cadence, which, heard from where we sat, was not unpleasing, and not loud enough to prevent conversation. When the saw started on its second journey through the log, Julius observed, in a lugubrious tone, and with a perceptible shudder:—

"Ugh! but dat des do cuddle my blood!"

"What's the matter, Uncle Julius?" inquired my wife, who is of a very sympathetic turn of mind. "Does the noise affect your nerves?"

"No, Mis' Annie," replied the old man, with emotion, "I ain' nervous; but dat saw, a-cuttin' en grindin' thoo dat stick er timber, en moanin', en groanin,' en sweekin', kyars my 'memb'ance back ter ole times, en 'min's me er po' Sandy." The pathetic intonation with which he lengthened out the "po' Sandy" touched a responsive chord in our own hearts.

"And who was poor Sandy?" asked my wife, who takes a deep interest in the stories of plantation life which she hears from the lips of the older colored people. Some of these stories are quaintly humorous; others wildly extravagant, revealing the Oriental cast of the negro's imagination; while others, poured freely into the sympathetic ear of a Northern-bred woman, disclose many a tragic incident of the darker side of slavery.

"Sandy," said Julius, in reply to my wife's question, "was a nigger w'at useter b'long ter ole Mars Marrabo McSwayne. Mars Marrabo's place wuz on de yuther side'n de swamp, right nex' ter yo' place. Sandy wuz a monst'us good nigger, en could do so many things erbout a plantation, en alluz 'ten' ter his wuk so well, dat w'en Mars Marrabo's chilluns growed up en married off, dey all un 'em wanted dey daddy fer ter gin 'em Sandy fer a weddin' present. But Mars Marrabo knowed de res' would n' be satisfied ef he gin Sandy ter a'er one un 'em; so w'en dey wuz all done married, he fix it by 'lowin' one er his chilluns ter take Sandy fer a mont' er so, en den ernudder for a mont' er so, en so on dat erway tel dey had all had 'im de same lenk er time; en den dey would all take him roun' ag'in, 'cep'n' oncet in a w'ile w'en Mars Marrabo would len' 'im ter some er his yuther kinfolks 'roun' de country, w'en dey wuz short er han's; tel bimeby it got so Sandy did n' hardly knowed whar he wuz gwine ter stay fum one week's een' ter de yuther.

"One time w'en Sandy wuz lent out ez yushal, a spekilater come erlong wid a lot er niggers, en Mars Marrabo swap' Sandy's wife off fer a noo 'oman. W'en Sandy come back, Mars Marrabo gin 'im a dollar, en 'lowed he wuz monst'us sorry fer ter break up de fambly, but de spekilater had gin 'im big boot, en times wuz hard en money skase, en so he wuz bleedst ter make de trade. Sandy tuk on some 'bout losin' his wife, but he soon seed dey want no use cryin' ober spilt merlasses; en bein' ez he lacked de looks er de noo 'oman, he tuk up wid her atter she'd be'n on de plantation a mont' er so.

"Sandy en his noo wife got on mighty well tergedder, en de niggers all 'mence' ter talk about how lovin' dey wuz. Wen Tenie wuz tuk sick oncet, Sandy useter set up all night wid 'er, en den go ter wuk in de mawnin' des lack he had his reg'lar sleep; en Tenie would 'a' done anythin' in de worl' for her Sandy.

"Sandy en Tenie had n' be'n libbin' tergedder fer mo' d'n two mont's befo' Mars Marrabo's old uncle, w'at libbed down in Robeson County, sent up ter fin' out ef Mars Marrabo could n' len' 'im er hire 'im a good han' fer a mont' er so. Sandy's marster wuz one er dese yer easy-gwine folks w'at wanter please eve'ybody, en he says yas, he could len' 'im Sandy. En Mars Marrabo tol' Sandy fer ter git ready ter go down ter Robeson nex' day, fer ter stay a mont' er so.

"It wuz monst'us hard on Sandy fer ter take 'im 'way fum Tenie. It wuz so fur down ter Robeson dat he did n' hab no chance er comin' back ter see her tel de time wuz up; he would

n' 'a' mine comin' ten er fifteen mile at night ter see Tenie,
but Mars Marrabo's uncle's plantation wuz mo' d'n forty mile
off. Sandy wuz mighty sad en cas' down atter w'at Mars
Marrabo tol' 'im, en he says ter Tenie, sezee:—

"'I'm gittin' monst'us ti'ed er dish yer gwine roun' so
much. Here I is lent ter Mars Jeems dis mont', en I got ter do
so-en-so; en ter Mars Archie de nex' mont', en I got ter do so-
en-so; den I got ter go ter Miss Jinnie's: en hit's Sandy dis en
Sandy dat, en Sandy yer en Sandy dere, tel it 'pears ter me I
ain' got no home, ner no marster, ner no mistiss, ner no nuffin. I can't eben keep a wife: my yuther ole 'oman wuz sol' away
widout my gittin' a chance fer ter tell her good-by; en now I got
ter go off en leab you, Tenie, en I dunno whe'r I'm eber gwine
ter see you ag'in er no. I wisht I wuz a tree, er a stump, er a
rock, er sump'n w'at could stay on de plantation fer a w'ile.'

"Atter Sandy got thoo talkin', Tenie didn' say near word,
but des sot dere by de fier, studyin' en studyin'. Bimeby she up
'n' says:—

"'Sandy, is I eber tol' you I wuz a cunjuh 'oman?'

"Co'se Sandy had n' nebber dremp' er nuffin lack dat, en
he made a great 'miration w'en he hear w'at Tenie say. Bimeby
Tenie went on:—

"'I ain' goophered nobody, ner done no cunjuh wuk, fer fifteen year er mo'; en w'en I got religion I made up my mine I
would n' wuk no mo' goopher. But dey is some things I doan
b'lieve it's no sin fer ter do; en ef you doan wanter be sent
roun' fum pillar ter pos', en ef you doan wanter go down ter
Robeson, I kin fix things so you won't haf ter. Ef you'll des say
de word, I kin turn you ter w'ateber you wanter be, en you kin
stay right whar you wanter, ez long ez you mineter."

"Sandy say he doan keer; he's will-in' fer ter do anythin' fer

ter stay close ter Tenie. Den Tenie ax 'im ef he doan wanter be
turnt inter a rabbit.

"Sandy say, 'No, de dogs mought git atter me.'

"'Shill I turn you ter a wolf?' sez Tenie.

"'No, eve'ybody 's skeered er a wolf, en I doan want nobody
ter be skeered er me.'

"'Shill I turn you ter a mawkin'-bird?'

"'No, a hawk mought ketch me. I wanter be turnt inter
sump'n w'at'll stay in one place.'

"'I kin turn you ter a tree,' sez Tenie. 'You won't hab no
mouf ner years, but I kin turn you back oncet in a w'ile, so you
kin git sump'n ter eat, en hear w'at 's gwine on.'

"Well, Sandy say dat'll do. En so Tenie tuk 'im down by de
aidge er de swamp, not fur fum de quarters, en turnt 'im inter
a big pine-tree, en sot 'im out 'mongs' some yuther trees. En
de nex' mawnin', ez some er de fiel' han's wuz gwine long
dere, dey seed a tree w'at dey did n' 'member er habbin' seed
befo'; it wuz monst'us quare, en dey wuz bleedst ter 'low dat
dey had n' 'membered right, er e'se one er de saplin's had
be'n growin' monst'us fas'.

"W'en Mars Marrabo 'skiver' dat Sandy wuz gone, he 'lowed
Sandy had runned away. He got de dogs out, but de las' place
dey could track Sandy ter wuz de foot er dat pine-tree. En dere
de dogs stood en barked, en bayed, en pawed at de tree, en tried
ter climb up on it; en w'en dey wuz tuk roun' thoo de swamp ter
look fer de scent, dey broke loose en made fer dat tree ag'in. It
wuz de beatenis' thing de w'ite folks eber hearn of, en Mars
Marrabo 'lowed dat Sandy must 'a' clim' up on de tree en jump'
off on a mule er sump'n, en rid fur ernuff fer ter spile de scent.
Mars Marrabo wanted ter 'cuse some er de yuther niggers er
heppin' Sandy off, but dey all 'nied it ter de las'; en eve'ybody

knowed Tenie sot too much sto' by Sandy fer ter he'p 'im run away whar she could n' nebber see 'im no mo'.

"W'en Sandy had be'n gone long ernuff fer folks ter think he done got clean away, Tenie useter go down ter de woods at night en turn 'im back, en den dey 'd slip up ter de cabin en set by de fire en talk. But dey ha' ter be monst'us keerful, er e'se somebody would 'a' seed 'em, en dat would 'a' spile' de whole thing; so Tenie alluz turnt Sandy back in de mawnin' early, befo' anybody wuz a-stirrin'.

"But Sandy did n' git erlong widout his trials en tribberlations. One day a woodpecker come erlong en 'mence' ter peck at de tree; en de nex' time Sandy wuz turnt back he had a little roun' hole in his arm, des lack a sharp stick be'n stuck in it. Atter dat Tenie sot a sparrer-hawk fer ter watch de tree; en w'en de woodpecker come erlong nex' mawnin' fer ter finish his nes', he got gobble' up mos' 'fo' he stuck his bill in de bark.

"Nudder time, Mars Marrabo sent a nigger out in de woods fer ter chop tuppentime boxes. De man chop a box in dish yer tree, en hack' de bark up two er th'ee feet, fer ter let de tuppentime run. De nex' time Sandy wuz turnt back he had a big skyar on his lef' leg, des lack it be'n skunt; en it tuk Tenie nigh 'bout all night fer ter fix a mixtry ter kyo it up. Atter dat, Tenie sot a hawnet fer ter watch de tree; en w'en de nigger come back ag'in fer ter cut ernudder box on de yuther side'n de tree, de hawnet stung 'im so hard dat de ax slip en cut his foot nigh 'bout off.

"W'en Tenie see so many things happenin' ter de tree, she 'eluded she 'd ha' ter turn Sandy ter sump'n e'se; en atter studyin' de matter ober, en talkin' wid Sandy one ebenin', she made up her mine fer ter fix up a gopher mixtry w'at would turn herse'f en Sandy ter foxes, er sump'n, so dey could run away en go some'rs whar dey could be free en lib lack w'ite folks.

"But dey ain' no tellin' w'at's gwine ter happen in dis worl'.

Tenie had got de night sot fer her en Sandy ter run away, w'en dat ve'y day one er Mars Marrabo's sons rid up ter de big house in his buggy, en say his wife wuz monst'us sick, en he want his mammy ter len' 'im a 'oman fer ter nuss his wife. Tenie's mistiss say sen' Tenie; she wuz a good nuss. Young mars wuz in a tarrible hurry fer ter git back home. Tenie wuz washin' at de big house dat day, en her mistiss say she should go right 'long wid her young marster. Tenie tried ter make some 'scuse fer ter git away en hide 'tel night, w'en she would have eve'ything fix' up fer her en Sandy; she say she wanter go ter her cabin fer ter git her bonnet. Her mistiss say it doan matter 'bout de bonnet; her head-hankcher wuz good ernuff. Den Tenie say she wanter git her bes' frock; her mistiss say no, she doan need no mo' frock, en w'en dat one got dirty she could git a clean one whar she wuz gwine. So Tenie had ter git in de buggy en go 'long wid young Mars Dunkin ter his plantation, w'ich wuz mo' d'n twenty mile away; en dey wa'n't no chance er her seein' Sandy no mo' 'tel she come back home. De po' gal felt monst'us bad 'bout de way things wuz gwine on, en she knowed Sandy mus' be a wond'rin' why she didn' come en turn 'im back no mo'.

"Wiles Tenie wuz away nussin' young Mars Dunkin's wife, Mars Marrabo tuk a notion fer ter buil' 'im a noo kitchen; en bein' ez he had lots er timber on his place, he begun ter look 'roun' fer a tree ter hab de lumber sawed out'n. En I dunno how it come to be so, but he happen fer ter hit on de ve'y tree w'at Sandy wuz turnt inter. Tenie wuz gone, en dey wa'n't nobody ner nuffin fer ter watch de tree.

"De two men w'at cut de tree down say dey nebber had sech a time wid a tree befo': dey axes would glansh off, en did n' 'pear ter make no progress thoo de wood; en of all de creakin', en shakin', en wobblin' you eber see, dat tree done it w'en it commence' ter fall. It wuz de beatenis' thing!

"W'en dey got de tree all trim' up, dey chain it up ter a timber waggin, en start fer de sawmill. But dey had a hard time gittin' de log dere: fus' dey got stuck in de mud w'en dey wuz gwine crosst de swamp, en it wuz two er th'ee hours befo' dey could git out. W'en dey start' on ag'in, de chain kep' a-comin' loose, en dey had ter keep a-stoppin' en a-stoppin' fer ter hitch de log up ag'in. W'en dey commence' ter climb de hill ter de sawmill, de log broke loose, en roll down de hill en in 'mongs' de trees, en hit tuk nigh 'bout half a day mo' ter git it haul' up ter de sawmill.

"De nex' mawnin' atter de day de tree wuz haul' ter de sawmill, Tenie come home. W'en she got back ter her cabin, de fus' thing she done wuz ter run down ter de woods en see how Sandy wuz gittin' on. Wen she seed de stump standin' dere, wid de sap runnin' out'n it, en de limbs layin' scattered roun', she nigh 'bout went out'n her min'. She run ter her cabin, en got her goopher mixtry, en den follered de track er de timber waggin ter de sawmill. She knowed Sandy could n' lib mo' d'n a minute er so ef she turnt him back, fer he wuz all chop' up so he'd 'a' be'n bleedst ter die. But she wanted ter turn 'im back long ernuff fer ter 'splain ter 'im dat she had n' went off a-purpose, en lef 'im ter be chop' down en sawed up. She did n' want Sandy ter die wid no hard feelin's to'ds her.

"De han's at de sawmill had des got de big log on de ker-ridge, en wuz startin' up de saw, w'en dey seed a 'oman runnin' up de hill, all out er bref, cryin' en gwine on des lack she wuz plumb 'stracted. It wuz Tenie; she come right inter de mill, en th'owed herse'f on de log, right in front er de saw, a-hollerin' en cryin' ter her Sandy ter fergib her, en not ter think hard er her, fer it wa'n't no fault er hern. Den Tenie 'membered de tree did n' hab no years, en she wuz gittin' ready fer ter wuk her goopher mixtry so ez ter turn Sandy back, w'en de mill-hands kotch holt er her en tied her arms wid a rope, en fasten'

her to one er de posts in de sawmill; en den dey started de saw
up ag'in, en cut de log up inter bo'ds en scantlin's right befo'
her eyes. But it wuz mighty hard wuk; fer of all de sweekin', en
moanin', en groanin', dat log done it w'iles de saw wuz a-
cuttin' thoo it. De saw wuz one er dese yer ole-timey, up-en-
down saws, en hit tuk longer dem days ter saw a log 'en it do
now. Dey greased de saw, but dat did n' stop de fuss; hit kep'
right on, tel fin'ly dey got de log all sawed up.

"W'en de oberseah w'at run de sawmill come fum breakfas',
de han's up en tell him 'bout de crazy 'oman—ez dey s'posed
she wuz—w'at had come runnin' in de sawmill, a-hollerin' en
gwine on, en tried ter th'ow herse'f befo' de saw. En de
oberseah sent two er th'ee er de han's fer ter take Tenie back
ter her marster's plantation.

"Tenie 'peared ter be out'n her min' fer a long time, en her
marster ha' ter lock her up in de smoke-'ouse 'tel she got ober
her spells. Mars Marrabo wuz monst'us mad, en hit would 'a'
made yo' flesh crawl fer ter hear him cuss, 'caze he say de
spekilater w'at he got Tenie fum had fooled 'im by wukkin' a
crazy 'oman off on him. Wiles Tenie wuz lock up in de smoke-
'ouse, Mars Marrabo tuk 'n' haul de lumber fum de sawmill,
en put up his noo kitchen.

"Wen Tenie got quiet' down, so she could be 'lowed ter go
'roun' de plantation, she up'n' tole her marster all erbout
Sandy en de pine-tree; en w'en Mars Marrabo hearn it, he
'lowed she wuz de wuss 'stracted nigger he eber hearn of. He
did n' know w'at ter do wid Tenie: fus' he thought he'd put her
in de po'house; but fin'ly, seein' ez she did n' do no harm ter
nobody ner nuffin, but des went 'roun' moanin', en groanin',
en shakin' her head, he 'cluded ter let her stay on de plantation en nuss de little nigger chilluns w'en dey mammies wuz
ter wuk in de cotton-fiel'.

"De noo kitchen Mars Marrabo buil' wuz n' much use, fer it had n' be'n put up long befo' de niggers 'mence' ter notice quare things erbout it. Dey could hear sump'n moanin' en groanin' 'bout de kitchen in de night-time, en w'en de win' would blow dey could hear sump'n a-hollerin' en sweekin' lack it wuz in great pain en sufferin'. En it got so atter a w'ile dat it wuz all Mars Marrabo's wife could do ter git a 'oman ter stay in de kitchen in de daytime long ernuff ter do de cookin'; en dey wa'n't near nigger on de plantation w'at would n' rudder take forty dan ter go 'bout dat kitchen atter dark,—dat is, 'cep'n' Tenie; she did n' 'pear ter min' de ha'nts. She useter slip 'roun' at night, en set on de kitchen steps, en lean up agin de do'-jamb, en run on ter herse'f wid some kine er foolishness w'at nobody could n' make out; fer Mars Marrabo had th'eaten' ter sen' her off'n de plantation ef she say anything ter any er de yuther niggers 'bout de pine-tree. But somehow er 'nudder de niggers foun' out all erbout it, en dey all knowed de kitchen wuz ha'nted by Sandy's sperrit. En bimeby hit got so Mars Marrabo's wife herse'f wuz skeered ter go out in de yard atter dark.

"Wen it come ter dat, Mars Marrabo tuk en to' de kitchen down, en use' de lumber fer ter buil' dat ole school'ouse w'at you er talkin' 'bout pullin' down. De school'ouse wuz n' use' 'cep'n' in de daytime, en on dark nights folks gwine 'long de road would hear quare soun's en see quare things. Po' ole Tenie useter go down dere at night, en wander 'roun' de school'ouse; en de niggers all 'lowed she went fer ter talk wid Sandy's sperrit. En one winter mawnin', w'en one er de boys went ter school early fer ter start de fire, w'at should he fin' but po' ole Tenie, layin' on de flo', stiff, en col', en dead. Dere did n' 'pear ter be nuffin pertickler de matter wid her,—she had des grieve' herse'f ter def fer her Sandy. Mars Marrabo didn' shed no tears. He thought Tenie wuz crazy, en dey wa'n't no tellin' w'at she mought do nex'; en dey ain' much room in dis worl' fer crazy w'ite folks, let 'lone a crazy nigger.

"Hit wa'n't long atter dat befo' Mars Marrabo sol' a piece er his track er lan' ter Mars Dugal' McAdoo,—*my* ole marster,— en dat's how de ole school'ouse happen to be on yo' place. Wen de wah broke out, de school stop', en de ole school'ouse be'n stannin' empty ever sence,—dat is, 'cep'n' fer de ha'nts. En folks sez dat de ole school'ouse, er any yuther house w'at got any er dat lumber in it w'at wuz sawed out'n de tree w'at Sandy wuz turnt inter, is gwine ter be ha'nted tel de las' piece er plank is rotted en crumble' inter dus'."

Annie had listened to this gruesome narrative with strained attention.

"What a system it was," she exclaimed, when Julius had finished, "under which such things were possible!"

"What things?" I asked, in amazement. "Are you seriously considering the possibility of a man's being turned into a tree?"

"Oh, no," she replied quickly, "not that"; and then she murmured absently, and with a dim look in her fine eyes, "Poor Tenie!"

We ordered the lumber, and returned home. That night, after we had gone to bed, and my wife had to all appearances been sound asleep for half an hour, she startled me out of an incipient doze by exclaiming suddenly,—

"John, I don't believe I want my new kitchen built out of the lumber in that old schoolhouse."

"You wouldn't for a moment allow yourself," I replied, with some asperity, "to be influenced by that absurdly impossible yarn which Julius was spinning to-day?"

"I know the story is absurd," she replied dreamily, "and I am not so silly as to believe it. But I don't think I should ever be able to take any pleasure in that kitchen if it were built out of that lumber. Besides, I think the kitchen would look better and last longer if the lumber were all new."

Of course she had her way. I bought the new lumber, though not without grumbling. A week or two later I was called away from home on business. On my return, after an absence of several days, my wife remarked to me,—

"John, there has been a split in the Sandy Run Colored Baptist Church, on the temperance question. About half the members have come out from the main body, and set up for themselves. Uncle Julius is one of the seceders, and he came to me yesterday and asked if they might not hold their meetings in the old schoolhouse for the present."

"I hope you didn't let the old rascal have it," I returned, with some warmth. I had just received a bill for the new lumber I had bought.

"Well," she replied, "I couldn't refuse him the use of the house for so good a purpose."

"And I'll venture to say," I continued, "that you subscribed something toward the support of the new church?"

She did not attempt to deny it.

"What are they going to do about the ghost?" I asked, somewhat curious to know how Julius would get around this obstacle.

"Oh," replied Annie, "Uncle Julius says that ghosts never disturb religious worship, but that if Sandy's spirit *should* happen to stray into meeting by mistake, no doubt the preaching would do it good."

JUNOT DÍAZ

JUNOT DÍAZ is a preeminent young American fiction writer. Born in 1968 in Santo Domingo, Dominican Republic, Díaz grew up there and in New Jersey. Like the stories in his widely acclaimed collection *Drown*, "The Brief Wondrous Life of Oscar Wao" travels between New Jersey and the Dominican Republic, bringing the same sharp observations and ironic humor to both locations. In fifteen brief sections, the story—almost a novella—chronicles the life of "ghettonerd" Oscar de Léon. Narrator Yunior, who appeared in *Drown*, recounts Oscar's travails during elementary school in Paterson, New Jersey; all-boys Catholic school ("for a fat, girl-crazy nigger like Oscar, a source of endless anguish"); Rutgers University; and finally a set of momentous trips to Santo Domingo.

THE BRIEF WONDROUS LIFE OF OSCAR WAO

(2000)

The Golden Age

Oscar de León was not one of those Dominican cats every-body's always going on about. He wasn't no player. Except for one time, he'd never had much luck with women.

He'd been seven then.

It's true: Oscar was a carajito who was into girls mad young. Always trying to kiss them, always coming up behind them during a merengue, the first nigger to learn the perrito and the one who danced it every chance he got. Because he was a Dominican boy raised in a relatively "normal" Dominican family, his nascent pimp-liness was encouraged by family and friends alike. During the parties—and there were many, many parties in those long-ago seventies days, before Washington Heights was Washington Heights, before the Bergenline became a straight shot of Spanish for almost a hundred blocks—some drunk relative inevitably pushed Oscar onto some little girl, and then everyone would howl as boy and girl approximated the hipmotism of the adults.

You should have seen him, his mother sighed. He was our little Porfirio Rubirosa.

He had "girlfriends" early. (Oscar was a stout kid, heading straight to fat, but his mother kept him nice in haircuts, and before the proportions of his head changed he'd had these lovely flashing eyes and these cute-ass cheeks.) The girls—his older sister's friends, his mother's friends, even his neighbor, a twenty-something postal employee who wore red on her lips and walked like she had a brass bell for an ass—all fell for him. Ese muchacho está bueno! Once, he'd even had two girl-friends at the same time, his only ménage à trois ever. With Maritza Chacón and Olga Polanca, two girls from his school.

The relationship amounted to Oscar's standing close to both girls at the bus stop, some undercover hand holding, and some very serious kissing on the lips, first Maritza, then Olga, while the three of them hid behind some bushes. (Look at that little macho, his mother's friends said. Qué hombre.)

The threesome lasted only a week. One day after school, Maritza cornered Oscar behind the swing set and laid down the law. It's either her or me! Oscar held Maritza's hand and talked seriously and at great length about his love for her and sug-gested that maybe they could all share, but Maritza wasn't hav-ing any of it. Maritza, with her chocolate skin and gray eyes, already expressing the Ogún energy that would chop down obstacles for her the rest of her life. Didn't take him long to decide: after all, Maritza was beautiful, and Olga was not. His logic as close to the yes/no math of insects as a nigger could get. He broke up with Olga the next day on the playground, Maritza at his side, and how Olga cried! Snots pouring out of her nose and everything! In later years, when he and Olga had both turned into overweight freaks, Oscar could not resist feel-ing the occasional flash of guilt when he saw Olga loping across a street or staring blankly out near the New York bus stop, won-dering how much his cold-as-balls breakup had contributed to her present fuckedupness. (Breaking up with her, he would remember, hadn't felt like anything; even when she started cry-ing, he hadn't been moved. He'd said, Don't be a baby.)

What *had* hurt, however, was when Maritza dumped *him*. The Monday after he'd shed Olga, he arrived at the bus stop only to discover beautiful Maritza holding hands with butt-ugly Nelson Pardo. At first Oscar thought it a mistake; the sun was in his eyes, he'd not slept enough the night before. But Maritza wouldn't even smile at him! Pretended he wasn't there. We should get married, she was saying to Nelson, and Nelson grinned moronically, turning up the street to look for the bus. Oscar was too hurt to speak; he sat down on the curb and felt something overwhelming surge up from his chest, and before he knew it he was crying, and when his sister Lola walked over and asked him what was the matter he shook his head. Look at the mariconcito, somebody snickered. Somebody else kicked his beloved lunchbox. When he got on the bus, still crying, the driver, a famously reformed PCP addict, said, Christ, what a fucking *baby*.

Maybe coincidence, maybe self-serving Dominican hyperbole, but it seemed to Oscar that from the moment Maritza dumped him his life shot straight down the tubes. Over the next couple of years he grew fatter and fatter, and early adolescence scrambled his face into nothing you could call cute; he got uncomfortable with himself and no longer went anywhere near the girls, because they always shrieked and called him gordo asqueroso. He forgot the perrito, forgot the pride he felt when the women in the family had called him hombre. He did not kiss another girl for a long, long time. As though everything he had in the girl department had burned up that one fucking week. Olga caught the same bad, no-love karma. She got huge and scary—a troll gene in her somewhere—and started drinking 151 straight out of the bottle and was taken out of school because she had a habit of screaming NATAS! In the middle of homeroom. Sorry, loca, home instruction for you. Even her breasts, when they finally emerged, were huge and scary.

And the lovely Maritza Chacón? Well, as luck would have it, Maritza blew up into the flyest girl in Paterson, New Jersey, one of the queens of New Peru, and, since she and Oscar were neighbors, he saw her plenty, hair as black and lush as a thunderhead, probably the only Peruvian girl on the planet with curly hair (he hadn't heard of Afro Peruvians yet or of a town called Chincha), body fine enough to make old men forget their infirmities, and from age thirteen steady getting in or out of some roughneck's ride. (Maritza might not have been good at much—not sports, not school, not work—but she was good at boys.) Oscar would watch Maritza's getting in and out all through his cheerless, sexless adolescence. The only things that changed in those years were the models of the cars, the size of Maritza's ass, and the music volting out of the car's speakers. First freestyle, then Special Ed–era hip-hop, and right at the very end, for just a little while, Hector Lavoe and the boys.

Oscar didn't imagine that she remembered their kisses but of course he remembered.

The Moronic Inferno

High school was Don Bosco Tech and since Don Bosco Tech was an all-boys Catholic school run by the Salesian Fathers and Brothers and packed with a couple of hundred insecure, hyperactive adolescents it was, for a fat, girl-crazy nigger like Oscar, a source of endless anguish.

Sophomore year Oscar's weight stabilized at about two-ten (two-twenty when he was depressed, which was often), and it had become clear to everybody, especially his family, that he'd become the neighborhood pariguayo. He wore his semikink hair in a Puerto Rican Afro, had enormous Section-8 glasses (his anti-pussy devices, his boys Al and Miggs called them), sported an unappealing trace of mustache, and possessed a pair of close-set eyes that made him look somewhat retarded. The Eyes of Mingus (a comparison he made himself one day, going through his mother's record collection; she was the only old-school Dominicana he knew who loved jazz; she'd arrived in the States in the early sixties and shacked up with morenos for years until she met Oscar's father, who put an end to that particular chapter of the All-African World Party). Throughout high school he did the usual ghettonerd things: he collected comic books, he played role-playing games, he worked at a hardware store to save money for an outdated Apple IIe. He was an introvert who trembled with fear every time gym class rolled around. He watched nerd shows like *Doctor Who* and *Blake's 7*, could tell you the difference between a Veritech fighter and a Zentraedi battle pod, and he used a lot of huge-sounding nerd words like "indefatigable" and "ubiquitous" when talking to niggers who would barely graduate from high school. He read Margaret Weis and Tracy Hickman novels (his favorite character was, of course, Raistlin) and became an early devotee of the End of the World. He devoured every book he could find that dealt with the End Times, from John Christopher's *Empty World* to Hal Lindsey's *The Late Great Planet Earth*. He didn't date no one. Didn't even come close. Inside, he was a passionate person who fell in love easily and deeply. His affection—that gravitational mass of love, fear, longing, desire, and lust that he directed at any and every girl in the vicinity—roamed across all Paterson, affixed itself everywhere without regard to looks, age, or availability. Despite the fact that he considered his affection this tremendous, sputtering force, it was actually more like a ghost because no girl ever seemed to notice it.

Anywhere else, his triple-zero batting average with the girls might have passed unremarked, but this is a Dominican kid, in a Dominican family. Everybody noticed his lack of game and everybody offered him advice. His tío Rodolfo (only recently released from Rahway State) was especially generous in his tutelage. We wouldn't want you to turn into one of those Greenwich Village maricones, Tío Rodolfo muttered ominously. You have to grab a muchacha, broder, y méteselo. That will take care of everything. Start with a fea. Coge that fea y méteselo! Rodolfo had four kids with three different women, so the nigger was without doubt the family's resident metiéndolo expert.

Oscar's sister Lola (who I'd start dating in college) was a lot more practical. She was one of those tough Jersey Latinas, a girl soccer star who drove her own car, had her own checkbook, called men bitches, and would eat a fat cat in front of you without a speck of vergüenza. When she was in sixth grade, she was raped by an older acquaintance, and surviving that urikán of pain, judgment, and bochinche had stripped her of cowardice. She'd say anything to anybody and she cut her hair short (anathema to late-eighties Jersey Dominicans) partially, I think, because when she'd been little her family had let it grow down past her ass—a source of pride, something I'm sure her rapist noticed and admired.

Oscar, Lola warned repeatedly, you're going to die a virgin.

Don't you think I know that? Another five years of this and I'll bet you somebody tries to name a church after me.

Cut the hair, lose the glasses, exercise. And get rid of those porn magazines. They're disgusting, they bother Mami, and they'll never get you a date.

Sound counsel, which he did not adopt. He was one of those niggers who didn't have any kind of hope. It wouldn't have been half bad if Paterson and its surrounding precincts had been, like Don Bosco, all male. Paterson, however, was girls the way NYC was girls. And if that wasn't guapas enough for you, well, then, head south, and there'd be Newark, Elizabeth, Jersey City, the Oranges, Union City, West New York, Weehawken—an urban swath known to niggers everywhere as Negrapolis One. He wasn't even safe in his own house; his sister's girlfriends were always hanging out, and when they were around he didn't need no *Penthouses*. Her girls were the sort of hot-as-balls Latinas who dated only weight-lifting morenos or Latino cats with guns in their cribs. (His sister was the anomaly—she dated the same dude all four years of high school, a failed Golden Gloves welterweight who was excruciatingly courteous and fucked her like he was playing connect the dots, a pretty boy she'd eventually dump after he dirty-dicked her with some Pompton Lakes Irish bitch.) His sister's friends were the Bergen County All-Stars, New Jersey's very own Ciguapas: primera was Gladys, who complained constantly about her chest being too big; Marisol, who'd end up in MIT and could out-salsa even the Goya dancers; Leticia, just off the boat, half Haitian, half Dominican, that special blend the Dominican government swears no existe, who spoke with the deepest accent, a girl so good she refused to sleep with three consecutive boyfriends! It wouldn't have been so bad if these girls hadn't treated Oscar like some deafmute harem guard; they blithely went on about the particulars of their sex lives while he sat in the kitchen clutching the latest issue of *Dragon*. Hey, he would yell, in case you're wondering, there's a male unit in here. Where? Marisol would say blandly. I don't see one.

Oscar Is Brave

Senior year found him bloated, dyspeptic, and, most cruelly, alone in his lack of a girlfriend. His two nerd boys, Al and Miggs, had, in the craziest twist of fortune, both succeeded in landing themselves girls that summer. Nothing special, skanks really, but girls nonetheless. Al had met his at Menlo Park Mall, near the arcade; she'd come on to him, he bragged, and when she informed him, after she sucked his dick, that she had a girlfriend *desperate* to meet somebody, Al had dragged Miggs away from his Atari and out to a movie, and the rest was, as they say, history. By the end of the week, Miggs had his, too, and only then did Oscar find out about any of it, while they were in his room setting up for another "hair-raising" Champions adventure against the Death-Dealing Destroyers. At first, he didn't say much. He just rolled his dice over and over. Said, You guys sure got lucky. Guess I'm next. It killed him that they hadn't thought to include him in their girl heists; he hated Al for inviting Miggs instead of him, and he hated Miggs for getting a girl, period. Al's getting a girl Oscar could comprehend; Al looked completely normal, and he had a nice gold necklace he wore everywhere. It was Miggs's girl-getting that astounded him. Miggs was an even bigger freak than Oscar. Acne galore and a retard's laugh and gray fucking teeth from having been given some medicine too young. What little faith Oscar had in the world took an SS-N-17 Snipe to the head. When, finally, he couldn't take it no more, he asked pathetically, What, these girls don't have any other friends?

Al and Miggs traded glances over their character sheets. I don't think so, dude.

And right there he realized something he'd never known: his fucked-up, comic-book-reading, role-playing, game-loving, no-sports-playing friends were embarrassed by *him.*

Knocked the architecture right out of his legs. He closed the game early—the Exterminators found the Destroyers' hideout right away; that was bogus, Al groused as Oscar showed them the door. Locked himself in his room, lay in bed for a couple of stunned hours, then got up, undressed in the bathroom he no longer had to share because his sister was at Rutgers, and examined himself in the mirror. The fat! The miles of stretch marks! The tumescent horribleness of his proportions! He looked straight out of a Daniel Clowes comic book. Like the fat, blackish kid in Beto Hernández's Palomar.

Jesus Christ, he whispered. I'm a Morlock.

Spent a week looking at himself in the mirror, turned himself every which way, took stock, didn't flinch, and then he went to Chucho's and had the barber shave his Puerto Rican 'fro off, lost the mustache, then the glasses, bought contacts, was already trying to stop eating, starving himself dizzy, and the next time Al and Miggs saw him Miggs said, Dude, what's the matter with you?

Changes, Oscar said pseudo-cryptically.

He, Miggs, and Al were never quite the same friends again. He hung out, saw movies, talked Los Brothers Hernández, Frank Miller, and Alan Moore with them but, over all, he kept his distance. Listened to their messages on the machine and resisted the urge to run over to their places. Didn't see them but once, twice a week. I've been finishing up my first novel, he told them when they asked about his absences.

Oscar Comes Close

In December, after all his college applications were in (Fairleigh Dickinson, Montclair, Rutgers, Drew, Glassboro State, William Paterson; he also sent an application to NYU, a one-in-a-million shot, and they rejected him so fast he was amazed the shit hadn't come back Pony Express) and winter was settling its pale, miserable ass across northern New Jersey,

Oscar fell in love with a girl in his SAT-prep class. Ana Acuña was a pretty, loudmouthed gordita who read Henry Miller books while she should have been learning to defeat problem sets. Their fifth class, he noticed her reading *Sexus*, and she noticed him noticing and, leaning over, she showed him a passage and he got an erection like a motherfucker.

You must think I'm weird, right? she said, during the break.

You ain't weird, he said. Believe me—I'm the top expert in the state.

Ana was a talker, had beautiful Caribbean-girl eyes, pure anthracite, and was the sort of heavy that almost every Island nigger dug (and wasn't shy about her weight, either), and, like every other girl in the neighborhood, wore tight black stirrup pants and the sexiest underwear she could afford. She was a peculiar combination of badmash and little girl—even before he visited her house, he knew there'd be an avalanche of stuffed animals on the bed—and there was something in the ease with which she switched between these two Anas that convinced him that there existed a third Ana, who was otherwise obscure and impossible to know. She'd got into Miller because her ex-boyfriend Manny had given her the books before he joined the Army. She'd been thirteen when they started dating, he'd been twenty-four, a recovering coke addict—Ana talking about these things like they weren't nothing at all.

You were thirteen and your mother *let* you date some old-ass nigger?

My parents *loved* Manny, she said. My mom used to cook dinner for him.

He said, That's crazy. (And later, at home, he asked his sister, back on winter break, Would you let your thirteen-year-old daughter date some twenty-four-year-old guy? Sure, she

snorted, right after they killed me. But they better cut my fucking head off because, believe me, I'd come back from the dead
and get them both.)

Oscar and Ana in SAT class, Oscar and Ana in the parking lot
afterward, Oscar and Ana at the McDonald's, Oscar and Ana
become friends. Each day, Oscar expected her to be adiós,
each day she was still there. They got into the habit of talking
on the phone a couple times a week, about nothing, really,
spinning words out of their everyday; the first time *she* called
him, offering him a ride to the SAT class; a week later, he called
her, just to try it. His heart beating so hard he thought he
would die, but all she did was say, Oscar, listen to the *bullshit* my
sister pulled, and off they'd go, building another one of their
word-scrapers. By the fifth time he called, he no longer
expected the Big Blowoff. She was the first girl outside his family who admitted to having a period, who actually said to him,
I'm bleeding like a hog, an astounding confidence that he
kept turning over and over in his head. Because her appearance in his life was sudden, because she'd come in under his
radar, he didn't have time to raise his usual wall of nonsense or
throw some wild-ass expectations her way. Maybe, after four
years of not getting ass, he'd finally found his zone, because
amazingly enough, instead of making an idiot of himself as
one might have expected, given the hard fact that this was the
first girl he'd ever had a conversation with, he actually took it a
day at a time. He spoke to her plainly and without effort, and
discovered that his sharp, self-deprecating world view pleased
her immensely. He would say something obvious and unin-
spired, and she'd say, Oscar, you're really fucking smart. When

she said, I *love* men's hands, he spread both of his across his face and said faux-casual-like, Oh, *really?* It cracked her up.

Man, she said, I'm glad I got to know you.

And he said, I'm glad I'm me knowing you.

One night while he was listening to New Order and trying to chug through "Clay's Ark," his sister knocked on his door. At Rutgers, she'd shaved her head down to the bone, Sinéad style, and now everybody, including their mother, was convinced she was a jota.

You got a visitor, she said.

I do?

Yup. But you might want to clean up some, she warned.

It was Ana. Standing in his foyer, in full-length leather, her trigueña skin blood-charged from the cold, her face gorgeous with eyeliner, mascara, base, lipstick, and blush.

Freezing out, she said. She had her gloves in one hand like a crumpled bouquet.

Hey, was all he managed to say. He knew his sister was upstairs, listening.

What you doing? Ana asked.

Nothing.

Like let's go to a movie then.

Like OK, he said.

When he went upstairs to change, his sister was jumping up and down on his bed, low screaming, It's a date, it's a date, and she jumped onto his back and nearly toppled him clean through the bedroom window.

So is this some kind of date? he said as he slipped into her car.

She smiled wanly. You could call it that.

Ana drove a Cressida, and instead of taking them to the local theatre she headed down to the Amboy Multiplex. It was so hard for Oscar to believe what was happening that he couldn't take it seriously. The whole time the movie was on, Oscar kept expecting niggers to jump out with cameras and scream, Surprise! Boy, he said, trying to remain on her map, this is some movie. Ana nodded; she smelled of a perfume, and when she pressed close the heat of her body was *vertiginous.*

On the ride home, Ana complained about having a headache and they didn't speak for a long time. He tried to turn on the radio but she said, No, my head's really killing me. So he sat back and watched the Hess Building and the rest of Woodbridge slide past through a snarl of overpasses. The longer they went without speaking, the more morose he became. It's just a movie, he told himself. It's not like it's a date.

Ana seemed unaccountably sad and she chewed her bottom lip, a real bembe, until most of her lipstick was on her teeth and he was going to make a comment about it, but he decided not to.

I'm reading *Dune,* he said, finally.

She nodded. I *hate* that book.

They reached the Elizabeth exit, which is what New Jersey is really known for, industrial wastes on both sides of the turnpike, when Ana let loose a scream that threw him against the door.

Elizabeth! she shrieked. Close your fucking legs! Then she looked over at him, threw back her head, and laughed.

When he returned to the house, his sister said, Well?

Well, what?

Did you *fuck* her?

Jesus, Lola.

Don't lie to me. I know you Dominican men. She held up her hands and flexed the fingers in playful menace. Son pulpos.

The next day he woke up feeling like he'd been unshackled from his fat, like he'd been washed clean of his misery, and for a long time he couldn't remember why he felt this way and then finally he said her name. Little did he know that he'd entered into the bane of nerds everywhere: a let's-be-friends relationship.

In April, Oscar learned he was heading to Rutgers–New Brunswick. You'll love it, his sister promised him. I know I will, he said. I was meant for college. Ana was on her way to Penn State, honors program, full ride. It was also in April that her ex-boyfriend Manny returned from the Army—Ana told Oscar during one of their trips to Yaohan, the Japanese mall in Edgewater. Manny's sudden reappearance and Ana's joy over it shattered the hopes Oscar had cultivated. He's back, Oscar asked, like forever? Ana nodded. Apparently, Manny had got into trouble again, drugs, but this time, Ana insisted, he'd been set up by these three cocolos, a word he'd never heard her use, so he figured she'd got it from Manny. Poor Manny, she said.

Yeah, poor Manny, Oscar muttered.

Poor Manny, poor Ana, poor Oscar. Things changed quickly. First, Ana stopped being home all the time, and Oscar found himself stacking messages on her machine: This is Oscar, a bear is chewing my legs off, please call me. This is Oscar, they want a million dollars or it's over, please call me. She always got back to him after a couple of days and was pleasant about it, but still. Then she cancelled three Fridays in a row, and he had to settle for the clearly reduced berth of Sunday after church. She picked him up, and they drove out to Boulevard East and parked the car, and together they stared out at the Manhattan skyline. It wasn't an ocean, or a mountain range; it was, at least to Oscar, better.

On one of these little trips, she let slip, God, I'd forgotten how big Manny's cock is.

Like I really need to hear that, Oscar snapped.

I'm sorry, she said hesitantly. I thought we could talk about everything.

Well, it actually wouldn't be bad if you kept Manny's anatomical enormity to yourself.

With Manny and his *big cock* around, Oscar began dreaming about nuclear annihilation, how through some miracle he was first to hear about a planned attack, and without pausing to think he stole his tío's car, drove it to the store, stocked it full of supplies (shooting a couple of looters on the way), and then fetched Ana. What about Manny? she wailed. There's no time! he'd insisted, peeling out. When he was in a better mood, he let Ana discover Manny, who would be hanging from a light fixture in his apartment, his tongue bulbous in his mouth. The news of the imminent attack on the TV, a note pinned to his chest. *I koona taek it.* And then Oscar would comfort Ana and say something like, He was too weak for this hard new world.

Oscar even got—joy of joys!—the opportunity to meet the famous Manny, which was about as much fun as being called a fag during a school assembly (which had happened). Met him outside Ana's house. He was this intense emaciated guy with voracious eyes.

When they shook hands, Oscar was sure the nigger was going to smack him; he acted so surly. Manny was muy bald and completely shaved his head to hide it, had a hoop in each ear, and this leathery out-in-the-sun look of an old cat straining for youth.

So you're Ana's little friend, Manny said derisively.

That's me, Oscar said in a voice so full of cheerful innocuousness that he could have shot himself for it.

He snorted. I hope you ain't trying to chisel in on my girl.

Oscar said, Ha-ha. Ana flushed red, looked at the ground.

With Manny around, Oscar was exposed to an entirely new side of Ana. All they talked about now, the few times they saw each other, was Manny and the terrible things he did to her. Manny smacked her, Manny kicked her, Manny called her a fat twat, Manny cheated on her, she was sure, with this Cuban chickie from the middle school. They couldn't talk ten minutes without Manny beeping her and her having to call him back and assure him she wasn't with anybody else.

What am I going to do? she asked over and over, and Oscar always found himself holding her awkwardly and telling her, Well, I think if he's this bad you should break up with him, but she shook her head and said, I know I should, but I can't. I love him.

Oscar liked to kid himself that it was only cold, anthropological interest that kept him around to see how it would all end, but the truth was he couldn't extricate himself. He was totally and irrevocably in love with Ana. What he used to feel for those girls he'd never really known was nothing compared with the amor he was carrying in his heart for Ana. It had the density of a dwarf motherfucking star and at times he was a hundred percent sure it would drive him mad. Every Dominican family has stories about niggers who take love too far, and Oscar was beginning to suspect that they'd be telling one of these stories about him real soon.

Miraculous things started happening. Once, he blacked out while crossing an intersection. Another time, Miggs was goofing on him, talking smack, and for the first time ever Oscar lost his temper and swung on the nigger, connected so hard that homeboy's mouth spouted blood. Jesus Christ, Al said. Calm down! I didn't mean to do it, Oscar said unconvincingly. It was an accident. Mudafuffer, Miggs said. Mudafuffer! Oscar got so bad that one desperate night, after listening to Ana sobbing to him on the phone about Manny's latest bullshit, he said, I have to go to church now, and put down the phone, went to his tío's room and stole his antique Dragoon pistol, that oh-so-famous First Nation exterminating Colt .44, stuck its impressive snout down the front of his pants, and proceeded to stand in front of Manny's apartment. Come on, motherfucker, he said calmly. I got a nice eleven-year-old girl for you. He didn't care that he would more than likely be put away forever and that niggers like him got ass- and mouth-raped in jail, or that if the cops picked him up and found the gun they'd send his tío's ass up the river for parole violation. He didn't care about jack. His head contained nothing, it felt like it had been excavated, a perfect vacuum.

Folks started noticing that he was losing it. His mother, his tío, even Al and Miggs, not known for their solicitude, were like, Dude, what the fuck's the matter with you?

After he went on his third Manny hunt, he broke down and confessed to his sister, and she got them both on their knees in front of the altar she'd built to their dead abuela and had him swear on their mother's soul that he'd never pull anything like that again as long as he lived. She even cried, she was so worried about him.

You need to stop this, Mister.

I know I do, he said. But it's hard.

That night, he and his sister both fell asleep on the couch, she first. Her shins were covered in bruises. Before he joined her, he decided that this would be the end of it. He would tell Ana how he felt, and if she didn't come away with him then he wouldn't speak to her ever again.

They met at the Yaohan mall. Ordered two chicken-katsu curries and then sat in the large cafeteria with the view of Manhattan, the only gaijin in the whole joint.

He could tell by Ana's clothes that she had other plans that night. She was in a pair of black leather pants and had on one of those fuzzy light-pink sweaters that girls with nice chests can rock forever. Her face was so swollen from recent crying it looked like she was on cortisone.

You have beautiful breasts, he said as an opener.

Confusion, alarm. Oscar! What's the matter with you?

He looked out through the glass at Manhattan's western flank, looked out like he was some deep nigger. Then he told her.

There were no surprises. Her eyes went soft, she put a hand on his hand, her chair scraped closer, there was a strand of yellow in her teeth. Oscar, she said gently, I have a boyfriend.

So you don't love me?

Oscar. She breathed deep. I love you as a *friend*.

She drove him home; at the house, he thanked her for her time, walked inside, lay in bed. They didn't speak again.

In June, he graduated from Don Bosco. He heard in passing that, of everybody in their section of P-town, only he and Olga, poor, fucked-up Olga, had not attended even one prom. Dude, Miggs joked, maybe you should have asked her out.

He spent the summer working at the hardware store. Had so much time on his hands he started writing a novel for real. In September, he headed to Rutgers, and quickly buried himself in what amounted to the college version of what he'd majored in throughout high school: getting no ass. Despite swearing to be different, he went back to his nerdy ways, eating, not exercising, using flash words, and after a couple consecutive Fridays alone he joined the university's resident geek organization, RU Gamers.

Sentimental Education

The first time I met Oscar was at Rutgers. We were roommates our sophomore year, cramped up in Demarest, the university's official homo dorm, because Oscar wanted to be a writer and because I'd pulled the last number in the housing lottery. You never met more opposite niggers in your life. He was a dork, totally into Dungeons & Dragons and comic books; he had like a billion science-fiction paperbacks, all in his closet; and me, I was into girls, weight lifting, and Danocrine. (What is it with us niggers and our bodies? Not even Fanon can explain it to me.) I had this beautiful Irish-Puerto Rican girlfriend, a Plainfield girl I couldn't get enough of, a firefighter's daughter who didn't speak a word of Spanish, and I was into clubs like a motherfucker—Illusions, Foxes, Mercedes and Mink (on Springfield Ave. in Newark, the only club on the planet with a Ghettogirl Appreciation Night). Those were the Boricua Posse days, and I never got home before six in the morning, so mostly what I saw of Oscar was a big, dormant hump crashed out under a sheet. When we were in the dorm together, he was either working on his novel or talking on the phone to his sister, who I'd seen a few times at Douglass. (I'd tried to put a couple of words on her because she was no joke in the body department, but she cold-crumbed me.) Those first months, me and my boys ragged on Oscar a lot—I mean, he was a nerd, wasn't he?—and right before Halloween I told him he looked like that fat homo Oscar Wilde, which was bad news for him, because then all of us started calling him Oscar Wao. The sad part? After a couple of weeks, he started *answering* to it.

Besides me fucking with him, we never had no problems; he never got mad at me when I said shit, just sat there with a hurt stupid smile on his face. Made a brother feel kinda bad, and after the others left I would say, You know I was just kidding, right? By second semester, I even started to like the kid a little. Wasn't it Turgenev who said, Whom you laugh at you forgive and come near to loving? I didn't invite him out to no clubs, but we did start going to Brower Commons to eat, even checked out an occasional movie. We talked a little, mostly about girls, comic books, and our corny white-boy neighbors who were pussy asshole cocksuckers. Girls, though, were point zero; they were the world to Oscar. I mean, they were the world to me, too, but with him it was on some next shit. He got around a cute one and the nigger would almost start shaking. Easy to understand; our first month as roommates, he'd told me he'd never kissed one! Never! Jesus fucking Christ! The horror! It wasn't like I couldn't sympathize, but I didn't think acting like a nut around the mamacitas was going to help his case. I tried to give him advice—first off, cristiano, you have to stop gunning on the superbabes—but he wouldn't listen. He said, Nothing else works, I might as well make a fool out of myself.

It wasn't until the middle of spring semester that I ever saw Oscar really in love. Catalyn Sangre de Toro Luperón. Catalyn was this Puerto Rican Goth girl—in 1990, niggers were having trouble wrapping their heads around Goths, period, but a Puerto Rican Goth, that was as strange to us as a black Nazi. Anyway, Catalyn was her real name, but her around-the-cauldron name was La Jablesse. You think I'm kidding? Every standard a brother like me had, this girl short-circuited. Her hair she wore in this black Egypto cut, her eyes caked with eyeliner and mascara, her lips painted black, a Navajo tattoo across her whole back, and none of it mattered, because homegirl was *luminous*. She had no waist, big perfect tits, wore black spiderweb clothes, and her accent in Spanish and English was puro Guayama. Even I had been hot for Catalyn, but the one time I'd tried to mack her at the Douglass Library she picked up her books and moved to another table, and when I tried to come over to apologize she did it again.

Ice.

So: one day I caught Oscar talking to La Jablesse in Brower, and I had to watch, because I figured if I got roasted she was going to vaporize his ass. Of course, he was full on, and homegirl was holding her tray and looking at him askance, like, What the fuck does this freak want? She started walking away, and Oscar yelled out, We'll talk later, OK? And she shot back a Sure, all larded with sarcasm.

You have to give it to Oscar. He didn't let up. He just kept hitting on her with absolutely no regard for self or dignity, and eventually she must have decided he was harmless, because she started treating him civil. Soon enough, I saw them walking together down College Avenue. One day, I came home from classes and found La Jablesse sitting on my bed, Oscar sitting on his. I was speechless. She remembered me. You can always tell. She said, You want me to get off your bed? I said, Nah, picked up my gym bag, and ran out of there like a pussy. When I got back from the weight room, Oscar was on his computer. On page one billion of his novel.

I said, What's up with you and Miss Scarypants?

Nothing much. Then he smiled and I knew he'd heard about my lame-ass pickup attempt.

I was one sore loser; I said, Well, good luck, Wao. I just hope she doesn't sacrifice you to Beelzebub or anything.

Later, the two of them started going to movies together. Some narratives never die. She was the first person to get him to try mushrooms, and once, right at the end, when he was starting to talk about her like she was the Queen of Everything, she took him to her room, turned off the lights, lit some witchy candles, and danced for him.

What the hell was this girl thinking?

In less than a week, Oscar was in bed crying, and La Jablesse had a restraining order on his ass. Turns out Oscar walked in on Catalyn while she was "entertaining" some Goth kid, caught them both naked, probably covered with blood or something, and he berserked. Started tearing her place up, and Gothdude jumped butt-naked out the window. Same night, I found Oscar on his top bunk, bare-chested, the night he said, I fucked up real bad, Yunior.

He had to attend counselling, to keep from losing his housing, but now everybody in the dorm though he was some kind of major psycho. This is how our year together ended. Him at his computer, typing, me being asked in the hall how I liked dorming with Mr. Crazyman.

Would probably never have chilled with him again, but then, a year later, I started speaking to his sister, Lola de León. Femme-matador. The sort of girlfriend God gives you young, so you'll know loss the rest of your life. The head of every black and brown women's progressive organization at Douglass, beloved Phi Chi hermana, blah, blah, blah. She didn't have no kind of tact and talked too much for my taste, but, man, could she move, and her smile was enough to pull you across a room. I began noticing every time she was around, it was like she was on a high wire; I couldn't keep my eyes off her. I asked my boys what they thought about her and they laughed, said, Yo, she looks like a slave. Never forgave any of them for that.

Our first night together was at her place on Commercial Ave., and before I put my face between her legs she dragged me up by my ears. Why is this the face I cannot forget? Tired from finals, swollen from kissing. She said, Don't ever cheat on me.

I won't, I promised her. Don't laugh. My intentions were good.

We were still together at graduation, and we took pictures with each other's families—there's even a couple of me and Oscar. We look like a couple of circus freaks: I'm muscle-bound, hands as big as hams, and Oscar's heavy, squinting into the camera like we just pulled him out of a trunk and he doesn't know where the fuck he is.

The Dark Age

After college, Oscar moved back home. Left a virgin, returned one. Took down his childhood posters (Star Blazers, Captain Harlock) and tacked up his college ones (Akira and Terminator II). These were the early Bush years, the economy still sucked, and he kicked around doing nada for almost seven months until he started substituting at Don Bosco. A year later, the substituting turned into a full-time job. He could have refused, could have made a "saving throw" versus Death Magic, but instead he went with the flow. Watched his horizons collapse, told himself it didn't matter.

Had Don Bosco, since last we visited, been miraculously transformed by the spirit of Christian brotherhood? Had the eternal benevolence of the Lord cleansed the students of their bile? Negro, please. The only change that Oscar saw was in the older brothers, who all seemed to have acquired the inbred Innsmouth "look"; everything else (like white arrogance and the self-hate of people of color) was the same, and a familiar gleeful sadism still electrified the halls. Oscar wasn't great at teaching, his heart wasn't in it, and boys of all grades and dispositions shitted on him effusively. Students laughed when they spotted him in the halls. Pretended to hide their sandwiches. Asked in the middle of lectures if he ever got laid, and no matter how he responded they guffawed mercilessly. How demoralizing was that? And every day he found himself watching the "cool" kids torture the crap out of the fat, the ugly, the smart, the poor, the dark, the black, the unpopular, the African, the Indian, the Arab, the immigrant, the strange, the femenino, the gay—and in every one of these clashes he must have been seeing himself. Sometimes he tried to reach out to the school's whipping boys—You ain't alone, you know?—but the last thing a freak wants is a helping hand from another freak. In a burst of enthusiasm, he attempted to start a science-fiction club, and for two Thursdays in a row he sat in his classroom after school, his favorite books laid out in an attractive pattern, listened to the roar of receding footsteps in the halls, the occasional shout outside his door of Beam me up! and Nanoo-Nanoo! Then, after thirty minutes, he collected his books, locked the room, and walked down those same halls, alone, his footsteps sounding strangely dainty.

Social life? He didn't have one. Once a week he drove out to Woodbridge Mall and stared at the toothpick-thin black girl who worked at the Friendly's, who he was in love with but to whom he would never speak.

At least at Rutgers there'd been multitudes and an institutional pretense that allowed a mutant like him to approach without causing a panic. In the real world, girls turned away in disgust when he walked past. Changed seats at the cinema, and one woman on the crosstown bus even told him to stop thinking about her. I know what you're up to, she hissed. So stop it.

I'm a permanent bachelor, he told his sister.

There's nothing permanent in the world, his sister said tersely.

He pushed his fist into his eye. There is in me.

The home life? Didn't kill him, but didn't sustain him, either. His moms, smaller, rounder, less afflicted by the suffering of her youth, still the work golem, still sold second-rate clothes out of the back of her house, still allowed her Peruvian boarders to pack as many relatives as they wanted into the first floors. And Tío Rodolfo, Fofo to his friends, had reverted back to some of his hard pre-prison habits. He was on the caballo again, broke into lightning sweats at dinner, had moved into Lola's room, and now Oscar got to listen to him chicken-boning his stripper girlfriends almost every single night. Hey Tío, he yelled out, try to use the headboard a little less.

Oscar knew what he was turning into, the worst kind of human on the planet: an old, bitter dork. He was depressed for long periods of time. The Darkness. Some mornings, he would wake up and not be able to get out of bed. Had dreams that he was wandering around the evil planet Gordo, searching for parts for his crashed rocket ship, but all he encountered were burned-out ruins. I don't know what's wrong with me, he said to his sister over the phone. He threw students out of class for breathing, told his mother to fuck off, went into his tío's closet and put the Colt up between his eyes, then lay in bed and thought about his mother fixing him his plate for the rest of his life. (He heard her say into the phone when she thought he wasn't around, I don't care, I'm happy he's here.)

Afterward—when he no longer felt like a whipped dog inside, when he could go to work without wanting to cry—he suffered from overwhelming feelings of guilt. He would apologize to his mother. He would take the car and visit Lola. She lived in the city now, was letting her hair grow, had been pregnant once, a real moment of excitement, but she aborted it because I was cheating on her with a neighbor. (Our only baby.) He went on long rides. He drove as far as Amish country, would eat alone at a roadside diner, eye the Amish girls, imagine himself in a preacher suit, sleep in the back of the car, and then drive home.

Oscar Takes a Vacation

When Oscar had been at Don Bosco nearly three years, his moms asked him what plans he had for the summer. Every year, the family spent the better part of June, July, and August in Santo Domingo; Oscar hadn't accompanied them since Abuela had screamed out *Haitians!* once and died.

It's strange. If he'd said no, nigger would probably still be alive. But this ain't no Marvel Comics "What if?"—this ain't about stupid speculation, and time, as they say, is growing short. That May, Oscar was, for once, in better spirits. A couple of months earlier, after a particularly nasty bout with the Darkness, he'd started another one of his diets and combined it with long, lumbering walks around the neighborhood, and guess what? The nigger stuck with it and lost close on twenty pounds! A milagro! He'd finally repaired his ion drive; the evil planet Gordo was pulling him back but his fifties-style rocket, the Hijo de Sacrificio, wouldn't quit. Behold our cosmic explorer: eyes wide, lashed to his acceleration couch, his hand over his mutant heart.

He wasn't svelte by any stretch of the imagination, but he wasn't Joseph Conrad's wife no more, either. Earlier in the month, he'd even spoken to a bespectacled black girl on a bus, said, So, you're into photosynthesis, and she'd actually lowered her issue of *Cell* and said, Yes, I am. So what if he hadn't ever got past Earth Sciences and hadn't been able to convert that slight communication into a phone number or a date? Homeboy was, for the first time in ten years, feeling resurgent; nothing seemed to bother him, not his students, not the fact that *Doctor Who* had gone off the air, not his loneliness; he felt *insuperable,* and summers in Santo Domingo . . . Well, Santo Domingo summers have their own particular allure. For two months, Santo Domingo slaps the diaspora engine into reverse, yanks back as many of its expelled children as it can; airports choke with the overdressed; necks and luggage carousels groan under the accumulated weight of that year's cadenas and paquetes; restaurants, bars, clubs, theatres, malecones, beaches, resorts, hotels, moteles, extra rooms, barrios, colonias, campos, ingenios swarm with quisqueyanos from the world over: from Washington Heights to Roma, from Perth Amboy to Tokyo, from Brijeporr to Amsterdam, from Anchorage to San Juan; it's one big party; one big party for everybody but the poor, the dark, the jobless, the sick, the Haitian, their children, the bateyes, the kids whom certain Canadian, American, German, and Italian tourists love to rape—yes, sir, nothing like a Santo Domingo summer, and so for the first time in years Oscar said, My elder spirits have been talking to me, Ma. I think I might go. He was imagining himself in the middle of all that ass-getting, imagining himself in love with an Island girl. (A brother can't be wrong forever, can he?)

So curious a change in policy was this that even Lola quizzed him about it. You never go to Santo Domingo.

He shrugged. I guess I want to try something new.

Return to a Native Land

Family de León flew down to the capital on the fourteenth of June. (Oscar told his bosses, My aunt got eaten by a shark, it's horrible, so he could bail out of work early. His mother couldn't believe it. You lied to a *priest?*)

In the pictures Lola brought home—she had to leave early; her job gave her only two weeks and she'd already killed off all her aunts—there are shots of Oscar in the back of the house reading Octavia Butler, shots of Oscar on the Malecón with a bottle of Presidente in his hand, shots of Oscar at the Columbus lighthouse, where half of Villa Duarte used to stand, shots of Oscar in Villa Juana buying spark plugs, shots of Oscar trying on a hat on the Conde, shots of Oscar standing next to a burro. You can tell he's trying. He's smiling a lot, despite the bafflement in his eyes.

He's also, you might notice, not wearing his fat-guy coat.

Oscar Meets a Babe

After his initial two weeks on the Island, after he'd got somewhat used to the scorching weather and the surprise of waking up in another country, after he refused to succumb to that whisper that all long-term immigrants carry inside themselves, the whisper that says You Do Not Belong, after he'd gone to about ten clubs and, because he couldn't dance salsa or merengue or bachata, had sat and drunk his Presidentes while Lola and his

cousins burned holes in the floor, after he'd explained to people a hundred times that he'd been separated from his sister at
birth, after he spent a couple of quiet mornings on his own on
the Malecón, after he'd given out all his taxi money to beggars
and had to call his cousin to get home, after he'd watched shirt-
less, shoeless seven-year-olds fighting each other for the scraps
he'd left on his plate at an outdoor café, after the family visited
the shack in Baitoa where his moms had been born, after he
had taken a dump in a latrine and wiped his ass with a corncob,
after he'd got somewhat used to the surreal whirligig that was
life in the capital—the guaguas, the cops, the mind-boggling
poverty, the Dunkin' Donuts, the beggars, the Pizza Huts, the
tígueres selling newspapers at the intersections, the snarl of
streets and shacks that were the barrios, the masses of niggers
he waded through every day and who ran him over if he stood
still, the mind-boggling poverty, the skinny watchmen standing
in front of stores with their shotguns, the music, the raunchy
jokes heard on the streets, the Friday-night strolls down the
Avenida, the mind-boggling poverty—after he'd gone to Boca
Chica and Villa Mella, after the relatives berated him for having
stayed away so long, after he heard the stories about his father
and his mother, after he stopped marvelling at the amount of
political propaganda plastered up on every spare wall, after the
touched-in-the-head tío who'd been tortured during Balaguer's
reign came over and cried, after he'd swum in the Caribbean,
after Tío Rodolfo had got the clap from a puta (Man, his tío
cracked, what a pisser! Har-har!), after he'd seen his first
Haitians kicked off a guagua because niggers claimed they
"smelled," after he'd nearly gone nuts over all the bellezas he
saw, after all gifts they'd brought had been properly distributed,
after he'd brought flowers to his abuela's grave, after he had
diarrhea so bad his mouth watered before each detonation,

after he'd visited all the rinky-dink museums in the capital, after he stopped being dismayed that everybody called him gordo, after he'd been overcharged for almost everything he wanted to buy, after the terror and joy of his return subsided, after he settled down in his abuela's house, the house that the diaspora had built, and resigned himself to a long, dull, quiet summer, after his fantasy of an Island girlfriend caught a quick dicko (who the fuck had he been kidding? he couldn't dance, he didn't have loot, he didn't dress, he wasn't confident, he wasn't handsome, he wasn't from Europe, he wasn't fucking no Island girl), after Lola flew back to the States, Oscar fell in love with a semiretired puta.

Her name was Yvón Pimentel. Oscar considered her the start of his *real* life. (She was the end of it, too.)

She lived two houses over and was a newcomer to Mirador Norte. She was one of those golden mulatas that French-speaking Caribbeans call "chabines," that my boys call chicas de oro; she had snarled apocalyptic hair, amber eyes, and was one white-skinned relative away from jabao.

At first Oscar thought she was only a visitor, this tiny, slightly paunchy babe who was always high-heeling it out to her Pathfinder. (She didn't have the Mirador Norte wanna-be American look.) The two times Oscar bumped into her at the local café she smiled at him and he smiled at her. The second time—here, folks, is where the miracles begin—she sat at his table and chatted him up. At first he didn't know what was happening and then he realized, *Holy shit!* A girl was rapping to *him.* Turned out Yvón had known his abuela, even attended her funeral. You I don't remember. I was little, he said defensively. And, besides, that was before the war changed me.

She didn't laugh. That's probably what it is. You were a boy. On went the shades, up went the ass, out went the girl, Oscar's erection following her like a dowser's wand.

Yvón had attended the UASD a long time ago, but she was no college girl. She had lines around her eyes and seemed, to Oscar at least, mad open, mad worldly, and had the sort of intense zipper gravity that hot middle-aged women exude effortlessly. The next time he ran into her, in front of her house (he had watched for her), she screamed, Oscar, querido! Invited him into her near-empty casa—Haven't had the time to move in yet, she said offhandedly—and because there wasn't any furniture besides a kitchen table, a chair, a bureau, a bed, and a TV, they had to sit on the bed. (Oscar peeped at the astrology books under the bed and the complete collection of Paulo Coelho's novels. She followed his gaze and said with a smile, Paulo Coelho saved my life.) She gave him a beer, had a double Scotch, then for the next six hours regaled him with tales from her life. It wasn't until midway through their chat that it hit Oscar that the job she talked so profusely about was prostitution. It was *Holy shit!* the Sequel. Even though putas were one of Santo Domingo's premier exports, Oscar had never been near one in his entire life.

Yvón was an odd, odd bird. She was talkative, the sort of easygoing woman a brother can relax around, but there was also something slightly detached about her, as though (Oscar's words now) she were some marooned alien princess who existed partially in another dimension. She was the sort of woman who, cool as she was, slipped out of your head a little too quickly, a quality she recognized and was thankful for, as though she relished the short bursts of attention she provoked from niggers, but didn't want anything sustained. She didn't seem to mind being the girl you called every couple of months at eleven at night, just to see what she was up to. As much relationship as she could handle.

Her Jedi mind tricks did not, however, work on Oscar. When it came to girls, the brother had a mind like a four-hundred-year-old yogi. He latched on and stayed latched. By the time he left her house that night and walked home through the Island's million attack mosquitoes, he was lost. He was head over heels. (Did it matter that Yvón started mixing Italian in with her Spanish after her fourth drink or that she almost fell flat on her face when she showed him out? Of course not!) He was in love.

His mother met him at the door and couldn't believe his sinvergüencería. Do you know that woman's a PUTA? Do you know she bought that house CULEANDO?

He shot back, Do you know her mother was a DOCTOR? Do you know her father was a JUDGE?

The next day at one, Oscar pulled on a clean chacabana and strolled over to her house. (Well, he sort of trotted.) A red Jeep was parked outside, nose to nose with her Pathfinder. A Policía Nacional plate. And felt like a stooge. Of course she had boyfriends. His optimism, that swollen red giant, collapsed down to a bone-crushing point of gloom. Didn't stop him coming back the next day, but no one was home, and by the time he saw her again three days later he was convinced that she had warped back to whatever Forerunner world had spawned her. Where were you? he said, trying not to sound as miserable as he felt. I thought maybe you fell in the tub or something. I thought maybe you'd got amnesia.

She smiled and gave her ass a little shiver. I was making the patria strong, mi amor.

He had caught her in front of the TV, doing aerobics in a pair of sweatpants and what might have been described as a halter top. It was hard for him not to stare at her body. When she first let him in she'd screamed, Oscar, querido! Come in! Come in!

I know what niggers are going to say. Look, he's writing Suburban Tropical now. A puta and she's not an underage, snort-addicted mess? Not believable. Should I go down to the Feria and pick me up a more representative model? Would it be better if I turned Yvón into Jahyra, a friend and a neighbor in Villa Juana, who still lives in one of those old-style pink wooden houses with a tin roof? Jahyra—your quintessential Caribbean puta, half cute, half not—who'd left home at the age of fifteen and lived in Curaçao, Madrid, Amsterdam, and Rome, has two kids and a breast job bigger than Luba's in *Love and Rockets,* and who claimed, proudly, that her aparato had paved half the streets in her mother's home town. Or would it be better if I had Oscar meet Yvón at the World Famous Lavacaro, the car-wash where a brother can get his head and his fenders polished (talk about convenience!). Would this be better?

But then I'd be lying. This is a true account of the Brief Wondrous Life of Oscar Wao. Can't we believe that an Yvón can exist and that a brother like Oscar might be due a little luck after twenty-three years?

This is your chance. If yes, continue. If no, return to the Matrix.

The Girl from Sabana Iglesia

In their photos, Yvón looks young. It's her smile and the way she perks up her body for every shot as if she's presenting her-self to the world, as if she's saying, ta-da, here I am, take it or leave it. It doesn't hurt that she's barely five feet tall or that she doesn't weigh nothing. She dressed young, too, but she was a solid thirty-six, a perfect age for anybody but a puta. In the close-ups, you can see the crow's-feet, and the little belly she complains all the time about, and the way her breasts and her ass are starting to lose their swell, which was why, she said, she had to be in the gym five days a week. When you're sixteen, a body like this is free; when you're forty—pffft!—it's a full-time occupation. The third time Oscar came over, Yvón doubled up on the Scotches again and then took down her photo albums from the closet and showed him all the pictures of herself when she was sixteen, seventeen, eighteen, always on a beach, always in an eighties bikini, always smiling, always with her arms around some middle-aged eighties yakub. Looking at those old hairy blancos, Oscar couldn't help but feel hopeful. Each photo had a date and a place at the bottom, and this was how he was able to follow Yvón's puta's progress through Italy, Portugal, and Spain. I was so beautiful in those days, she said wistfully. It was true—her smile could have put out a sun, but Oscar didn't think she was any less fine now; the slight declensions in her appearance only seemed to add to her luster and he told her so.

You're so sweet, mi amor. She knocked back another double and rasped, What's your sign?

How lovesick he became! He began to go over to her house nearly every day, even when he knew she was working, just in case she was sick or decided to quit the profession so she could marry him. The gates of his heart had swung open and he felt light on his feet, he felt weightless, he felt lithe. His moms steady gave him shit, told him that not even God loves a puta. Yeah, his tío laughed, but everybody knows that God loves a puto. His tío seemed thrilled that he no longer had a pájaro for a nephew. I can't believe it, he said proudly. The palomo is finally a man. He put Oscar's neck in the New Jersey State Police patented niggerkiller lock. When did it happen? What was the date? I want to play that número as soon I get home.

Here we go again: Oscar and Yvón at her house, Oscar and Yvón at the movies, Oscar and Yvón at the beach, Oscar and Yvón talking, voluminously. She told him about her two sons, Sterling and Perfecto, who lived with their grandparents in Puerto Rico, who she saw only on holidays. She told him about the two abortions she had, which she called Marisol and Pepita, and about the time she'd been jailed in Madrid and how hard it was to sell your ass, and asked, Can something be impossible and not impossible at once? She told him about her Dominican boyfriend, the Capitán, and her foreign boyfriends, the Italian, the German, and the Canadian, the three benditos, how they each visited her on different months. You're lucky they all have families, she said, or I'd have been working this whole summer. (He wanted to ask her not to talk about any of these dudes, but she would only have laughed.)

Maybe we should get married, he said once, not joking, and she said, I make a terrible wife. He was around so often that he even got to see her in a couple of her notorious "moods," when her alien princess took over and she became very cold and uncommunicative and called him an idiot americano for spilling his beer. On these days, she threw herself into bed and didn't want to do anything. Hard to be around her, but he would convince her to see a movie and afterward she'd be a little easier. She'd take him to an Italian restaurant, and no matter how much her mood had improved she'd insist on drinking herself ridiculous—so bad he'd have to put her in the truck and drive her home through a city he did not know. (Early on, he hit on a great scheme: he called Clives, the evangelical taxista his family always used, who would swing by—no sweat—and lead him home.) When he drove, she always put her head in his lap and talked to him, sometimes in Italian, sometimes in Spanish, sometimes sweet, sometimes not, and having her mouth so close to his nuts was finer than your best yesterday.

Oh, they got close, all right, but we have to ask the hard questions: Did they ever kiss in her Pathfinder? Did he ever put his hands up her super-short skirt? Did she ever push up against him and say his name in a throaty whisper? Did they ever fuck?

Of course not. Miracles go only so far. He watched her for the signs that would tell him she loved him. He began to suspect that it might not happen this summer, but already he had plans to come back for Thanksgiving and then for Christmas. When he told her, she looked at him strangely and said only his name, Oscar, a little sadly.

She liked him, it was obvious. It seemed to Oscar that he was one of her few real friends. Outside the boyfriends, foreign and domestic, outside her psychiatrist sister in San Cristóbal and her ailing mother in Sabana Iglesia, her life seemed as spare as, say, her house.

Travel light, was all she ever said about the house when he suggested buying her a lamp or something, and he suspected that she would have said the same thing about having more friends. He knew, of course, that he wasn't her only visitor. One day, he found three discarded condom foils on the floor and asked, Are you having trouble with incubuses? She smiled. This is one man who doesn't know the word quit.

Poor Oscar. At night he dreamed that his rocket ship, the Hijo de Sacrificio, was up and off but that it was heading for the Ana Acuña Barrier at the speed of light.

Oscar at the Rubicon

At the beginning of August, Yvón started mentioning her ex-boyfriend the Capitán a lot more. Seems he'd heard about Oscar and wanted to meet him. He's really jealous, Yvón said, rather weakly. Just have him meet me, Oscar said. I make all boyfriends feel better about themselves. I don't know, Yvón said. Maybe we shouldn't spend so much time together. Shouldn't you be looking for a girlfriend?

I got one, he said.

A jealous Third World cop ex-boyfriend? Maybe we shouldn't spend so much time together? Any other nigger would have pulled a Scooby-Doo double take—Eeuoooorr?—would have thought twice about staying in Santo Domingo another day, but not Oscar.

Two days later, Oscar found his tío examining the front door. What's the matter? His tío showed him the door and pointed at the concrete-block wall on the other side of the foyer. I think somebody shot our house last night. He shook his head. Fucking Dominicans. Probably hosed the whole neighborhood down.

For a second, Oscar felt this strange tugging in the back of his head, what someone else might have called Instinct, but instead of hunkering down and sifting through it he said, We probably didn't hear it because of all our air-conditioners. Then he walked over to Yvón's. They were going to the Duarte that day.

Oscar Gets Beat

In the middle of August, Oscar finally met the Capitán. Yvón had passed out again. It was super-late and he'd been following Clives in the Pathfinder, the usual routine, when a crowd of cops up ahead let Clives pass and then asked Oscar to please step out of the vehicle. These were the DR's new highway police, brand-new uniforms and esprit de corps up to here. It's not my truck, he explained, it's hers. He pointed to sleeping Yvón. We understand. If you could please step out of the truck. It wasn't until these two plainclothes—who we'll call Solomon Grundy and Gorilla Grodd, for simplicity's sake—tossed him into the back of a black Volkswagen bug that he realized something was up. Wait a minute, he said as they pulled out, where the hell are you taking me? Wait! Gorilla Grodd gave him one cold glance and that was all it took to quiet his ass down. This is fucked up, he said under his breath. I didn't *do* nothing.

The Capitán was waiting for him on a noticeably unelectrified stretch of road. A skinny forty-something-year-old jabao standing near his spotless red Jeep, dressed nice in slacks and a crisply pressed white button-down, his shoes bright as scarabs. The Capitán was one of those tall, arrogant, handsome niggers that most of the planet feels inferior to. (The Capitán was also one of those very bad men who not even postmodernism can explain away.)

So you're the New Yorker, he said with great cheer. When Oscar saw the Capitán's close-set eyes he knew he was fucked. (He had the Eyes of Lee Van Cleef!) If it hadn't been for the courage of his sphincter, Oscar's lunch and his dinner and his breakfast would have whooshed straight out of him.

I didn't do anything, Oscar quailed. Then he blurted out, I'm an American citizen.

The Capitán waved away a mosquito. I'm an American citizen, too. I was sworn in in the city of Buffalo, in the State of New York.

I bought mine in Miami, Gorilla Grodd said.

Not me, Solomon Grundy lamented. I only got my damn residency.

Please, you have to believe me, I didn't do anything.

The Capitán smiled. Motherfucker even had First World teeth. Oscar was lucky; if he had looked like my pana Pedro, the Dominican Superman, he probably would have got shot right there. But because he was a young homely slob the Capitán punched him only a couple of times, warned him away from Yvón in no uncertain terms, and then remanded him to Messrs. Grundy and Grodd, who squeezed him back into the bug and drove out to the cane fields between Santo Domingo and Villa Mella.

Oscar was too scared to speak. He was a shook daddy. He couldn't believe it. He was going to die. He tried to imagine Yvón at the funeral in her nearly see-through black sheath and couldn't. Watched Santo Domingo race past and felt impossibly alone. Thought about his mother and his sister and started crying.

You need to keep it down, Grundy said, but Oscar couldn't stop, even when he put his hands in his mouth.

At the cane fields, Messrs. Grodd and Grundy pulled Oscar out of the car, walked him into the cane, and then with their pistol butts proceeded to give him the beating to end all beatings. It was the Götterdämmerung of beatdowns, a beatdown so cruel and relentless that even Camden, the City of the Ultimate Beatdown, would have been impressed. (Yessir, nothing like getting smashed in the face with those patented Pachmayr Presentation Grips.) He shrieked, but that didn't stop the beating; he begged, but that didn't stop it, either, he blacked out, but that was no relief; the niggers kicked him in the nuts and perked him right up! It was like one of those nightmare 8 A.M. MLA panels that you think will never, ever end. Man, Gorilla Grodd said, this kid is making me *sweat*. Toward the end, Oscar found himself thinking about his old dead abuela, who used to scratch his back and fry him yaniqueques; she was sitting in her rocking chair and when she saw him she snarled, What did I tell you about those putas?

The only reason he didn't lie out in that rustling endless cane for the rest of his life was because Clives the evangelical taxista had had the guts to follow the cops on the sly, and when they broke out he turned on his headlights and pulled up to where they'd last been and found poor Oscar. Are you alive? Clives whispered. Oscar said, Blub, blub. Clives couldn't hoist Oscar into the car alone so he drove to a nearby batey and recruited a couple of Haitian braceros to help him. This is a big one, one of the braceros joked. The only thing Oscar said the whole ride back was her name. *Yvón*. Broken nose, broken zygomatic arch, crushed seventh cranial nerve, three of his front teeth snapped off at the gum, concussion, alive.

That was the end of it. When Moms de León heard it was the police, she called first a doctor and then the airlines. She wasn't no fool; she'd lived through Trujillo and the Devil Balaguer; knew that the cops hadn't forgotten shit from those days. She put it in the simplest of terms. You stupid, worthless, no-good son of a whore are going home. No, he said, through demolished lips. He wasn't fooling, either. When he first woke up and realized that he was still alive, he insisted on seeing Yvón. I love her, he whispered, and his mother said, Shut up, you! Just shut up!

The doctor ruled out epidural hematoma but couldn't guarantee that Oscar didn't have brain damage. (She was a cop's girlfriend? Tío Rodolfo whistled. I'll vouch for the brain damage.) Send him home right now, homegirl said, but for four whole days Oscar resisted any attempt to be packed up in a plane, which says a lot about this fat kid's fortitude; he was eating morphine by the handful and his grill was in agony, he had an around-the-clock quadruple migraine and couldn't see squat out of his right eye; motherfucker's head was so swollen he looked like John Merrick, Jr., and anytime he attempted to stand, the ground whisked right out from under him. My God! he thought. So this is what it feels like to get your ass *kicked*. It wasn't all bad, though; the beating granted him strange insights: he heard his tío, three rooms over, stealing money from his mother's purse; and he realized that had he and Yvón not been serious the Capitán would probably never have fucked with him. Proof positive that he and Yvón had a relationship.

Yvón didn't answer her cell, and the few times Oscar managed to limp to the window he saw that her Pathfinder wasn't there. I love you, he shouted into the street. I love you! Once, he made it to her door and buzzed before his tío realized that he was gone and dragged him back inside.

And, then, on Day Three, she came. While she sat on the edge of his bed, his mother banged pots in the kitchen and said "puta" loudly enough for them to hear.

Forgive me if I don't get up, Oscar whispered. I'm having a little trouble with my face.

She was dressed in white, like an angel, and her hair was still wet from the shower, a tumult of brownish curls. Of course the Capitán had beaten the shit out of her, too; of course she had two black eyes. (He'd also put his .44 Magnum in her vagina and asked her who she really loved.) There was nothing about her that Oscar wouldn't have gladly kissed. She put her fingers on his hand and told him that she could never be with him again. For some reason, Oscar couldn't see her face; it was a blur, she had retreated completely into that other plane of hers. Heard only the sorrow of her breathing. He tried to focus but all he saw was his love for her. Yvón? he croaked, but she was already gone.

Se acabó. Oscar refused to look at the ocean as they drove to the airport. It's beautiful today, Clives remarked. On the flight over, Oscar sat between his tío and his moms. Jesus, Oscar, Rodolfo said nervously. You look like they put a shirt on a turd.

P-Town Blues

Oscar returned to Paterson. He lay in bed, he stared at his games, he read Andre Norton books, he healed. He talked to the school, and they told him not to worry about the job; it was his when he was ready. You're lucky you're alive, his mother told him. Maybe you could save up your money and get an operation for your face, his tío suggested. Oscar, his sister sighed, Oscar. On the darkest days, he sat in his tío's closet, the Dragoon on his lap, looked back over the past two decades of his life, saw nothing but cowardice and fear. So why was there still a fortress in his heart? Why did he feel like he could be Minas Tirith if he wanted to? He really tried to forget, but he couldn't. He dreamed that he was adrift, alone in his spacesuit, and that she was calling to him.

Me and Lola were living up in the Heights—this was before the white kids started their invasion, when you could walk the entire length of Harlem and see not a single "homesteader." September, October? I was home for the week, curling ninety, when Oscar buzzed me from the street. Hadn't seen him in weeks. Jesus, Oscar, I said. Come up, come up. I waited for him in the hall and when he stepped out of the elevator I put the mitts on him. How are you, bro?

I'm fine, he said, smiling sheepishly.

We sat down and I broke up a dutch, asked him how it was going.

I'm going back to Don Bosco soon.

Word? I said.

Word, he said. His face was still fucked up, the left side was paralyzed and wouldn't get better anytime soon, but he wasn't hiding it anymore. I still got the Two-Face going on bad, he said, laughing.

You gonna smoke?

Just a little. I don't want to cloud my faculties.

That last day on our couch, he looked like a man at peace with himself. You should have seen him. He was so thin, had lost all the weight, and was still, still.

I want to know, Yunior, if you can do me a favor.

Anything, bro. Just ask it.

He needed money for a security deposit, was finally moving into his own apartment, and of course I gave it to him. All I had, but if anybody was going to pay me back it was Oscar.

We smoked the dutch and talked about the problems me and Lola were having.

You should never have had carnal relations with that Paraguayan girl, he pointed out.

I know, I said, I know. He seemed confident that it would work itself out, though, and there was something in his tone that made me hopeful. You ain't going to wait for Lola?

Have to get back to Paterson. I got a date.

You're shitting me?

He shook his head, the tricky fuck.

On Saturday, he was gone.

The Last Days

As soon as he hit the airport exit, Oscar called Clives and homeboy picked him up an hour later. Cristiano, Clives said, eyes tearing, what are you doing here?

It's the Ancient Powers, Oscar said. They won't leave me alone.

They parked in front of her house and waited almost seven hours before she returned. Pulled up in the Pathfinder. She looked thinner. For a moment, he thought about letting the whole thing go, returning to Bosco and getting on with his life, but then she stooped over to pick up her gym bag, as if the whole world were watching, and that settled it. He winched down the window and called her name. She stopped, shaded her eyes, and then recognized him. She said his name, terrified, *Oscar*. He popped the door and walked over to where she was standing and embraced her and she said, Mi amor, you have to leave right now.

In the middle of the street, he told her how it was. He was in love with her. He'd been hurt, but now he was all right, and if he could just have a week alone with her, one short week, then everything would be fine, and he would be able to go on with his life, and he said it again, that he loved her more than the universe, and it wasn't something that he could shake, so, please, come away with him for a little while, and then it would be over if she wanted.

Maybe she did love him a little bit. Maybe in her heart of hearts she left the gym bag on the concrete and got in the taxi with him. But she'd known men like the Capitán all her life. Knew, also, that in the DR they called a bullet a cop's divorce. The gym bag was not left on the street.

I'm going to call him, Oscar, she said, misting up a little. So, please, go, before he gets here.

I'm not going anywhere, he said.

For twenty-seven days he chased her. He sat in front of her house, he called her on her cell, he went to the World Famous Riverside, a casa de putas where she worked. The neighbors, when they saw him on the curb, shook their heads and said, Look at that loco.

She was miserable when she saw him and miserable, she would tell him later, when she didn't, convinced that he'd been killed. He slipped long passionate letters under her gate, written in English, and the only response he got was when the Capitán and his friends called and threatened to chop him in pieces. After each threat, he recorded the time and then phoned the Embassy and told them that the Capitán had threatened to kill him, and asked, Could you please help?

She started scribbling back notes and passed them to him at the club or had them mailed to his house. Please, Oscar, I haven't slept in a week. I don't want you to end up hurt or dead. Go home.

But, beautiful girl above all beautiful girls, he wrote back. This *is* my home.

Your real home, mi amor.

A person can't have two?

Night Nineteen, she honked her horn, and he opened his eyes and knew it was her. She leaned over and unlocked the truck door, and when he got in he tried to kiss her, but she said, Please stop it. They drove out toward La Romana, where the Capitán didn't have no friends. Nothing new was discussed, but he said, I like your new haircut, and she started laughing and crying and said, Really? You don't think it makes me look cheap?

You and cheap do not compute, Yvón.

What could we do? Lola flew down to see him, begged him to come home, told him that he was only going to get Yvón and himself killed; he listened and then said angrily that she didn't understand how he felt, never had. How incredibly short are twenty-seven days.

One night, the Capitán and his friends came into the Riverside, and Oscar stared at the man for a good ten seconds and then, whole body shaking, he left. Didn't bother to call Clives, jumped in the first taxi he could find. The next night Oscar was back and, in the parking lot of the Riverside, he tried again to kiss Yvón; she turned her head away (but not her body). Please don't, she said. He'll kill us.

Twenty-seven days, and then the expected happened. One night, he and Clives were driving back from the World Famous Riverside and at a light two men got into the cab with them. It was, of course, Gorilla Grodd and Solomon Grundy. Good to see you again, Grodd said, and then they beat him as best they could, given the limited space inside the cab.

This time, Oscar didn't cry when they drove him back to the cane fields. Zafra would be here soon, and the cane had grown well and thick and in places you could hear the stalks clack-clack-clacking against each other like triffids, and you could hear the kriyol voices lost in the night. There was a moon, and Clives begged the men to spare Oscar, but they laughed. You should be worrying, Grodd said, about yourself. Oscar sent telepathic messages to his moms (I love you, Señora), to Rodolfo (Quit, Tío, and live), to Lola (I'm so sorry it happened; I always loved you), and the longest to Yvón.

They walked him into the cane and then turned him around. (Clives they left tied up in the cab.) They looked at him and he looked at them, and then he started to speak. He told them that what they were doing was wrong, that they were going to take a great love out of the world. Love was a rare thing, he told them, easily confused with a million other things, and if anybody knew this to be true it was him. He told them about Yvón and the way he loved her and how much they had risked and that they'd started to dream the same dreams and say the same words, and he told them that if they killed him they would probably feel nothing and their children would probably feel nothing, either, not until they were old and weak or about to be struck by a car, and then they would sense his waiting for them on the other side, and over there he wouldn't be no fat boy or dork or kid no girl had ever loved, over there he'd be a hero, an avenger. Because anything you can dream (he put his hand up) you can be.

They waited for him to finish, and then they shot him to pieces.

Oscar—

The End of the Story

Lola and I flew down to claim the body. We went to the funeral. A year later, we broke up.

Four times, the family hired lawyers, but no charges were ever filed. The Embassy didn't help and neither did the government. Yvón, I hear, is still living in Mirador Norte, still dancing at the Riverside. The de Leóns sold their house a year later.

Lola swore she would never return to that terrible country, and I don't think she ever has. On one of our last nights, she said, Eight million Trujillos is all we are.

(Of course things like this don't happen in Santo Domingo no more. We have enlightened, uncorrupt politicians and a kind benevolent President and a people who are clearheaded and loving. The country is kind, no Haitian or dark-skinned person is hated, the élites fuck nobody, and the police measure their probity by the mile.)

Almost eight weeks after Oscar died, a package arrived at the house in Paterson. Two manuscripts enclosed. One was chapters of his never-to-be-completed opus, an E. E. (Doc) Smithesque space opera called "Starscourge." The other was a long letter to Lola. Turns out that toward the end the palomo *did* get Yvón away from the capital. For two whole days, they hid out on some beach in Barahona while the Capitán was away on "business," and guess what? Yvón actually kissed him! Guess what else? Yvón actually fucked him. Yahoo! He reported that he'd liked it and that Yvón's you-know-what hadn't tasted the way he had expected. She tastes like Heineken, he said. He wrote that at night Yvón had nightmares that the Capitán had found them; once, she'd woken up and said in the voice of true fear, Oscar, he's here, really believing he was, and Oscar woke up and threw himself at the Capitán but it turned out to be only a turtle shell the hotel had hung on the wall for decoration. Almost busted my nose! He wrote that Yvón had little hairs coming up almost to her bellybutton and that she crossed her eyes when she fucked but what really got him were the little intimacies that he'd never in his whole life anticipated, like combing her hair or getting her underwear off a

line or watching her walk naked to the bathroom or the way
she would suddenly sit on his lap and put her face into his
neck. The intimacies like listening to her tell him about being
a little girl and him telling her that he'd been a virgin all his
life. He wrote that he couldn't believe he'd had to wait for this
so goddam long. (Yvón was the one who suggested calling the
wait something else. Yeah, like what? Maybe, she said, you
could call it life.) He wrote: So this is what everybody's always
talking about! Diablo! If only I'd known. The beauty! The
beauty!

PATRICIA GRACE

WITH SEVERAL NOVELS and short story collections to her name, Patricia Grace is renowned in New Zealand for her portrayals of the many layers of contemporary Maori life. Born in Wellington in 1937, she began writing as a teacher in North Auckland, and later moved to her ancestral land in Plimmerton, New Zealand. In "Letters from Whetu," sixth-former Whetu o te Moana (Star of the Sea; "I was named after a church") gets through what could be a stultifying day at his new, elite school by writing letters to his friends Lenny, Iosefa, Ani, and Andy—some of whom he will see again within minutes—simply to "beat boredom" and re-create life outside school. "I'm a bit sick of being her honourable statistic, her minority person MAKING IT," Whetu writes, echoing the recurrent themes of education and identity often explored by vernacular literature. Writing, for Whetu, becomes a way to preserve the self in the face of potential cultural domination.

LETTERS FROM WHETU

(1980)

English,
Room 12,
Period 1.
Friday.

Dear Lenny,

Be like Whetu o te Moana,
Beat Boredom,
Write a Letter.

How slack finding myself the only one of the old gang in the sixth form. How slack and BORING. And it's so competitive round here—No chance of copying a bit of homework or sharing a few ideas. Everyone's after marks and grades coz that's what counts on ACCREDITING DAY and Nobody Never tells Nobody Nothing—No Way. ACCREDITING DAY—it's ages away yet everyone's in a panic. It's like we're all going to be sorted out for heaven or hell, or for DECIDING DAY, and I really don't know what it's all for. I've thought and thought but just don't get it. I tell yuh it just doesn't add up. Must tell you about DECIDING DAY inaminnit.

See . . . it seems we get put through this machine so that we can come out well-educated and so we can get interesting jobs. I think it's supposed to make us better than some other people—like our mothers and fathers for example, and some of our friends. And somehow it's supposed to make us happier and more FULFILLED. Well I dunno.

I quite like Fisher, I kind of appreciate her even though she thinks she, and she alone, got me through S.C. last year, and even though she thinks I've got no brayne of my own. Little does she know that I often wish now that I'd fayled. How was I to know I'd be sitting here alone and so lonely learning boring things. Why do we learn such boring things? We learned boring things last year and now we're learning boring things again. I bet this letter's getting boring.

I sometimes do a bit of a stir with Fisher, like I say 'yous' instead of 'you' (pl.). It always sends her PURPLE. The other day I wrote it in my essay and she had a BLUE fit. She scratched it out in RED and wrote me a double underlined note—'I have told you many times before that there is no such word as "yous" (I wonder if it hurt her to write it). Please do not use (yous heh heh) it again.' So I wrote a triple underlined note underneath—'How can I yous it if it does not exist?' Now that I think of it that's really slack—what lengths I go to, it's really pathetic. I mean she's OKAY, but I'm a bit sick of being her honourable statistic, her minority person MAKING IT.

I'll tell you something else, that lady sure does go on. And on. And on. She's trying to make us enjoy K.M. Kay Em is what she calls Katherine Mansfield, as though she and K.M. were best mates. Well I suppose Fisher could be just about old enough to have been a mate of K.M.s. . . . I'll tell you what she's doing. She's prancing about reading like she's gonna bust. Her lips are wobbling and popping, and she's sort of poised like an old ballet dancer. She does a couple of tip-toes now and again. Sometimes she flaps the book about and makes circles in the air with it. I don't think she'll burst into tears.

Do you know what? When she waves and flaps the book about she doesn't stop 'reading', so I suppose that means she knows her K.M. off by heart, bless her HART (Halt All Racist Tours), punctuation and all. I don't think her glasses will quite fall off—Beat Boredom, wait and hope for Fisher's glasses to fall off and cut her feet to ribbons.

Gee I enjoyed our day at the beach last weekend, and us being all together again first time for ages. Andy looks great. All those hours in the sea and those big waves lopping over us. Hey why don't we save up and get us a surfboard?

I got my beans when I got home though, boy did I get my beans. Yes, and we'll take some food next time, and some togs and towels (to save our jeans from getting so clean). What about this weekend, but we'd have to contact Andy. Anyhows think on it. Really neat. It wuz tanfastic bowling round in those breakers hour after hour.

And what about those new songs we made up—haven't done that since fourth form. Soon as I got home, after having my ears laid back by Mum and Dad, I went and wrote that second song down so we wouldn't forget it. I like it, I really do. I'm writing out a copy for each of us and I'm sending Andy's with his letter which I'll write period 4. I'm writing letters to all of you today. Gonna post them too, even though I see you all at lunchtime (except Andy).

Can't remember the words to that first song, there must've been about twenty verses, and what rubbish. I can remember the 'Shake-a Shake-a' and the 'Culley bubba' bits, and I remember Iosefa's verse,

Tasi lua tolu fa,
Come a me a hugga hugga,

Shake-a Shake-a Shake-a,
   Culley bubba longa-a long-a.

And

Tangaroa Tangaroa,
Little fish belong-a he a,
Shake-a Shake-a. . . .

Then there was another one about a shitting seagull—well never mind. Great music you and Andy made for it though, and only the waves to hear.

She's still flapping, and poncing, and I swear there's a tear in her eye.

And yes. I said I was going to tell you about DECIDING DAY. Went to the library on Monday, and opened a book which I started reading in the middle somewhere. Well this story is all set in New Zealand in the future ay, and there's been a world war and wide devastation.

There are too many people and they're short of stuff—goods, manure, natural resources and all that, so it's been agreed that all the cripples, mentals, wrinklies and sickies have to be sorted out and killed, then recycled. DECIDING DAY is the day the computer comes up with who's human and who's 'animal'. They're going to make them (the dead mentals, etc.) into energy, and use their skins for purses, etc. The kid down the road becomes your new knife handles, buy a bottle of drink and it's your granny stoppered inside ready to fizz. Turn on your light and there's your nutty uncle. After that there'll be a perfect society and a life of ease so they reckon. Neat story?

After DECIDING DAY the fires are going for weeks and weeks, and there's smoke and stink everywhere. The remaining people (not very many coz the computer doesn't find too many 'humans') try to make out they can handle it, but they can't. They can't hack it at all, and they want to chunder over and over, or fall about mad screaming.

Well e hoa. Fisher's winding down, and period one almost over. Love talking to you, not bored at all. See you lunchtime but you won't get this til next week. Gonna get me some envelopes and stamps and do some lickin'.

> Arohanui,
> Whetu o te Moana.
> (I was named after a church.)

> Mathematics,
> Room 68,
> Period 2.
> Friday.

Dear Ani,

The new maths teacher is really strange. He never calls the roll but just barges in, goes straight to the rolling blackboard and starts writing. At the same time as he's writing he's mumbling into his whiskers and flinging the board up. His face is only about six inches from the board and you keep thinking he might catch his nose in it. I think he's half blind.

When he gets to the end of the rolling board he starts rubbing out with his left hand and keeps on scribbling his columns and numbers with his right. At the same time he keeps up his muttering and his peering. All he needs now is a foot drum and some side cymbals. When the bell goes he turns round as if he's just noticed us, his specs are all white and chalky and his whiskers are snowy, and he has a tiny pyramid of chalk pinched between his finger and thumb, all that's left of a whole stick. What a weird-o. Then he yells out page numbers and exercise numbers for homework and says, 'Out you go. Quickly.' As we go out he's cleaning his bi-fokes and getting out a new piece of chalk ready for the next lot of suckers. No wonder I'm no good at maths (not like Lenny who's got a mthmtcl brayne. What say we save up for a srfbrd and Lenny can be the treasurer).

Trust you to get stuck halfway up the cliff. Hey I got really scared looking at you, then I got wild with the boys just leaving you there and doing all that Juliet stuff with the guitar. Wasn't til I started up to help you that they decided to come up, and even so they were only assing round.

Then it was really beautiful up on that ledge after all. Wasn't it? You forget, living here. Living here you never really see the sun go down, or you don't think of it as being anything really good. Sometimes if you're outside picking up the newspaper or the milk bottles you see the sky looking a bit pink, or else it just gets dark and you know it's happened. But you don't think 'The sun's going down,' you only think 'It's getting dark.' Mostly we have the curtains over the windows because of people going past, and you think they might LOOK IN, or something TERRIBLE like that. and what if one of them HAD A GUN, and aimed it at you? What if there was a loud bang, and a little hole in the window the size of a peanut, and a big one in your head the size of an orange? What a splash of colour, what a sunset and a half that would be.

Yes and anyway we need the curtains over the windows because of telly being on. Telly is a sort of window too, with everything always on the other side of the glass. After a while you don't know the difference between 'looking out' and 'looking in'. Well you know what I mean fren, you don't ever think how it is sitting halfway up a cliff making up songs, with the sun dropping behind an island.

You weren't scared anymore once we all got up there, and the sun settled at the head of the island like a big bloodshot eye just for a sec. Then it dropped behind like a trick ball.

You don't ever think of the sky slapped all over red and orange, and the sea smothered in gold-pink curls. When you think back you can see it all again, but can't quite feel the same, like your skin is stretching tight over your body, like your eyes are just holes and it's all pouring in.

Well what a climb down in the dark, then the hunt in the dark for shoes. If we hadn't had to look for our shoes we'd have caught an earlier train home. God I got my beans when I got home. Then of course there was that long wait in the greasy shop for our greasies. I was *starving*.

When we were little we always used to go to the beach—every low tide even in the cold weather. But now that us kids have grown up I don't think Dad likes it anymore. Anyway he's so busy and on so many committees—marae committee, P.T.A., Tu Tangata, District Council—and Mum's almost as bad. We're never home together these days, especially now that Hepa's flatting and Amiria's married. As for Koro, he's never in one place for a day. He gets called north south east west, if not to a tangi then to a land meeting, if not to a land meeting then to a convention. Well it's no wonder we never get to the beach or see each other much.

Er um! Hepa turned up on Saturday, so Dad went and got Amiria and John. Er! Koro was back from Auckland, so, er, I was the only one not home. And NOBODY knew where I was. Tricky huh? Well we didn't know we were going to the beach did we? We started out to meet beautiful Andy off the train and ended up getting the next train north.

Hey old chalk-chewer is yelling out page numbers, he's remembered we're here. He looks like a sort of constipated old Santa—I'd better end this letter inaminnit.

Yes Dad cracked a fit and I took a good bit of flak from Mum as well. They were all dressed to go out and they'd been waiting hours for me. Of course what Dad really thought was that I was out getting myself popped, it's what they all think but won't say. Ding Dong. Got to bed midnight. Or was that the time we got home, heh heh?

The beach. It beats late shopping nights by a long way. Gotta go. I'm the only one left, goodbye fren. Writing to Iosefa next period. See you lunchtime, but you won't get this til next week.

> Much love,
> Yours ake, ake, ake,
> Star.
> (I'm a Star
> I'm a Star
> I'm a Mon*star*.)

> Geography,
> Room 3,
> Period 3,
> Friday.

Dear Sef,

I write to you amid a shower of topographical maps, aerial photos, fault lines and air masses. What a circus. Lattimer arrives loaded with books which he bangs on to a table. Then he starts spouting—So you SEE, So you SEE—producing his cross-sections, graphs, map keys, land formations like tricks out of a hat. After a while he bounces round the room dealing out worksheets and slamming books down in front of us, creating his own earthquakes.

Writing to Ani I remembered how we always used to go downtown on late shopping nights. She and I used to make up all sorts of excuses so we'd be allowed to go, and so did you. You used to tell your mother you were going on a training run, then you'd run into town and we'd all meet and spend our money on take-aways and junk. Then we'd hang round the fountain with the other kids and hope a fight might start up between our college and the one up the line. We always knew who was out to get who, and who was ripping off what from where. The night we caught the taxi home (with Lenny's money) you had to run up and down the road to get puffed and sweaty before you went inside. I got home wet from you throwing half the fountain on me. We'd all swapped clothes as usual.

Well parents get upset about funny things. Wasn't allowed downtown for ages and ages and used to feel really slacked off on late-shopping-nite-nites because I wanted to be out there having FUN, that was winter. Hey what babies we were, running round, hiding in doorways and hoping all the time that something really awful would happen.

Yes Lattimer's got a great act there. Maybe we should all crouch on our desks like circus tigers and spring from table to table and roar, and swipe the air with our paws.

What about the time we took your little cousins to the zoo, and Andy got smart to the ape and it went haywire. Then Andy walked away whistling and looking at the sky. Remember the ducks zooming in, and the tiger that turned its bum round at feed time and pissed on the people. And Ani pissed herself laughing. Oh Ani, what a roly-poly, what a ball. Ani's really neat.

Well the ape was bouncing all over its cage with its big open mouth as pink as undercoat paint, baring his old smoker's teeth and trying to wrench the bars apart. Then he began snatching and grabbing at his own arm, his own shoulder, his own head, and at the same time he kept opening his mouth and slamming it shut, and putting his bottom teeth almost up his nose. His eyes were as black as print and glinting like flicked pins.

Our mate Lenny looked at the ape and said, 'Honey baby come to my pipi farm and I'll give you a gink at my muscles.' Spare it! Poor monkey, with its thumbs on back to front. The palms of its hands looked like old cow turds.

I really wonder about Lattimer. The way he throws himself about the room you'd think he was really trying to knock the walls down and make a run for it, or perhaps he wants to give himself a crack on the head so he can be pulled out by the feet.

Anyway he's all right—busts out in a sick grin every so often. Remember Harris (harass) and her screwed-up face, and how she used to walk in and shove open all the windows because we all stank. I really wanted to walk out that time Andy left, if only I'd had the guts. Everytime she got on to him I felt like dying, even before I knew Andy properly. She'd never believe what Andy's really like, she was just so scared of him, of his looks, of the way he talks, of his poor clothes. Most of all she must have realised Andy had her taped, over and over, although he never said anything. On that last day I reckon it was his quietness and his acceptance that got to her. She was screwed up with hate, and screaming. Writing to Andy next period and won't forget to tell him about Palmer's DISGUISE.

Sometimes I can't hack the thought that I didn't follow Andy down the road that day, instead of sitting here waiting to 'realise' my 'potential'. Hey Sef, when and how does potential become whatever it's meant to become? I mean Mum and Dad have all these IDEAS, they're both getting their THRILLS over my education and I reckon I'll be sitting behind a desk FOREVER.

Funny though, if it had been either one of them they'd have gone out the door with Andy without thinking twice, because they really know what's important. It's only me they've got under glass. Anyhows I'll leave it before I start thinking what a sucker I am.

And now I'll talk about the beach. Nex' time we'll take all our gears, especially FOOD. If you're wrkng next wknd, or if Ani's wrkng, or if Andy can't come, we'll go another time. Soon. But gee Sef, the dropping sun and the bleeding sky and those great fat humping seas, the seagulls. . . .

I often dream about flying, and sometimes in the dream I'm afraid of what I'm doing, and other times I'm so happy and free flying about, up above everyone and everything, going anywhere I want. . . . If I wasn't me I'd be a seagull belting out over the sea and throwing myself at any storm, ANY STORM. What would you be, e hoa, if you weren't you?

Gotta go Iosefa, he's snapping up all his books and handouts, and now, slurp, they're all back in the trick box. Howzat? See ya lunchtime, which is now.

> Much love from,
> Star of the Sea.

> History,
> Room 42,
> Period 4.
> Friday.

Dear Andy,

Great to see you on Sunday, you and your old guitar. I hardly remember going to the beach, only being there. When we came to meet you off the train we didn't quite expect to find ourselves on the next one heading north. Suddenly we were off the train again and legging it to the beach all those miles. But it seemed no distance, the road just rolled away under us and only our talking tongues were in a sweat. Hey that neat car, 'You got the Mercedes, I got the Benz' (according to Len). I've been writing letters all morning as part of my anti-boredom campaign.

What I want to tell you is that Iosefa has got a black eye. On Tuesday, Palmer, who is the new VICE principal, disguised himself (as a flasher) and pounced on Lenny, Iosefa and some other boys who were all puffing up large on the bank by the top field. True. He put on an old raincoat, ankle length no less (a real flasher's job), and one of those work caps that have advertisements printed on them—Marple Paints. The boys thought it was a member of the public taking a short-cut to the road so didn't take much notice. Instead it was old P. ready to pounce, wearing his usual greaser's grin.

All the letters went home to parents as usual—'Dear   , I wish to bring to your notice that your son/daughter   was discovered (!!!) smoking in the school grounds on   (date, etc., etc.).'

Iosefa got thumped by his old man, and Lenny's mum screwed up the letter and laughed her wrinkled old head off. On Wednesday Palmer's blackboard was covered with compliments—'Palmer's a wanker' and all the usual things. Someone drew a spy glass with a gory eye looking through. And you know Rick Ossler? His old man came up and shook 'the letter' in Palmer's face and called him a Creeping Jesus. Well I laughed and laughed. Never heard that expression before, but when I told Mum she said it was an oldie.

Anyway enough of that. Neat fun sitting up on that ledge

singing up large, we must've been there for hours. Every now and then I'd think of all our mates from fourth form days, and how we'd all go over to D6 and sing and act like fools, and make up funny songs.

But Angie and Brian, Willy, Judy, Vasa, Hariata, lots of others . . . I was thinking too of how we all used to terrorise the town on late-shopping-nite-nites. Wonder what they're all doing now?

Before I went to bed on Saturday (and after I'd had my ears blasted for being back late), I wrote down the words of our song so we wouldn't forget them. It seems there are things to know about our songs, even the rubbish ones, things we don't really know yet. There are so many things to know, and I really envy you because you're learning some of them. I want to know important things, and also I want to know what's important.

Slitting the throat of a sheep and hanging it up kicking seems to be a real thing, like picking watercress, and even though it's something you can do and I can't, I still want to know about it. Even though I wouldn't want to cut the belly and haul the guts out I know it must sometimes be all right to have blood on your hands. Or if not blood then dirt, or shit— on the outside where you can see it. You see I've got this bad idea that I'm sitting here storing all the muck up inside me, getting slowly but surely shit ridden. As for you, you've never held any shit, ever, and never will.

But other things, so many things. I mean, I want to know what goes on in houses, especially in houses on hills with trees round them. What do the people there say to each other? What do they laugh about and what do they eat? Are their heads different from them being up higher? Do they chew gum, how can I know?

Are girls who work in clothes shops just like me, or do their faces fall away when night comes, and does someone hang them limp on a rack until morning? Does central heating dry people out and make them unable to face the weather? Well I could go on and on.

E hoa, I want to walk all over the world but how do I develop the skills for it sitting in a plastic bag fastened with a wire-threaded paper twist to keep the contents airtight. You sit cramped in there, with your head bowed, knees jack-knifed up under your chin.

If I walked round the world I'd wear two holes in my face in place of eyes and let everything pour in. I reckon I could play an alpine horn.

The other day two fifth formers bought pot from the care-taker then potted him. And a lot of fourth formers are getting high from sniffing cleaner fluid which they pour on their sleeves. Peter got his arm blown up when his mate lit a cigarette, and now he's in hospital (luckily). Were we *that* suicidal two years ago, screaming round town in our jackets wishing to see someone slit from eye to knee with a knife?

I saw a girl nick a bottle of the stuff from a stand in McKenzies yesterday but I didn't do anything. There were two rows of it on a glass shelf at 89c a bottle.

And now the bell rings and we're almost through the day. No more letters to write, but next period (last one) I'll write out THE SONG for everyone (see yours below). If I write slow enough it might use up the hour.

Well dear friend, write back straight away and tell us when you can come down again. WE'VE GOT PLANS, and WE SEND OUR LOVE.

Yours 4 eva,
Whetu.

Sky love earth
Shine light
Fall rai-ai-ain,
Earth give life
Turn breast
To chi-i-ild.

Child
Steal light
Turn away rai-ai-ain,
Thrust bright
Sword
Deep into ea-ea-earth.

Mother bleed
Your child
Die,
Bleed mother
Child
Already dead.
            W-o-te-M.

ZORA NEALE HURSTON

ZORA NEALE HURSTON'S contributions to American cultural and intellectual life during the first half of the twentieth century were widespread. Hurston was born in 1891 and grew up in the all-black community of Eatonville, Florida. She began writing short stories in the 1920s, with the encouragement of Harlem Renaissance godfather Alain Locke, conducted groundbreaking ethnographic research in Florida and Haiti, and published her first novel, *Jonah's Gourd Vine*, in 1934. By the time of her death in 1960 she had written plays, essays, and an autobiography. The relatively early short story "Spunk" shows Hurston experimenting—quite successfully—with the same mix of Standard English and Florida vernacular that would make her 1937 novel *Their Eyes Were Watching God* so compelling. Like that novel, "Spunk" addresses themes of passion, infidelity, and mortality. Hurston creates layers of prurient audiences so that the readers, in effect, mirror her gossiping crowd: Elijah Moseley, the story's first speaker, eggs Joe Kanty on to his unfortunate fate just as urban audiences clamored for tales of backwoods intrigue. "Story in Harlem Slang" shows how hard it can be for two good-time boys to keep up a constant swindle. For this story Hurston provided a seemingly authoritative glossary which provides its own fascinating angle on internal migration.

SPUNK

(1925)

I

A giant of a brown-skinned man sauntered up the one street of the village and out into the palmetto thickets with a small pretty woman clinging lovingly to his arm.

"Looka theah, folkses!" cried Elijah Mosley, slapping his leg gleefully, "Theah they go, big as life an' brassy as tacks."

All the loungers in the store tried to walk to the door with an air of nonchalance but with small success.

"Now pee-eople!" Walter Thomas gasped. "Will you look at 'em!"

"But that's one thing Ah likes about Spunk Banks—he ain't skeered of nothin' on God's green footstool—*nothin'*! He rides that log down at saw-mill jus' like he struts 'round wid another man's wife—jus' don't give a kitty. When Tes' Miller got cut to giblets on that circle-saw, Spunk steps right up and starts ridin'. The rest of us was skeered to go near it."

A round-shouldered figure in overalls much too large came nervously in the door and the talking ceased. The men looked at each other and winked.

"Gimme some soda-water. Sass'prilla Ah reckon," the newcomer ordered, and stood far down the counter near the open pickled pig-feet tub to drink it.

Elijah nudged Walter and turned with mock gravity to the new-comer.

"Say, Joe, how's everything up yo' way? How's yo' wife?"

Joe started and all but dropped the bottle he held in his hands. He swallowed several times painfully and his lips trembled.

"Aw 'Lige, you oughtn't to do nothin' like that," Walter grumbled. Elijah ignored him.

"She jus' passed heah a few minutes ago goin' thata way," with a wave of his hand in the direction of the woods.

Now Joe knew his wife had passed that way. He knew that the men lounging in the general store had seen her, moreover, he knew that the men knew *he* knew. He stood there silent for a long moment staring blankly, with his Adam's apple twitching nervously up and down his throat. One could actually *see* the pain he was suffering, his eyes, his face, his hands and even the dejected slump of his shoulders. He set the bottle down upon the counter. He didn't bang it, just eased it out of his hand silently and fiddled with his suspender buckle.

"Well, Ah'm goin' after her to-day. Ah'm goin' an fetch her back. Spunk's done gone too fur."

He reached deep down into his trouser pocket and drew out a hollow ground razor, large and shiny, and passed his moistened thumb back and forth over the edge.

"Talkin' like a man, Joe. 'Course that's *yo'* fambly affairs, but Ah like to see grit in anybody."

Joe Kanty laid down a nickel and stumbled out into the street.

Dusk crept in from the woods. Ike Clarke lit the swinging oil lamp that was almost immediately surrounded by candleflies. The men laughed boisterously behind Joe's back as they watched him shamble woodward.

"You oughtn't to said whut you did to him, Lige—look how it worked him up," Walter chided.

"And Ah hope it did work him up. Tain't even decent for a man to take and take like he do."

"Spunk will sho' kill him."

"Aw, Ah doan't know. You never kin tell. He might turn him up an' spank him fur gettin' in the way, but Spunk wouldn't shoot no unarmed man. Dat razor he carried outa heah ain't gonna run Spunk down an' cut him, an' Joe ain't got the nerve to go up to Spunk with it knowing he totes that Army .45. He makes that break outa heah to bluff us. He's gonna hide that razor behind the first palmetto root an' sneak back home to bed. Don't tell me nothin' 'bout that rabbit-foot colored man. Didn't he meet Spunk an' Lena face to face one day las' week an' mumble sumthin' to Spunk 'bout lettin' his wife alone?"

"What did Spunk say?" Walter broke in—"Ah like him fine but tain't right the way he carries on wid Lena Kanty, jus' 'cause Joe's timid 'bout fightin'."

"You wrong theah, Walter. Tain't 'cause Joe's timid at all, it's 'cause Spunk wants Lena. If Joe was a passle of wile cats Spunk would tackle the job just the same. He'd go after anything he wanted the same way. As Ah wuz sayin' a minute ago, he tole Joe right to his face that Lena was his. 'Call her and see if she'll come. A woman knows her boss an' she answers when he calls.' 'Lena, ain't I yo' husband?' Joe sorter whines out. Lena looked at him real disgusted but she don't answer and she don't move outa her tracks. Then Spunk reaches out an' takes hold of her arm an' says: 'Lena, youse mine. From now on Ah works for you an' fights for you an' Ah never wants you to look to nobody for a crumb of bread, a stitch of close or a shingle to go over yo' head, but *me* long as Ah live. Ah'll git the lumber foh owah house to-morrow. Go home an' git yo' things together!' 'Thass mah house,' Lena speaks up. 'Papa gimme that.' 'Well,' says

Spunk, 'doan give up whut's yours, but when youse inside doan forgit youse mine, an' let no other man git outa his place wid you!'

"Lena looked up at him with her eyes so full of love that they wuz runnin' over, an' Spunk seen it an' Joe seen it too, and his lip started to tremblin' and his Adam's apple was galloping up and down his neck like a race horse. Ah bet he's wore out half a dozen Adam's apples since Spunk's been on the job with Lena. That's all he'll do. He'll be back heah after while swallowin' en' workin' his lips like he wants to say somethin' an' can't."

"But didn't he do nothin' to stop 'em?"

"Nope, not a frazzlin' thing—jus' stood there. Spunk took Lena's arm and walked off jus' like nothin' ain't happened and he stood there gazin' after them till they was outa sight. Now you know a woman don't want no man like that. I'm jus' waitin' to see whut he's goin' to say when he gits back."

II

But Joe Kanty never came back, never. The men in the store heard the sharp report of a pistol somewhere distant in the palmetto thicket and soon Spunk came walking leisurely, with his big black Stetson set at the same rakish angle and Lena clinging to his arm, came walking right into the general store. Lena wept in a frightened manner.

"Well," Spunk announced calmly, "Joe come out there wid a meat axe an' made me kill him."

He sent Lena home and led the men back to Joe—crumpled and limp with his right hand still clutching his razor.

"See mah back? Mah close cut clear through. He sneaked

up en' tried to kill me from the back, but Ah got him, an' got him good, first shot," Spunk said.

The men glared at Elijah, accusingly.

"Take him up an' plant him in Stony Lonesome," Spunk said in a careless voice. "Ah didn't wanna shoot him but he made me do it. He's a dirty coward, jumpin' on a man from behind."

Spunk turned on his heel and sauntered away to where he knew his love wept in fear for him and no man stopped him. At the general store later on, they all talked of locking him up until the sheriff should come from Orlando, but no one did anything but talk.

A clear case of self-defense, the trial was a short one, and Spunk walked out of the court house to freedom again. He could work again, ride the dangerous log-carriage that fed the singing, snarling, biting circle-saw; he could stroll the soft dark lanes with his guitar. He was free to roam the woods again; he was free to return to Lena. He did all of these things.

III

"Whut you reckon, Walt?" Elijah asked one night later. "Spunk's gittin' ready to marry Lena!"

"New! Why, Joe ain't had time to git cold yit. Nohow Ah didn't figger Spunk was the marryin' kind."

"Well, he is," rejoined Elijah. "He done moved most of Lena's things—and her along wid'em—over to the Bradley house. He's buying it. Jus' like Ah told yo' all right in heah the night Joe wuz kilt. Spunk's crazy 'bout Lena. He don't want folks to keep on talkin' 'bout her—thass reason he's rushin' so. Funny thing 'bout that bob-cat, wasn't it?"

"What bob-cat, 'Lige? ah ain't heered 'bout none."

"Ain't cher?? Well, night befo' las' was the fust night Spunk an' Lena moved together an' just then as they was goin' to bed, a big black bob-cat, black all over, you hear me, black, walked round and round that house and howled like forty, an' when Spunk got his gun an' went to the winder to shoot it, he says it stood right still an' and looked him in the eye, an' howled right at him. The thing got Spunk so nervoused up he couldn't shoot. But Spunk says twan't no bob-cat nohow. He says it was Joe done sneaked back from Hell!"

"Humph!" sniffed Walter, "he oughter be nervous after what he done. Ah reckon Joe come back to dare him to marry Lena, or to come out an' fight. Ah bet he'll be back time and again, too. Know what Ah think? Joe wuz a braver man than Spunk."

There was a general shout of derision from the group.

"Thass a fact," went on Walter. "Lookit whut he done; took a razor an' went out to fight a man he knowed toted a gun an' wuz a crack shot, too; 'nother thing Joe wuz skeered of Spunk, skeered plumb stiff! But he went jes' the same. It took him a long time to get his nerve up. Tain't nothin' for Spunk to fight when he ain't skeered of nothin'. Now, Joe's done come back to have it out wid the man that's got all he ever had. Y'all know Joe ain't never had nothin' or wanted nothin' besides Lena. It musta been a h'ant 'cause ain't nobody never seen no black bob-cat."

"'Nother thing," cut in one of the men, "Spunk wuz cussin' a blue streak to-day 'cause he 'lowed dat saw wuz wobblin'— almos' got 'im once. The machinist come, looked it over an' said it wuz alright. Spunk musta been leanin' t'wards it some. Den he claimed somebody pushed 'im but twan't nobody close

to 'im. Ah wuz glad when knockin' off time come. I'm skeered
of dat man when he gits hot. He'd beat you full of button holes
as quick as he's look etcher."

IV

The men gathered the next evening in a different mood, no
laughter. No badinage this time.

"Look, 'Lige, you goin' to set up wid Spunk?"

"New, Ah reckon not, Walter. Tell yuh the truth, Ah'm a li'l
bit skittish, Spunk died too wicket—died cussin' he did. You
know he thought he was done outa life."

"Good Lawd, who'd he think done it?"

"Joe."

"Joe Kanty? How come?"

"Walter, Ah b'leeve Ah will walk up thata way an' set. Lena
would like it Ah reckon."

"But whut did he say, 'Lige?"

Elijah did not answer until they had left the lighted store
and were strolling down the dark street.

"Ah wuz loadin'a wagon wid scantlin' right near the saw
when Spunk fell on the carriage but 'fore Ah could git to him
the saw got him in the body—awful sight. Me an' Skint Miller
got him off but it was too late. Anybody could see that. The fust
thing he said wuz: 'He pushed me, 'Lige—the dirty hound
pushed me in the back!'—he was spittin' blood at ev'ry breath.
We laid him on the sawdust pile with his face to the east so's he
could die easy. He helt mah hen' till the last, Walter, and said: 'It
was Joe, 'Lige . . . the dirty sneak shoved me . . . he didn't dare
to come to mah face . . . but Ah'll git the son-of-a-wood louse
soon's Ah get there an' make Hell too hot for him. . . . Ah felt
him shove me . . . !' Thass how he died."

"If spirits kin fight, there's a powerful tussle goin' on somewhere ovah Jordan 'cause Ah b'leeve Joe's ready for Spunk an' ain't skeered any more—yas, Ah b'leeve Joe pushed 'im mahself."

They had arrived at the house. Lena's lamentations were deep and loud. She had filled the room with magnolia blossoms that gave off a heavy sweet odor. The keepers of the wake tipped about whispering in frightened tones. Everyone in the Village was there, even old Jeff Kanty, Joe's father, who a few hours before would have been afraid to come with ten feet of him, stood leering triumphantly down upon the fallen giant as if his fingers had been the teeth of steel that laid him low.

The cooling board consisted of three sixteen-inch boards on saw horses, a dingy sheet was his shroud.

The women ate heartily of the funeral baked meats and wondered who would be Lena's next. The men whispered coarse conjectures between guzzles of whiskey.

STORY IN HARLEM SLANG

(1942)

Wait till I light up my coal-pot and I'll tell you about this Zigaboo called Jelly. Well, all right now. He was a seal-skin brown and papa-tree-top-tall. Skinny in the hips and solid built for speed. He was born with this rough-dried hair, but when he laid on the grease and pressed it down overnight with his stocking-cap, it looked just like that righteous moss, and had so many waves you got seasick from looking. Solid, man, solid!

His mama named him Marvel, but after a month on Lenox Avenue, he changed all that to Jelly. How come? Well, he put it in the street that when it came to filling that long-felt need, sugar-curing the ladies' feelings, he was in a class by himself and nobody knew his name, so he had to tell 'em. "It must be Jelly, 'cause jam don't shake." Therefore, his name was Jelly. That was what was on his sign. The stuff was there and it was mellow. Whenever he was challenged by a hard-head or a frail eel on the right of his title he would eye-ball the idol-breaker with a slice of ice and put on his ugly-laugh, made up of scorn and pity, and say: "Youse just dumb to the fact, baby. If you don't know what you talking 'bout, you better ask Granny Grunt. I wouldn't mislead you, baby. I don't need to—not with the help I got." Then he would give the pimps'* sign, and percolate on down the Avenue. You can't go behind a fact like that.

So this day he was airing out on the Avenue. It had to be late afternoon, or he would not have been out of bed. All you did by rolling out early was to stir your stomach up. That made you hunt for more dishes to dirty. The longer you slept, the less you had to eat. But you can't collar nods all day. No matter how long you stay in bed, and how quiet you keep, sooner or later that big gut is going to reach over and grab that little one and start to gnaw. That's confidential right from the Bible. You got to get out on the beat and collar yourself a hot.

So Jelly got into his zoot suit with the reet pleats and got out to skivver around and do himself some good. At 132nd Street, he spied one of his colleagues on the opposite sidewalk, standing in front of a café. Jelly figured that if he bull-skated just right, he might confidence Sweet Back out of a thousand on a plate. Maybe a shot of scrap-iron or a reefer. Therefore, Jelly took a quick backward look at his shoe soles to see how his leather was holding out. The way he figured it after the peep was that he had plenty to get across and maybe do a little more cruising besides. So he stanched out into the street and made the crossing.

"Hi there, Sweet Back!" he exploded cheerfully. "Gimme some skin!"

"Lay de skin on me, pal!" Sweet Back grabbed Jelly's outstretched hand and shook hard. "Ain't seen you since the last time, Jelly. What's cookin'?"

*In Harlemese, *pimp* has a different meaning than its ordinary definition as a procurer for immoral purposes. The Harlem pimp is a man whose amatory talents are for sale to any woman who will support him, either with a free meal or on a common law basis; in this sense, he is actually a male prostitute. [Hurston's note]

"Oh, just like de bear—I ain't nowhere. Like de bear's brother, I ain't no further. Like de bear's daughter—ain't got a quarter."

Right away, he wished he had not been so honest. Sweet Back gave him a top-superior, cut-eye look. Looked at Jelly just like a showman looks at an ape. Just as far above Jelly as fried chicken is over branch water.

"Cold in hand, hunh?" He talked down to Jelly. "A red hot pimp like you *say* you is, ain't got no business in the barrel. Last night when I left you, you was beating up your gums and broadcasting about how hot you was. Just as hot as July-jam, you told me. What you doing cold in hand?"

"Aw, man, can't you take a joke? I was just beating up my gums when I said I was broke. How can I be broke when I got de best woman in Harlem? If I ask her for a dime, she'll give me a ten dollar bill: ask her for drink of likker, and she'll buy me a whiskey still. If I'm lying, I'm flying!"

"Gar, don't hang out dat dirty washing in my back yard! Didn't I see you last night with dat beat chick, scoffing a hot dog? Dat chick you had was beat to de heels. Boy, you ain't no good for what you live."

"If you ain't lying now, you flying. You ain't got de first thin. You ain't got nickel one."

Jelly threw back the long skirt of his coat and rammed his hand down into his pants pocket. "Put your money where your mouth is!" he challenged, as he mock-struggled to haul out a huge roll. "Back your crap with your money. I bet you five dollars!"

Sweet Back made the same gesture of hauling out non-existent money.

"I been raised in the church. I don't bet, but I'll doubt you. Five rocks!"

"I thought so!" Jelly crowed, and hurriedly pulled his empty hand out of his pocket. "I knowed you'd back up when I drawed my roll on you."

"You ain't drawed no roll on me, Jelly. You ain't drawed nothing but your pocket. You better stop dat boogerbooing. Next time I'm liable to make you do it." There was a splinter of regret in his voice. If Jelly really had had some money, he might have staked him, Sweet Back, to a hot. Good Southern cornbread with a piano on a platter. Oh, well! The right broad would, or might, come along.

"Who boogerbooing?" Jelly snorted. "Jig, I don't have to. Talking about *me* with a beat chick scoffing a hot dog! You must of not seen me, 'cause last night I was riding round in a Yellow Cab, with a yellow gal, drinking yellow likker and spending yellow money. Tell 'em 'bout me, tell 'em!"

"Git out of my face, Jelly! Dat broad I seen you with wasn't no pe-ola. She was one of them coal-scuttle blondes with hair just as close to her head as ninety-nine is to a hundred. She look-ted like she had seventy-five pounds of clear bosom, guts in her feet, and she look-ted like six months in front and nine months behind. Buy you a whiskey still! Dat broad couldn't make the down payment on a pair of sox."

"Sweet Back, you fixing to talk out of place." Jelly stiffened.

"If you trying to jump salty, Jelly, that's your mammy."

"Don't play in de family, Sweet Back. I don't play de dozens. I done told you."

"Who playing de dozens? You trying to get your hips up on your shoulders 'cause I said you was with a beat broad. One of them lam blacks."

"Who? Me? Long as you been knowing me, Sweet Back, you ain't never seen me with nothing but pe-olas. I can get any frail eel I wants to. How come I'm up here in New York? You don't know, do you? Since youse dumb to the fact, I reckon I'll have to make you hep. I had to leave from down south 'cause Miss Anne used to worry me so bad to go with me. Who, me? Man, I don't deal in no coal. Know what I tell 'em? If they's white, they's right! If they's yellow, they's mellow! If they's brown, they can stick around. But if they come black, they better git way back! Tell 'em 'bout me!"

"Aw, man, you trying to show your grandma how to milk ducks. Best you can do is to confidence some kitchen-mechanic out of a dime or two. Me, I knocks de pad with them cack-broads up on Sugar Hill, and fills 'em full of melody. Man, I'm quick death and easy judgment. Youse just a home-boy, Jelly. Don't try to follow me."

"Me follow *you!* Man, I come on like the Gang Busters, and go off like The March of Time! If dat ain't so, God is gone to Jersey City and you know He wouldn't be messing 'round a place like that. Know what my woman done? We hauled off and went to church last Sunday, and when they passed 'round the plate for the *penny* collection, I throwed in a dollar. De man looked at me real hard for dat. Dat made my woman mad, so she called him back and throwed in a twenty dollar bill! Told him to take dat and go! Dat's what he got for looking at me 'cause I throwed in a dollar."

"Jelly, de wind may blow and de door may slam; dat what you shooting ain't worth a damn!"

Jelly slammed his hand in his bosom as if to draw a gun. Sweet Back did the same.

"If you wants to fight, Sweet Back, the favor is in me."

"I was deep-thinking then, Jelly. It's a good thing I ain't short-tempered. 'T'aint nothing to you, nohow. You ain't hit me yet."

Both burst into a laugh and changed from fighting to lounging poses.

"Don't get too yaller on me, Jelly. You liable to get hurt some day."

"You over-sports your hand your ownself. Too blamed astor-perious. I just don't pay you no mind. Lay de skin on me!"

They broke their handshake hurriedly, because both of them looked up the Avenue and saw the same thing. It was a girl and they both remembered that it was Wednesday afternoon. All of the domestics off for the afternoon with their pay in their pock-ets. Some of them bound to be hungry for love. That meant a dinner, a shot of scrap-iron, maybe room rent and a reefer or two. Both went into the pose and put on the look.

"Big stars falling!" Jelly said out loud when she was in hear-ing distance. "It must be just before day!"

"Yeah, man!" Sweet Back agreed. "Must be a recess in Heaven—pretty angel like that out on the ground."

The girl drew abreast of them, reeling and rocking her hips.

"I'd walk clear to Diddy-Wah-Diddy to get a chance to speak to a pretty lil' ground-angel like that," Jelly went on.

"Aw, man, you ain't willing to go very far. Me, I'd go slap to Ginny-Gall, where they eat cow-rump, skin and all."

The girl smiled, so Jelly set his hat and took the plunge.

"Baby," he crooned, "what's on de rail for de lizard?"

The girl halted and braced her hips with her hands. "A Zigaboo down in Georgy, where I come from, asked a woman that one time and the judge told him 'ninety days.'"

"Georgy!" Sweet Back pretended to be elated. "Where 'bouts in Georgy is you from? Delaware?"

"Delaware?" Jelly snorted. "My people! My people! Free schools and dumb jigs! Man, how you going to put Delaware in Georgy? You ought to know dat's in Maryland."

"Oh, don't try to make out youse no northerner, you! Youse from right down in 'Bam your ownself!" The girl turned on Jelly.

"Yeah, I'm *from* there and I aims to stay from there."

"One of them Russians, eh?" the girl retorted. "Rushed up here to get away from a job of work."

That kind of talk was not leading towards the dinner table.

"But baby!" Jelly gasped. "Dat shape you got on you! I bet the Coca Cola Company is paying you good money for the patent!"

The girl smiled with pleasure at this, so Sweet Back jumped in.

"I know youse somebody swell to know. Youse real people. You grins like a regular fellow." He gave her his most killing look and let it simmer in. "These dickty jigs round here tries to smile. S'pose you and me go inside the café here and grab a hot?"

"You got any money?" the girl asked, and stiffened like a ramrod. "Nobody ain't pimping on me. You dig me?"

"Aw, now, baby!"

"I seen you two mullet-heads before. I was uptown when Joe Brown had you all in the go-long last night. Dat cop sure hates a pimp! All he needs to see is the pimps' salute, and he'll out with his night-stick and whip your head to the red. Beat your head just as flat as a dime!" She went off into a great blow of laughter.

"Oh, let's us don't talk about the law. Let's talk about us," Sweet Back persisted. "You going inside with me to holler 'Let one come flopping! One come grunting! Snatch one from de rear!'"

"Naw indeed!" the girl laughed harshly. "You skillets is trying to promote a meal on me. But it'll never happen, brother. You barking up the wrong tree. I wouldn't give you air if you was stopped up in a jug. I'm not putting out a thing. I'm just like the cemetery—I'm not putting out, I'm taking in! Dig?"

"I'll tell you like the farmer told the potato—plant you now and dig you later."

The girl made a movement to switch on off. Sweet Back had

not dirtied a plate since the day before. He made a weak but desperate gesture.

"Trying to snatch my pocketbook, eh?" she blazed. Instead of running, she grabbed hold of Sweet Back's draping coat-tail and made a slashing gesture. "How much split you want back here? If your feets don't hurry up and take you 'way from here, you'll *ride* away. I'll spread my lungs all over New York and call the law. Go ahead, Bedbug! Touch me! And I'll holler like a pretty white woman!"

The boys were ready to flee, but she turned suddenly and rocked on off with her ear-rings snapping and her heels popping.

"My people! My people!" Sweet Back sighed.

"I know you feel chewed," Jelly said, in an effort to make it appear that he had had no part in the fiasco.

"Oh, let her go," Sweet Back said magnanimously. "When I see people without the periodical principles they's supposed to have, I just don't fool with 'em. What I want to steal her old pocketbook with all the money I got? I could buy a beat chick like her and give her away. I got money's mammy and Grandma change. One of my women, and not the best one I got neither, is buying me ten shag suits at one time."

He glanced sidewise at Jelly to see if he was convincing. But Jelly's thoughts were far away. He was remembering those full, hot meals he had left back in Alabama to seek wealth and splendor in Harlem without working. He had even forgotten to look cocky and rich.

Glossary of Harlem Slang

Air out: leave, flee, stroll

Astorperious: haughty, biggity

Aunt Hagar: Negro race (also *Aunt Hagar's chillun*)

Bad hair: Negro-type hair

Balling: having fun

'Bam, and *down in 'Bam:* down South

Battle-hammed: badly formed about the hips

Beating up your gums: talking to no purpose

Beluthahatchie: next station beyond Hell

Big boy: stout fellow. But in the South, it means fool and is a prime insult.

Blowing your top: getting very angry; occasionally used to mean, "He's doing fine!"

Boogie-woogie: type of dancing and rhythm. For years, in the South, it meant secondary syphilis.

Brother-in-black: Negro

Bull-skating: Bragging

Butt sprung: a suit or a skirt out of shape in the rear

Coal scuttle blonde: black woman

Cold: exceeding, well, etc., as in "He was cold on that trumpet!"

Collar a nod: sleep

Collar a hot: eat a meal

Color scale: high yaller, yaller, high brown, vaseline brown, seal brown, low brown, dark black

Conk buster: cheap liquor; also an intellectual Negro

Cruising: parading down the Avenue. Variations: *oozing, percolating,* and *free-wheeling.* The

latter implies more briskness.

Cut: doing something well

Dark black: a casually black person. Superlatives: *low black,* a blacker person; *lam black,* still blacker; and *damn black,* blackest man, of whom it is said: "Why, lightning bugs follow him at 12 o'clock in the day, thinking it's midnight."

Dat thing: sex of either sex

Dat's your mammy: same as, "So is your old man."

Diddy-Wah-Diddy: a far place, a measure of distance. (2) another suburb of Hell, built since way before Hell wasn't no bigger than Baltimore. The folks in Hell go there for a big time.

Dig: understand. "Dig me?" means, "Do you get me? Do you collar the jiver?"

Draped down: dressed in the height of Harlem fashion; also *togged down*

Dumb to the fact: "You don't know what you're talking about."

Dusty butt: cheap prostitute

Eight-rock: very black person

Every postman on his beat: kinky hair

First thing smoking: a train. "I'm through with this town. I mean to grab the first thing smoking."

Frail eel: pretty girl

Free schools: a shortened expression of deprecation derived from "free schools and dumb Negroes," sometimes embellished with "free schools, pretty yellow teachers and dumb Negroes."

Function: a small, unventilated dance, full of people too casually bathed

Gator-faced: long, black face with big mouth

Getting on some stiff time: really doing well with your racket

Get you to go: power, physical or otherwise, to force the opponent to run

Ginny Gall: a suburb of Hell, a long way off

Git up off of me: quit talking about me, leave me alone

Go when the wagon comes: another way of saying, "You may be acting biggity now, but you'll cool down when enough power gets behind you."

Good hair: Caucasian-type hair

Granny Grunt: a mythical character to whom most questions may be referred

Ground rations: sex, also under rations

Gum beater: a blowhard, a braggart, idle talker in general

Gut-bucket: low dive, type of music, or expression from same

Gut-foot: bad case of fallen arches

Handkerchief-head: sycophant type of Negro; also an Uncle Tom

Hauling: fleeing on foot. "Man! He cold hauled it!"

I don't deal in coal: "I don't keep company with black women."

I'm cracking but I'm facking: "I'm wisecracking, but I'm telling the truth."

Inky dink: very black person

I shot him lightly and he died politely: "I completely outdid him."

Jar head: Negro man

Jelly: sex

Jig: Negro, a corrupted shortening of Zigaboo

Jook: a pleasure house, in the class of gut-bucket; now common all over the South

Jooking: playing the piano, guitar, or any musical instrument in the manner of the Jooks (pronounced like "took") (2) dancing and "scronching," ditto

Juice: liquor

July-jam: something very hot

Jump salty: get angry

Kitchen mechanic: a domestic

Knock yourself out: have a good time

Lightly, slightly and politely: doing things perfectly

Little sister: measure of hotness: "Hot as little sister!"

Liver-lip: pendulous, thick purple lips

Made hair: hair that has been straightened

Mammy: a term of insult. Never used in any other way by Negroes.

Miss Anne: a white woman

Mister Charlie: a white man

Monkey chaser: a West Indian

Mug Man: small-time thug or gangster

My people! My people!: Sad and satiric expression in the Negro language; sad when a Negro comments on the backwardness of some members of his race; at other times, used for satiric or comic effect.

Naps: kinky hair

Nearer my God to Thee: good hair

Nothing to the bear but his curly hair:

"I call your bluff," or "Don't be afraid of him; he won't fight."

Now you cookin' with gas: now you're talking, in the groove, etc.

Ofay: white person

Old cuffee: Negro (genuine African word for the same thing)

Palmer House: walking flat-footed, as from fallen arches

Pancake: a humble type of Negro

Park ape: an ugly, underprivileged Negro

Peckerwood: poor and unloved class of Southern whites

Peeping through my likkers: carrying on even though drunk

Pe-ola: a very white Negro girl

Piano: spare ribs (white rib-bones suggest piano keys)

Pig meat: young girl

Pilch: house or apartment; residence

Pink toes: yellow girl

Playing the dozens: low-rating the ancestors of your opponent

Red neck: poor Southern white man

Reefer: marijuana cigarette, also *a drag*

Righteous mass or *grass:* good hair

Righteous rags: the components of a Harlem-style suit

Rug-cutter: originally a person frequenting house-rent parties, cutting up the rugs of the host with his feet; a person too cheap or poor to patronize regular dance halls; now means a good dancer

Russian: a Southern Negro up north. "Rushed up here," hence a Russian.

Scrap iron: cheap liquor

Sell out: run in fear

Sender: he or she who can get you to go, i.e., has what it takes. Used often as a compliment: "He's a solid sender!"

Smoking, or *smoking over:* looking someone over

Solid: perfect

Sooner: anything cheap and mongrel, now applied to cheap clothes, or a shabby person

Stanch, or *stanch out:* to begin, commence, step out

Stomp: low dance, "but hat man!"

Stormbuzzard: shiftless, homeless character

Stroll: doing something well

Sugar Hill: northwest sector of Harlem, near Washington Heights, site of the newest apartment houses, mostly occupied by professional people. (The expression has been distorted in the South to mean a Negro red light district.)

The bear: confession of poverty

The big apple, also *the big red apple:* New York City

The man: the law, or powerful boss

Thousand on a plate: beans

Tight head: one with kinky hair

Trucking: strolling. (2) dance step from the strolling motif

V and X: five-and-ten-cent store

West Hell: another suburb of Hell, worse than the original

What's on the rail for the lizard?: suggestion for moral turpitude

Whip it to the red: beat your head until it is bloody

Woofing: aimless talk, as a dog barks on a moonless night

Young suit: ill-fitting, too small. Observers pretend to believe you're breaking in your little brother's suit for him.

Your likker told you: misguided behavior

Zigaboo: a Negro

Zoot suit with the reet pleat: Harlem-style suit, padded shoulders, 43-inch trousers at the knee with cuff so small it needs a zipper to get into, high waistline, fancy lapels, bushels of buttons, etc.

JOHN KASAIPWALOVA

JOHN KASAIPWALOVA was born in 1949 in Kiriwana Island of the Trobriand Island Group, Papua New Guinea. He studied at the University of Queensland and the University of Papua New Guinea. As well as fiction, he has written poetry and an opera; he is now a tribal chief in Trobriand Island. In this brief but vivid story, set during the Australian administration of Papua New Guinea, Kasaipwalova assembles a montage of linguistic and cultural codes. While asserting the right to chew betel nut (or buwa) in an airport, his student hero also demonstrates his ability to shift effortlessly among Standard English, pidgin, and Hiri Motu. He narrates "he knewed and we knewed that he wronged all the time," but can also demand that a belligerent police officer produce "that ordinance which specifically lays down that we natives are not allowed to chew betel nut within the precincts of an air terminal, in our own country." Kasaipwalova puts his own twist on the now-familiar code-switching format used by Zora Neale Hurston and others, in which only an omniscient narrator has the capacity to employ language strategically.

BETEL NUT IS BAD MAGIC
FOR AIRPLANES

(1972)

O ne Saturday afternoon in May 22 this year some of we university students went to meet our people at Jacksons Airport in Seven Mile. They arrived and we happy very much. Then we all comes to that backyard corner. That one place where Ansett and TAA capsize boxes for native people who go by plane.

We was standing about thirty of we, waiting to catch our things. We was chewing plenty buwa like civilized people. We was not spitting or making rubbish. Only feeling very good from the betel nuts our people had bringed to Moresby.

Then for nothing somebody in brown uniform with cap like pilot, and wearing boots like dimdim and black belt, he comes up to one our people and he gives some Motu and English. That one our people didn't understood. So soon that uniform man was redding his eyes and rubbing his teeths just like white man's puppy dog. Maybe something like five minutes died but still he talk. Bloody bastard! He wanted our people to stop chewing buwa because TAA and Ansett jets had come and plenty plenty white people inside the terminal. They must not be offended to see us chew betel nut. Anyways, this brown puppy dog of white man angried himself for nothing. His anger now made big big pumpkin inside his throat for because he was "educated native" and he didn't wanted kanaka natives doing like that in front of Europeans.

Soon quickly one native uni. gel student seen what's happening. She goes and she asks why he was giving Motu and English to our people. He whyed. She seen quickly that his why is no good. So the uni. gel student she says to him to go away. Chewing buwa is our custom for many, many civilizations. Bloody bastard! Maybe this one first time natives talked him like that way, because quickly he becomes more angry. He started talking big and making his fingers round like hard cricket ball.

I seen what's hairpin too and I fright really true. But I walks over and I asks. The uni. gel she explains and he talks also. We talk loud and many peoples they see us too and he say, "Stop being cheeky. Just shut up and do what I tell you. You are breaking the law!" So I says, "What law are we breaking? Tell me! What ordinance are we breaking?"

The puppy he gets very angry and he say "Don't be smart! Just shut up and stop chewing betel nut. You are breaking the law!"

Then my anger really wanted to stand its feet, so I says "Bull shit. We are neither spitting nor throwing rubbish. Black people never made that law and this is black people's land. There's no such law."

"All right you think you smart! You want me to report the boss?"

"I don't know your boss. Run to him if you want to smell his boots. Go on report if you want!"

His face smoked and he walked away to get his boss. I says good words to our people and we continue chewing our buwa. We was really getting tired. Our boxes sleeping somewhere we donno. I chewed my buwa but little bit my stomach was frighten because the security man will bring his boss. Then maybe big trouble! Bloody bastard!

Not long. Soon the brown puppy dog comes with their white papa dog and two other brown puppy dogs too. They was all wearing khaki uniforms, caps, boots and black belts. They seen us and we seen them too. They come to us. My heart started winking and breathing very fast. The white papa dog, his face like one man I seen one day near Boroko R. S. L. Club.

O sori! I looks at him and truly my chest wanted to run away. His bigness, his face red and especially his big big beer stomach, they frighten me already. Maybe if you seen him too, ei, you will really laugh. Bloody bastard! His stomach was too big for him. I can seen how his belt was trying its best to hold the big swelling together. His brown shirt was really punished and all of we can sees how it wanted to break. But no matter, because the stomach was trying to fall down over the black belt like one full up bilum bag.

Me, it was already nearly too much. I straighten my legs quickly because something like water was falling down my leg inside my long trousers. I dunno what something and maybe only my fright trying his luck on me. But I didn't look at my long trousers. Too many people watching and also my head was boding sweat from the hotness.

Anyways, the security guards came to us. But now we three university students, we was standing together and looking them very proudly. Too late now. We was not going to run any more. We decided to defend our rights. At first they didn't know what to say and only they talked quietly inside their throats. Then their boss, the Australian papa with big stomach, he started showing we his teeths. Oi, we was frighten by his hard voice. He says to me, "Listen boy, who gave you permission to chew betel nut here? You are breaking the law, the legal laws of this land. And when they (pointing to his puppies) told you to stop, you said you didn't believe in the law and will continue to break the law!"

Straightaway my face blooded because many black, white and yellow people, they was watching us too and this white papa dog, he was talking bad like that way to me. Plenty times I hear white people calling black men "bois" so this time I hear it and my mind was already fire. I wanted to give him some. Maybe good English or maybe little bit Strine. So I says loudly to him, "All right white man, on what moral grounds is it unlawful for me to chew betel nut here? This is a free country of which we black people are citizens and unless you can show me the moral basis for your 'so called laws' I cannot recognize and therefore comply to that law!"

Well, he was very very angry now because one black man answering him in very good English. Maybe he didn't understand what I say.

"Listen boy, don't be smart. You are breaking the law and the law is laid down by the lawful government in the book."

I knows straightaway that he is another one of those ignorant, uneducated white men. I getting very angry too.

"O.K. then, show me that ordinance which specifically lays down that we natives are not allowed to chew betel nut within the precincts of an air terminal, in our own country. As a citizen I have at least the right to be shown that law before you crassly accuse me of breaking the law. Until such times as you do so we shall consider you a liar and one using his delegated authority to intimidate the black people of Niugini."

"Shut up! You are nothing more than a cheeky brat!"

"Your resorting to insults is unwarranted here. All I'm demanding from you is the proof for the existence of such a law. Come on show me the exact ordinance."

"I don't have to show you the written ordinance. The lawful authority is vested in me as an officer to arrest you if I want to. It's written in Commonwealth Safety Regulations Act, section 32."

"Bull shit. I want to see it with my own eyes! Listen mate. Why aren't you arresting those white kids inside the terminal for chewing P.K. What's the difference between their P.K inside the terminal and our betel nut outside on the road pavement?"

"Shut up you cheeky brat!" Then he wanted to grab my little neck. I was only short so I jumped back and he missed. But his face was red fire. "Since you are not going to obey, we shall arrest you!"

He was making we feel like we was some "bad cowboys" or criminals. All we three university students we was already hotted up and we was arguing with him very loudly. But when he tried that one on me, that was finish for everything. I lost my manners. I lost my calmness and also my boiling anger and fear. My heart was knocking my chest very hard. Only one thing I wanted to be—a true kanaka. So I threw my voice at him nearly spitting his face.

"Don't you dare lay hands on me white boi. This is black man's country and we have the right to make our laws to suit us. Commonwealth government is not the Niugini House of Assembly. If you think your laws are justified, you are nothing more than a bloody white racist! A bloody white racist, you hear!"

I was shaking. The overseas people who was arrived and also black people, they was watching. Our people was just waiting for him to hit me and then they would finish him on the spot. Maski Bomana. We will only eat rice and have good times there. The Australian papa dog, he seen too many black faces around him. Too much for him. I think our argument already full him up. He starts walking away and threatening we.

"We'll fix you, you cheeky brat! Don't you run away. I'm going to ring the police."

"Ring the police if you want to! Always like you white racists. Each time you know you are wrong or want to bully us black people, you have to use the police on us."

The brown puppy dogs didn't know what to do so they followed their white boss, the papa dog with big stomach. I think all the water in my blood was all red now. I breathing very fast but maybe that was because I already frighten about the coming of the police. I seen many times how they do to protect white men's lives or property. Only last week I seen them hitting some Chimbu men because they was enjoying life from drinks. I wanted to throw some stones at the police cars but they was too fast and they took the Chimbu men away to kalabus.

Then something maybe like five minutes and we hear big siren noise. Two blue polis cars and one big lorry. That one had gorilla wire all around it and truly big enough to capture maybe twenty or thirty natives inside it. The cars and the lorry was all for we three university students. They stopped the traffic and about six black polis bois jumped down. I was really frighten. But papa dog he gets his courage and they march to us. We was standing calmly, because we was ready now. Any time! The polis bois they seen us not making big trouble so they run away with the big lorry, but they stopped the two blue cars.

They comes marching up to we and our people. Also university bus already come and we busy loading up the boxes, bags of yams and drums. But papa dog he no play now. Bloody bastard! His teeths was already making noise to the polis bois.

"Officer I want you to charge him now."

The polis bois they look very stupid because they didn't know what's up. Only I can seen their eyes. They was very hungry and truly wanted to catch us because white man he said to them. My anger comes back to my head very quickly. I happy little bit, but, because the polis bois was black men and not white.

"Officer before you charge me, I would like to know what you are charging me for and perhaps, allow me to give my side of the story."

The officer he stands very stupidly. He has no words to say. So white papa dog he tells him more.

"Officer, I want you to charge him with the use of obscene language in public and also breach of the Commonwealth Safety Regulations Act, section thirty-two."

All of we was too surprised and we make one big whistle because he was already lying.

"Obscene language, my foot! All right if you reckon I used obscene language, just exactly what words did I use? Go on, tell the officer the exact words I used."

"Officer charge him. I wouldn't even repeat the words in front of the lady, in any case."

The lady who papa dog was pointing to, she was the university gel student with us. So she says, "Officer I don't mind at all, just ask him to prove to us what obscene words we used."

The polis bois they says nothing only wanting to take us away to kalabus.

"Officer they have breached the law under section 32 of the Commonwealth Safety Regulations Act and he was using very insulting language something like 'this is bloody, black fella's country.' I have my witnesses here." He showed them his puppy dogs.

We knewed fully he was truly telling lie. He only want to kalabus we because we was opened our mouths against him.

"Look officer this man is lying and we have here at least thirty witnesses to tell you exactly what I said. I called him a bloody white racist which is what he really is. I had simply questioned him his rights to force us to stop chewing betel nut here. We weren't throwing rubbish or spitting."

The polis bois was getting very annoyed and they wanted to catch me. But I was only very small and I jumped back. Then one officer he say, "You have to come to the police station."

"What for?" I asks very angry. "We've done nothing wrong. If you are going to believe the word of this white man against our thirty witnesses right here, then I suggest that you are nothing more than puppet tools for white man."

My words hit their shame because many black people was watching them too. Quickly they didn't like me. Bloody bastards! They want to friend with white man.

"Just shut up and come to the police station!"

Truly by now I wanted to give them some. But of, their size and also their big boots! If they give me one, I will really have many holes in my bottom. But I says naski.

"You can't arrest me without telling me what the charges are. Let go my hands! We came to see that our people get to the university and I'm not going anywhere until our people are comfortably seen back to the university!"

I run away free and we start our people into the bus. The polis bois and the white papa dog, they didn't know what to do, so they was standing there like bamboo, all empty. Soon our peoples they come back to university in the bus and we three university students, we goes and we argue some more.

In the end, they tells we three to get into the police car. We goes in but then we sees how the polis bois was going to leave the papa dog behind and take us to Boroko Police Station. So we quickly opens the doors and we runs out. They catch us very quickly again then I says loudly, "We are not going to the police station unless that white man also comes with us. It's hardly justifiable for the police to be his spokesman because this will conveniently screen him from any embarrassment."

What can they do? They knows they was wrong so they calls him back. They pushed we into the back seat, then they opens the front door for the papa dog. So he talks loudly and strong.

"Get in there white man!"

He blooded more and we laugh inside. The polis they was all very silent. We speeded to Boroko Police Station. I knows that place often.

They bringed us to one big table and many police men behind it. The papa dog he didn't waste time. He open one book and he show them.

"I want you to charge them for trespassing under section thirty-two. Under this regulation I have the authority to arrest or have arrested any persons I see to be causing danger to the safety of aeroplanes. . . ."

Then I know he was truly telling more lies and I shout straightaway. "What a lot of rubbish. We weren't carrying anything inflammable. We were simply chewing betel nut on the road pavement outside the terminal."

The white sergeant police, he turns fastly and like one lion's mouth, he yells me, "Listen boy, keep your mouth shut!"

His voice was too big for me. His eyes wanted to shoot and his blue uniform swelling from his fatness. I wanted to say more. But too late! I see his bigness and I hear his voice and that one finished me up quick. Anyways we was very tired now and we shut up good. Maybe we let him give us some now and maybe later we fight him inside court house. So the papa dog gives more lies.

"I also want to charge him with the use of obscene language in a public place. He was using the words and I quote 'this is fuckin black fellas' country.'"

He tell them more and he shows them more from his book. But the police sergeant and his bois didn't knew what means "obscene language." They look for one dictionary and we was standing there like five or maybe ten minutes waiting for them. They didn't find what means that word. I seen the sergeant pull one telephone and talks to it.

Like two minutes later, we was took to one office inside, near the back. That one office, his name CIB office. We walks in, the four of we and we seen one man sitting inside. He looks like very important man. Long trousers, shoes and tie. We sit down and again the papa dog he starts more talking. Ei, he talks very long, and this making me feel like one real "bad" cowboy or something. Finally the important man shut him up.

"You can either charge him with one or the other. With regards to the section thirty-two, a similar case took place in Lae last year and I remember clearly the new precedent set then. If you want to charge him with that you have to write away for the Controller General's permission from Melbourne."

The papa dog, he nearly cried because he knewed and we knewed that he wronged all the time. Then my turn for explain. I told him about the argument and everything.

"I have my two witnesses here to testify. I didn't use 'fuckin black fellas' country.' I do admit having spoken to him in a firm voice but what I called him was a 'bloody white racist.' As far as I'm concerned these are not obscene words. They are political terms which I often ascribe to persons committing injustice to others, and I would just as readily call a black man a 'bloody black racist' if I saw him committing an injustice to a man of another ethnic origin."

The important man held his head for long time and we wait like sleeping pigs. Then he looks up and writes down the white man's name, address and phone. After that he told him to go. I wanted to say something but my mouth shut very quickly. The important man, he writes our names in his book then he say, "I will notify you on Monday as to what the charge will be. In the meantime you may go."

We walk out and we was feeling little bit happy. But I remember we have no money for bus to Waigani. The police they should pay us. So I walks back to the CIB office. "Sir the police had inconvenienced us in the first place and I think it is only right they should take us back to the university."

The important man walk out with us to the front office and he called on sergeant.

"Sergeant, arrange for a car to take these students safely to the university, will you?"

That one sergeant same one before. He didn't like it, to treat us good. We three university students, we come back to Waigani. We was chewing our betel nut on the way.

EARL LOVELACE

EARL LOVELACE has contributed greatly to West Indian literature with his mastery of multiple genres. Lovelace was born in
Toco, Trinidad, in 1935, grew up in Tobago, studied at Howard
and Johns Hopkins universities, and has worked as a forest
ranger and journalist as well as writer. "Joebell and America"
offers a commentary on language, its richness and its limitations. When the "classy" chameleon Joebell decides to immigrate illegally to the United States, he feels certain that his
longtime immersion in American popular culture will get him
through. The story's narrative voice switches between an
anonymous gambling buddy of Joebell's, who sets up the story,
and the protagonist himself, who narrates his moment of
greatest stress as well as his bittersweet victory. Ultimately
Joebell finds himself still marked by his island's history of
British colonization. The story provides a masterful illustration
of how British and U.S. culture compete to win the souls of the
Caribbean—and how those souls maintain their own integrity.

JOEBELL AND AMERICA

(1988)

ONE

Joebell find that he seeing too much hell in Trinidad so he make up his mind to leave and go away. The place he find he should go is America, where everybody have a motor car and you could ski on snow and where it have seventy-five channels of color television that never sign off and you could sit down and watch for days, all the boxing and wrestling and basketball, right there as it happening. Money is the one problem that keeping him in Cunaripo; but that year as Christmas was coming, luck hit Joebell in the gamble, and for three days straight he win out the wappie. After he give two good pardners a stake and hand his mother a raise and buy a watch for his girl, he still have nineteen hundred and seventy-five Trinidad and Tobago dollars that is his own. That was the time. If Joebell don't go to America now, he will never go again.

But, a couple years earlier, Joebell make prison for a wounding, and before that they had him up for resisting arrest and using obscene language. Joebell have a record; and for him to get a passport he must first get a letter from the police to say that he is of good character. All the bribe Joebell try to bribe, he can't get this letter from the police. He prepare to pay a thousand dollars for the letter; but the police pardner who he had working on the matter keep telling him to come back and come back and come back. But another pardner tell him that with the same thousand dollars he could get a whole new American passport, with new name and everything. The only thing a little ticklish is Joebell will have to talk Yankee.

Joebell smile, because if is one gift he have it is to talk languages, not Spanish and French and Italian and such, but he could talk English and American and Grenadian and Jamaican; and of all of them the one he love best is American. If that is the only problem, well, Joebell in America already.

But it have another problem. The fellar who fixing up the passport business for him tell him straight, if he try to go direct from Trinidad to America with the US passport, he could get arrest at the Trinidad airport, so the pardner advise that the best thing to do is for Joebell to try to get in through Puerto Rico where they have all those Spanish people and where the immigration don't be so fussy. Matter fix. Joebell write another pardner who he went to school with and who in the States seven years, and tell him he coming over, to look out for him, he will ring him from Puerto Rico.

Up in Independence Recreation Club where we gamble, since Joebell win this big money, he is a hero. All the fellars is suddenly his friend, everybody calling out, "Joebell! Joebell!" some asking his opinion and some giving him advice on how to gamble his money. But Joebell not in no hurry. He know just as how you could win fast playing wappie, so you could lose fast too; and, although he want to stay in the wappie room and hear how we talk up his gambling ability, he decide that the safer thing to do is to go and play poker where if he have to lose he could lose more slow and where if he lucky he could win a good raise too. Joebell don't really have to be in the gambling club at all. His money is his own; but Joebell have himself down as a hero, and to win and run away is not classy. Joebell have himself down as classy.

Fellars' eyes open big big that night when they see Joebell heading for the poker room, because in there it have Japan and Fisherman from Mayaro and Captain and Papoye and a fellar named Morgan who every Thursday does come up from Tunapuna with a paper bag full with money and a knife in his shoe. Every man in there could real play poker.

In wappie, luck is the master; but in poker skill is what make luck work for you. When day break that Friday morning, Joebell stagger out the poker room with his whole body wash down with perspiration, out five hundred of his good dollars. Friday night he come back with the money he had give his girl to keep. By eleven he was down three. Fellars get silent and all of us vex to see how money he wait so long to get he giving away so easy. But, Joebell was really to go America in truth. In the middle of the poker, he leave the game to pee. On his way back, he walk into the wappie room. If you see Joebell: the whole front of his shirt open and wiping sweat from all behind his head. "Heat!" somebody laugh and say. On the table that time is two card: Jack and Trey. Albon and Ram was winning everybody. The both of them like Trey. They gobbling up all bets. Was a Friday night. Waterworks get pay, County Council get pay. It had men from Forestry. It had fellars from the Housing Project. Money high high on the table. Joebell favorite card is Jack.

Ram was a loser the night Joebell win big; now, Ram on top. "Who against Trey?" Ram say. He don't look at Joebell, but everybody know is Joebell he talking to. Out of all Joebell money, one thousand gone to pay for the false passport, and, already in the poker he lose eight. Joebell have himself down as a hero. A hero can't turn away. Everybody waiting to see.

They talking, but, they waiting to see what Joebell will do. Joebell wipe his face, then wipe his chest, then he wring out the perspiration from the handkerchief, fold the kerchief and put it round his neck, and bam, just like that, like how you see in pictures when the star boy, quiet all the time, begin to make his move, Joebell crawl right up the wappie table, fellars clearing the way for him, and, everything, he empty out everything he had in his two pocket, and, lazy lazy, like he really is that star boy, he say, "Jack for this money!"

Ram was waiting, "Count it, Casa," Ram say.

When they count the money was two hundred and thirteen dollars and some change. Joebell throw the change for a broken hustler, Ram match him. Bam! Bam! Bam! In three card, Jack play.

"Double!" Joebell say. "For all," which mean that Joebell betting that another Jack play before any Trey.

Ram put some, and Albon put the rest, they sure is robbery. Whap! Whap! Whap! Jack play. "Devine!" Joebell say. That night Joebell leave the club with fifteen hundred dollars. Fellars calling him The Gambler of Natchez.

When we see Joebell next, his beard shave off, his head cut in a GI trim, and he walking with a fast kinda shuffle, his body leaned forward and his hands in his pockets and he talking Yankee: "How ya doin, Main! Hi-ya, Baby!" And then we don't see Joebell in Cunaripo.

"Joebell gone away," his mother, Miss Myrtle say, "Praise God!"

If they have to give a medal for patience in Cunaripo, Miss Myrtle believe that the medal is hers just from the trials and tribulations she undergo with Joebell. Since he leave school his best friend is Trouble and wherever Trouble is, right there is Joebell.

"I shoulda mind my child myself," she complain. "His grandmother spoil him too much, make him feel he is too much of a star, make him believe that the world too easy."

"The world don't owe you anything, boy," she tell him. "Try to be decent, son," she say. Is like a stick break in Joebell two ears, he don't hear a word she have to say. She talk to him. She ask his uncle Floyd to talk to him. She go by the priest in Mount St. Benedict to say a novena for him. She say the ninety-first psalm for him. She go by a *obeah* woman in Moruga to see what really happening to him. The *obeah* woman tell her to bring him quick so she could give him a bath and a guard to keep off the evil spirit that somebody have lighting on him. Joebell fly up in one big vexation with his mother for enticing him to go to the *obeah* woman: "Ma, what stupidness you trying to get me in? You know I don't believe in the negromancy business. What blight you want to fall on me now? That is why it so hard for me to win in gamble, you crossing up my luck."

But Miss Myrtle pray and she pray and at last, praise God, the answer come, not as how she did want it—you can't get everything the way you want it—but, praise God, Joebell gone away. And to those that close to her, she whisper, "America!" for that is the destination Joebell give her.

But Joebell aint reach America yet. His girl Alicia, who working at Last Chance snackette on the Cunaripo road is the only one he tell that Puerto Rico is the place he trying to get to. Since she take up with Joebell, her mother quarreling with her every day, "How a nice girl like you could get in with such a vagabond fellar? You don't have eyes in your head to see that the boy is only trouble?" They talk to her, they tell her how he stab a man in the gambling club and went to jail. They tell her how he have this ugly beard on his face and this ugly look in his face. They tell her how he don't work nowhere regular, "Child,

why you bringing this cross into your life?" they ask her. They
get her Uncle Matthew to talk to her. They carry her to Mount
St. Benedict for the priest to say a novena for her. They give
her the ninety-first psalm to say. They carry her to Moruga to a
obeah woman who bathe her in a tub with bush, and smoke
incense all over her to untangle her mind from Joebell.

But there is a style about Joebell that she like. Is a dream in
him that she see. And a sad craziness that make her sad too but
in a happy kinda way. The first time she see him in the snackette, she watch him and don't say nothing but, she think, Hey!
Who he think he is? He come in the snackette with this foolish
grin on his face and this strolling walk and this kinda com-
manding way about him and sit down at the table with his legs
wide open, taking up a big space as if he spending a hundred
dollars, and all he ask for is a coconut roll and a juice. And
then he call her again, this time he want a napkin and a tooth-
pick. Napkins and toothpicks is for people who eating food;
but she give them to him. And still he sit down there with some
blight, some trouble hanging over him, looking for somebody
to quarrel with or for something to get him vex so he could
parade. She just do her work, and not a word she tell him. And
just like that, just so by himself he cool down and start talking
to her though they didn't introduce.

Everything he talk about is big: big mountains and big cars
and race horses and heavyweight boxing champions and people in America—everything big. And she look at him from
behind the counter and she see his sad craziness and she hear
him talk about all this bigness far away, that make her feel too
that she would like to go somewhere and be somebody, and
just like that, without any words, or touching it begin.

Sometimes he'd come in the snackette, walking big and
singing, and those times he'd be so broke all he could afford to

call for'd be a glass of cold water. He wanted to be a calypso-
nian, he say; but he didn't have no great tune and his compositions wasn't so great either and everything he sing had a
kinda sadness about it, no matter how he sing it. Before they
start talking direct to one another he'd sing, closing his eyes
and hunching his shoulders, and people in the snackette'd
think he was just making joke; but, she know the song was for
her and she'd feel pretty and sad and think about places far
away. He used to sing in a country and western style, this song:
his own composition:

> *Gonna take ma baby*
> *Away on a trip*
> *Gonna take ma baby*
> *Yip yip yip*
> *We gonna travel far*
> *To New Orleans*
> *Me and ma baby*
> *Be digging the scene*

If somebody came in and had to be served, he'd stop
singing while she served them, then he'd start up again. And
just so, without saying anything or touching or anything, she
was his girl.

She never tell him about the trouble she was getting at
home because of him. In fact she hardly talk at all. she'd just sit
there behind the counter and listen to him. He had another
calypso that he thought would be a hit.

> *Look at Mahatma Gandhi*
> *Look at Hitler and Mussolini*
> *Look at Uriah Butler*

> *Look at Kwame Nkrumah*
> *Great as they was*
> *Every one of them had to stand the pressure*

He used to take up the paper that was on one side of the counter and sit down and read it, "Derby day," he would say. "Look at the horses running," and he would read out the horses' names. Or it would be boxing, and he would say Muhammed boxing today, or Sugar. He talked about these people as if they were personal friends of his. One day he brought her five pounds of deer wrapped in a big brown paper bag. She was sure he pay a lot of money for it. "Put this in the fridge until you going home." Chenette, mangoes, oranges, sapodillas, he was always bringing things for her. When her mother ask her where she was getting these things, she tell her that the owner of the place give them to her. For her birthday Joebell bring her a big box wrapped in fancy paper and went away, so proud and shy, he couldn't stand to see her open it, and when she open it it was a vase with a whole bunch of flowers made from colored feathers and a big birthday card with an inscription: From guess who?

"Now, who give you this? The owner?" her mother asked. She had to make up another story.

When he was broke she would slip him a dollar or two of her own money and if he win in the gamble he would give her some of the money to keep for him, but she didn't keep it long, he mostly always came back for it next day. And they didn't have to say anything to understand each other. He would just watch her and she would know from his face if he was broke and want a dollar or if he just drop in to see her, and he could tell from her face if she want him to stay away altogether that day or if he should make a turn and come again or what. He didn't get to go no place with her, cause in the night when the snackette close her big brother would be waiting to take her home.

"Thank God!" her mother say when she hear Joebell gone away. "Thank you, Master Jesus, for helping to deliver this child from the clutches of that vagabond." She was so happy she hold a thanksgiving feast, buy sweet drinks and make cake and invite all the neighbor's little children; and she was surprise that Alicia was smiling. But Alicia was thinking, Lord, just please let him get to America, they will see who is vagabond. Lord, just let him get through that immigration they will see happiness when he send for me.

The fellars go round by the snackette where Alicia working and they ask for Joebell.

"Joebell gone away," she tell them.

"Gone away and leave a nice girl like you? If was me I would never leave you."

And she just smile that smile that make her look like she crying and she mumble something that don't mean nothing, but if you listen good is, "Well, is not you."

"Why you don't let me take you to the dance in the Centre Saturday? Joey Lewis playing. Why you don't come and forget that crazy fellar?"

But Alicia smile no, all the time thinking, wait until he send for me, you will see who crazy. And she sell the cake and the coconut roll and sweet drink and mauby that they ask for and take their money and give them their change and move off with that soft, bright, drowsy sadness that stir fellars, that make them sit down and drink their sweet drink and eat their coconut roll and look at her face with the spread of her nose and the lips stretch across her mouth in a full round soft curve and her far away eyes and think how lucky Joebell is.

When Joebell get the passport he look at the picture in it and he say, "Wait! This fellar aint look like me. A blind man could see this is not me."

"I know you woulda say that," the pardner with the passport say, "You could see you don't know nothing about the American immigration. Listen, in America, every black face is the same to white people. They don't see no difference. And this fellar here is the same height as you, roughly the same age. That is what you have to think about, those little details, not how his face looking." That was his pardner talking.

"You saying this is me, this fellar here is me?" Joebell ask again. "You want them to lock me up or what, man? This is what I pay a thousand dollars for? A lock up?"

"Look, you have no worry. I went America one time on a passport where the fellar had a beard and I was shave clean and they aint question me. If you was white you mighta have a problem, but black, man, you easy."

And in truth when he think of it, Joebell could see the point, cause he aint sure he could tell the difference between two Chinese.

"But, wait!" Joebell say, "Suppose I meet up a black immigration?"

"Ah!" the fellar say, "You thinking. Anyhow, it aint have that many, but, if you see one stay far from him."

So Joebell, with his passport in his pocket, get a fellar who running contraband to carry him to Venezuela where his brother was living. He decide to spend a couple days by his brother and from there take a plane to Puerto Rico, in transit to America.

His brother had a job as a motor car mechanic.

"Why you don't stay here?" his brother tell him, "It have

work here you could get. And TV does be on whole day."

"The TV in Spanish," Joebell tell him.

"You could learn Spanish."

"By the time I finish learn Spanish I is a old man," Joebell say, "*Caramba! Caramba! Habla! Habla!* No. And besides I done pay my thousand dollars. I have my American passport. I is an American citizen. And," he whisper, softening just at the thought of her, "I have a girl who coming to meet me in America."

Joebell leave Venezuela in a brown suit that he get from his brother, a strong-looking pair of brown leather boots that he buy, with buckles instead of laces, a cowboy hat on his head and an old camera from his brother over his shoulder and in his mouth is a cigar, and now he is James Armstrong Brady of the one hundred and twenty-fifth infantry regiment from Alabama, Vietnam Veteran, twenty-six years old. And when he reach the airport in Puerto Rico he walk with a stagger and he puff his cigar like he already home in the United States of America. And not for one moment it don't strike Joebell that he doing any wrong.

No. Joebell believe the whole world is a hustle. He believe everybody running some game, putting on some show and the only thing that separate people is that some have power and others don't have none, that who in in and who out out, and that is exactly what Joebell kick against, because Joebell have himself down as a hero too and he not prepare to sit down timid timid as if he stupid and see a set of bluffers take over the world, and he stay wasting away in Cunaripo; and that is Joebell's trouble. That is what people call his craziness, is that that mark him out. That is the "light" that the *obeah* woman in Moruga see burning on him, is that that frighten his mother and charm Alicia and make her mother want to pry her loose from him. Is that that fellars see when they see him throw down his last hundred dollars on a single card, as if he know it going to play. The thing is that Joebell really don't be betting on the card, Joebell does be betting on himself. He don't be trying to guess about which card is the right one, he is trying to find that power in himself that will make him call correct. And that power is what Joebell searching for as he queue up in the line leading to the immigration entering Puerto Rico. Is that power that he calling up in himself as he stand there, because if he can feel that power, if that power come inside him, then, nothing could stop him. And now this was it.

"Mr. Brady?" The immigration man look up from Joebell passport and say, same time turning the leaves of the passport. And he glance at Joebell and he look at the picture. And he take up another book and look in it, and look again at Joebell; and maybe it is that power Joebell reaching for, that thing inside him, his craziness that look like arrogance, that put a kinda sneer on his face that make the immigration fellar take another look.

"Vietnam Veteran? Mr. Brady, where you coming from?"

"Venezuela."

The fellar ask a few more questions. He is asking Joebell more questions than he ask anybody.

"Whatsamatta? Watsa problem?" Joebell ask, "Man, I aint never seen such incompetency as you got here. This is boring. Hey, I've got a plane to catch. I aint got all day."

All in the airport people looking at Joebell 'cause Joebell not talking easy, and he biting his cigar so that his words coming to the immigration through his teeth. Why Joebell get on so is because Joebell believe that one of the main marks of a real American is that he don't stand no nonsense. Any time you get a real American in an aggravating situation, the first thing he do is let his voice be heard in objection: in other words, he does get on. In fact that is one of the things Joebell admire most about Americans: they like to get on. They don't care who hear them, they going to open their mouth and talk for their rights. So that is why Joebell get on so about incompetency and missing his plane and so on. Most fellars who didn't know what it was to be a real American woulda take it cool. Joebell know what he doing.

"Sir, please step into the first room on your right and take a seat until your name is called." Now is the immigration talking, and the fellar firm and he not frighten, cause he is American too. I don't know if Joebell didn't realize that before he get on. That is the kind of miscalculation Joebell does make sometimes in gambling and in life.

"Maan, just you remember I gotta plane to catch," and Joebell step off, with that slow, tall insolence like Jack Palance getting off his horse in *Shane,* but he take off his hat and go and sit down where the fellar tell him to sit down.

It had seven other people in the room but Joebell go and sit down alone by himself because with all the talk he talking big, Joebell is just playing for time, just trying to put them off; and now he start figuring serious how he going to get through this one. And he feeling for that power, that craziness that sometimes take him over when he in a wappie game, when every bet he call he call right; and he telling himself they can't trap him with any question because he grow up in America right there in Trinidad. In his grandmother days was the British; but he know from Al Jolson to James Brown. He know Tallahashie bridge and Rocktow mountain. He know Doris Day and Frank Sinatra. He know America. And Joebell settle himself down not bothering to remember anything, just calling up his power. And then he see this tall black fellar over six foot five enter the room. At a glance Joebell could tell he's a crook, and next thing he know is this fellar coming to sit down side of him.

TWO

I sit down there by myself alone and I know they watching me. Everybody else in the room white. This black fellar come in the room, with beads of perspiration running down his face and his eyes wild and he looking round like he escape. As soon as I see him I say "Oh God!" because I know with all the empty seats all about the place is me he coming to. He don't know my troubles. He believe I want friends. I want to tell him "Listen, man, I love you. I really dig my people, but now is not the time to come and talk to me. Go and be friendly by those other people, they could afford to be friends with you." But I can't tell him that 'cause I don't want to offend him and I have to watch how I talking in case in my situation I slip from American to Trinidadian. He shake my hand in the Black Power sign. And we sit down there side by side, two crooks, he and me, unless he's a spy they send to spy on me.

I letting him do all the talking, I just nodding and saying yeah, yeah.

He's an American who just come out of jail in Puerto Rico for dope or something. He was in Vietnam too. He talking, but I really aint listening to him. I thinking how my plane going. I thinking about Alicia and how sad her face will get when she don't get the letter that I suppose to send for her to come to America. I thinking about my mother and about the fellars up in Independence Recreation Club and around the wappie table when the betting slow, how they will talk about me,

"Natchez," who win in the wappie and go to America—nobody ever do that before—and I thinking how nice it will be for me and Alicia after we spend some time in America to go back home to Trinidad for a holiday and stay in the Hilton and hire a big car and go to see her mother. I think about the Spanish I woulda have to learn if I did stay in Venezuela.

At last they call me inside another room. This time I go cool. It have two fellars in this room, a big tough one with a stone face and a jaw like a steel trap, and a small brisk one with eyes like a squirrel. The small one is smoking a cigarette. The tough one is the one asking questions. The small one just sit down there with his squirrel eyes watching me, and smoking his cigarette.

"What's your name?"

And I watching his jaw how they clamping down on the words. "Ma name is James Armstrong Brady."

"Age?"

And he go through a whole long set of questions.

"You're a Vietnam Veteran, you say? Where did you train?"

And I smile cause I see enough war pictures to know, "Nor' Carolina," I say.

"Went to school there?"

I tell him where I went to school. He ask questions until I dizzy.

The both of them know I lying, and maybe they coulda just throw me in jail just so without no big interrogation; but, America. That is why I love America. They love a challenge. Something in my style is a challenge to them, and they just don't want to lock me up because they have the power, they want to trap me plain for even me to see. So now is me, Joebell, and these two Yankees. And I waiting, cause I grow up on John Wayne and Gary Cooper and Audie Murphy and James Stewart and Jeff Chandler. I know the Dodgers and Phillies, the Redskins and the Dallas Cowboys, Green Bay Packers and the Vikings. I know Walt Frazier and Doctor J, and Bill Russell and Wilt Chamberlain. Really, in truth, I know America so much, I feel American. Is just that I aint born there.

As fast as the squirrel-eye one finish smoke one cigarette, he light another one. He aint saying nothing, only listening. At last he put out his cigarette, he say, "Recite the alphabet."

"Say what?"

"The alphabet. Recite it."

And just so I know I get catch. The question too easy. Too easy like a calm blue sea. And, pardner, I look at that sea and I think about Alicia and the warm soft curving sadness of her lips and her eyes full with crying, make me feel to cry for me and Alicia and Trinidad and America and I know like when you make a bet you see a certain card play that it will be a miracle if the card you bet on play. I lose, I know. But I is still a hero. I can't bluff forever. I have myself down as classy. And, really, I wasn't frighten for nothing, not for nothing, wasn't afraid of jail or of poverty or of Puerto Rico or America and I wasn't vex with the fellar who sell me the passport for the thousand dollars, nor with Iron Jaw and Squirrel Eyes. In fact, I kinda respect them. "A . . . B . . . C . . ." And Squirrel Eyes take out another cigarette and don't light it, just keep knocking it against the pack, Tock! Tock! Tock! K . . . L . . . M . . . And I feel I love Alicia . . . V . . . W . . . and I hear Paul Robeson sing "Old Man River" and I see Sammy Davis Junior dance Mr. Bojangle's dance and I hear Nina Simone humming humming "Suzanne," and I love Alicia; and I hear Harry Belafonte's rasping call, "Daay-o, Daaay-o! Daylight come and me want to go home," and Aretha Franklin screaming screaming, " . . . Y . . . Zed."

"Bastard!" the squirrel eyes cry out, "Got you!"

And straightaway from another door two police weighed down with all their keys and their handcuffs and their pistols and their night stick and torch light enter and clink their handcuffs on my hands. They catch me. God! And now, how to go? I think about getting on like an American, but I never see an American lose. I think about making a performance like the British, steady, stiff upper lip like Alec Guinness in *The Bridge over the River Kwai,* but with my hat and my boots and my piece of cigar, that didn't match, so I say I might as well take my losses like a West Indian, like a Trinidadian. I decide to sing. It was the classiest thing that ever pass through Puerto Rico airport, me with these handcuffs on, walking between these two police and singing.

> *Gonna take ma baby*
> *Away on a trip*
> *Gonna take ma baby*
> *Yip yip yip*
> *We gonna travel far*
> *To New Orleans*
> *Me and ma baby*
> *Be digging the scene*

ROHINTON MISTRY

THE RENOWNED FICTION WRITER Rohinton Mistry was born in 1952 in Bombay, India (now Mumbai), and moved to Canada in 1975. His 1987 collection *Tales from Firozsha Baag* depicts life in a largely Parsi apartment complex in Bombay; his more recent work includes the novel *A Fine Balance.* In this story, Mistry crosses lines of gender, class, religion, and language to channel the voice of Jacqueline, a Goan Catholic ayah who has worked for the same family since she was "fifteen. Yes, fifteen." Superficially the tale of a benign apparition, "Ghost" gently describes the lifetime of small and large injustices endemic to Jacqueline's situation. As she succinctly puts it, "I learned forty-nine years ago that life as ayah means living close to floor." Form mirrors content here, as Jacqueline's daily domestic tasks constantly interrupt her storytelling. The story offers many meditations on the politics of language. As Mene does in Ken Saro-Wiwa's *Sozaboy,* Jacqueline now answers to the distorted name she has been given by people who hardly know her. And in another commonality with *Sozaboy,* English provides a neutral ground in ways that would surprise anyone familiar with Macaulay's "Minute on Indian Education." Here, Mistry uses English to convey the internal language Jacqueline has developed after years of reluctantly speaking Hindi and Gujarati instead of her native Konkani.

THE GHOST OF FIROZSHA BAAG

(1987)

I always believed in ghosts. When I was little I saw them in my father's small field in Goa. That was very long ago, before I came to Bombay to work as ayah.

Father also saw them, mostly by the well, drawing water. He would come in and tell us, the *bhoot* is thirsty again. But it never scared us. Most people in our village had seen ghosts. Everyone believed in them.

Not like in Firozsha Baag. First time I saw a ghost here and people found out, how much fun they made of me. Calling me crazy, saying it is time for old ayah to go back to Goa, back to her *muluk,* she is seeing things.

Two years ago on Christmas Eve I first saw the *bhoot.* No, it was really Christmas Day. At ten o'clock on Christmas Eve I went to Cooperage Stadium for midnight mass. Every year all of us Catholic ayahs from Firozsha Baag go for mass. But this time I came home alone, the others went somewhere with their boyfriends. Must have been two o'clock in the morning. Lift in B Block was out of order, so I started up slowly. Thinking how easy to climb three floors when I was younger, even with a full bazaar-bag.

After reaching first floor I stopped to rest. My breath was coming fast-fast. Fast-fast, like it does nowadays when I grind curry *masala* on the stone. Jaakaylee, my *bai* calls out, Jaakaylee, is *masala* ready? Thinks a sixty-three-year-old ayah can make *masala* as quick as she used to when she was fifteen. Yes, fifteen. The day after my fourteenth birthday I came by bus from Goa to Bombay. All day and night I rode the bus. I still remember when my father took me to bus station in Panjim. Now it is called Panaji. Joseph Uncle, who was mechanic in Mazagaon, met me at Bombay Central Station. So crowded it was, people running all around, shouting, screaming, and coolies with big-big trunks on their heads. Never will I forget that first day in Bombay. I just stood in one place, not knowing what to do, till Joseph Uncle saw me. Now it has been forty-nine years in this house as ayah, believe or don't believe. Forty-nine years in Firozsha Baag's B Block and they still don't say my name right. Is it so difficult to say Jacqueline? But they always say Jaakaylee. Or worse, Jaakayl.

All the fault is of old *bai* who died ten years ago. She was in charge till her son brought a wife, the new *bai* of the house. Old *bai* took English words and made them Parsi words. Easy chair was *igeechur*, French beans was *ferach beech*, and Jacqueline became Jaakaylee. Later I found out that all old Parsis did this, it was like they made their own private language.

So then new *bai* called me Jaakaylee also, and children do the same. I don't care about it now. If someone asks my name I say Jaakaylee. And I talk Parsi-Gujarati all the time instead of Konkani, even with other ayahs. Sometimes also little bits of English.

But I was saying. My breath was fast-fast when I reached first floor and stopped for rest. And then I noticed someone, looked like in a white gown. Like a man, but I could not see the face, just body shape. *Kaun hai?* I asked in Hindi. Believe or don't believe, he vanished. Completely! I shook my head and started for second floor. Carefully, holding the railing, because the steps are so old, all slanting and crooked.

Then same thing happened. At the top of second floor he was waiting. And when I said, *kya hai?* believe or don't believe, he vanished again! Now I knew it must be a *bhoot*. I knew he would be on third floor also, and I was right. But I was not scared or anything.

I reached the third floor entrance and found my bedding which I had put outside before leaving. After midnight mass I always sleep outside, by the stairs, because *bai* and *seth* must not be woken up at two A.M., and they never give me a key. No ayah gets key to a flat. It is something I have learned, like I learned forty-nine years ago that life as ayah means living close to floor. All work I do, I do on floors, like grinding *masala*, cutting vegetables, cleaning rice. Food also is eaten sitting on floor, after serving them at dining-table. And my bedding is rolled out at night in kitchen-passage, on floor. No cot for me. Nowadays, my weight is much more than it used to be, and is getting very difficult to get up from floor. But I am managing.

So Christmas morning at two o'clock I opened my bedding and spread out my *saterunjee* by the stairs. Then stopped. The *bhoot* had vanished, and I was not scared or anything. But my father used to say some ghosts play mischief. The ghost of our field never did, he only took water from our well, but if this ghost of the stairs played mischief he might roll me downstairs, who was to say. So I thought about it and rang the doorbell.

After many, many rings *bai* opened, looking very mean. Mostly she looks okay, and when she dresses in nice sari for a wedding or something, and puts on all bangles and necklace, she looks really pretty, I must say. But now she looked so mean. Like she was going to bite somebody. Same kind of look she has every morning when she has just woken up, but this was much worse and meaner because it was so early in the morning. She was very angry, said I was going crazy, there was no ghost or anything, I was just telling lies not to sleep outside.

Then *seth* also woke up. He started laughing, saying he did not want any ghost to roll me downstairs because who would make *chai* in the morning. He was not angry, his mood was good. They went back to their room, and I knew why he was feeling happy when crrr-crr crrr-crr sound of their bed started coming in the dark.

When he was little I sang Konkani songs for him. *Mogacha Mary* and *Hanv Saiba.* Big man now, he's forgotten them and so have I. Forgetting my name, my language, my songs. But complaining I'm not, don't make mistake. I'm telling you, to have a job I was very lucky because in Goa there was nothing to do. From Panjim to Bombay on the bus I cried, leaving behind my brothers and sisters and parents, and all my village friends. But I knew leaving was best thing. My father had eleven children and very small field. Coming to Bombay was only thing to do. Even schooling I got first year, at night. Then *bai* said I must stop because who would serve dinner when *seth* came home from work, and who would carry away dirty dishes? But that was not the real reason. She thought I stole her eggs. There were six eggs yesterday evening, she would say, only five this morning, what happened to one? She used to think I took it with me to school to give to someone.

I was saying, it was very lucky for me to become ayah in Parsi house, and never will I forget that. Especially because I'm Goan Catholic and very dark skin colour. Parsis prefer Manglorean Catholics, they have light skin colour. For themselves also Parsis like light skin, and when Parsi baby is born that is the first and most important thing. If it is fair they say,

O how nice light skin just like parents. But if it is dark skin they say, *arré* what is this *ayah no chhokro,* ayah's child.

All this doing was more in olden days, mostly among very rich *bais* and *seths.* They thought they were like British only, ruling India side by side. But don't make mistake, not just rich Parsis. Even all Marathi people in low class Tar Gully made fun of me when I went to buy grocery from *bunya.* Blackie, blackie, they would call out. Nowadays it does not happen because very dark skin colour is common in Bombay, so many people from south are coming here, Tamils and Keralites, with their funny *illay illay poe poe* language. Now people more used to different colours.

But still not to ghosts. Everybody in B Block found out about the *bhoot* of the stairs. They made so much fun of me all the time, children and grown-up people also.

And believe or don't believe, that *was* a ghost of mischief. Because just before Easter he came back. Not on the stairs this time but right in my bed. I'm telling you, he was sitting on my chest and bouncing up and down, and I couldn't push him off, so weak I was feeling (I'm a proper Catholic, I was fasting), couldn't even scream or anything (not because I was scared— he was choking me). Then someone woke up to go to WC and put on a light in the passage where I sleep. Only then did the rascal *bhoot* jump off and vanish.

This time I did not tell anyone. Already they were making so much fun of me. Children in Firozsha Baag would shout, ayah *bhoot!* ayah *bhoot!* every time they saw me. And a new Hindi film had come out, *Bhoot Bungla,* about a haunted house, so they would say, like the man on the radio, in a loud voice: SEE TODAY, at APSARA CINEMA, R. K. Anand's NEW fillum *Bhoooot Bungla,* starring JAAKAYLEE of BLOCK B! Just like that! O they made a lot of fun of me, but I did not care, I knew what I had seen.

Jaakaylee, bai *calls out, is it ready yet? She wants to check curry* masala. *Too thick, she always says, grind it again, make it smoother. And she is right, I leave it thick purposely. Before, when I did it fine, she used to send me back anyway. O it pains in my old shoulders, grinding this* masala, *but they will never buy the automatic machine. Very rich people, my* bai-seth. *He is a chartered accountant. He has a nice motorcar, just like A Block priest, and like the one Dr Mody used to drive, which has not moved from the compound since the day he died.* Bai *says they should buy it from Mrs Mody, she wants it to go shopping. But a* masala *machine they will not buy. Jaakaylee must keep on doing it till her arms fall out from shoulders.*

How much teasing everyone was doing to me about the *bhoot.* It became a great game among boys, pretending to be ghosts. One who started it all was Dr Mody's son, from third floor of C Block. The one they call Pesi *paadmaroo* because he makes dirty wind all the time. Good thing he is in boarding-school now. That family came to Firozsha Baag only few years ago, he was doctor for animals, a really nice man. But what a terrible boy. Must have been so shameful for Dr Mody. Such a kind man, what a shock everybody got when he died. But I'm telling you, that boy did a bad thing one night.

Vera and Dolly, the two fashionable sisters from C Block's first floor, went to nightshow at Eros Cinema, and Pesi knew. After nightshow was over, tock-tock they came in their high-heel shoes. It was when mini-skirts had just come out, and that is what they were wearing. Very *esskey-messkey,* so short I don't know how their *mai-baap* allowed it. They said their daughters were going to for-eign for studies, so maybe this kind of dressing was practice for over there. Anyway, they started up, the stairs were very dark. Then Pesi, wearing a white bedsheet and waiting under the stair-case, jumped out shouting *bowe ré.* Vera and Dolly screamed so loudly, I'm telling you, and they started running.

Then Pesi did a really shameful thing. God knows where he got the idea from. Inside his sheet he had a torch, and he took it out and shined up into the girls' mini-skirts. Yes! He ran after them with his big torch shining in their skirts. And when Vera and Dolly reached the top they tripped and fell. That shameless boy just stood there with his light shining between their legs, seeing undies and everything, I'm telling you.

He ran away when all neighbours started opening their doors to see what is the matter, because everyone heard them screaming. All the men had good time with Vera and Dolly, pretending to be like concerned grown-up people, saying, it is all right, dears, don't worry, dears, just some bad boy, not a real ghost. And all the time petting squeezing them as if to comfort them! Sheeh, these men!

Next day Pesi was telling his friends about it, how he shone the torch up their skirts and how they fell, and everything he saw. That boy, sheeh, terrible.

Afterwards, parents in Firozsha Baag made a very strict rule that no one plays the fool about ghosts because it can cause serious accident if sometime some old person is made scared and falls downstairs and breaks a bone or something or has heart attack. So there was no more ghost games and no more making fun of me. But I'm telling you, the *bhoot* kept coming every Friday night.

Curry is boiling nicely, smells very tasty. Bai *tells me don't forget about curry, don't burn the dinner. How many times have I burned the dinner in forty-nine years, I should ask her. Believe or don't believe, not one time.*

Yes, the *bhoot* came but he did not bounce any more upon my chest. Sometimes he just sat next to the bedding, other times he lay down beside me with his head on my chest, and if I tried to push him away he would hold me tighter. Or would try to put his hand up my gown or down from the neck. But I sleep with buttons up to my collar, so it was difficult for the rascal. O what a ghost of mischief he was! Reminded me of Cajetan back in Panjim always trying to do same thing with girls at the cinema or beach. His parents' house was not far from Church of St Cajetan for whom he was named, but this boy was no saint, I'm telling you.

Calunqute and Anjuna beaches in those days were very quiet and beautiful. It was before foreigners all started coming, and no hippie-bippie business with *charas* and *ganja,* and no big-big hotels or nothing. Cajetan said to me once, let us go and see the fishermen. And we went, and started to wade a little, up to ankles, and Cajetan said let us go more. He rolled up his pants over the knees and I pulled up my skirt, and we went in deeper. Then a big wave made everything wet. We ran out and sat on the beach for my skirt to dry.

Us two were only ones there, fishermen were still out in boats. Sitting on the sand he made all funny eyes at me, like Hindi film hero, and put his hand on my thigh. I told him to stop or I would tell my father who would give him solid pasting and throw him in the well where the *bhoot* would take care of him. But he didn't stop. Not till the fishermen came. Sheeh, what a boy that was.

Back to kitchen. To make good curry needs lots of stirring while boiling.

I'm telling you, that Cajetan! Once, it was feast of St Francis Xavier, and the body was to be in a glass case at Church of Bom Jesus. Once every ten years is this very big event for Catholics. They were not going to do it any more because, believe or don't believe, many years back some poor crazy woman took a bite from toe of St Francis Xavier. But then they changed their minds. Poor St Francis, it is not his luck to have a whole body—one day, Pope asked for a bone from the right arm, for people in Rome to see, and never sent it back; that is where it is till today.

But I was saying about Cajetan. All boys and girls from my village were going to Bom Jesus by bus. In church it was so crowded, and a long long line to walk by St Francis Xavier's glass case. Cajetan was standing behind my friend Lily, he had finished his fun with me, now it was Lily's turn. And I'm telling you, he kept bumping her and letting his hand touch her body like it was by accident in the crowd. Sheeh, even in church that boy could not behave.

And the ghost reminded me of Cajetan, whom I have not seen since I came to Bombay—what did I say, forty-nine years ago. Once a week the ghost came, and always on Friday. On Fridays I eat fish, so I started thinking, maybe he likes smell of fish. Then I just ate vegetarian, and yet he came. For almost a whole year the ghost slept with me, every Friday night, and Christmas was not far away.

And still no one knew about it, how he came to my bed, lay down with me, tried to touch me. There was one thing I was feeling so terrible about—even to Father D'Silva at Byculla Church I had not told anything for the whole year. Every time in confession I would keep completely quiet about it. But now Christmas was coming and I was feeling very bad, so first Sunday in December I told Father D'Silva everything and then I was feeling much better. Father D'Silva said I was blameless because it was not my wish to have the *bhoot* sleeping with me. But he gave three Hail Marys, and said eating fish again was okay if I wanted.

So on Friday of that week I had fish curry rice and went to bed. And believe or don't believe, the *bhoot* did not come. After midnight, first I thought maybe he is late maybe he has somewhere else to go. Then the clock in *bai*'s room went three times and I was really worried. Was he going to come in early morning while I was making tea? That would be terrible.

But he did not come. Why, I wondered. If he came to the bedding of a fat and ugly ayah all this time, now what was the matter? I could not understand. But then I said to myself, what are you thinking Jaakaylee, where is your head, do you really want the ghost to come sleep with you and touch you so shamefully?

After drinking my tea that morning I knew what had happened. The ghost did not come because of my confession. He was ashamed now. Because Father D'Silva knew about what he had been doing to me in the darkness every Friday night.

Next Friday night also there was no ghost. Now I was completely sure my confession had got rid of him and his shameless habits. But in a few days it would be Christmas Eve and time for midnight mass. I thought, maybe if he is ashamed to come into my bed, he could wait for me on the stairs like last year.

Time to cook rice now, time for seth *to come home. Best quality Basmati rice we use, always, makes such a lovely fragrance while cooking, so tasty.*

For midnight mass I left my bedding outside, and when I returned it was two A.M. But for worrying there was no reason. No ghost on any floor this time. I opened the bedding by the stairs, thinking about Cajetan, how scared he was when I said I would tell my father about his touching me. Did not ask me to go anywhere after that, no beaches, no cinema. Now same thing with the ghost. How scared men are of fathers.

And next morning *bai* opened the door, saying good thing ghost took a holiday this year, if you had woken us again I would have killed you. I laughed a little and said Merry Christmas, *bai,* and she said same to me.

When *seth* woke up he also made a little joke. If they only knew that in one week they would say I had been right. Yes, on New Year's Day they would start believing, when there was really no ghost. Never has been since the day I told Father D'Silva in confession. But I was not going to tell them they were mistaken, after such fun they made of me. Let them feel sorry now for saying Jaakaylee was crazy.

Bai and *seth* were going to New Year's Eve dance, somewhere in Bandra, for first time since children were born. She used to say they were too small to leave alone with ayah, but that year he kept saying please, now children were bigger. So she agreed. She kept telling me what to do and gave telephone number to call in case of emergency. Such fuss she made, I'm telling you, when they left for Bandra I was so nervous.

I said special prayer that nothing goes wrong, that children would eat dinner properly, not spill anything, go to bed without crying or trouble. If *bai* found out she would say, what did I tell you, children cannot be left with ayah. And then she would give poor *seth* hell for it. He gets a lot anyway.

Everything went right and children went to sleep. I opened my bedding, but I was going to wait till they came home. Spreading out the *saterunjee*, I saw a tear in the white bedsheet used for covering—maybe from all pulling and pushing with the ghost—and was going to repair it next morning. I put off the light and lay down just to rest.

Then cockroach sounds started. I lay quietly in the dark, first to decide where it was. If you put a light on they stop singing and then you don't know where to look. So I listened carefully. It was coming from the gas stove table. I put on the light now and took my *chappal*. There were two of them, sitting next to cylinder. I lifted my *chappal*, very slowly and quietly, then phut! phut! Must say I am expert at cockroach-killing.

The poison which *seth* puts out is really not doing much good, my *chappal* is much better.

I picked up the two dead ones and threw them outside, in Baag's backyard. Two cockroaches would make nice little snack for some rat in the yard, I thought. Then I lay down again after switching off light.

Clock in *bai-seth*'s room went twelve times. They would all be giving kiss now and saying Happy New Year. When I was little in Panjim, my parents, before all the money went, always gave a party on New Year's Eve. I lay on my bedding, thinking of those days. It is so strange that so much of your life you can remember if you think quietly in the darkness.

Must not forget rice on stove. With rice, especially Basmati, one minute more or one minute less, one spoon extra water or less water, and it will spoil, it will not be light and every grain separate.

So there I was in the darkness remembering my father and mother, Panjim and Cajetan, nice beaches and boats. Suddenly it was very sad, so I got up and put a light on. In *bai-seth*'s room their clock said two o'clock. I wished they would come home soon. I checked children's room, they were sleeping.

Back to my passage I went, and started mending the torn sheet. Sewing, thinking about my mother, how hard she used to work, how she would repair clothes for my brothers and sisters. Not only sewing to mend but also to alter. When my big brother's pants would not fit, she would open out the waist and undo trouser cuffs to make longer legs. Then when he grew so big that even with alterations it did not fit, she sewed same pants again, making a smaller waist, shorter legs, so little brother could wear. How much work my mother did, sometimes even helping my father outside in the small field, especially if he was visiting a *taverna* the night before.

But sewing and remembering brought me more sadness. I put away the needle and thread and went outside by the stairs. There is a little balcony there. It was so nice and dark and quiet, I just stood there. Then it became a little chilly. I wondered if the ghost was coming again. My father used to say that whenever a ghost is around it feels chilly, it is a sign. He said he always did in the field when the *bhoot* came to the well.

There was no ghost or anything so I must be chilly, I thought, because it is so early morning. I went in and brought my white bedsheet. Shivering a little, I put it over my head, covering up my ears. There was a full moon, and it looked so good. In Panjim sometimes we used to go to the beach at night when there was a full moon, and father would tell us about when he was little, and the old days when Portuguese ruled Goa, and about grandfather who had been to Portugal in a big ship.

Then I saw *bai-seth*'s car come in the compound. I leaned over the balcony, thinking to wave if they looked up, let them know I had not gone to sleep. Then I thought, no, it is better if I go in quietly before they see me, or *bai* might get angry and say, what are you doing outside in middle of night, leaving children alone inside. But she looked up suddenly. I thought, O my Jesus, she has already seen me.

And then she screamed. I'm telling you, she screamed so loudly I almost fell down faint. It was not angry screaming, it was frightened screaming, *bhoot! bhoot!* and I understood. I quickly went inside and lay down on my bedding.

It took some time for them to come up because she sat inside the car and locked all doors. Would not come out until he climbed upstairs, put on every staircase light to make sure the ghost was gone, and then went back for her.

She came in the house at last and straight to my passage, shaking me, saying wake up, Jaakaylee, wake up! I pretended to be sleeping deeply, then turned around and said, Happy New Year, *bai*, everything is okay, children are okay.

She said, yes yes, but the *bhoot* is on the stairs! I saw him, the one you saw last year at Christmas, he is back, I saw him with my own eyes!

I wanted so much to laugh, but I just said, don't be afraid, *bai*, he will not do any harm, he is not a ghost of mischief, he must have just lost his way.

Then she said, Jaakaylee, you were telling the truth and I was angry with you. I will tell everyone in B Block you were right, there really is a *bhoot*.

I said *bai*, let it be now, everyone has forgotten about it, and no one will believe anyway. But she said, when *I* tell them, they will believe.

And after that many people in Firozsha Baag started to believe in the ghost. One was *dustoorji* in A Block. He came one day and taught *bai* a prayer, *saykasté saykasté sataan*, to say it every time she was on the stairs. He told her, because you have seen a *bhoot* on the balcony by the stairs, it is better to have a special Parsi prayer ceremony there so he does not come again and cause any trouble. He said, many years ago, near Marine Lines where Hindus have their funerals and burn bodies, a *bhoot* walked at midnight in the middle of the road, scaring motorists and causing many accidents. Hindu priests said prayers to make him stop. But no use. *Bhoot* kept walking at midnight, motorists kept having accidents. So Hindu priests called me to do a *jashan*, they knew Parsi priest has most powerful prayers of all. And after I did a *jashan* right in the middle of the road, everything was all right.

Bai listened to all this talk of *dustoorji* from A Block, then said she would check with *seth* and let him know if they wanted a balcony *jashan*. Now *seth* says yes to everything, so he told her, sure sure, let *dustoorji* do it. It will be fun to see the exkoriseesum, he said, some big English word like that.

Dustoorji was pleased, and he checked his Parsi calendar for a good day. On that morning I had to wash whole balcony floor specially, then *dustoorji* came, spread a white sheet, and put all prayer items on it, a silver thing in which he made fire with sandalwood and *loban*, a big silver dish, a *lotta* full of water, flowers, and some fruit.

When it was time to start saying prayers *dustoorji* told me to go inside. Later, *bai* told me that was because Parsi prayers are so powerful, only a Parsi can listen to them. Everyone else can be badly damaged inside their soul if they listen.

So *jashan* was done and *dustoorji* went home with all his prayer things. But when people in Firozsha Baag who did not believe in the ghost heard about prayer ceremony, they began talking and mocking.

Some said Jaakaylee's *bai* has gone crazy, first the ayah was seeing things, and now she has made her *bai* go mad. *Bai* will not talk to those people in the Baag. She is really angry, says she does not want friends who think she is crazy. She hopes *jashan* was not very powerful, so the ghost can come again. She wants everyone to see him and know the truth like her.

Busy eating, bai-seth *are. Curry is hot, they are blowing whooshwhoosh on their tongues but still eating, they love it hot. Secret of good curry is not only what spices to put, but also what goes in first, what goes in second, and third, and so on. And never cook curry with lid on pot, always leave it open, stir it often, stir it to urge the flavour to come out.*

So *bai* is hoping the ghost will come again. She keeps asking me about ghosts, what they do, why they come. She thinks because I saw the ghost first in Firozsha Baag, it must be my speciality or something. Especially since I am from village—she says village people know more about such things than city people. So I tell her about the *bhoot* we used to see in the small field, and what my father said when he saw the *bhoot* near the well. *Bai* enjoys it, even asks me to sit with her at table, bring my separate mug, and pours a cup for me, listening to my ghost-talk. She does not treat me like servant all the time.

One night she came to my passage when I was saying my rosary and sat down with me on the bedding. I could not believe it, I stopped my rosary. She said, Jaakaylee, what is it Catholics say when they touch their head and stomach and both sides of chest? So I told her, Father, Son, and Holy Ghost. Right right! she said, I remember it now, when I went to St Anne's High School there were many Catholic girls and they used to say it always before and after class prayer, yes, Holy Ghost. Jaakaylee, you don't think this is that Holy Ghost you pray to, do you? And I said, no *bai*, that Holy Ghost has a different meaning, it is not like the *bhoot* you and I saw.

Yesterday she said, Jaakaylee, will you help me with something? All morning she was looking restless, so I said, yes *bai*. She left the table and came back with her big scissors and the flat cane *soopra* I use for winnowing rice and wheat. She said, my granny showed me a little magic once, she told me to keep it for important things only. The *bhoot* is, so I am going to use it. If you help me. It needs two Parsis, but I'll do it with you.

I just sat quietly, a little worried, wondering what she was up to now. First, she covered her head with a white *mathoobanoo*, and gave me one for mine, she said to put it over my head like a scarf. Then, the two points of scissors she poked through one side of *soopra,* really tight, so it could hang from the scissors. On two chairs we sat face to face. She made me balance one ring of scissors on my finger, and she balanced the other ring on hers. And we sat like that, with *soopra* hanging from scissors between us, our heads covered with white cloth. Believe or don't believe, it looked funny and scary at the same time. When *soopra* became still and stopped swinging around she said, now close your eyes and don't think of anything, just keep your hand steady. So I closed my eyes, wondering if *seth* knew what was going on.

Then she started to speak, in a voice I had never heard before. It seemed to come from very far away, very soft, all scary. My hair was standing. I felt chilly, as if a *bhoot* was about to come. This is what she said: if the ghost is going to appear again, then *soopra* must turn.

Nothing happened. But I'm telling you, I was so afraid I just kept my eyes shut tight, like she told me to do. I wanted to see nothing which I was not supposed to see. All this was something completely new for me. Even in my village, where everyone knew so much about ghosts, magic with *soopra* and scissors was unknown.

Then *bai* spoke once more, in that same scary voice: if the ghost is going to appear again, upstairs or downstairs, on balcony or inside the house, this year or next year, in daylight or in darkness, for good purpose or for bad purpose, then *soopra* must surely turn.

Believe or don't believe, this time it started to turn, I could feel the ring of the scissors moving on my finger. I screamed and pulled away my hand, there was a loud crash, and *bai* also screamed.

Slowly, I opened my eyes. Everything was on the floor, scissors were broken, and I said to *bai*, I'm very sorry I was so frightened, *bai*, and for breaking your big scissors, you can take it from my pay.

She said, you scared me with your scream, Jaakaylee, but it

is all right now, nothing to be scared about, I'm here with you. All the worry was gone from her face. She took off her *mathoobanoo* and patted my shoulder, picked up the broken scissors and *soopra,* and took it back to kitchen.

Bai was looking very pleased. She came back and said to me, don't worry about broken scissors, come, bring your mug, I'm making tea for both of us, forget about *soopra* and ghost for now. So I removed my *mathoobanoo* and went with her.

Jaakaylee, O Jaakaylee, she is calling from dining room. They must want more curry. Good thing I took some out for my dinner, they will finish the whole pot. Whenever I make Goan curry, nothing is left over. At the end seth *always takes a piece of bread and rubs it round and round in the pot, wiping every little bit. They always joke, Jaakaylee, no need today for washing pot, all cleaned out. Yes, it is one thing I really enjoy, cooking my Goan curry, stirring and stirring, taking the aroma as it boils and cooks, stirring it again and again, watching it bubbling and steaming, stirring and stirring till it is ready to eat.*

MARK TWAIN

MARK TWAIN is one of the foremost figures in nineteenth-century American literature. Born Samuel Clemens in 1835 in Florida, Missouri, he grew up in Hannibal, Missouri, and worked as a printer, newspaper reporter, riverboat pilot, and miner before turning to fiction. He first began writing as Mark Twain in 1863. His two best-known books were *The Adventures of Tom Sawyer*, published in 1876, and *The Adventures of Huckleberry Finn*, published in 1884. Before his death in 1910, Twain also wrote plays, nonfiction, and dozens of short stories, and helped to organize the Anti-Imperialist League. These two stories—one a staple of short-fiction anthologies and the other relatively unknown—exemplify Twain's range as well as his often bittersweet wit. The quintessential American tall tale "The Celebrated Jumping Frog" leaves its audience unsure of exactly who is being hustled. In relating the story of how an inveterate gambler was duped, the narrator suspects that he himself may have been tricked into hearing the tale; but it is the narrator's recounting of the "monotonous narrative" to which he was forced to listen that we cannot help doubting. "A True Story" is another frame tale, but one constructed for a quite different purpose: Twain invents and ventriloquizes "Aunt Rachel" in order to point out the condescending credulity of his equally manufactured author-persona. Using Aunt Rachel's dialect, Twain carefully dispels the lingering myth of the happy slave.

THE CELEBRATED JUMPING FROG OF CALAVERAS COUNTY

(1867)

In compliance with the request of a friend of mine, who wrote me from the East, I called on good-natured, garrulous old Simon Wheeler, and inquired after my friend's friend, *Leonidas W.* Smiley, as requested to do, and I hereunto append the result. I have a lurking suspicion that *Leonidas W.* Smiley is a myth; that my friend never knew such a personage; and that he only conjectured that, if I asked old Wheeler about him, it would remind him of his infamous *Jim* Smiley, and he would go to work and bore me nearly to death with some infernal reminiscence of him as long and tedious as it should be useless to me. If that was the design, it certainly succeeded.

I found Simon Wheeler dozing comfortably by the bar-room stove of the old, dilapidated tavern in the ancient mining camp of Angel's, and I noticed that he was fat and bald-headed, and had an expression of winning gentleness and simplicity upon his tranquil countenance. He roused up and gave me good-day. I told him a friend of mine had commissioned me to make some inquiries about a cherished companion of his boyhood named *Leonidas W.* Smiley—*Rev. Leonidas W.* Smiley—a young minister of the Gospel, who he had heard was at one time a resident of Angel's Camp. I added that, if Mr. Wheeler could tell me any thing about this Rev. Leonidas W. Smiley, I would feel under many obligations to him.

Simon Wheeler backed me into a corner and blockaded me there with his chair, and then sat me down and reeled off the monotonous narrative which follows this paragraph. He never smiled, he never frowned, he never changed his voice from the gentle-flowing key to which he tuned the initial sentence, he never betrayed the slightest suspicion of enthusiasm; but all through the interminable narrative there ran a vein of impressive earnestness and sincerity, which showed me plainly that, so far from his imagining that there was any thing ridiculous or funny about his story, he regarded it as a really important matter, and admired its two heroes as men of transcendent genius in *finesse.* To me, the spectacle of a man drifting serenely along through such a queer yarn without ever smiling, was exquisitely absurd. As I said before, I asked him to tell me what he knew of Rev. Leonidas W. Smiley, and he replied as follows. I let him go on in his own way, and never interrupted him once:

There was a feller here once by the name of *Jim* Smiley, in the winter of '49—or may be it was the spring of '50—I don't recollect exactly, somehow, though what makes me think it was one or the other is because I remember the big flume wasn't finished when he first came to the camp; but any way, he was the curiosest man about always betting on any thing that turned up you ever see, if he could get any body to bet on the other side; and if he couldn't, he'd change sides. Any way that suited the other man would suit him—any way just so's he got a bet, *he* was satisfied. But still he was lucky, uncommon lucky; he most always come out winner. He was always ready and laying for a chance; there couldn't be no solitry thing mentioned but that feller'd offer to bet on it, and take any side you please, as I was just telling you. If there was a horse-race, you'd find him flush, or you'd find him busted at the end of it; if there was a dog-fight, he'd bet on it; if there was a cat-fight, he'd bet on it; if there was a chicken-fight, he'd bet on it; why, if there was two birds setting on a fence, he would bet you which one would fly first; or if there was a camp-meeting, he would be there reg'lar, to bet on Parson Walker, which he judged to be the best exhorter about here, and so he was, too, and a good man. If he even seen a straddle-bug start to go anywheres, he would bet you how long it would take him to get wherever he was going to, and if you took him up, he would foller that straddle-bug to Mexico but what he would find out where he was bound for and how long he was on the road. Lots of the boys here has seen that Smiley, and can tell you about him. Why, it never made no difference to *him*—he would bet on *any* thing—the dangdest feller. Parson Walker's wife laid very sick once, for a good while, and it seemed as if they warn't going to save her; but one morning he come in, and Smiley asked how she was, and he said she was considerable better—thank the Lord for his inf'nit mercy—and coming on so smart that, with the blessing of Prov'dence, she'd get well yet; and Smiley, before he thought, says, "Well, I'll risk two-and-a-half that she don't, any way."

Thish-yer Smiley had a mare—the boys called her the fifteen-minute nag, but that was only in fun, you know, because, of course, she was faster than that—and he used to win money on that horse, for all she was so slow and always had the asthma, or the distemper, or the consumption, or something of that kind. They used to give her two or three hundred yards start, and then pass her under way; but always at the fag-end of the race she'd get excited and desperate-like, and come cavorting and straddling up, and scattering her legs around limber, sometimes in the air, and sometimes out to one side amongst the fences, and kicking up m-o-r-e dust, and raising m-o-r-e racket with her coughing and sneezing and blowing her nose—and always fetch up at the stand just about a neck ahead, as near as you could cipher it down.

And he had a little small bull pup, that to look at him you'd think he wan't worth a cent, but to set around and look ornery, and lay for a chance to steal something. But as soon as money was up on him, he was a different dog; his under-jaw'd begin to stick out like the fo'castle of a steamboat, and his teeth would uncover, and shine savage like the furnaces. And a dog might tackle him, and bully-rag him, and bite him, and throw him over his shoulder two or three times, and Andrew Jackson— which was the name of the pup—Andrew Jackson would never let on but what *he* was satisfied, and hadn't expected nothing else—and the bets being doubled and doubled on the other side all the time, till the money was all up; and then all of a sudden he would grab that other dog jest by the j'int of his hind leg and freeze to it—not chew, you understand, but only jest grip and hang on till they throwed up the sponge, if it was a year. Smiley always come out winner on that pup, till he harnessed a dog once that didn't have no hind legs, because they'd been sawed off by a circular saw, and when the thing had gone along far enough, and the money was all up, and he come to make a snatch for his pet holt, he saw in a minute how he'd been imposed on, and how the other dog had him in the door, so to speak, and he 'peared surprised, and then he looked sorter discouraged-like, and didn't try no more to win the fight, and so he got shucked out bad. He give Smiley a look, as much as to say his heart was broke, and it was *his* fault, for putting up a dog that hadn't no hind legs for him to take holt of, which was his main dependence in a fight, and then he limped off a piece and laid down and died. It was a good pup, was that Andrew Jackson, and would have made a name for his-

self if he'd lived, for the stuff was in him, and he had genius—
I know it, because he hadn't had no opportunities to speak of,
and it don't stand to reason that a dog could make such a fight
as he could under them circumstances, if he hadn't no talent.
It always makes me feel sorry when I think of that last fight of
his'n, and the way it turned out.

Well, thish-yer Smiley had rat-tarriers, and chicken cocks,
and tom-cats, and all them kind of things, till you couldn't rest,
and you couldn't fetch nothing for him to bet on but he'd
match you. He ketched a frog one day, and took him home,
and said he cal'klated to edercate him; and so he never done
nothing for three months but set in his back yard and learn
that frog to jump. And you bet you he *did* learn him, too. He'd
give him a little punch behind, and the next minute you'd see
that frog whirling in the air like a doughnut—see him turn
one summerset, or may be a couple, if he got a good start, and
come down flat-footed and all right, like a cat. He got him up
so in the matter of catching flies, and kept him in practice so
constant, that he'd nail a fly every time as far as he could see
him. Smiley said all a frog wanted was education, and he could
do most any thing—and I believe him. Why, I've seen him set
Dan'l Webster down here on this floor—Dan'l Webster was the
name of the frog—and sing out, "Flies, Dan'l, flies!" and quick-
er'n you could wink, he'd spring straight up, and snake a fly
off'n the counter there, and flop down on the floor again as
solid as a gob of mud, and fall to scratching the side of his head
with his hind foot as indifferent as if he hadn't no idea he'd
been doin' any more'n any frog might do. You never see a frog
so modest and straightfor'ard as he was, for all he was so gifted.
And when it come to fair and square jumping on a dead level,
he could get over more ground at one straddle than any animal of his breed you ever see. Jumping on a dead level was his

strong suit, you understand; and when it come to that, Smiley would ante up money on him as long as he had a red. Smiley was monstrous proud of his frog, and well he might be, for fellers that had traveled and been everywheres, all said he laid over any frog that ever *they* see.

Well, Smiley kept the beast in a little lattice box, and he used to fetch him down town sometimes and lay for a bet. One day a feller—a stranger in the camp, he was—come across him with his box, and says:

"What might it be that you've got in the box?"

And Smiley says, sorter indifferent like, "It might be a parrot, or it might be a canary, may be, but it an't—it's only just a frog."

And the feller took it, and looked at it careful, and turned it round this way and that, and says, "H'm—so 'tis. Well, what's *he* good for?"

"Well," Smiley says, easy and careless, "He's good enough for *one* thing, I should judge—he can outjump any frog in Calaveras county."

The feller took the box again, and took another long, particular look, and give it back to Smiley, and says, very deliberate, "Well, I don't see no p'ints about that frog that's any better'n any other frog."

"May be you don't," Smiley says. "May be you understand frogs, and may be you don't understand 'em; may be you've had experience, and may be you an't only a amature, as it were. Anyways, I've got *my* opinion, and I'll risk forty dollars that he can outjump any frog in Calaveras county."

And the feller studied a minute, and then says, kinder sad like, "Well, I'm only a stranger here, and I an't got no frog; but if I had a frog, I'd bet you."

And then Smiley says, "That's all right—that's all right—if

you'll hold my box a minute, I'll go and get you a frog." And so the feller took the box, and put up his forty dollars along with Smiley's, and set down to wait.

So he set there a good while thinking and thinking to his-self, and then he got the frog out and prized his mouth open and took a teaspoon and filled him full of quail shot—filled him pretty near up to his chin—and set him on the floor. Smiley he went to the swamp and slopped around in the mud for a long time, and finally he ketched a frog, and fetched him in, and give him to this feller, and says:

"Now, if you're ready, set him alongside of Dan'l, with his fore-paws just even with Dan'l, and I'll give the word." Then he says, "One—two—three—jump!" and him and the feller touched up the frogs from behind, and the new frog hopped off, but Dan'l give a heave, and hysted up his shoulders—so—like a Frenchman, but it wan't no use—he couldn't budge; he was planted as solid as an anvil, and he couldn't no more stir than if he was anchored out. Smiley was a good deal surprised, and he was disgusted too, but he didn't have no idea what the matter was, of course.

The feller took the money and started away; and when he was going out at the door, he sorter jerked his thumb over his shoulders—this way—at Dan'l, and says again, very deliberate, "Well, *I* don't see no p'ints about that frog that's any better'n any other frog."

Smiley he stood scratching his head and looking down at Dan'l a long time, and at last he says, "I do wonder what in the nation that frog throw'd off for—I wonder if there an't some-thing the matter with him—he 'pears to look mighty baggy, somehow." And he ketched Dan'l by the nap of the neck, and lifted him up and says, "Why, blame my cats, if he don't weigh five pound!" and turned him upside down, and he belched out a double handful of shot. And then he see how it was, and he was the maddest man—he set the frog down and took out after that feller, but he never ketched him. And—

[Here Simon Wheeler heard his name called from the front yard, and got up to see what was wanted.] And turning to me as he moved away, he said: "Just set where you are, stranger, and rest easy—I an't going to be gone a second."

But, by your leave, I did not think that a continuation of the history of the enterprising vagabond *Jim* Smiley would be likely to afford me much information concerning the Rev. *Leonidas W.* Smiley, and so I started away.

At the door I met the sociable Wheeler returning, and he buttonholed me and recommenced:

"Well, thish-yer Smiley had a yaller one-eyed cow that didn't have no tail, only jest a short stump like a bannanner, and—"

"Oh! hang Smiley and his afflicted cow!" I muttered, good-naturedly, and bidding the old gentleman good-day, I departed.

A TRUE STORY, REPEATED WORD FOR WORD AS I HEARD IT

(1874)

It was summer time, and twilight. We were sitting on the porch of the farm-house, on the summit of the hill, and "Aunt Rachel" was sitting respectfully below our level, on the steps—for she was our servant, and colored. She was of mighty frame and stature; she was sixty years old, but her eye was undimmed and her strength unabated. She was a cheerful, hearty soul, and it was no more trouble for her to laugh than it is for a bird to sing. She was under fire, now, as usual when the day was done. That is to say, she was being chaffed without mercy, and was enjoying it. She would let off peal after peal of laughter, and then sit with her face in her hands and shake with throes of enjoyment which she could no longer get breath enough to express. At such a moment as this a thought occurred to me, and I said:—

"Aunt Rachel, how is it that you've lived sixty years and never had any trouble?"

She stopped quaking. She paused, and there was a moment of silence. She turned her face over her shoulder toward me, and said, without even a smile in her voice:—

"Misto C——, is you in 'arnest?"

It surprised me a good deal; and it sobered my manner and my speech, too. I said:—

"Why, I thought—that is, I meant—why, you can't have had

any trouble. I've never heard you sigh, and never seen your eye when there was n't a laugh in it."

She faced fairly around, now, and was full of earnestness.

"Has I had any trouble? Misto C——, I 's gwyne to tell you, den I leave it to you. I was bawn down 'mongst de slaves; I knows all 'bout slavery, 'cause I ben one of 'em my own se'f. Well, sah, my ole man—dat's my husban'—he was lovin' an' kind to me, jist as kind as you is to yo' own wife. An' we had chil'en—seven chil'en—an' we loved dem chil'en jist de same as you loves yo' chil'en. Dey was black, but de Lord can't make no chil'en so black but what dey mother loves 'em an' would n't give 'em up, no, not for anything dat 's in dis whole world.

"Well, sah, I was raised in ole Fo'ginny, but my mother she was raised in Maryland; an' my *souls!* she was turrible when she'd git started! My *lan'!* but she'd make de fur fly! When she'd git into dem tantrums, she always had one word dat she said. She'd straighten herse'f up an' put her fists in her hips an' say, 'I want you to understan' dat I wa'n't bawn in de mash to be fool' by trash! I 's one o' de ole Blue Hen's Chickens, *I* is!' 'Ca'se, you see, dat's what folks dat's bawn in Maryland calls deyselves, an' dey's proud of it. Well, dat was her word. I don't ever forgit it, beca'se she said it so much, an' beca'se she said it one day when my little Henry tore his wris' awful, an' most busted his head, right up at de top of his forehead, an' de niggers did n't fly aroun' fas' enough to 'tend to him. An' when dey talk' back at her, she up an' she says, 'Look-a-heah!' she says, 'I want you niggers to understan' dat I wa'n't bawn in de mash to be fool' by trash! I's one o' de ole Blue Hen's Chickens, *I* is!' an' den she clar' dat kitchen an' bandage' up de chile herse'f. So I says dat word, too, when I 's riled.

"Well, bymeby my ole mistis say she's broke, en' she got to sell all de niggers on de place. An' when I heah dat dey gwyne to sell us all off at oction in Richmon', oh de good gracious! I know what dat mean!"

Aunt Rachel had gradually risen, while she warmed to her subject, and now she towered above us, black against the stars.

"Dey put chains on us an' put us on a stan' as high as dis po'ch,—twenty foot high,—an' all de people stood aroun', crowds an' crowds. An' dey 'd come up dah an' look at us all roun', an' squeeze our arm, an' make us git up an' walk, an' den say, 'Dis one too ole,' or 'Dis one lame,' or 'Dis one don't 'mount to much.' An' dey sole my ole man, an' took him away, an' dey begin to sell my chil'en an' take *dem* away, an' I begin to cry; an' de man say, 'Shet up yo' dam blubberin',' en' hit me on de mouf wid his han'. An' when de las' one was gone but my little Henry, I grab' *him* clost up to my breas' so, an' I ris up an' says, 'You shan't take him away,' I says; 'I'll kill de man dat tetches him!' I says. But my little Henry whisper an' say, 'I gwyne to run away, an' den I work an' buy yo' freedom.' Oh, bless de chile, he always so good! But dey got him—dey got him, de men did; but I took and tear de clo'es mos' off of 'em, an' beat 'em over de head wid my chain; an' *dey* give it to *me*, too, but I did n't mine dat.

"Well, dah was my ole man gone, an' all my chil'en, all my seven chil'en—an' six of 'em I hain't set eyes on ag'in to dis day, an' dat's twenty-two year ago las' Easter. De man dat bought me b'long' in Newbern, an' he took me dah. Well, bymeby de years roll on an' de waw come. My marster he was a Confedrit colonel, an' I was his family's cook. So when de Unions took dat town, dey all run away an' lef' me all by myse'f wid de other niggers in dat mons'us big house. So de big Union officers move in dah, an' dey ask me would I cook for *dem.* 'Lord bless you,' says I, 'dat's what I 's *for.*'

"Dey wa' n't no small-fry officers, mine you, dey was de

biggest dey *is*; an' de way dey made dem sojers mosey roun'! De Gen'l he tole me to boss dat kitchen; an' he say, 'If anybody come meddlin' wid you, you jist make 'em walk chalk; don't you be afeard,' he say; 'you's 'mong frens, now.'

"Well, I thinks to myse'f, if my little Henry ever got a chance to run away, he'd make to de Norf, o' course. So one day I comes in dah whah de big officers was, in de parlor, an' I drops a kurtchy, so, an' I up an' tole 'em 'bout my Henry, dey a-listenin' to my troubles jist de same as if I was white folks; an' I says, 'What I come for is beca'se if he got away and got up Norf whah you gemmen comes from, you might 'a' seen him, maybe, an' could tell me so as I could fine him ag'in; he was very little, an' he had a sk-yar on his lef' wris', an' at de top of his forehead.' Den dey look mournful, an' de Gen'l say, 'How long sence you los' him?' an' I say, 'Thirteen year.' Den de Gen'l say, "He would n't be little no mo', now—he's a man!'

"I never thought o' dat befo'! He was only dat little feller to *me*, yit. I never thought 'bout him growin' up an' bein' big. But I see it den. None o' de gemmen had run across him, so dey could n't do nothin' for me. But all dat time, do' *I* did n't know it, my Henry *was* run off to de Norf, years an' years, an' he was a barber, too, an' worked for hisse'f. An' bymeby, when de waw come, he ups an' he says, 'I's done barberin',' he says; 'I's gwyne to fine my ole mammy, less'n she's dead.' So he sole out an' went to whah dey was recruitin', an' hired hisse'f out to de colonel for his servant; an' den he went all froo de battles everywhah, huntin' for his ole mammy; yes indeedy, he'd hire to fust one officer an' den another, tell he'd ransacked de whole Souf; but you see *I* didn't know nuffin 'bout *dis*. How was *I* gwyne to know it?

"Well, one night we had a big sojer ball; de sojers dah at Newbern was always havin' balls an' carryin' on. Dey had 'em in my kitchen, heaps o' times, 'ca'se it was so big. Mine you, I was *down* on sich doin's; beca'se my place was wid de officers, an' it rasp' me to have dem common sojers cavortin' roun' my kitchen like dat. But I alway' stood aroun' an' kep' things straight, I did; an' sometimes dey'd git my dander up, an' den I'd make 'em clar dat kitchen, mine I *tell* you!

"Well, one night—it was a Friday night—dey comes a whole platoon f'm a *nigger* ridgment dat was on guard at de house,—de house was head-quarters, you know,—an' den I was jist a-*bilin*'! Mad? I was jist a-*boomin*'! I swelled aroun', an' swelled aroun'; I jist was a-itchin' for 'em to do somefin for to start me. An' dey was a-waltzin' an a-dancin'! *my!* but dey was havin' a time! an' I jist a-swellin' an' a-swellin' up! Pooty soon, 'long comes *sich* a spruce young nigger a-sailin' down de room wid a yaller wench roun' de wais'; an' roun' an' roun' an' roun' dey went, enough to make a body drunk to look at 'em; an' when dey got abreas' o' me, dey went to kin' o' balancin' aroun', fust on one leg an' den on t'other, an' smilin' at my big red turban, an' makin' fun, an' I ups an' says, '*Git* along wid you!—rubbage!' De young man's face kin' o' changed, all of a sudden, for 'bout a second, but den he went to smilin' ag'in, same as he was befo'. Well, 'bout dis time, in comes some niggers dat played music an' b'long' to de ban', an' dey *never* could git along widout puttin' on airs. An' de very fust air dey put on dat night, I lit into 'em! Dey laughed, an' dat made me wuss. De res' o' de niggers got to laughin', an' den my soul *alive* but I was hot! My eyes was jist a-blazin'! I jist straightened myself up, so,—jist as I is now, plum to de ceilin', mos',—an' I digs my fists into my hips, an' I says, 'Look-a-heah!' I says, 'I want you niggers to understan' dat I wa'n't bawn in de mash to be fool' by trash! I's one o' de ole Blue Hen's Chickens, *I* is!' an' den I see dat young man stan' a-starin' an' stiff, lookin' kin' o' up at de ceilin' like he fo'got somefin, an' couldn't 'member it no mo'. Well, I jist march' on dem niggers,—so, lookin' like a gen'l,— an' dey jist cave' away befo' me an' out at de do'. An' as dis young man was a-goin' out, I heah him say to another nigger, 'Jim,' he says, 'you go 'long an' tell de cap'n I be on han' 'bout eight o'clock in de mawnin'; dey's somefin on my mine,' he says; 'I don't sleep no mo' dis night. You go 'long,' he says, 'an' leave me by my own se'f.'

"Dis was 'bout one o'clock in de mawnin'. Well, 'bout seven, I was up an' on han', gittin' de officers' breakfast. I was a-stoopin' down by de stove,—jist so, same as if yo' foot was de stove,—an' I'd opened de stove do' wid my right han',—so, pushin' it back, jist as I pushes yo' foot,—an' I'd jist got de pan o' hot biscuits in my han' an' was 'bout to raise up, when I see a black face come aroun' under mine, an' de eyes a-lookin' up into mine, jist as I's a-lookin' up clost under yo' face now; an' I jist stopped *right dah*, an' never budged! jist gazed, an' gazed, so; an' de pan begin to tremble, an' all of a sudden I *knowed*! De pan drop' on de flo' an' I grab his lef' han' an' shove back his sleeve,—jist so, as I's doin' to you,—an' den I goes for his forehead an' push de hair back, so, an' 'Boy!' I says, 'if you an't my Henry, what is you doin' wid dis welt on yo' wris' an' dat sk-yar on yo' forehead? De Lord God ob heaven be praise', I got my own ag'in!'

"Oh, no, Misto C——, *I* hain't had no trouble. An' no *joy*!"

IRVINE WELSH

IRVINE WELSH was born in Leith, Scotland, in 1958, and grew up in Edinburgh. After working as a television repairman in Edinburgh and a punk-rock guitarist in London, he published his first novel, *Trainspotting*, in 1993. Since then Welsh has written several other novels, short story collections, and a screenplay, in addition to directing film and producing music. *Trainspotting* instantly transformed Welsh into Scotland's best-known contemporary writer. "A Soft Touch" echoes many of that novel's themes in a brief and hard-hitting format. In "Granny's Old Junk," Welsh parodies some of the defining elements of *Trainspotting*: heroin addiction, familial dissolution, and general depravity.

A SOFT TOUCH

(1994)

It wis good fir a while wi Katriona, but she did wrong by me. And that's no jist something ye can forget; no jist like that. She came in the other day, intae the pub, while ah was oan the bandit likes. It was the first time ah'd seen her in yonks.

—Still playing the bandit, John, she sais, in that radge, nasal sortay voice she's goat.

Ah wis gaunny say something like, naw, ah'm fuckin well swimming at the Commie Pool, but ah jist goes:—Aye, looks like it.

—No goat the money to get ays a drink, John? she asked ays. Katriona looked bloated: mair bloated than ever. Maybe she wis pregnant again. She liked being up the stick, liked the fuss people made. Bairns she had nae time fir but she liked being up the stick. Thing wis, every time she wis, people made less ay a thing about it than they did the time before. It goat boring; besides, people kent what she wis like.

—You in the family wey again, ah asked, concentrating oan getting a nudge oan the bandit. A set ay grapes. That'll dae me.

Gamble.

Collect.

Hit collect.

Tokens. Eywis fuckin tokens. Ah thought Colin sais tae ays that the new machine peyed cash.

—Is it that obvious, Johnny? she goes, lifting up her checked blouse and pulling her leggings ower a mound ay gut. Ah thought ay her tits and arse then. Ah didnae look at them likes, didnae stare or nowt like that; ah jist thought ay them. Katriona had a great pair ay tits and a nice big arse. That's what ah like in a bird. Tits and arse.

—Ah'm oan the table, ah sais, moving past her, ower tae the pool. The boy fae Crawford's bakeries had beat Bri Ramage. Must be a no bad player. Ah goat the baws oot and racked up. The boy fae Crawford's seemed awright.

—How's Chantel? Katriona goes.

—Awright, ah sais. She should go doon tae ma Ma's and see the bairn. No that she'd be welcome thair mind you. It's her bairn though, and that must count fir something. Mind you, ah should go n aw. It's ma bairn n aw, but ah love that bairn. Everybody kens that. A mother though, a mother that abandons her bairn, that's no bothered aboot her bairn; that's no a mother, no a real mother. No tae me. That's a fucking slag, a slut, that's what that is. A common person as ma Ma says.

Ah wonder whae's bairn she's cairrying now. Probably Larry's. Ah hope so. It would serve the cunts right; the baith ay them. It's the bairn ah feels sorry for but. She'll leave that bairn like she left Chantel; like she left the two other bairns she's hud. Two other bairns ah nivir even kent aboot until ah saw them at oor weddin reception.

Aye, ma Ma wis right aboot her. She's common, Ma said. And no jist because she wis a Doyle. It wis her drinking; no like a lassie, Ma thought. Mind you, ah liked that. At first ah liked it, until ah got peyed oaf and the hirey's wir short. That wis me toiling. Then the bairn came. That wis when her drinking goat tae be a total pain; a total fuckin pain in the erse.

She eywis laughed at ays behind ma back. Ah'd catch sight ay her twisted smile when she thought ah wisnae looking. This wis usually when she wis wi her sisters. The three ay them would laugh when ah played the bandit or the pool. Ah'd feel them looking at me. After a while, they stopped kidding that they wirnae daein it.

Ah nivir coped well wi the bairn; ah mean as a really wee bairn like. It seemed to take everything over; aw that noise fae that wee size. So ah suppose ah went oot a lot eftir the bairn came. Maybe a bit ay it wis my fault; ah'm no saying otherwise. There wis things gaun oan wi her though. Like the time ah gied her that money.

She wis skint so ah gies her twenty notes and sais: You go oot doll, enjoy yirself. Go oot wi yir mates. Ah mind that night fine well because she goes n gits made up like a tart. Make-up, tons ay it, and that dress she wore. Ah asked her where she wis gaun dressed like that. She just stood thair, smiling at me. Where, ah sais. You wanted ays tae go out, so ah'm fuckin well gaun oot, she telt ays. Where but? ah asked. Ah mean, ah wis entitled tae ken. She just ignored ays but, ignored ays and left, laughing in ma face like a fuckin hyena.

When she came back she wis covered in love bites. Ah checked her purse when she wis oan the toilet daein a long, drunken pish. Forty quid she had in it. Ah gave her twenty quid and she came back wi forty fuckin bar in her purse. Ah wis fuckin demented. Ah goes, whit's this, eh? She just laughed at ays. Ah wanted tae check her fanny; tae see if ah could tell that she'd been shagged. She started screaming and saying that if ah touched her, her brothers would be roond. They're radge, the Doyles, every fucker in the scheme kens that. Ah'm radge, if the truth be telt, ever getting involved wi a Doyle. Yir a soft touch son, ma Ma once said. These people, they see that in ye. They ken yir a worker, they ken yir easy meat fir thum.

Funny thing was, a Doyle can dae what they like, but ah thought that if ah goat in wi the Doyles then ah could dae what ah liked. And ah could fir a bit. Nae cunt messed wi ays, ah wis well in. Then the tapping started; the bumming ay fags, drinks, cash. Then they had ays, or that cunt Alec Doyle, he had ays looking eftir stuff fir um. Drugs. No hash or nowt like that; wir talking aboot smack here.

Ah could've gone doon. Done time; fuckin years ah could have done. Fuckin years for the Doyles and thir hoor ay a sister. Anywey, ah never messed wi the Doyles. Never ever. So ah didnae touch Katriona that night and we slept in different rooms; me oan the couch, likes.

It wis jist eftir that ah started knocking around wi Larry upstairs. His wife had just left um and he wis lonely. For me it wis, likesay, insurance: Larry wis a nutter, one ay the few guys living in the scheme even the Doyles gied a bit ay respect tae.

Ah wis working oan the Employment Training. Painting. Ah wis daein the painting in the Sheltered Hooses fir the auld folks, like. Ah wis oot maist ay the time. Thing is when ah came back in ah'd either find Larry in oor place or her up at his. Half-fuckin-bevvied aw the time; the baith ay thum. Ah kent he wis shagging her. Then she started tae stey up thair some nights. Then she jist moved upstairs wi him aw the gither; leaving me doonstairs wi the bairn. That meant ah hud tae pack in the painting; fir the bairn's sake, like, ken?

When ah took the bairn doon tae ma Ma's or tae the shops in the go-cart, ah'd sometimes see the two ay thum at the windae. They'd be laughing at ays. One day ah gits back tae the

hoose and it's been broken intae; the telly and video are away.
Ah kent whae had taken thum, but thir wis nothing ah could
dae. No against Larry and the Doyles.

Their noise kept me and the bairn awake. Her ain bairn.
The noise ay them shagging, arguing, partying.

Then one time thir wis a knock at the door. It wis Larry. He jist
pushed past ays intae the flat, blethering away in that excited,
quick wey he goes on. Alright mate, he sais. Listen, ah need a wee
favour. Fuckin electric cunts have only gone and cut ays off, eh.

He goes ower tae ma front windae and opens it and pulls in
this plug that's swingin doon fae his front room above. He
takes it and plugs it intae one ay ma sockets. That's me sorted
oot, he smiles at ays. Eh, ah goes. He tells ays that he's got an
extension cable wi a block upstairs but he jist needs access tae
a power point. Ah tell him that he's ootay order, it's ma electric
he's using and ah goes ower tae switch it oaf. He goes: See if
you ivir touch that fuckin plug or that switch, you're fuckin
deid, Johnny! Ah'm fuckin telling ye! He means it n aw.

Larry then starts telling ays that he still regards me and him
as mates, in spite ay everything. He sais tae ays that we'll go
halfers oan the bills, which ah knew then wouldnae happen.
Ah sais that his bills would be higher than mine because ah've
no got anything left in the hoose that uses electricity. Ah wis
thinking aboot ma video and telly which ah kent he had up the
stair. He goes: What's that supposed tae mean then, Johnny?
Ah just goes: Nowt. He says: It better fuckin no mean nowt. Ah
sais nowt eftir that because Larry's crazy; a total radge.

Then his face changed and he sortay broke intae this smile.
He nodded up at the ceiling: No bad ride, eh John? Sorry tae
huv tae move in thair, mate. One ay these things though, eh?
Ah jist nodded. Gies a barry gam though, he sais. I felt like
shite. Ma electricity. Ma woman.

Ever fucked it up the erse? he asked. Ah jist shrugged. He crosses one ay his airms ower the other one. Ah've started giein it the message that wey, he said, jist cause ah dinnae want it up the stick. Bairn daft, that cunt. Once ye git a cunt up the stick, they think thuv goat thir hand in yir poakit fir the rest ay yir puff. Yir dough's no yir ain. Isnae ma fuckin scene, ah kin tell ye. Ah'll keep ma money. Tell ye one thing, Johnny, he laughed, ah hope you've no goat AIDS or nowt like that, cause if ye huv ye'd've gied it tae me by now. Ah never use a rubber when ah shaft her up the stairs thair. No way. Ah'd rather have a fuckin wank man.

Naw, ah've no goat nowt like that, ah telt him, wishing for the first time in ma life that ah did.

Just as well, ya dirty wee cunt, Larry laughed.

Then he stretched intae the playpen and patted Chantel on the heid. Ah started tae feel sick. If he tried tae touch that bairn again, ah'd've stabbed the cunt; disnae matter whae he is. Ah jist wouldnae care. It's awright, he goes, ah'm no gaunny take yir bairn away. She wants it mind, and ah suppose that a bairn belongs wi its Ma. Thing is, John, like ah sais, ah'm no intae huving a bairn aroond the house. So yuv goat me to thank fir still huvin the bairn, think aboot it like that. He went aw upset and angry and pointed tae hisel. Think aboot it that wey before ye start making accusations aboot other people. Then he goes cheery again; this cunt can jist change like that, and sais: See that draw for the quarter-finals? The winners ay St Johnstone v. Kilmarnock. At Easter Road, likes, he smiles at ays, then twists his face aroond the room. Fuckin pit this, he sais, before turning tae go. Just as he's at the front door he stops and turns tae me. One other thing, John, if ye want a poke at it again, he points at the ceiling, jist gies a shout. A tenner tae you. Gen up, likes.

Ah mind ay aw that, cause just after it ah took the bairn tae ma Ma's. That wis that; Ma goat ontae the Social Work; goat things sorted oot. They went and saw her; she didnae want tae ken. Ah goat a kicking fir that, fae Alec and Mikey Doyle. Ah goat another yin, a bad yin, fae Larry and Mikey Doyle when ma electric wis cut oaf. They grabbed ays in the stair and dragged ays through the back. They goat ays doon and started kicking ays. Ah wis worried cause ah hud a bit ay money ah'd won fae the bandit. Ah wis shitein it in case they'd go through ma poakits. Fifteen quid ah hud taken the bandit fir. They just booted intae ays but. Booted ays and she wis screamin: KICK THE CUNT! KILL THE CUNT! OOR FUCKIN ELECTRIC! IT WIS OOR FUCKIN ELECTRICITY! HE'S GOAT MA FUCKIN BAIRN! HIS FUCKIN AULD HOOR AY A MOTHER'S GOAT MA FUCKIN BAIRN! GO BACK TAE YIR FUCKIN MA! LICK YIR MA'S FUCKIN PISS-FLAPS YA CUNT!

Thank fuck they left ays withoot checking ma poakits. Ah thoat; well, that's seekened they cunts' pusses anywey, as ah staggered tae ma Ma's tae git cleaned up. Ma nose wis broken and ah hud two cracked ribs. Ah hud tae go tae the A and E at the Infirmary. Ma sais that ah should nivir huv goat involved wi Katriona Doyle. That's easy tae say now but, ah telt her, but see if ah hudnae, jist sayin like, jist supposin ah hudnae; we would nivir huv hud Chantel, like. Yuv goat tae think aboot it that wey. Aye, right enough, ma Ma said, she's a wee princess.

The thing wis thit some cunt in the stair hud called the polis. Ah wis thinking that it could mean criminal injuries compensation money fir me. Ah gied them a false description ay two guys thit looked nowt like Larry n Mikey. But then the polis talked like they thought ah wis the criminal, that ah wis the cunt in the wrong. Me, wi a face like a piece ay bad fruit, two cracked ribs and a broken nose.

Her and Larry moved away fae upstairs eftir that and ah just thought: good riddance tae bad rubbish. Ah think the council evicted them fir arrears; rehoosed them in another scheme. The bairn wis better oaf at ma Ma's and ah goat a job, a proper job, no just oan some training scheme. It wis in a supermarket; stackin shelves and checking stock levels, that kind ay thing. No a bad wee number: bags ay overtime. The money wisnae brilliant but it kept ays oot ay the pub, ken wi the long hours, like.

Things are gaun awright. Ah've been shaggin one or two burds lately. There's this lassie fae the supermarket, she's mairried, but she's no wi the guy. She's awright, a clean lassie, like. Then there's the wee burds fae roond the scheme, some ay them are jist at the school. A couple ay thum come up at dinnertime if ah'm oan backshift. Once ye git tae ken one, yir well in. They aw come roond; just fir somewhere tae muck aboot cause thirs nowt fir thum tae dae. Ye might git a feel or a gam. Like ah sais, one or two, especially that wee Wendy, thir game fir a poke. Nae wey dae ah want tae git involved again aw heavy like but.

As fir her, well, this is the first ah've seen ay her fir ages.

—How's Larry? ah ask, gaun doon tae connect wi a partially covered stripe. One guy's squinting his eye and saying that's no oan. The Crawford's bakery boy goes:—Hi you! Admiral Fuckin Nelson thair! Let the boy play his ain game. Nae coaching fae the touchline!

—Oh him, she goes as the cue clips the stripe and heads towards the boatum cushion.—He's gaun back inside. Ah'm back at ma Ma's.

Ah jist looked at her.

—He found oot that ah wis pregnant and he jist fucked off, she sais.—He's been steying wi some fucking slut, she goes. Ah felt like saying, ah fuckin well ken that, ah'm staring her in the fuckin face.

But ah says nowt.

Then her voice goes aw that high, funny way, like it eywis goes when she wants something.—Why don't we go oot fir a drink the night, Johnny? Up the toon likes? We wir good, Johnny, good the gither you n me. Everybody said, mind? Mind we used tae go tae the Bull and Bush up Lothian Road, Johnny?

—Ah suppose so, ah sais. Thing wis, ah supposed ah still loved her; ah suppose ah never really stoaped. Ah liked gaun up the Bull and Bush. Ah wis always a bit lucky oan the bandit up there. It's probably a new one now though; but still.

GRANNY'S OLD JUNK

(1994)

The warden, Mrs French I think they call her, is looking me up and down. It's fairly obvious that she doesn't like what she sees; her gaze has a steely ice to it; it's definitely a negative evaluation I'm getting here.

—So, she says, hands on hips, eyes flitting suspiciously in that glistening yellow-brown foundation mask topped by a brittle head of brown hair,—you're Mrs Abercrombie's grandson?

—Aye, I acknowledge. I shouldn't resent Mrs French. She's only doing her job. Were she less than vigilant in keeping her eye on the auld doll, complaints from the family would ensue. I also have to acknowledge that I am less than presentable; lank, greasy black hair, a scrawny growth sprouting from a deathly white face broken up by a few red and yellow spots. My overcoat has seen better days and I can't remember when I changed into these jeans, sweatshirt, t-shirt, trainers, socks and boxer-shorts.

—Well, I suppose you'd better come in, Mrs French said, reluctantly shifting her sizeable bulk. I squeezed past, still brushing against her. Mrs French was like an oil tanker, it took a while for her to actually change direction.—She's on the second floor. You don't come to see her very often, do you? she said with an accusatory pout.

No. This is the first time I've been to see the auld doll

since she moved into this Sheltered Housing scheme. That must be over five years ago now. Very few families are close nowadays. People move around, live in different parts of the country, lead different lives. It's pointless lamenting something as inevitable as the decline of the extended family network; in a way it's a good thing because it gives people like Mrs French jobs.

—Ah don't stay local, I mumble, making my way down the corridor, feeling a twinge of self-hate for justifying myself to the warden.

The corridors have a rank, fetid smell of pish and stale bodies. Most people here seem in such an advanced state of infirmity it merely confirms my intuitive feeling that such places are just ante-chambers to death. It follows from this that my actions won't alter the auld doll's quality of life: she'll scarcely notice that the money's gone. Some of it would probably be mine anyway, when she finally snuffs it; so what the fuck's the point of waiting until it's no good to me? The auld doll could hang on for donkey's years as a cabbage. It would be utterly perverse, self-defeating nonsense not to rip her off now, to allow oneself to be constrained by some stupid, irrelevant set of taboos which pass as morality. I need what's in her tin.

It's been in the family for so long: Gran's shortbread tin. Just sitting there under her bed, crammed full of bundles of notes. I remember, as a sprog, her opening it up on our birthdays and peeling off a few notes from what seemed to be a fortune, the absence of which made no impact on the wad.

Her life savings. Savings for what? Savings for us, that's what, the daft auld cunt: too feeble, too inadequate to enjoy or even use her wealth. Well I shall just have my share now, Granny, thank you very much.

I rap on the door. Abercrombie, with a red tartan background. My back chills and my joints feel stiff and aching. I haven't got long.

She opens the door. She looks so small, like a wizened puppet, like Zelda out of *Terrahawks*.

—Gran, I smile.

—Graham! she says, her face expanding warmly.—God, ah cannae believe it! Come in! Come in!

She sits me down, babbling excitedly, hobbling back and forth from her small adjoining kitchen as she slowly and cumbersomely prepares tea.

—Ah keep askin yir mother how ye nivir come tae see me. Ye always used tae come oan Saturday for yir dinner, mind? For yir mince, remember, Graham? she says.

—Aye, the mince, Gran.

—At the auld place, mind? she said wistfully.

—Ah remember it well, Gran, I nodded. It was a vermin-infested hovel unfit for human habitation. I hated that grotty tenement: those stairs, the top floor surprise surfuckingprise, with the backs of my legs already fucked from the sickening ritual of walking up and down Leith Walk and Junction Street; her standing oblivious to our pain and discomfort as she prattled on a load of irrelevant, mundane shite with every other auld hound that crossed our path; big brother Alan taking his exasperation out on me by punching me or booting me or twisting my airm when she wisnae looking, and if she was she didnae bother. Mickey Weir gets more protection from Syme at Ibrox than I ever did from that auld cunt. Then, after all that, the fuckin stairs. God, I detested those fuckin stairs!

She comes in and looks at me sadly, and shakes her head with her chin on her chest.—Your mother was saying that yuv been gettin intae trouble. Wi these drugs n things. Ah sais, no oor Graham, surely no.

—People exaggerate, Gran, I said as a spasm of pain shot through my bones, and a delirious shivering tremor triggered off an excretion of stale perspiration from my pores. Fuck fuck fuck.

She re-emerges from the kitchen, popping out like a crumpled jack-in-the-box.—Ah thoat so. Ah sais tae oor Joyce: No oor Graham, he's goat mair sense thin that.

—Ma goes oan a bit. Ah enjoy masel, Gran, ah'm no sayin otherwise, bit ah dinnae touch drugs, eh. Ye dinnae need drugs tae enjoy yirself.

—That's whit ah sais tae yir mother. The laddie's an Abercrombie, ah telt her, works hard and plays hard.

My name was Millar, not Abercrombie, that's the auld lady's side. This auld hound seemed to believe that being referred to as an Abercrombie is the highest possible accolade one can aspire to; though perhaps, if you want to demonstrate expertise in alcoholism and theft, this may very well be the case.

—Aye, some crowd the Abercrombie, eh Gran?

—That's right, son. Ma Eddie—yir grandfaither—he wis the same. Worked hard n played hard, n a finer man nivir walked the earth. He nivir kept us short, she smiled proudly. Short.

I have my works in my inside pocket. Needle, spoon, cotton balls, lighter. All I need is a few grains of smack, then just add water and it's all better. My passport's in that tin.

—Whair's the lavvy, Gran?

Despite the small size of the flat, she insisted on escorting me to the bog, as if I'd get lost on the way. She fussed, clucked and farted as if we were preparing to go on safari. I tried a quick slash, but couldn't pee, so I stealthily tiptoed into the bedroom.

I lifted up the bedclothes that hung to the floor. The large old shortbread tin with the view of Holyrood Palace sat in full magnificent view under the bed. It was ridiculous, an act of absolute criminal stupidity to have that just lying around in this day and age. I was more convinced than ever that I had to rip her off. If I didn't somebody else would. Surely she'd want me to have the money, rather than some stranger? If I didn't take the cash, I'd be worried sick about it. Anyway, I was planning to get clean soon; maybe get a job or go to college or something. The auld hound would get it back right enough. No problem.

Prising open the lid of the fucker was proving extremely difficult. My hands were trembling and I couldn't get any purchase on it. I was starting to make headway when I heard her voice behind me.

—So! That's whit this is aw aboot! She was standing right over me. I thought I'd have heard the clumsy auld boot sneaking up on me, but she was like a fuckin ghost.—Yir mother wis right. Yir a thief! Feeding yir habit, yir drugs habit, is that it?

—Naw Gran, it's jist . . .

—Dinnae lie, son. Dinnae lie. A thief, a thief thit steals fae his ain is bad, but a liar's even worse. Ye dinnae ken whair ye stand wi a liar. Get away fae that bloody tin! she snapped so suddenly that I was taken aback, but I sat where I was.

—I need something, right?

—Yill find nae money in thair, she said, but I could tell by the anxiety in her voice that she was lying. I prised, and it transpired that she wasn't. On top of a pile of old photos lay some whitish-brown powder in a plastic bag. I'd never seen so much gear.

—What the fuckin hell's this . . .

—Git away fae thair! Git away! Fuckin thief! Her bony, spindly leg lashed out and caught me in the side of the face. It didn't hurt but it shocked me. Her swearing shocked me even more.

—Ya fuckin auld . . . I sprang to my feet, holding the bag in the air, beyond her outstretched hands.—Better call the warden, Gran. She'll be interested in this.

She pouted bitterly and sat down on the bed.—You got works? she asked.

—Aye, I said.

—Cook up a shot then, make yourself useful.

I started to do as she said.—How Gran? How? I asked, relieved and bemused.

—Eddie, the Merchant Navy. He came back wi a habit. We had contacts. The docks. The money wis good, son. Thing is, ah kept feedin it, now ah huv tae sell tae the young ones tae keep gaun. The money aw goes upfront. She shook her head, looking hard at me.—Thir's a couple ay young yins ah git tae run messages fir me, but that fat nosey yin doonstairs, the warden, she's gittin suspicious.

I took up her cue. Talk about falling on your feet.—Gran, maybe we kin work the gither on this.

The animal hostility on her small, pinched face dissolved into a scheming grin.—Yir an Abercrombie right enough, she told me.

—Aye, right enough, I acknowledged with a queasy defeatism.

THOMAS WOLFE

AMERICAN NOVELIST THOMAS WOLFE was born in 1900 and grew up in Asheville, North Carolina. After attending the University of North Carolina and Harvard University, he initially tried his hand at writing plays, but soon switched to an expansive and experimental prose. Wolfe's masterpiece *Look Homeward, Angel* was published in 1929, eleven years before he died suddenly of pneumonia and tuberculosis. This economical story, unusual within Wolfe's oeuvre, describes an encounter between a pragmatic Brooklynite and an odd stranger naïve enough to navigate the formidable borough "wit a map." The map, incorporating all that is codified and knowable, provides a clever analogue to Standard English. The vernacular, on the other hand, conveys a murkier reality and thus is the only appropriate code for "the sprawl and web of jungle desolation that is Brooklyn t'roo and t'roo."

ONLY THE DEAD KNOW BROOKLYN

(1935)

Now is the winter of our discontent made glorious by dis mont' of May, and all the long-drowned desolation of our souls in the green fire and radiance of the Springtime buried.

We are the dead—ah! We were drowned so long ago—and now we thrust our feelers in distressful ooze upon the sea-floors of the buried world. We are the drowned—blind crawls and eyeless gropes and mindless sucks that swirl and scuttle in the jungle depths, immense and humid skies bend desolately upon us, and our flesh is gray.

We are lost, the eyeless atoms of the jungle depth, we grope and crawl and scuttle with blind feelers, and we have no way but this.

Dere's no guy livin' dat knows Brooklyn t'roo an' t'roo (only the dead know Brooklyn t'roo and t'roo), because it'd take a lifetime just to find his way aroun' duh goddam town (—only the dead know Brooklyn t'roo and t'roo, even the dead will quarrel an' bicker over the sprawl and web of jungle desolation that is Brooklyn t'roo an' t'roo).

So like I say, I'm waitin' for my train t' come when I sees dis big guy standin' deh—dis is duh foist I eveh see of him. Well, he's lookin' wild, y'know, an' I can see dat he's had plenty, but still he's holdin' it; he talks good, an' he's walkin' straight

283

enough. So den dis big guy steps up to a little guy dat's standin' deh, an' says, "How d'yuh get t' Eighteent' Avenoo an' Sixty-sevent' Street?" he says.

"Jesus! Yuh got me, chief," duh little guy says to him. "I ain't been heah long myself. Where is duh place?" he says. "Out in duh Flatbush section somewhere?"

"Nah," duh big guy says. "It's out in Bensonhoist. But I was neveh deh befoeh. How d'yuh get deh?"

"Jesus," duh little guy says, scratchin' his head, y'know—yuh could see duh little guy didn't know his way about—"yuh got me, chief. I neveh hoid of it. Do any of youse guys know where it is?" he says to me.

"Sure," I says. "It's out in Bensonhoist. Yuh take duh Fourt' Avenoo express, get off at Fifty-nint' Street, change to a Sea Beach local deh, get off at Eighteent' Avenoo an' Sixty-toid, and den walk down foeh blocks. Dat's all yuh got to do," I says.

"G'wan!" some wise guy dat I neveh seen befoeh pipes up. "Watcha talkin' about?" he says—oh, he was wise, y'know. "Duh guy is crazy! I'll tell yuh wht yuh do," he says to duh big guy. "Yuh change to duh West End line at Toity-sixt'," he tells him. "Get off at Noo Utrecht an' Sixteent' Avenoo," he says. "Walk two blocks oveh, foeh blocks up," he says, "an' you'll be right deh." Oh, a *wise* guy, y'know.

"Oh, yeah?" I says. "Who told *you* so much?" He got me sore because he was so wise about it. "How long you been livin' heah?" I says.

"All my life," he says. "I was bawn in Williamsboig," he says. "An' I can tell you t'ings about dis town you neveh hoid of," he says.

"Yeah?" I says.

"Yeah," he says.

"Well, den, yuh can tell me t'ings about dis town dat nobody else has eveh hoid of, either. Maybe yuh make it all up yoehself at night," I says, "befoeh yuh go to sleep—like cuttin' out papeh dolls, or somep'n."

"Oh, yeah?" he says. "You're pretty wise, ain't yuh?"

"Oh, I don't know," I says. "Duh boids ain't usin' my head for Lincoln's statue yet," I says. "But I'm wise enough to know a phony when I see one."

"Yeah?" he says. "A wise guy, huh? Well, you're so wise dat someone's goin' t'bust yuh one right on duh snoot some day," he says. "Dat's how wise *you* are."

Well, my train was comin', or I'da smacked him den an' dere, but when I seen duh train was comin' all I said was, "All right, mugg! I'm sorry I can't stay to take keh of yuh, but I'll be seein' yuh sometime, I hope, out in duh cemetery." So den I says to duh big guy, who'd been standin' deh all duh time, "You come wit me," I says. So when we gets onto duh train, I says to him, "Where yuh goin' out in Bensonhoist?" I says. "What numbeh are yuh looking for?" I says. *You* know—I t'ought if he told me duh address I might be able to help him out.

"Oh," he says, "I'm not lookin' for no one. I don't know no one out deh."

"Then whatcha goin' out deh for?" I says.

"Oh," duh guy says, "I'm just goin' out to see duh place," he says. "I like duh sound of duh name"—Bensonhoist, y'know— "so I t'ought I'd go out an' have a look at it."

"Whatcha tryin' t' hand me?" I says. "Whatcha tryin' to do, kid me?" *You* know, I t'ought duh guy was bein' wise wit me.

"No," he says, "I'm tellin yuh duh troot. I like to go out an' take a look at places wit nice names like dat. I like to go out an' look at all kinds of places," he says.

"How'd yuh know deh was such a place," I says, "if yuh neveh been deh befoeh?"

"Oh," he says, "I got a map."

"A *map*?" I says.

"Sure," he says, "I got a map dat tells me about all dese places. I take it wit me every time I come out heah," he says.

And Jesus! Wit dat, he pulls it out of his pocket, an' so help me, but he's *got* it—he's tellin' duh troot—a big map of duh whole goddam place wit all duh different pahts. Mahked out, y'know—Canarsie an' East Noo Yawk and Harbush, Bensonhoist, Sout' Brooklyn, duh Heights, Bay Ridge, Greenpernt—duh whole goddam layout, he's got it right deh on duh map.

"You been to any of dose places?" I says.

"Sure," he says, "I been to most of 'em. I was down in Red Hook just last night," he says.

"Jesus! Red Hook!" I says. "Whatcha do down deh?"

"Oh," he says, "nuttin' much. I just walked aroun'. I went into a coupla places an' had a drink," he says, "but most of the time I just walked aroun'."

"Just walked aroun'?" I says.

"Sure," he says, "just lookin' at t'ings, y'know."

"Where'd yuh go?" I asts him.

"Oh," he says, "I don't know duh name of duh place, but I could find it on my map," he says. "One time I was walkin' across some big fields where deh ain't no houses," he says, "but I could see ships oveh deh all lighted up. Dey was loadin'. So I walks across duh fields," he says, "to where duh ships are."

"Sure," I says, "I know where yuh was. Yuh was down to duh Erie Basin."

"Yeah," he says, "I guess dat was it. Dey had some of dose big elevators an' cranes, and dey was loadin' ships, an' I could see some ships in drydock all lighted up, so I walks across duh fields to where dey are," he says.

"Den what did yuh do?" I says.

"Oh," he says, "nuttin' much. I came on back across duh fields after a while an' went into a coupla places an' had a drink."

"Didn't nuttin' happen while yuh was in dere?" I says.

"No," he says. "Nuttin' much. A coupla guys was drunk in one of duh places an' started a fight, an' dey bounced 'em out," he says, "an' den one of duh guys stahted to come back again, but duh bartender gets his baseball bat out from under duh counteh, so duh guy goes on."

"Jesus!" I said. "Red Hook!"

"Sure," he says. "Dat's where it was, all right."

"Well, you keep outa deh," I says. "You stay away from deh."

"Why?" he says. "What's wrong wit it?"

"Oh," I says, "it's a good place to stay away from, dat's all. It's a good place to keep out of."

"Why?" he says. "Why is it?"

Jesus! Whatcha gonna do wit a guy as dumb as dat? I saw it wasn't no use to try to tell him nuttin', he wouldn't know what I was talkin' about, so I just says to him, "Oh, nuttin' Yuh might get lost down deh, dat's all."

"Lost?" he says. "No, I wouldn't get lost. I got a map," he says.

A map! Red Hook! Jesus!

So den duh guy begins to ast me all kinds of nutty questions: how big was Brooklyn an' could I find my way aroun' in it, how long would it take a guy to know duh place.

"Listen!" I says. "You get dat idea outa youeh head right now," I says. "You ain't eveh gonna get to know Brooklyn," I says. "Not in a hunderd yeahs. I been livin' heah all my life," I says, "an' I don't even know all deh is to know about it, so how do you expect to know duh town," I says, "when yuh don't even live heah?"

"Yes," he says, "but I got a map to help me find my way about."

"Map or no map," I says, "yuh ain't gonna get to know Brooklyn wit no map," I says.

"Can yuh swim?" he says, just like dat. Jesus! By dat time, y'know, I begun to see dat duh guy was some kind of nut. He'd had plenty to drink, of course, but he had dat crazy look in his eye I didn't like. "Can yuh swim?" he says.

"Sure," I says. "Can't you?"

"No," he says. "Not more'n a stroke or two. I neveh loined good."

"Well, it's easy," I says. "All yuh need is a little confidence. Duh way I loined, me oldeh bruddeh pitched me off duh dock one day when I was eight yeahs old, cloes an' all. 'You'll swim,' he says. 'You'll swim all right—or drown.' An', believe me, I swam! When yuh know yuh got to, you'll do it. Duh only t'ing yuh need is confidence. An' once you've loined," I says, "you've got nuttin' else to worry about. You'll neveh ferget it. It's somep'n dat stays wit yuh as long as yuh live."

"Can yuh swim good?" he says.

"Like a fish," I tells him. "I'm a regleh fish in duh wateh," I says. "I loined to swim right off duh docks wit duh odeh kids," I says.

"What would yuh do if yuh saw a man drownin'," duh guy says.

"Do? Why, I'd jump in an' pull him out," I says. "Dat's what I'd do."

"Did yuh eveh see a man drown?" he says.

"Sure," I says. "I see two guys—bot' times at Coney Island. Dey got out too far, an' neider one could swim. Dey drowned befoeh anyone could get to 'em."

"What becomes of people after dey have drowned out heah?" he says.

"Drowned out where?" I says.

"Out heah in Brooklyn."

"I don't know whatcha mean," I says. "Neveh hoid of no one drownin' heah in Brooklyn, unless yuh mean in a swimmin' pool. Yuh can't drown in Brooklyn," I says. "Yuh gotta drown somewhere else—in duh ocean, where dere's watch."

"Drownin'," duh guy says, lookin' at his map. "Drownin'."

Jesus! By den I could see he was some kind of nut, he had dat crazy expression in his eyes when he looked at yuh, an' I didn't know what he might do. So we was comin' to a station, an' it wasn't my stop, but I got off, anyway, an' waited for duh next train.

"Well, so long, chief," I says. "Take it easy, now."

"Drownin'," duh guys say, lookin' at his map. "Drownin'."

Jesus! I've t'ought about dat guy a t'ousand times since den an' wondered what eveh happed to 'm goin' out to look at Bensonhoist because he liked duh name! Walkin' aroun' t'roo Red Hook by himself at night an' lookin' at his map! How many people did I see drowned out heah in Brooklyn! How long would it take a guy wit a good map to know all deh was to know about Brooklyn!

Jesus! What a nut *he* was! I wondeh what eveh happened to 'm, anyway! I wondeh if someone knocked 'm on duh head, or if he's still wanderin' aroun' in duh subway in duh middle of duh night wit his little map! Duh poor guy! Say, I've got to laugh, at dat, when I t'ink about him! Maybe he's found out by now dat he'll neveh live long enough to know duh whole of Brooklyn. It'd take a guy a lifetime to know Brooklyn t'roo and t'roo. An' even den, yuh wouldn't know it all.

Only the dead know Brooklyn t'roo an' t'roo.

SECTION THREE · "I WANNA SAY I AM SOMEBODY" · SELECTIONS FROM VERNACULAR NOVELS · SECTION THREE · "I WANNA SAY I AM SOMEBODY" ·

SELECTIONS FROM VERNACULAR NOVELS · SECTION THREE · "I WANNA SAY I AM SOMEBODY" · SELECTIONS FROM VERNACULAR NOVELS · SECTION THREE · "I WANNA SAY I AM SOMEBODY"

SELECTIONS FROM VERNACULAR NOVELS

SECTION THREE · "I WANNA SAY I AM SOMEBODY" · SELECTIONS FROM VERNACULAR NOVELS ·

IF VERNACULAR POETRY feeds on music, and vernacular short stories on the tall tale, the type of writing to which vernacular novels owe the most is revisionist history. Most of the books excerpted here are *bildungsromans,* or novels of individual growth and development, which render untold biographies from trying times. From Peter Carey's *True History of the Kelly Gang,* which sympathetically chronicles the emergence of an outlaw hero, to Sapphire's *Push,* which allows a pregnant teenage incest victim to express herself for the first time, these novels tell stories that have been obscured by the official record. Carey's Ned Kelly, for example, narrates with the explicit goal that the new generation may "finally comprehend the injustice we poor Irish suffered in this present age." Accordingly, most of these novels—Carey's and Sapphire's as well as Frances Molloy's *No Mate for the Magpie* and Ken Saro-Wiwa's *Sozaboy*—have first-person narrators. Others, like Roddy Doyle's *The Snapper,* force their readers to negotiate among the competing needs and voices of many strong characters.

The novels excerpted here include honest representations of ugly mindframes—racism, misogyny, violence, and homophobia—that can go along with being part of a marginalized population. Carey shows us how unsettling it is for Ned Kelly to find his tenuous place in a nineteenth-century social hierarchy threatened when he sees "blackfellows" wearing boots: "we was raised to think the blacks the lowest of the low but they had boots not us and we damned and double damned them as we ran." Sapphire's Precious Jones firmly believes that "crack addicts is *disgusting*!" until she learns that her dear friend Rita had been one. Nonetheless, these novels generally maintain a warm and good-hearted tone, ultimately granting their sometimes shortsighted characters a chance to redeem themselves through the telling.

PETER CAREY

PETER CAREY is a versatile and accomplished novelist whose work ranges freely over continents and centuries. Born in 1943 in Bacchus Marsh, Victoria, Australia, Carey worked in advertising in Melbourne, Sydney, and London, and began writing novels and short stories in 1964. Carey's Booker Prize–winning novel *True History of the Kelly Gang* allows the nineteenth-century Australian outlaw Ned Kelly to tell his own story. Realistically, it is a story told on the run, scrawled on any scrap of paper Carey's fictionalized Ned could grab, and narrated in a gorgeous, metaphor-laden Irish Australian lingo whose sentences tumble on breathlessly. This excerpt is taken from the novel's first "parcel" (as opposed to the traditional "chapter"), which describes Ned's early childhood, his family's constant confrontations with the law, and the unjust situation of the Irish in Australia.

From TRUE HISTORY OF THE KELLY GANG

(2001)

I lost my own father at 12 yr. of age and know what it is to be raised on lies and silences my dear daughter you are presently too young to understand a word I write but this history is for you and will contain no single lie may I burn in Hell if I speak false.

God willing I shall live to see you read these words to witness your astonishment and see your dark eyes widen and your jaw drop when you finally comprehend the injustice we poor Irish suffered in this present age. How queer and foreign it must seem to you and all the coarse words and cruelty which I now relate are far away in ancient time.

Your grandfather were a quiet and secret man he had been ripped from his home in Tipperary and transported to the prisons of Van Diemen's Land I do not know what was done to him he never spoke of it. When they had finished with their tortures they set him free and he crossed the sea to the colony of Victoria. He were by this time 30 yr. of age red headed and freckled with his eyes always slitted against the sun. My da had sworn an oath to evermore avoid the attentions of the law so when he saw the streets of Melbourne was crawling with policemen worse than flies he walked 28 mi. to the township of Donnybrook and then or soon thereafter he seen my mother. Ellen Quinn were 18 yr. old she were dark haired and slender the prettiest figure on a horse he ever saw but your grandma was like a snare laid out by God for Red Kelly. She were a Quinn and the police would never leave the Quinns alone.

My 1st memory is of Mother breaking eggs into a bowl and crying that Jimmy Quinn my 15 yr. old uncle were arrested by the traps. I don't know where my daddy were that day nor my older sister Annie. I were 3 yr. old. While my mother cried I scraped the sweet yellow batter onto a spoon and ate it the roof were leaking above the camp oven each drop hissing as it hit.

My mother tipped the cake onto the muslin cloth and knotted it. Your Aunt Maggie were a baby so my mother wrapped her also then she carried both cake and baby out into the rain. I had no choice but follow up the hill how could I forget them puddles the colour of mustard the rain like needles in my eyes.

We arrived at the Beveridge Police Camp drenched to the bone and doubtless stank of poverty a strong odour about us like wet dogs and for this or other reasons we was excluded from the Sergeant's room. I remember sitting with my chilblained hands wedged beneath the door I could feel the lovely warmth of the fire on my fingertips. Yet when we was finally permitted entry all my attention were taken not by the blazing fire but by a huge red jowled creature the Englishman who sat behind the desk. I knew not his name only that he were the most powerful man I ever saw and he might destroy my mother if he so desired.

Approach says he as if he was an altar.

My mother approached and I hurried beside her. She told the Englishman she had baked a cake for his prisoner Quinn and would be most obliged to deliver it because her husband were absent and she had butter to churn and pigs to feed.

No cake shall go to the prisoner said the trap I could smell his foreign spicy smell he had a handlebar moustache and his scalp were shining through his hair.

Said he No cake shall go to the prisoner without me inspecting it 1st and he waved his big soft white hand thus indicating my mother should place her basket on his desk. He untied the muslin his fingernails so clean they looked like they was washed in lye and to this day I can see them livid instruments as they broke my mother's cake apart.

Tis not poverty I hate the most
nor the eternal groveling
but the insults which grow on it
which not even leeches can cure

I will lay a quid that you have already been told the story of how your grandma won her case in court against Bill Frost and then led wild gallops up and down the main street of Benalla. You will know she were never a coward but on this occasion she understood she must hold her tongue and so she wrapped the warm crumbs in the cloth and walked out into the rain. I cried out to her but she did not hear so I followed her skirts across the muddy yard. At 1st I thought it an outhouse on whose door I found her hammering it come as a shock to realise my young uncle were locked inside. For the great offence of duffing a bullock with cancer of the eye he were interred in this earth floored slab hut which could not have measured more than 6 ft. × 6 ft. and here my mother were forced to kneel in the mud and push the broken cake under the door the gap v. narrow perhaps 2 in. not sufficient for the purpose.

She cried God help us Jimmy what did we ever do to them that they should torture us like this?

My mother never wept but weep she did and I rushed and

clung to her and kissed her but still she could not feel that I were there. Tears poured down her handsome face as she forced the muddy mess of cake and muslin underneath the door.

She cried I would kill the b———ds if I were a man God help me. She used many rough expressions I will not write them here. It were eff this and ess that and she would blow their adjectival brains out.

These was frightening sentiments for a boy to hear his mamma speak but I did not know how set she were until 2 nights later when my father returned home and she said the exact same things again to him.

You don't know what you're talking about said he.

You are a coward she cried. I blocked my ears and buried my face into my floursack pillow but she would not give up and neither would my father turn against the law. I wish I had known my parents when they truly loved each other.

RODDY DOYLE

THE IRISH NOVELIST RODDY DOYLE was born in 1959 in Dublin. He graduated from University College Dublin and taught English and geography in North Dublin, where most of his novels are set, before he began writing full-time in 1993. His first three novels, *The Commitments, The Snapper,* and *The Van,* have all been made into movies; collectively known as the Barrytown Trilogy, they treat the lives of the Rabbitte family and their unpredictable working-class circle. Doyle has also written several other novels as well as children's books, plays, a screenplay, a teleplay, and a work of nonfiction. *The Snapper* follows Sharon Rabbitte through the pregnancy that results from a miserable (and secret) drunken encounter with Georgie Burgess, her friend Yvonne's father. These two scenes connect Sharon and her own supportive but often bumbling father Jimmy Sr., as Sharon's interactions with her tight group of friends (Yvonne as well as Jackie and Mary) closely parallel those of Jimmy Sr.'s with his gang (Bimbo, Paddy, and Bertie). In both cases, each relies upon the closest and most reliable friend—Jackie, in Sharon's case, and Bimbo, in Jimmy Sr.'s— to set the tone of the group's reaction. As in Zora Neale Hurston's story "Spunk," a nosy community becomes a significant character in its own right, as the excerpt ends with Sharon imagining the sorts of responses she will indeed face later in the novel.

From THE SNAPPER

(1990)

—How much did it cost yeh, Jackie? Yvonne asked.

She dipped two wetted fingers into her crisp bag and dredged it for crumbs.

—Fifteen pound, ninety-nine, said Jackie.

—Really? said Yvonne. —That's brilliant, isn't it?

—Is it hand wash, Jackie? said Mary.

—Yeah, it is.

—It's very nice now.

—Thanks.

Yvonne wiped her fingers on the stool beside her.

Sharon saw this as she walked over to join them so she parked herself on the stool opposite Yvonne.

—Hiyis, she said.

—Hiyeh, Sharon.

—Ah howyeh, Sharon.

—Hiyis, said Sharon.

—Are they new, Sharon?

—No, not really.

A lounge boy was passing. Sharon stopped him.

—A vodka an' a Coke, please, she said.

—Don't bother abou' the Coke, Sharon, said Jackie. —I've loads here, look it.

—Okay. Thanks, Jackie. A vodka just, she told the lounge boy.

—Anyway, Jackie, said Mary.

The real business of the night was starting.

—Will yeh be seein' Greg again?

—Tha' prick! said Jackie.

They laughed.

Jackie had given Greg the shove the Saturday before—or so she said anyway—in one of those café places in the ILAC Centre, after he'd accused her of robbing the cream out of his chocolate eclair.—An' I paid for the fuckin' thing! she'd told them the night before.

She was in good form tonight as well. She tapped the table with her glass.

—If he was the last man on earth I wouldn't go with him.

She took a fair sip from the glass.

—I'd shag the Elephant Man before I'd let him go near me again, the prick.

They roared.

—Yis should've seen him with that fuckin' eclair. I was so embarrassed, I was scarleh, I'm not jokin' yis, I was burnin'. In his leather jacket an' his fuckin' keys hangin' off his belt, yeh know, givin' the goo goo eyes to a fuckin' eclair. It was pat'etic, it was.

—Were yeh goin' to break it off anyway? Sharon asked her.

—Yeah, said Jackie. —I was thinkin' about it alrigh'. I was givin' the matter, eh, my serious consideration.

They laughed.

—Then when I saw him sulkin'; Jesus!

—He was very good lookin' though, wasn't he? said Yvonne. —Very handsome.

—Not really, said Jackie. —Not when yeh got up close to him. D'yeh know what I mean?

—Beauty is only skin deep, said Mary.

—It wasn't even tha' deep, Mary, Jackie told her. —He had loads o' little spots on his chin. Tiny little ones now. Millions o' them. You only noticed them when you were right up against him, an' then you'd want to throw up. ——There was nothin' under the leather jacket really. That's all he was now that I think of it.

Jackie sighed and took a slug from her glass.

—A leather jacket. ——He was thick as well.

—Come here, Jackie, said Mary. —Was he passionate?

—No, said Jackie. —But he thought he was. Yeh know? He was just a big thick monkey.

—Lookin' for somewhere to stick his banana, wha', said Yvonne.

They screamed.

—Yvonne Burgess!

Sharon wiped her eyes.

—He stuck his tongue in me ear once, Jackie told them when they'd settled down again. —An', I'm not jokin' yis, I think he was tryin' to get it out the other one. I don't know what he fuckin' thought I had in there.

She laughed with them.

—He licked half me brains ou'. Like a big dog, yeh know.

They roared.

Jackie waited.

—His sense o' direction wasn't the best either, d'yis know what I mean?

They roared again.

—Jesus!

—Jackie O'Keefe! You're fuckin' disgustin'!

—Wha'?

More vodkas and Cokes and a gin and a tonic were ordered. And crisps.

Then Sharon told them her bit of news.

—I'm pregnant, did I tell yis?

Mary laughed, but the others didn't. Then Mary stopped.

—Yeah, well, said Sharon. —I am.

—She's fuckin' serious, said Yvonne.

No one said anything for a bit. Sharon couldn't look anywhere. The others looked at one another, their faces held blank. Sharon picked up her glass but she was afraid to put it to her mouth.

Then Jackie spoke.

—Well done, Sharon, she said.

—Thanks, Jackie.

She put the glass down. She was starting to shake. Suddenly she couldn't breathe in enough air to keep her going.

—Yeah, Sharon. Congrats, said Mary.

—Thanks, Mary.

—Well done, Sharon, said Yvonne. —Yeh thick bitch yeh.

Then they all started laughing. They looked at one another and kept laughing. Sharon was delighted. They were all blushing and laughing. The tears were running out of her and the snot would be as well in a minute. She took up her bag from the floor to look for a hankie.

The laughing died down and became fits of the giggles. They all blew their noses and wiped their eyes.

—Jesus though, Sharon, said Jackie, but she was grinning. Sharon reddened again.

—I know, she said. —It's terrible really.

Some questions had to be asked.

First an easy one.

—How long are yeh gone, Sharon? Yvonne asked her.

—Fourteen weeks.

They converted that into months.

—Jesus! Tha' long? said Mary.

They looked at Sharon.

—You don't look it, said Yvonne.

—I do, said Sharon.

—I won't argue with you, said Yvonne. —You're the expert.

They screamed.

—I'm only messin', said Yvonne.

Sharon wiped her eyes.

—I know tha'.

—You look the same, said Mary.

—I'll start gettin' bigger in a few weeks.

—Well, said Jackie, —you can start hangin' round with someone else when tha' happens. No fellas'll come near us if one of us is pregnant.

They laughed.

—Sharon, said Yvonne. —Who're yeh havin' it for?

Your fat da, thought Sharon.

—I can't tell, she said. —Sorry.

She looked at her drink. She could feel herself going red again.

—Ah, Sharon!

She grinned and shook her head.

—Meany, said Jackie.

Sharon grinned.

—Give us a hint.

—No.

—Just a little one.

Nothing.

—Do we know him?

—No, said Sharon.

—Ah Sharon, go on. Tell us.

—No.

—We won't tell annyone.

—Leave Sharon alone, said Jackie. —It's none o' your fuckin' business. Is he married, Sharon?

—Oh Jesus! Said Mary.

—No, said Sharon.

She laughed.

—You're scarleh. He must be.

—He's not. I swear. He's not—

—Are yeh gettin' married? Mary asked.

—No. I mean—I mean I don't want to marry him.

—Are yeh sure we don't know him?

—Yeah.

—Is he in here?

—Jesus, said Jackie. —If we don't know him he isn't here. An' anyway, would you do it with annyone here?

—I was only fuckin' askin', said Yvonne.

She looked around. The lounge was fairly full.

—You're righ' though, she said. —It was a stupid question. Sorry for insultin' yeh, Sharon.

—That's okay.

—Serious though, Sharon, said Mary. —Do we really not know him?

—No. I swear to God.

—I believe yeh, thousands wouldn't, said Yvonne.

—Where did yeh meet him?

—Ah look, said Sharon. —I don't want to talk about it annymore; righ'?

—Let's get pissed, will we? said Jackie.

—Ah yeah, said Sharon.

—Hey! Jackie roared at the lounge boy. —Get your body over here.

They laughed.

The lounge boy was sixteen and looked younger.

—Three vodkas an' two Cokes an' a gin an' tonic, said Jackie. —Got tha'?

—Yeah, said the lounge boy.

—An' a package o' crisps, said Yvonne.

—Ah yeah, said Sharon. —Two packs.

—Do yeh have anny nuts? Mary asked him.

—Jesus, Mary, yeh dirty bitch yeh!

They screamed.

—I didn't mean it tha' way, said Mary.

The very red lounge boy backed off and headed for the bar. Yvonne shouted after him.

—Come back soon, chicken.

—Leave him alone or he'll never come back, said Jackie.

—Who's goin' to sub me till Thursday? said Yvonne.

—Me, said Sharon. —I will. A tenner?

—Lovely.

—He'll be nice when he's older, won't he? said Mary.

—Who? The lounge boy?

Jackie looked over at him.

—He's a bit miserable lookin'.

—He's a nice little arse on him all the same, said Yvonne.

—Pity there's a dickie bow under it, said Jackie.

They stopped looking at the lounge boy.

—Annyway, Sharon, said Jackie. —What's it like? Are yeh pukin' up in the mornin's?

—No, said Sharon. —Well, yeah. Only a couple o' times. It's not tha' bad.

—I'd hate tha'.

—Yeah. It's bad enough havin' to get up without knowin you're goin' to be vomitin' your guts up as well.

—It's not tha' bad, said Sharon.

—Are you goin' to give up work? Mary asked her.

—I don't know, said Sharon. —I haven't thought about it really. I might.

—It's nice for some, said Yvonne. —Havin' a job to think abou' givin' it up.

—Ah, stop whingin', said Jackie.

—I wasn't whingin'.

—Would you really like to be doin' wha' Sharon does, would yeh? Stackin' shelves an' tha'?

—No.

—Then fuck off an' leave her alone.

—Are you havin' your periods or somethin'?

—Yeah, I am actually. Wha' about it?

—You're stainin' the carpet.

The row was over. They nearly got sick laughing. The lounge boy was coming back.

—Here's your bit o' fluff, Mary, said Sharon.

—Ah stop.

—Howyeh, Gorgeous, said Jackie. —Did yeh make your holy communion yet?

The lounge boy tried to get everything off the tray all at once so he could get the fuck out of that corner.

He said nothing.

—Wha' size do yeh take? Yvonne asked him.

The lounge boy legged it. He left too much change on the table and a puddle where he'd spilt the Coke. Mary threw a beer-mat on top of it.

—Jesus, Sharon, said Jackie. —I thought you were goin' to have a miscarriage there you were laughin' so much.

—I couldn't help it. —Wha' size d'yeh take.

They started again.

—I meant his shirt, said Yvonne.

They giggled, and wiped their eyes and noses and poured the Coke and tonic on top of the vodka and gin.

—Are yeh eatin' annythin' weirdy? Mary asked Sharon.

—No, said Sharon.

—Debbie ate coal, Jackie told them.

—Jesus!

—I wouldn't eat fuckin' coal, said Sharon.

—How d'you eat coal? Mary asked.

—I don't know! said Jackie. —The dust, I suppose.

—My cousin, Miriam. Yeh know her, with the roundy glasses? She ate sardines an' Mars Bars all squashed together.

—Yeuhh! Jesus!

—Jesus!

—That's disgustin'.

—Was she pregnant? said Jackie.

—Of course she——Fuck off, you.

They all attacked their drinks.

—He won't come back, said Jackie. —We'll have to go up ourselves.

—Come here, Sharon, said Yvonne. —Was it Dessie Delaney?

—No!

—I was on'y askin'.

—Well, don't, said Sharon. —I'm not tellin', so fuck off.

—Was it Billy Delaney then?

Sharon grinned, and they laughed.

Sharon put her bag under her arm.

—Are yeh comin', Jackie?

—The tylet?

—Yeah.

—Okay.

Jackie got her bag from under the table. They stood up. Sharon looked down at Yvonne and Mary.

—Me uterus is pressin' into me bladder, she told them.

—Oh Jesus!

They roared.

—Annyway, said Bimbo. —I gave him his fiver an' I said, Now shag off an' leave me alone.

—A fiver! said Paddy. —I know wha' I'd've given the cunt.

—I owed him it but.

—So wha'? said Paddy. —Tha' doesn't mean he can come up to yeh outside o' mass when you're with your mot an' your kids an' ask yeh for it.

—The kids weren't with us. Just Maggie an' her mother.

—Jimmy!

—Wha'? said Jimmy Sr from the bar.

—Stick on another one, said Paddy. —Bertie's here.

Bertie saluted those looking his way and then sat down at the table with Paddy and Bimbo.

—There y'are, Bertie, said Bimbo.

—Buenas noches, compadre, said Bertie.

—How's business, Bertie? said Paddy.

—Swings an' roundabouts, said Bertie. —Tha' sort o' way, yeh know.

—Tha' seems to be the story everywhere, said Bimbo. —Doesn't it?

—Are you goin' to nigh' classes or somethin'? said Paddy.

Bertie laughed.

—Ah fuck off, you now, said Bimbo. —Every time I open me mouth yeh jump down it.

—There's plenty o' room in there annyway, said Bertie, —wha'.

They heard Jimmy Sr.

—D'yis want ice in your pints?

He put two pints of Guinness down on the table, in front of Paddy and Bimbo. There was a little cocktail umbrella standing up in the head of Bimbo's pint.

Jimmy Sr came back with the other two pints.

—How's Bertie?

—Ah sure.

—It's the same everywhere, isn't it? said Paddy.

Bertie sniggered.

Bimbo was spinning the umbrella.

—Mary Poppins, said Jimmy Sr.

—Who? said Bimbo. —Oh yeah.

He held the umbrella up in the air and sang.

—THE HILLS ARE A—

Paddy squirmed, and looked around.

—LIVE WITH THE SOUND O' —no, that's wrong. That's not Mary Poppins.

—It was very good, all the same, said Jimmy Sr.

—It fuckin' was, alrigh', Bertie agreed. —Yeh even looked like her there for a minute.

Bimbo stuck his front teeth out over his bottom lip, and screeched.

—JUST A SPOONFUL OF SHUGEH—

HELPS THE MEDICINE——GO DOWN—

THE MEDICINE——GO DOW—

            WOWN—

THE MEDICINE——GO DOWN—

—Are yeh finished? said Paddy.

—Do your Michael O'Hehir, said Jimmy Sr.

—Ah, for fuck sake, said Paddy. —Not again. All o' them horses are fuckin' dead.

—Weuahh!

That was Bertie.

—Jesus!——fuck!

He gasped. His mouth was wide open. He shook his face. He was holding his pint away from his mouth like a baby trying to get away from a full spoon.

He pointed the pint at Jimmy Sr.

—Taste tha'.

—I will in me hole taste it. What's wrong with it?

—Nothin', said Bertie.

And he knocked back a bit less than half of it.

—Aah, he said when he came up for air. —Mucho good.

Bimbo put the umbrella into his breast pocket.

—Wha' d'yeh want tha' for? said Paddy.

—Jessica, said Bimbo. —She collects them. Maggie brings all hers home to her.

Paddy looked across to Jimmy Sr and Bertie for support. Jimmy Sr grinned and touched his forehead.

—Oh yeah, said Bertie.

He'd remembered something. He picked the bag he'd brought in with him off the floor and put it on his lap.

—You don't follow Liverpool, said Paddy.

—It's Trevor's, said Bertie. —I had to take all his bukes an' copies ou' of it cos I'd nothin' else. There was a lunch in the bottom of it an', fuckin' hell. Did yis ever see blue an' green bread, did yis?

—Ah fuck off, will yeh.

—The fuckin' meat. Good Christ. It stuck its head ou' from between the bread an' it said, Are The Tremeloes still Number One?

He put his face to the opening and sniffed.

—Yeh can still smell it. The lazy little bastard. Annyway,

Jimmy, he said. —Compadre mio. How many bambinos have yeh got that are goin' to school.

—Eh——three. Why?

Bertie took three Casio pocket calculators in their boxes out of the bag.

—Uno, dos, tres. There you are, my friend. For your bambinos so tha' they'll all do well for themselves an' become doctors.

—Are yeh serious? said Jimmy Sr.

He picked up one of the calculators and turned it round.

—Si, said Bertie.

He explained.

—There's a bit of a glut in the calculator market, yeh know. I took three gross o' them from a gringo tha' we all know an' think he's a fuckin' eejit—

—An' whose wife does bicycle impressions when he isn't lookin'?

—That's him, said Bertie. —I gave him fuck all for them. I was laughin' before I'd the door shut on the cunt, yeh know. Only now I can't get rid o' the fuckin' things. No one wants them. I even tried a few o' the shops. Which was stupid. But they were gettin' on me wick. I can't live with failure, yeh know. So I'm givin' them away. Righ', Bimbo. How many do you need?

—Five, said Bimbo.

—Five!?

—He only has four, said Jimmy Sr. —He wants one for himself.

Bimbo held up his left hand. He pointed to his little finger.

—Glenn.

He moved on to the next finger.

—Wayne.

The middle one.

—Jessica.

—Okay okay, said Bertie. —There'll be six by the time you've finished.

He dealt the boxes out to Bimbo.

—Uno, dos, tres, four, five.

—Thanks very much, Bertie.

—No problem, said Bertie. —See if yeh can get them to lose them, so I can give yeh more. I still have two gross in intervention. A fuckin' calculator mountain. ——Cal-cul-ators! We don't need your steenking cal-cul-ators! I speet on your cal-cul-ators!——Paddy?

—Wha'?

—How many?

—I don't want your charity.

Bertie, Jimmy Sr and Bimbo laughed. Paddy was serious, but that made it funnier.

—None o' those kids he has at home are his annyway, said Jimmy Sr.

The stout in Bimbo's throat rushed back into his mouth and bashed against his teeth.

—My round, compadres, said Bertie.

He stood up.

—Three pints, isn't that it? he said.

They looked up at him.

—Do yeh want me charity, Paddy, or will yeh stay on your own?

—Fuck off.

—Four pints, said Bertie.

Jimmy Sr and Bimbo laughed and grinned at each other. Paddy spoke.

—Fuck yis.

Bertie took two more calculators out of the bag.

—For my amigos, the barmen.

When he got back from the bar Bimbo had one of the calculators out of its wrapper.

—The round costs five pound, forty-four, he told them.

—Go 'way! said Jimmy Sr.

—That's very fuckin' dear all the same, isn't it? said Bimbo.

—It was just as dear before yeh got the calculator, said Bertie.

—I know, I know tha'. It's just when yeh see it like tha' in black an', eh, silvery grey it makes it look worse. ——I think annyway.

—My Jaysis, said Paddy.

He looked at Bertie.

—Fuckin' hell, said Bimbo. —If there was six of us the round'd cost—

—Put it away, Bimbo, for fuck sake, said Jimmy Sr.

—I've got two kids in school, Paddy told Bertie.

—Is tha' right'? said Bertie.

—Yeah.

—Well, I hope they're good at their sums, said Bertie. —Cos they're not gettin' anny calculators.

—Young Sharon's after getting' herself up the pole, Jimmy Sr told them.

He rubbed his hands and picked up his pint.

—Is tha' YOUR Sharon, like? said Bimbo.

—That's righ', said Jimmy Sr. —Gas, isn't it?

—One calculator for Sharon, said Bertie, and he passed one across to Jimmy Sr, and then another one. —And one for the bambino. A good start in life.

—She's not married, said Bimbo.

—I know tha'! said Jimmy Sr.

—Is tha' the tall girl tha' hangs around with Georgie Burgess's young one? Paddy asked.

—That's righ', said Jimmy Sr.

—Is she gettin' married? said Bimbo.

—No, said Jimmy Sr. —Why should she? They've more cop-on these days. Would you get married if you were tha' age again these days?

—I think I'm goin' to cry, said Bertie.

—I'd say I would, yeah, said Bimbo.

—What're yeh askin' him for, for fuck sake? said Paddy.

—He brings home little umbrellas for his kids. He goes to meetin's. He brought his mot to the flicks last week.

—Only cos her sister's in hospital, said Bimbo. —She usually goes with her sister, he told Jimmy Sr. —The Livin' Daylights, we went to. The James Bond one.

—Is it anny good?

—Ah it is, yeah. It's good alrigh'. ——There's a lovely lookin' bird in it. Lovely.

—Oh, I've seen her, said Bertie.

—Isn't she lovely?

—Oh si. Si. A little ride.

—Ah no. She's not. She's the sort o' bird, said Bimbo, —that yeh wouldn't really want to ride. D'yeh know wha' I mean?

—No.

Paddy shook his head and looked at Bertie, and grinned.

—Is she a cripple or somethin'?

—No! said Bimbo. —No.——She's TOO nice, yeh know?

—You'd give her little umbrellas, would yeh?

—Fuck off, you, said Bimbo.

Bertie put a calculator in front of Bimbo.

—Give her tha' the next time yeh see her.

—Who did the damage? Paddy asked Jimmy Sr.

—We don't know, to tell yeh the truth, said Jimmy Sr. —She won't tell us.

—Well, you'd want to fuckin' find ou', said Paddy.

—What's it you who it is? said Bimbo.

—I couldn't give a fuck who it is, said Paddy. —It's Jimmy. I'm not goin' to be buyin' food for it, an' nappies an' little fuckin' tracksuits. Jimmy is.

—I am in me hole, said Jimmy Sr. —Hang on though. Maybe I will be.

He thought about it.

—So wha' though. I don't care.

—Good man, said Bimbo.

—An' she'll have her allowance, said Bertie.

—Will she? said Jimmy Sr. —I don't know. I s'pose she will. I don't care.

—Of course yeh don't, said Bimbo. —Such a thing to be worryin' abou'! Who's goin' to pay for it!

—Will yeh listen to him, said Paddy. —The singin' fuckin' nun.

—Fuck off.

—I believe Gerry Foster's young fella's after puttin' some young one from Coolock up the stick, Bertie told them.

—Wha'? said Jimmy Sr. —Jimmy's pal? What's this they call him? Outspan.

—Yeah. Him.

Jimmy Sr laughed.

—I'd say tha' made his hair go curly.

—Is he marryin' her? Bimbo asked.

—Yes indeed, said Bertie. —A posse came down from Coolock. Mucho tough hombres. They hijacked the 17A. Take us to Barrytown, signor.

They laughed.

—I believe the poor fucker's walkin' around with half an 8 iron stuck up his arse.

—Where's he goin' to be livin'?

They knew the answer they wanted to hear.

—Coolock, said Bertie.

—There's no need for all tha' fuss, said Jimmy Sr, when they'd stopped laughing. —Sure there's not?

—Not at all, said Bimbo. —It's stupid.

Bertie agreed.

—Thick, he said.

—It's only a baby, said Bimbo. —A snapper.

—Doctor Kildare, Bertie said to Paddy.

—That's it, said Paddy.

—Fuck off, youse, said Bimbo.

—I wouldn't want Sharon gettin' married tha' young, said Jimmy Sr.

—She's her whole life ahead of her, said Bimbo.

—Unless she drinks an iffy pint, said Bertie.

—Annyway, said Jimmy Sr.

He lifted his glass.

—To Sharon, wha'.

—Oh yeah. Def'ny. Sharon.

Bertie picked up his pint.

—To the Signorita Rabbeete that is havin' the bambino out of wedlock, fair play to her.

He gave Jimmy Sr another calculator.

—In case it's twins.

—Stop, for fuck sake.

Bimbo filled his mouth, swallowed, filled it again, swallowed and put his glass back on its mat.

—Havin' a baby's the most natural thing in the world, he said.

Jimmy Sr loved Bimbo.

—D'you know wha' Sharon is, Jimmy? said Bimbo.

——Wha'?

—She's a modern girl.

—Oh good fuck, said Paddy.

Sharon was lying in bed.

Well, they knew now. They'd been great. It'd been great.

She was a bit pissed. But not too bad. She shut her eyes, and the bed stayed where it was.

She'd never laughed as much in her life. And when Yvonne had pinched the lounge boy's bum, the look on his face. And Jackie's joke about the girl in the wheelchair at the disco. It'd been brilliant.

Then, near closing time, they'd all started crying. And that had been even better. She didn't know how it had started. Outside, they'd hugged one another and said all sorts of stupid, corny things but it had been great. Mary said that the baby would have four mothers. If she'd said it any other time Sharon would have told her to cop on to herself but outside the car-park it had sounded lovely.

Then they'd gone for chips. And Jackie asked the poor oul' one that put the stuff in the bags how she kept her skin so smooth.

Sharon laughed—

Soon everyone would know. Good. She could nearly hear them.

—Sharon Rabbitte's pregnant, did yeh hear?

—Your one, Sharon Rabbitte's up the pole.

—Sharon Rabbitte's havin' a baby.

—I don't believe yeh!

—Jaysis.

—Jesus! Are yeh serious?

—Who's she havin' it for?

—I don't know.

—She won't say.

—She doesn't know.

—She can't remember.

—Oh God, poor Sharon.

—That's shockin'.

—Mm.

—Dirty bitch.

—Poor Sharon.

—The slut.

—I don't believe her.

—The stupid bitch.

—She had tha' comin'.

—Serves her righ'.

—Poor Sharon.

—Let's see her gettin' into those jeans now.

Sharon giggled.

Fuck them. Fuck all of them. She didn't care. The girls had been great.

Mister Burgess would know by tomorrow as well. He probably knew now. He might have been up when Yvonne got home.

——Fuck him too. She wasn't going to start worrying about that creep.

She couldn't help it though.

THE CONTROVERSIAL and accomplished New Zealand novelist Alan Duff was born in 1950 in Rotorua. He ran away from home at a young age, served time as a teenager for a number of petty offenses, and began writing full-time in 1985. *Once Were Warriors* is his best-known work, largely due to its 1994 film adaptation. Duff has also written several novels (including two more about *Warriors* antihero Jake Heke), a memoir, and a polemical work on what he sees as the failures of Maori leadership. Showing a dramatically different side of Maori life from Patricia Grace's hopeful short story, *Warriors* depicts a family falling apart in Wellington's miserable urban fringe. Beth and Jake Heke and their children count, in Beth's own estimation, among "the going-nowhere nobodies who populate this state-owned, half of us state-fed, slum." In this excerpt, a family outing becomes an opportunity for Jake to ruminate bitterly on the legacy of slavery within the Maori community. Jake remembers his childhood as marked by fissures of class and race, of "having to cop the shit from having been descended from this weakling arsehole of an ancestor." The novel's action is filtered through the consciousness of alternating characters; here, Beth's parenthetical observations punctuate Jake's acerbic monologue.

From ONCE WERE WARRIORS

(1990)

Hey kids. Know what I inherited as a Maori? Jake asking out of the blue, as sheep and cattle countryside sped by on one side, the lake in bits between trees the other. A freshly lit fag in his big left mit. Slaves. (Oh?) Taking the big motor around a hard bend as casual as could be, right driving elbow out the window, big fingertips just controlling the wheel, and a wife thinking her husband, for all these years of being carless, could sure drive. Wonder he'd even had a licence when she went to hire the car, but he did and it was up to date. My family were slaves. Beth waited for the joke. Aw, Dad. It's true. What you mean, slaves? Slaves. Like I said, kids; slaves. Ya haven't hearda slaves? And everyone gone quiet. My branch of the Heke line was descended from a slave. A fulla taken prisoner by the enemy when he shoulda—he *woulda*—been better off dyin. In the fight. Beth hearing the rustle of the kids coming forward in their seat.

Yep. Slave he was, this ancestor of mine. And Beth getting worried by Jake's tone.

When I was a kid—me and my brothers and sisters—we weren't allowed to play with many other families in our pa. No way, not the Hekes, man. Don't play with them, you'll get the slave disease. Thas what they used to say. Jake drawing on his fag, inhaling deeply, blowing out a jet stream of smoke.

And Beth in total confusion, wonderment: I ain't ever
heardim mention this before. See, kids, to be a warrior and
get captured in battle was the pits. Just the pits, eh. Better to
die. So us Hekes—*innocent*—having to cop the shit from
being descended from this weakling arsehole of an ancestor.
Jeez . . . Shaking his head, and everyone able to hear his teeth
grating together. Five hundred years, that's what they used to
tell us Heke kids. Five hundred years of the slave curse bein on
our heads. Teeth clacking together, jaw muscles pulsing out
and in. (You never *told* me, Jake. You never told me . . .) As for
the kids related to the chief: if we went within a hundred
fuckin yards ofem they'd be throwin stones, yelling and
screaming at us to get away, go home, you Hekes're juss a
packa fuckin slaves. Ooooo! Jake letting out a kind of growl yet
sounding half like a moan. (Of hurt, my husband? Oh, poor
Jake. I never dreamed . . .) Bullying us. Picking on us. Hitting
us. Beating us up—Dad! No! Abe in outburst. How *come*? How
come what, son? How come you got beaten by them? Only
when I was little, boy. Jake chuckling grimly. Not when I got to
about your age. No fuckin way. Eh son? No fu—no way, Dad.
And Beth telling Abe, Lucky for you, boy. And Jake going, Aw,
Mum. It's only a word. We all use it. Even the Maori's got it in
his language: whaka—whatever. It comes natural to us. Maybe
so, Jake Heke, but I ain't having it come natural to no kid a
mine till they're old enough. And that's final. Poll saying, Dad,
but you're not a slave now eh? Nah, girl. Do I look like one?
And the three of them: No way! Their laughter with an edge.
(Poor little fuckers: only defending their father, the family
name. And who blames them? Oh, but I wish a man'd told me;
mighta been able to, you know, help in some way. Or at least
understand him better. Oh but maybe he's tricking us.)
Though a look at Jake told Beth no such thing.

So that's *your* family history on your father's side, kids. So Beth informing them all: Slaves, kids. Us Maoris used to practise slavery just like them poor Negroes had to endure in America. Surprised at the passion, the emotion in her voice. Yet to read the newspapers, on the TV every damn day, you'd think we're descended from a packa angels, and it's the Pakeha who's the devil. Clicking her tongue: Just shows, we're all good, and we're all bad. Thinking, Slaves . . . (How dare they bring my husband up believing he was a slave.)

Then it felt like an electric shock had hit her. It went racing up her arm from her fingers, into her tummy (where all my little ones got carried, seeded by this man, *my* man) and tears just sprang from her eyes. At Jake's fingers warm on hers.

JONATHAN SAFRAN FOER

AMERICAN NOVELIST JONATHAN SAFRAN FOER was born in 1977 in Washington, D.C. After attending Princeton University he took a post-undergraduate "roots" trip to Ukraine, which inspired his best-selling 2002 novel *Everything is Illuminated*. This excerpt from the opening chapter of the fanciful and affecting novel introduces the unforgettable sidekick Alexander Perchov and his overeducated, anti-idiomatic Ukrainian English.

From **EVERYTHING IS ILLUMINATED**

(2002)

An Overture to the Commencement of a Very Rigid Journey

My legal name is Alexander Perchov. But all of my many friends dub me Alex, because that is a more flaccid-to-utter version of my legal name. Mother dubs me Alexi-stop-spleening-me!, because I am always spleening her. If you want to know why I am always spleening her, it is because I am always elsewhere with friends, and disseminating so much currency, and performing so many things that can spleen a mother. Father used to dub me Shapka, for the fur hat I would don even in the summer month. He ceased dubbing me that because I ordered him to cease dubbing me that. It sounded boyish to me, and I have always thought of myself as very potent and generative. I have many many girls, believe me, and they all have a different name for me. One dubs me Baby, not because I am a baby, but because she attends to me. Another dubs me All Night. Do you want to know why? I have a girl who dubs me Currency, because I disseminate so much currency around her. She licks my chops for it. I have a miniature brother who dubs me Alli. I do not dig this name very much, but I dig him very much, so OK, I permit him to dub me Alli. As for his name, it is Little Igor, but Father dubs him Clumsy One, because he is always promenading into things. It was only four days previous that he made his eye blue from a mismanagement with a brick wall. If you're wondering what my bitch's name is, it is Sammy Davis, Junior, Junior. She has this name because Sammy Davis, Junior was Grandfather's beloved singer, and the bitch is his, not mine, because I am not the one who thinks he is blind.

As for me, I was sired in 1977, the same year as the hero of this story. In truth, my life has been very ordinary. As I mentioned before, I do many good things with myself and others, but they are ordinary things. I dig American movies. I dig Negroes, particularly Michael Jackson. I dig to disseminate very much currency at famous nightclubs in Odessa. Lamborghini Countaches are excellent, and so are cappuccinos. Many girls want to be carnal with me in many good arrangements, notwithstanding the Inebriated Kangaroo, the Gorky Tickle, and the Unyielding Zookeeper. If you want to know why so many girls want to be with me, it is because I am a very premium person to be with. I am homely, and also severely funny, and these are winning things. But nonetheless, I know many people who dig rapid cars and famous discotheques. There are so many who perform the Sputnik Bosom Dalliance—which is always terminated with a slimy underface—that I cannot tally them on all of my hands. There are even many people named Alex. (Three in my house alone!) That is why I was so effervescent to go to Lutsk and translate for Jonathan Safran Foer. It would be unordinary.

I had performed recklessly well in my second year of English at university. This was a very majestic thing I did because my instructor was having shit between his brains. Mother was so proud of me, she said, "Alexi-stop-spleening-me! You have made me so proud of you." I inquired her to purchase me leather pants, but she said no. "Shorts?" "No." Father was also so proud. He said, "Shapka," and I said, "Do not dub me that," and he said, "Alex, you have made Mother so proud."

Mother is a humble woman. Very, very humble. She toils at a small cafe one hour distance from our home. She presents food and drink to customers there, and says to me, "I mount the autobus for an hour to work all day doing things I hate. You want to know why? It is for you, Alexi-stop-spleening-me! One day you will do things for me that you hate. That is what it means to be a family." What she does not clutch is that I already do things for her that I hate. I listen to her when she talks to me. I resist complaining about my pygmy allowance. And did I mention that I do not spleen her nearly so much as I desire to? But I do not do these things because we are a family. I do them because they are common decencies. That is an idiom that the hero taught me. I do them because I am not a big fucking asshole. That is another idiom that the hero taught me.

Father toils for a travel agency, denominated Heritage Touring. It is for Jewish people, like the hero, who have cravings to leave that ennobled country America and visit humble towns in Poland and Ukraine. Father's agency scores a translator, guide, and driver for the Jews, who try to unearth places where their families once existed. OK, I had never met a Jewish person until the voyage. But this was their fault, not mine, as I had always been willing, and one might even write lukewarm, to meet one. I will be truthful again and mention that before the voyage I had the opinion that Jewish people were having shit between their brains. This is because all I knew of Jewish people was that they paid Father very much currency in order to make vacations from America to Ukraine. But then I met Jonathan Safran Foer, and I will tell you, he is not having shit between his brains. He is an ingenious Jew.

So as for the Clumsy One, who I never ever dub the Clumsy One but always Little Igor, he is a first-rate boy. It is now evident to me that he will become a very potent and generative man, and that his brain will have many muscles. We do not speak in volumes, because he is such a silent person, but I am certain that we are friends, and I do not think I would be lying if I wrote that we are paramount friends. I have tutored Little Igor to be a man of this world. For an example, I exhibited him a smutty magazine three days yore, so that he should be appraised of the many positions in which I am carnal. "This is the sixty-nine," I told him, presenting the magazine in front of him. I put my fingers—two of them—on the action, so that he would not overlook it. "Why is it dubbed sixty-nine?" he asked, because he is a person hot on fire with curiosity. "It was invented in 1969. My friend Gregory knows a friend of the nephew of the inventor." "What did people do before 1969?" "Merely blowjobs and masticating box, but never in chorus." He will be made a VIP if I have a thing to do with it.

This is where the story begins.

But first I am burdened to recite my good appearance. I am unequivocally tall. I do not know any women who are taller than me. The women I know who are taller than me are lesbians, for whom 1969 was a very momentous year. I have handsome hairs, which are split in the middle. This is because Mother used to split them on the side when I was a boy, and to spleen her I split them in the middle. "Alexi-stop-spleening-me!," she said, "you appear mentally unbalanced with your hairs split like that." She did not intend it, I know. Very often Mother utters things that I know she does not intend. I have an aristocratic smile and like to punch people. My stomach is very strong, although it presently lacks muscles. Father is a fat man, and Mother is also. This does not disquiet me, because my stomach is very strong, even if it appears very fat. I will describe my eyes and then begin the story. My eyes are blue and resplendent. Now I will begin the story.

UZODINMA IWEALA

UZODINMA IWEALA astonished readers and critics with his compact but powerfully resonant 2005 novel *Beasts of No Nation.* Iweala was born in 1982 in Washington, D.C., and grew up there and in Lagos, Nigeria. He began writing *Beasts,* the first-person story of a child combatant, as his undergraduate thesis at Harvard University. As Iweala explains it, "This person might have been in Uganda and this person might have been in Sierra Leone, and this person might have been in Sri Lanka, and this person might have been in Cambodia, but I'm trying to put all of these experiences into one character." This chapter shows Iweala's narrator Agu attempting to reconcile his sense of morality with the atrocities he has been forced to commit. Agu delves into sweet early memories of home, school, and church, "but these thing are before the war and I am only remembering them like dream." Like many others in *Beasts of No Nation,* this beautifully constructed chapter returns elegantly to its agonized opening.

From **BEASTS OF NO NATION**

(2005)

I am not bad boy. I am not bad boy. I am soldier and soldier is not bad if he is killing. I am telling this to myself because soldier is supposed to be killing, killing, killing. So if I am killing, then I am only doing what is right. I am singing song to myself because I am hearing too many voice in my head telling me I am bad boy. They are coming from all around me and buzzing in my ear like mosquito and each time I am hearing them, they are chooking my heart and making my stomach to turn. So I am singing,

Soldier Soldier
Kill Kill Kill.
That is how you live.
That is how you die.

This is my song that I am singing all of the time wherever we are going to be reminding myself that I am only doing what soldier is supposed to be doing. But it is never working because I am always feeling like bad boy. So I am thinking, how can I be bad boy? Me, bad boy—somebody who is having life like I am having and fearing God the whole time.

I am learning how to read very early in my life from my mother and my father. When I am very small, before even my sister is born, I am always sitting with my mother on the floor of the kitchen and watching her washing all the plate. In the evening, I am always sitting on the floor just watching her with her buttom sticking high into the air and her breast touching her knee while she is working to make the kitchen so clean that not even fruit fly is wanting to put its egg inside.

I am liking to read so much that my mother is calling me professor. I am pulling her dress and she is saying to me, two more minute professor. Only two more minute. Then she is locking the door and holding my hand as we are walking to the main house. Inside, my father is always just sleeping sleeping or listening to his radio, so we would be moving quietly, getting the matches from the wood table in the middle of the room and lighting the lamp just in case they are taking the light. All of this is making me to agitate because it is taking so long until finally she is coming to the bookshelf and pretending to search for just the right book. The shelf was having many book of different size and different color—some red, some yellow, some blue, and some brown—but the one I am always wanting her to pick, the only one that I am wanting to hear is the one that is holding all of the other book up, the big white Bible. I was so small and the book was so big that I am almost not even able to be carrying it. But I was enjoying how the cover is so soft, and how the letter saying HOLY BIBLE was made of gold. This was my favorite book because of how it is looking and because of all the story inside of it. Whenever my mother is touching it, I am shouting, that one, that one and she is saying, shhh don't be so loud or you will be waking your father. I was always sitting in her laps on our favorite chair and we are staring at the small small letter on the page. She was reading over my shoulder and I am feeling her lip moving in my ear as she was saying each word. My mother is reading very very slowly because she is not schoolteacher like my father who is knowing too much about book. She is not going to school for long enough like my father, but she was always saying, I am knowing enough to read the only book that is mattering. This is why Pastor is liking her so much.

She is reading to me about how Cain is killing his brother Abel, and how God is visiting Abraham, and about Jonah living in the fish. She was also reading about how God is making Job to suffer very much, but how He is rewarding him at the end, and how David is killing Goliath. Each time she is reading this story I would be thinking in my head that I am standing here looking at how all the army is shining with gold and bronze in the sun and how Goliath is laughing until David is cutting off his head. I am seeing all of these thing when she is reading and thinking that I am wanting to be warrior. And all the time my mother is reading I am pointing to each word and asking what is that what is that so she can be telling me and I can be learning. We were doing this every evening until my mother is saying, okay Agu it is enough now. My eye is tired.

When my mother is not there, I was going to the shelf to be reading The Bible myself. My mother was still reading to me every night, but I was also able to be reading by myself, and soon, when my father was coming back from work to be sitting in his short and singlet listening to the radio in his favorite chair, I was sitting with him and not my mother and I would be reading to him what I am teaching myself from The Bible. I was wanting to show him that I am big enough to be going to school so I can be learning everything that he is knowing that is making everybody in the village to like him so much. I was always asking him every day, tomorrow can I be going to school? Tomorrow can I go to school, and he was always saying to me, just wait just wait. Enh. Agu! Why are you wanting to grow so big so fast? Then I would be going to my mother to be begging her to help me go to school. I was wanting to go so much that each time I would be crying to her to make my father take me to school and she is saying to me that if I am crying like this, then at school they will just be laughing at me. So, when my father is coming home, I was first asking him how is his own school that he is teaching and then I was asking him if I am big enough and he was telling me to take my right hand and put it over my head to touch my left ear, but I was too small to be doing that so he was telling me, Agu you are not ready yet.

Until one day, I am running to my father and saying, look, and then taking my hand over my head and touching my ear. He is smiling and saying, okay, and then the next day we are going to the primary school where everybody is wearing uniform that is red short and white shirt if you are boy and red skirt and white shirt if you are girl. I was looking at all of them holding one red notebook and Biro in their hand and standing in line not making any noise. The boys were all having head shaved and the girls were all having plaits so that everybody is looking the same. I wanted to be wearing uniform and carrying red notebook and Biro too much so I was just standing there agitating.

My father was taking me to Mistress Gloria who is the head teacher and asking her if I can be going to school, but she was asking, this one? Isn't he too small? And I was looking at how Mistress Gloria is having very fat belly and big cheek and I wanted to be saying, I am only too small because you are so big, but my father is saying, no. He is not small and Mistress Gloria is having to take me in.

Because my father was schoolteacher and my mother is always reading to me from The Bible, I was already reading when the other children are just trying to learn. I was the smartest person in my class, so smart that the only thing I am having to learn is writing. Mrs. Gloria was seeing how smart I am and she is moving me up with the other people in primary one so I was just sitting on a bench with people bigger than me. When all of the other student are having their leg touch the ground while they are sitting, my own was just swinging back and forward in the air.

The school is just one big building with blackboard at the front of the classroom. This is where Mistress Gloria is standing when she is teaching lesson. All of the class are having their lesson in this one room so that Mistress Gloria was teaching every class up to primary six. She was always holding one large wooden ruler that she would be using to hit you on the head if you are not behaving well. Sometimes during the day we are having quiet time where the younger people is having to put their head down on their desk and all the older one is having to copy their lesson in their notebook. I am always doing my lesson at home so during quiet time I am sitting and thinking about different thing. I always liked thinking about everything that I am reading in book until it is time to play. Even though I am learning with the older children, I am always playing with all my mates. I am having one very good friend who is having Engineer for father so they are some of the rich people in the village. My friend's name was Dike. He was tall past me even if we are the same age, but he was still my best friend.

But these thing are before the war and I am only remembering them like dream. I am seeing my school and all of my friend. I am seeing Mistress Gloria and her curly black wig of hairs that she was always shifting around because it is not staying on her head well well. Some people were hating Mistress Gloria and always making fun of her by pushing out their belly big and walking around like fat goat, but I am liking Mistress

Gloria and she was liking me. She was always saying to me softly when I was leaving the classroom after helping her to clean up, Agu make sure you study book enh? If you are studying hard you can be going to the university to be Doctor or Engineer.

All of this thing that she was always telling me are making me to happying because I was seeing how the Doctor and the Engineer is being treated. I was putting all this thing in my head and remembering them but not letting them be taking up too much of my time as I am young. So after talking with her like this each day, I was then going to play with all my friend in the schoolyard. I was having many friend in my village because all of the other children were thinking that I am nice boy and also I am the best at all of the game and all of the lesson we are learning. So they were all liking me and wanting to be my friend, but the person who was really liking me and who I was really liking was my best friend Dike. We are always doing everything together in the village. So after going from Mistress Gloria, I was going with Dike to be going behind the school yard with some of the other boy to be playing football in the dust with one flat ball that is never very good to kick or we are having the race that I am always winning and I was flying up and down the school yard even if I am only wearing slipper. I am liking school very much and always thinking about going until the war is coming and then they are stopping school because there is no more government.

I am always going to church every Sunday where I am first going to the Sunday school to be sitting outside under the shade of one big tree in the church compound with all of my mate and sometimes, if she is not causing too much trouble, my sister, to be listening to the women reading us more story from The Bible about Jesus and Joseph and Mary and telling us that we should watch out so that we are taking the hard road

and not the easy road. And then we are saying prayer for for-
giveness and the Our Father and also singing many song
because God is liking music more than just talking so if we are
singing, then He is listening to us well well. They are always
telling us that God is liking children so much, that He is always
watching us. Sometimes after Sunday school is finishing I am
going into the big gray church and sitting with my mother and
father who are dressing in their nice clothe and listening to
Pastor shouting and sweating. I am feeling how the wood is
chooking my buttom with splinter and how the fan above us is
shaking so much that it is looking like it was going to fall and
be cutting off my head. I was always watching how the women
would be dancing well well so that their clothe is shaking and
they are having to tie it and tie it again and singing very loud
when it is time to put their money in the collection plate. And
the men are just shuffling their feets and bowing their head so
their chin is touching their chest.

And on Sunday there are other thing that we are doing in
my village. When there is no school and no chore, all my friend
and me are making all kind of game to be playing. Sometimes,
we are playing that we are grown up and doing grown-up thing
like driving car and flying plane, or being Doctor or Boatman.
And sometimes we are playing that we are soldier like we are
sometimes seeing in movie and taking stick and using them as
gun to be shooting at each other and falling down each time to
pretending we are dead. And each time we are playing all this
game we are having so much fun and laughing and running
and yelling all up and down the road of the village. All the small
small children are watching us and wanting to be like us and
even the grown people are watching us and even if they are
yelling at us to stop making so much noise, I am knowing from
the way that they are shouting through their teeths they are try-

ing not to be smiling because they are also wanting to be just like us. So we were playing all this game then and thinking that to be a soldier was to be the best thing in the world because gun is looking so powerful and the men in movie are looking so powerful and strong when they are killing people, but I am knowing now that to be a soldier is only to be weak and not strong, and to have no food to eat and not to eat whatever you want, and also to have people making you do thing that you are not wanting to do and not to be doing whatever you are wanting which is what they are doing in movie. But I am only knowing this now because I am soldier now.

So I am singing to myself,

Soldier Soldier
Kill Kill Kill.
That is how you live.
That is how you die.

And I am remembering to myself that I am doing all of this thing before I am soldier and it is making me to feel better. If I am doing all of this good thing and now only doing what soldier is supposed to be doing, then how can I be bad boy?

OONYA KEMPADOO was born in Sussex, England, in 1966, grew up in Guyana, and has also lived in Trinidad, St. Lucia, Tobago, and Grenada. Her first novel, *Buxton Spice,* appeared in 1998 to much acclaim. Kempadoo followed *Buxton Spice,* which depicts a young girl coming of age in Guyana, with what she describes as an attempt to explore teenage masculinity. *Tide Running* is largely narrated by Cliff, who lives in Plymouth, Tobago, with his mother, younger brother Ossi, older sister Lynette, and niece Baby Keisha. Here, Kempadoo brings to vivid life the competing cultural influences of North American television and the local soca-baptist preacher, each with its own conventions and idioms: on the one hand, "the girls in they high-cut bath-suits, bubbies squeezing out shiny and stiff-looking," and on the other, the preacher decrying *"young girls wearing skirt split up to they waist."*

From **TIDE RUNNING**

(2001)

Baywatch and de Preacher

Baywatch now showing, and is this night the soca-baptist preacher decide to preach. Park heself on the road corner by the Evertons' house, but we can still hear he speaker-funnel hailing clear over the TV.

And people, how are you tonight? preach out.

'Why dat damn man have to be tormenting people so?' Lynette set sheself with a cup'a cocoa-tea to watch the show, comb and curlers stick-up in she hair.

'You 'ave any more tea in de kitchen?" Ossi akse.

'Go see for yuhself nuh.'

The lifeguards and bouncy girls start smoothing on with the music. Big bare-chest muscly fellas with dark-shades, wet hair and slick smiles.

Was it a good day? Did you praise the Lord today? Or was it frauth with worry an' frustrashun?

The girls in they high-cut bath-suits, bubbies squeezing out shiny and stiff-looking. Ossi hand me a cup'a the thick spicy cocoa-tea.

Aren't ALL your days full of fatigue and woa?

'Why dat man don' rest he tail!" Lynette grumble. "He is de one giving people frustrashun. Huh.'

Island of Romance. Gulls clacking round, speedboats cruising, chicks and guys playing netball on the beach. Ceejay, one of the specially bubbilicious girls, mincing over to talk to Mitch, face set up like she going to kiss him or take off she bath-suit or something, but is only 'Hi' come out she mouth.

People of Plymuth, when are you going to come to your SENSES? Every DAY dat's passing is precious! Gaad didn' take he best heffort, take he good good time and make you, for you to stay here WANDAR-ING! LOST!

A ad about if you want love, call 1 800 psychic. Ceejay and Stephanie on they speedboat, just the two'a them, driving and smiling into the breeze. They flexy hair spinning out behind them like horse tail and they talking through they nose. Ceejay bend over, bam-bam up, bubbies down, sparky water skimming behind she.

'Da' one nice, eh?' Ossi slide down more on he seat.

Lynette cast she eye on he and steups.

Where are you going? What are you doing with your life? When Judgement Day come, where will you BE? With the sheeps or the goats?

Just so, the girls spy a boat ketching a'fire, the people on it jumping overboard. The girls' eyebrows serious-up, eyes come concern, pointing they arms, ready to rescue. 'Coastguard! Coastguard! Come in. Come in!' Speeding up, the people in the water bawling. Coastguard big boat coming.

'Dat is one t'ing I like da' place for, boy . . .'

Fire hose spraying, the girls done jump in the water already, saving them people but a body gone down. Stephanie diving down and coming up. Again and again, can't find the person. A coastguard fella, with all he tubes and t'ing, dive down. Pull up the sinking girl, she yellow hair moving like squid foot.

'She ain' dead nuh . . . dat is one t'ing I like foreign for, dem always have all de 'quipment for any kind'a 'mergency, boy.'

Ossi like to talk when he watching TV. Mouth always running. 'Watch nuh, dey go do dat t'ing 'pon de girl . . .'

The coastguards and Stephanie pulling the drownding girl up into they boat. Even though she half dead, she toes pose-off pointing, bath-suit and lipstick fix-up perfect.

'. . . Wha' dey call it, nuh. Dey go suck she mouth and press down on she chest. Eh. Dem lifeguard and dem does always do dat. She go wake up.'

The girl cough, sit up and smile. The rest'a the coastguards clapping. 'Yeah!'

Ads for Tums—now the man can eat a next cheeseburger. Sweet-talker Betty Crocker. Now Ceejay and Stephanie sitting on some rocks talking through they nose again. Rocks looking just like Plymuth Rocks, same gulls squalling, same kind'a sea slapping.

And where are your chi'ren? LOST! You lost yuh chi'ren! You say is de TV take dem. De rumshop, de DRUGS! Lost, Plymuth people. Wandaring. And only YOU, only you O Lord, can help yuhself. Amen-ah. But de Devil, ohh, he have plans-ah . . .

I see Lynette ain' really watching the TV. Them girls taking pictures of one another. Running round on the sand and posing like them magazine girls. Pushing they bubbies together, pulling up one knee so. They gallery theyself.

Ossi grinning and twisting he head when they bend down. 'Oh gawd, boy. Uh!'

They putting on they gears to go and dive. A ad for Pepsid come on.

'Dem Amerrycan can real eat plenty, boy.' He watching the man eating pizza, mouth henging.

Look around you-ah! Not even school can save yuh chi'ren. CHI'REN MAKING CHI'REN! Young girls wearing skirt split up to they waist. KARNAL KNOWLEDGE, INCES', fathers wit' they own

chi'ren, RAPE! Beastly-ality. YES! BEASTLY-ALITY! And de MEN?
Where are de men? NO FATHERS! Allelujah, oh yes. Look around
you-ah . . .

A woman come in front on the screen saying how all them
people behind she in a party having a good time, while she
out here with gas. No shame. She take a tablet. 'Not any
more!' she say.

'Aye! Da preacher need one'a dem tablet, boy. Tek-out all
he gas, ha!'

Lynette don't ketch Ossi joke. Is only when Ossi open he
mouth that Lynette watching at what going on. De preacher
man pulling she mind. Reminding she about things she don't
want to think 'bout. Even me can see that on she face. She
thinking 'bout Baby Keisha.

The girls down in the water admiring sea things: sea fans,
sea feathers, sea frost. I know all'a them same things. Li'l fish
passing and then the music changing, heavy, a man with a
knife down there too. But they don't see him. The darky music
getting louder, they swim into a undawater cave still admiring
the place: 'Gee, this is fantastic! It's so peace-full.' The t'iefing
fella digging round the treasure box with he knife. 'Wow . . .
let's take a picture before we go.' They have the camera down
in the water and all. The man setting a undawater dynamite . . .

Watch who leading you! De blind leading de blind, sweet Father in
heaven-ah . . . De politicians there telling you de same STUPIDNESS!
A EXCUSE! A excuse canna' save you, it canna' save yuh chi'ren!
Only Gaad can do dat, Amen. When t'ings bad, they tell you is
Trinidad fault, Trinidad ain' giving we enough money. Or is de
Amerrycans controlling we. Before dat, was de British. They telling
you watch dem foreigners coming in, de Germans buying land, big
hotel going up. Always somebody else fault, never they own . . . and
YOU SIT DOWN LIKE A MOO-MOO LISTENING! AMEN! You

ain' see where de money going? You ain' seeing NUTHING! Nuthing-ah! Satan'self could be in yuh house and you ain' go see HIM-AH . . .

The girls smiling for the camera in the cave. The wick t'ing burning to the dynamite. Undawater. The man swimming fast away . . . Booush!

'Dem girls go get trap, boy . . .'

Rocks falling down on them, they hold on together, mouth round. The hole for them to get out block up. No air. They air running out. Ceejay feeling faint, start closing she eye.

Look where yuh chi'ren going . . . give dem a better life, hallelujah. Before is too late, too late, too late-ah!

The coastguard fellas done notice the girls' boat on top, notice they missing too long.

'Dey coming, girl. You ain' go dead!' Ossi admiring the fellas, how they ever-ready. Coastguard fellas pulling out the rocks with a boat cable, giving the girls air. Carrying them up to the surface. On top the water the others done ketch the t'ief. 'Oh, wow! How can we ever thank you guys enough?' The two fellas holding them, smiling big, Ossi too. The girls bouncy selves, floating round the fellas' necks in the water. 'I'm sure we can think of a way!'

Lionheart with Van Damme showing later. Fire blazing behind the man naked steely chest, face scrench-up, kicking. Aagh. Gun down five fellas . . . aagh. Lynette get up and go outside.

R. ZAMORA LINMARK

AMERICAN POET, NOVELIST, and playwright R. Zamora Linmark was born in the Philippines in 1968 and grew up in Hawaii. His 1995 novel *Rolling the R's* consists of a series of linked fragments—letters, monologues, dialogues, short stories—all depicting the lives of "lovely faggot" Edgar Ramirez and his circle of teen misfits in 1970s Hawaii. *Leche*, a sequel to the novel, is forthcoming. In this excerpt from *Rolling the R's*, Linmark shows how Edgar's marginalization plays out as a clash of narratives in which his homosexual desire is deliberately excised from the collection of long-distance dedications Casey Kasem will include in his weekly "American Top Forty" countdown. As Edgar plaintively asks the unresponsive DJ, "How many times I sent you letters already? I so hungry for this boy, Casey."

From ROLLING THE R'S

(1995)

Face

Dear Casey Kasem,

You know, I one virgin when come for findin' the right words for explain that what I do and how I feel are not the same. That's why I always listen to the theme song from *Ice Castles,* or buy those expensive cards cuz got rainbows, poems, and all, like the one that says, "Your love brings / endless joy to / my life / I am bound to you," followed by three dots. For infinity. That's why I spend my Sundays countin' down the Top 40 with you when all I waitin' for is really the part where you read the letters that match the song dedications, like the one to the unrequited lover in Missouri, or the runaway father in Cincinnati, or the special, super-duper guy in Nebraska. Frustratin', you know. How many times I tried to write like Susie Polish Shutz, her words so true to my heart? How many times I sent you letters already? I so hungry for this boy, Casey. And even if I one boy when you get to my name, how come, Casey, how come you no pick my letter for the week? I so hungry for this boy. He look like one hapa–Andy Gibb. I see him on the weekends, playin' Galaxian and air hockey at Mitsukoshi game room. He even in my dreams, takin' Scott Baio's place. Such a doll, Casey. Not like the ete guys he hang around with, real bathroom truant types. I tell my friends for

scream my name out loud plenty times so he can notice me.
But he just walk on by. Slap in the face, Casey. I hate feelin'
like this. I hope he stay listenin' so he know the torture I expe-
riencin'. Could you please play "(Our Love) Don't Throw It
All Away" by Andy Gibb?

Sincerely yours,
Invisible Edgar

GAUTAM MALKANI

ENGLISH JOURNALIST and novelist Gautam Malkani was born in London in 1976. He studied at Cambridge University, where he wrote a thesis on South Asian rudeboy culture for his degree in social and political sciences. The thesis, which Malkani had originally intended to convert into a nonfiction book, left obvious marks on his 2006 novel *Londonstani* and its exploration of the complex dynamics of urban subcultures. The novel is marked as well by Malkani's extraordinary sensitivity to language. This excerpt, *Londonstani*'s opening chapter, considers the illogic of labels like "Paki" and "coloured," the "front" that vernacular expression can provide, and the psychic weight of constant code-switching. In this chapter—as throughout *Londonstani*—Malkani plays with the absurd notion of authenticity as his ex-nerd narrator Jas struggles to measure up to the "realness" of his new homeboys Hardjit, Ravi, and Amit. "I swear I've watched as much MTV Base an Juggy D videos as they have, but I still can't attain the right level a rudeboy finesse," bemoans Jas. "If I could, I wouldn't be using poncey words like attain an finesse, innit. I'd be sayin I couldn't keep it real or someshit."

From LONDONSTANI

(2006)

—Serve him right he got his muthafuckin face fuck'd, shudn't b callin me a Paki, innit.

After spittin his words out Hardjit stopped for a second, like he expected us to write them down or someshit. Then he sticks in an exclamation mark by kickin the white kid in the face again.—Shudn't b callin us Pakis, innit, u dirrty gora.

Again, punctuation came with a kick, but with his left foot this time so it was more like a semicolon.—Call me or any a ma bredrens a Paki again an I'ma mash u an yo family. In't dat da truth, Pakis?

—Dat's right, Amit, Ravi an I go,—dat be da truth.

The three a us spoke in sync like we belonged to some tutty boy band, the kind who sing the chorus like it's some blonde American cheerleader routine. Hardjit, Hardjit, he's our man, if he can't bruck-up goras, no one can. Ravi then delivers his standard solo routine:—Yeh, blud, safe, innit.

—Hear wat my bredren b sayin, sala kutta? Come out wid dat shit again n I'ma knock u so hard u'll b shittin out yo mouth 4 real, innit, goes Hardjit, with an eloquence an conviction that made me green with envy. Amit always liked to point out that brown people don't actually go green:—We don't go red when we been shamed an we don't go blue when we dead, he'd said to me one time.—We don't even go purple when we been bruised, jus a darker brown. An still goras got da front to call *us* coloured.

It was an old joke, but, green or not, I in't shamed to admit I'm envious a Hardjit. Most bredren round Hounslow were jealous a his designer desiness, with his perfectly built body, his perfectly shaped facial hair an his perfectly groomed garms that made it look like he went shopping with P Diddy. Me, I was jealous a his front—what someone like Mr Ashwood'd call a person's linguistic prowess or his debating dexterity or someshit. Hardjit always knew exactly how to tell others that it just weren't right to describe all desi boys as Pakis. Regarding it as some kind a civic duty to educate others in this basic social etiquette, he continued kickin the white kid in the face, each kick carefully planted so he din't get blood on his Nike Air Force Ones (the pair he'd bought even before Nelly released a track bout what wikid trainers they were).

—We ain't bein called no fuckin Paki by u or by any otha gora, u get me? Hardjit goes to the white boy as he squirms an splutters in a puddle on the concrete floor, lifting his head right back into the flight path a Hardjit's Air Force Ones.—U bhanchod b callin us lot Paki one more time an I swear we'll cut'chyu up, innit.

For a minute, the gora's given a time out as Hardjit stops to straighten his silver chain, keepin his metal dog tags hangin neatly in the centre a his black Dolce & Gabbana vest, slightly covering up the &. A little higher an he could've probly clenched the dog tags in the deep groove between his pecs.

—Ki dek ta paych? U like dis chain I got, white boy? Fuckin five-ounce white gold, innit. Call me a Paki again n I whip yo ass wid it.

—Yeh, blud, safe, innit, Ravi goes, cocking his head upwards. This weren't just cos most desi boys tended to tilt their heads up when they spoke, but also cos Ravi was just five foot five. The bredren was chubby too. Matter a fact, if you swapped

Ravi's waxed-back hair with a £5 crew cut an gave him boiled-chicken-coloured skin he could pass for one a them lager-lout football thugs, easy. The kind who say Enger-land cos they can't pronounce the name a their own country.

The boiled-chicken-coloured boy on the floor in front a us weren't no football hooligan nor no lager lout. He wouldn't want to be one an wouldn't want to look like one either. These days, lager louts had more to fear from us lot than us lot had to fear from them. Honest to God, in pinds like Hounslow an Southall, they feared us even more than they feared black kids. Round some parts, even black kids feared people like us. Especially when people like us were people like Hardjit. Standin there in his designer desi garms, a tiger tattooed on his left shoulder an a Sikh Khanda symbol on his right bicep. He probly could've fit a whole page a Holy Scriptures on his biceps if he wanted to. The guy'd worked every major muscle group, down the gym, every other day since he was fuckin fourteen years old. Since, despite his mum's best efforts, he hit puberty an became a proper desi boy. Even drinks that powdery protein shit they sell down there but she don't care cos he mixes it in with milk.

—How many us bredren u count here? Hardjit goes to the white boy.

—Uuuuurgh.

—Fuckin ansa me, u dirrty gora. Or is it dat your glasses r so smash'd up u can't count? Shud've gone 2 Specsavers, innit. How many a us bredren b here?

—F-F-F . . .

For a second I thought the gora was gonna say something stupid. Something like F-F-Fuck off perhaps, or maybe even F-F-Fuck you. F-F-Fuckin Paki would've also been inadvisable. Instead he answers Hardjit with a straightforward,—F-F-Four.

—Yeh, blud, safe, goes Ravi.—Gora in't seein double, innit.

So now it was Ravi's turn to make me jealous with his perfectly timed an perfectly authentic rudeboy front. I still use the word rudeboy cos it's been round for longer. People're always tryin to stick a label on our scene. That's the problem with havin a fuckin scene. First we was rudeboys, then we be Indian niggas, then rajamuffins, then raggastanis, Britasians, fuckin Indobrits. These days we try an use our own word for homeboy an so we just call ourselves desis but I still remember when we were happy with the word rudeboy. Anyway, whatever the fuck we are, Ravi an the others are better at being it than I am. I swear I've watched as much MTV Base an Juggy D videos as they have, but I still can't attain the right level a rudeboy finesse. If I could, I wouldn't be using poncey words like attain an finesse, innit. I'd be sayin I couldn't keep it real or someshit. An if I said it that way, then there'd be no need for me to say it in the first place so I wouldn't say it anyway. After all, it's all bout what you say an how you say it. Your linguistic prowess an debating dexterity (though whatever you do don't say it that way). The sort a shit my old schoolteachers told my parents I lacked an which Mr Ashwood'd even made me practise by watchin ponces read the news on the BBC. Honest to God. Why'd the fuck'd anyone wanna chat like that anyway? Or even *listen* to someone who chatted like that? I respect Mr Ashwood for tryin to help me lose my stammer or whatever kind a speech problem it was I'd got when I was at school. But I'd've wasted less a the man's time if I just sat down with Hardjit in the first place. Let's just say Hardjit'd make a more proper newsreader. An the white boy here was listenin to him.

—Dat's right, goes Hardjit,—we b four a us bredrens here. An out a us four bredrens, none a us got a mum an dad wat actually come from Pakistan, innit. So don't u b telling any a us Pakis dat we b Pakis like our Paki bredren from Pakistan, u get me.

A little more blood trickled down the gora's face as he screwed up his forehead. He wiped it away with his hands, still tryin to keep it from staining the sappy button-down collar a his checkered Ben Sherman shirt.

—It ain't necessary for u 2 b a Pakistani to call a Pakistani a Paki, Hardjit explains,—or for u 2 call any Paki a Paki for dat matter. But u gots 2 b call'd a Paki yourself. U gots 2 b, like, an honorary Paki or someshit. An dat's da rule. Can't be callin someone a Paki less u also call'd a Paki, innit. So if you hear Jas, Amit, Ravi or me callin anyone a Paki, dat don't mean u can call him one also. We b honorary Pakis n u ain't.

—Yeh, blud, safe, goes Ravi.

Don't ask me why the white boy still looked confused. It was the exact same for black people. They could call each other nigger but even us desi bredrens couldn't call them niggers. Or niggaz, if you spell it like that. At least that's how NWA was spelt when their name was spelt out in full. In fact, I figured that if Niggaz With Attitude followed the usual rules a acronyms, it'd be more accurate to use a capital letter, as in Nigga or Paki. I know I should've fuckin known better, but I decided to share this thought with the other guys.

—Yeh, motherfucker, an even when you allowed to call someone a Paki, it be Paki wid a capital P, innit.

—Jas, u khota, Hardjit goes, swiveling round so fast his dog tags would've flown af someone with a thinner neck,—why da fuck u teachin him how 2 spell?

I shrugged, deeply lamenting my lack a rudeboyesque panache.

—Da gora ain't no neo-Nazi graffiti artist n dis ain't no fuckin English lesson, innit.

So then I shut the fuck up an let Hardjit sum up his own lesson.

—A Paki is someone who comes from Pakistan. Us bredrens who don't come from Pakistan can still b call'd Paki by other bredrens if it means we can call dem Paki in return. But u people ain't allow'd 2 join in, u get me?

All a this shit was just academic a course. Firstly, Hardjit's thesis, though it was what Mr Ashwood's call internally coherent, failed to recognise the universality a the word Nigga compared with the word Paki. De-poncified, this means many Hindus an Sikhs'd spit blood if they ever got linked to anything to do with Pakistan. Indians are just too racist to use the word Paki. Secondly, the white kid couldn't call no one a Paki no more with his mouth all cut up. It was still bleedin in little bursts, thick gobfuls droppin onto the concrete floor like he was slowly pukin up blood or someshit. It made me feel like pukin up myself (the samosas an a can a Coke we got at the college canteen at break time). The blood trickled differently down his chin than down his cheeks. A closer look showed me that was cos he'd got this really short goatee beard that I hadn't noticed before. What's the point in havin a goatee if it's so blond no one can even see it unless your face is covered in blood? Amit'd always said goras couldn't ever get their facial hair right. If it weren't too blond, it was too curly or too bum-fluffy or just too gimpy-shaped. One time he said that they looked like batty boys when they had facial hair an baby boys when they din't. I told him I thought he was being racist. He goes to me it was the exact same thing as sayin black guys were good at growin dreadlocks but crap at growin ponytails. Amit probly had the wikidest facial hair in the whole a Hounslow, better than Hardjit's even. Thin heavy lines a carefully shaped, short, unstraggly black hair that from far back looked like it'd been drawn on with a felt-tip pen. Anyway, even if it was possible for a gora to have ungay facial hair, the gora in front a us now looked like he'd shaved himself with a chainsaw.

Hardjit was telling the gora something else, but I din't hear what. I'd zoned out during the short silence an tuned into the creaking a these mini goalposts Hardjit'd hung his Schott bomber jacket over. You could tell from the creaking that they'd rusted an were meant to be used inside the school sports hall rather than stuck out here opposite the dustbin an traffic cone that made up the other goal.

—Ansa me, you dirrty gora, Hardjit goes, before kneeling down an punchin him in the mouth so that his tongue an lower lip explodes again over the library books he'd tried to use as a shield. Even if the white kid could say something stead a just gurgling an spluttering blood, he was wise enough not to.

—Dat's right, the three a us go in boy-band mode again, —ansa da man or we bruck yo fuckin face.

—Yeh, blud, safe, goes Ravi.

We should've just left the white kid then an got our butts back to the car. We'd still got some other business to sort out before headin back to college that afternoon. We were also takin some serious liberties with our luck that none a teacher'd look out the classroom windows or step into the playground to pick up litter. They'd ID us for sure if they did. Not just cos we hung round this school's sixth-form common room now an then, but also cos up till last June we were sixth-formers here ourselves. We all fuckin failed, a course, despite all our parents' prayin an payin for private maths tuition. An so now we were down the road at Hounslow College a Higher Education, retakin our fuckin A levels at the age a fuckin nineteen when we should've been at King's

College or the London School a Economics or one a the other desi unis with nice halls a residence in central London.

Teachers or no teachers, fuck it. I had to redeem myself after my gimpy remark bout spellin Paki with a capital P. After all, Ravi had spotted the white kid in the first place an Amit'd helped Hardjit pin him against the brick wall. But me, I hadn't added anything to either the physical or verbal abuse a the gora. To make up for my useless shitness I decided to offer the following, carefully crafted comment:—Yeh, bredren, knock his fuckin teeth out. Bruck his fuckin face. Kill his fuckin . . . well, his fuckin, you know, him. Kill him.

This was probly a bit over the top but I think I'd got the tone just right an nobody laughed at me. At least I managed to stop short a sayin, Kill the pig, like the kids do in that film *Lord a the Flies*. It's also a book too, but I'm tryin to stop knowin shit like that.

—U hear wot ma bredren Jas b chattin? Hardjit says, welcoming my input.—If u b getting lippy wid me u b getting yo'self mashed up. I'll bruck yo face an it'll serve u right, fuckin bhanchod. Shudn't b callin us Pakis, innit.

There weren't much face left to bruck, a course. No way Hardjit could've done that damage with his bare fists. I weren't sure whether he'd used his keys or his kara. One time, when he sparked Imran I think, Hardjit slid his kara down from his wrist over his fingers an used it like some badass knuckleduster. Even though he was one a those Sardarjis who doesn't even wear a turban, Hardjit always wore a kara round his wrist an something orange to show he was a Sikh. Imran's face was so fucked up back then that we made Hardjit promise never to do that shit again. We weren't even Sikh like him but we told him he shouldn't use his religious stuff that way. Din't matter that he was fightin a Muslim. Din't matter that he was fightin a

Pakistani. His mum an dad got called into school an after dinner rinsed him big time for being a badmarsh delinquent ruffian who'd abused his religion an his culture. Then again, Imran did call it a bangle so served him right.

My fledgling rudeboy reputation redeemed, I was now ready to get the fuck away from there. But Hardjit weren't. He still needed to deliver his favourite line. An just like one a them chana-daal farts that take half an hour to brew, out it eventually came.

—U dissin ma mum?

The blood on the white kid's face seemed to evaporate just to make it easier for us to see his expression a what-the-fuck? If his mouth weren't mashed up he'd've probly been screamin denials an protesting his innocence. Hardjit'd have ignored him anyway so that he could deliver his second an third favourite lines,—U cussin ma mum? an the less venacular,—U be disrespectin my mother?

The rest a us knew where all a this was headed an Amit, who'd known Hardjit since the man was happy just being called Harjit, was the best placed to challenge him.

—Come now, bredren, dat's nuff batterings you given him. Da gora din't cuss no one's mum.

—Yeh, Amit, yeh he fuckin did.

—Nah, man, come now, we done good here, let's just allow it, blud.

—Allow him to dis my mother? Wat da fuck's wrong wid'chyu, pehndu? U turning into a batty boy wid all a dis let's-make-peace-an-drink-spunk-lassi shit?

—No, I mean allow as in, u know, leave it be, blud. He din't cuss your mum n no fuckin way he ever gonna call no one a Paki no more. Let's just leave it, blud. Let's just allow it n get goin wid our shit, innit.

—Da fuckin gora call'd me a Paki. He cuss'd da colour a my skin n my mama got the same colour skin as me, innit.

None a us dared argue, an Hardjit'd found a reason to kick the white kid in the face again, an again, an again, this time punctuating the rapid-fire beating with,—U fuckin gora, u cuss'd my mum, an then adding variations like,—U cuss'd my sister an ma bredren. U cuss'd my dad, my uncle Deepak, u cuss'd my aunty Sheetal, my aunty Meera, ma cousins in Leicester, u cuss'd ma granddad in Jalandhar.

Hardjit was so fast with his moves that the white boy hardly had time to scream before the next impact a the man's foot, fist, elbow. Hardjit's thuds against the gora's body, the gora's head against the concrete playground, had a kind a rhythm bout it that you just couldn't block out. Ravi starts cheering as if Ganguly had just scored six runs an there'd be no saving the boy's Ben Sherman shirt now. When it was done, stead a knockin the white kid out, Hardjit straightened himself up, took his Tag Heuer out his pocket an put his keys back in it. He could've done the same damage even if he'd just used his bare fists. He does four different types a martial arts as well as working every muscle group, like I said, down the gym, every other day. He says it don't really matter how many times you go down the gym, you can't be proper tough less you also have proper fights. It was the same with all his martial arts lessons. There weren't no point learning them if he didn't use them in the street or in the playground at least. His favourite martial art that time was kalaripayat, which in case you don't know was one a the first kindsa martial arts ever to be invented. A big bonus point if you know where it was invented. China? Japan? Tibet? Fuck, no. It's from India, innit. Chinese an Tibetan kung fu came later. People tend to forget this cos the British banned kalaripayat when they took over India. But now Hardjit'd found out bout it he wouldn't let no one forget. He reminded the white kid never to call anyone a Paki again before we all headed across the playground to the gate where Ravi'd parked the Beemer on the zigzag line. We were stridin slowly a course, so as not to look batty. With the gora gone quiet at last you could now hear screamin from inside the school. It was the usual voices. Four, maybe five different teachers yellin an shoutin at the usual kids for fuckin around in lessons, resulting in more laughter from the back rows followed by more shoutin from the front. From outside, the place sounded more like a mental home than a school. Lookin at where the sounds were coming from I figured no way any a the teachers would've spotted us through a classroom window. Even those that were clean were covered in masking tape cos they'd been broken by cricket balls. The result a special desi spin-bowling probly.

Nobody said jackshit to nobody in case it took the edge off Hardjit's warm-up for the proper fight he'd got lined up for tomorrow. But as the four a us got to the Beemer, Ravi remembered he'd left Hardjit's Schott bomber jacket wrapped round the goalposts in the playground.

—You fuckin gimp, was all Hardjit said. He weren't even referring to me for a change but still I volunteered to go get his jacket, even though it meant a spectacularly gimpy fifty-metre trot to the other side a the playground. Not exactly my most greatest idea seeing as how I'd just spent the last twelve months tryin to get upgraded from my former state a dicklessness.

As I got nearer the goalposts, I watched the white kid wipe his face with his shirt. You hardly ever saw a brown-on-white beating these days, not round these pinds anyway. It was when all those beatings stopped that Hardjit started hooking up with the Sikh boys who ran Southall whenever they took on the

Muslim boys who ran Slough. Hounslow's more a mix a Sikhs, Muslims an Hindus, you see, so the brown-on-browns tended to just be one-on-ones stead a thirty desis fighting side by side. Whenever those one-on-ones were between a Sikh an a Muslim an whenever the Sikh was Hardjit, people'd come from Southall an Slough just to watch his martial arts moves in action. If you don't believe me, wait till the big showdown with Tariq Khan he'd got lined up for tomorrow.

The white kid was now lookin me straight in the eye in a way that made me glad we hadn't made eye contact while he was being beaten.—What, white boy? I said.—Did you expect me to stop them? Do you think I'm some kind a fuckin fool?

—Jas, I didn't call nobody a Paki, he said, coughin.—You know that's the truth.

—I don't know shit, Daniel.

—I didn't even say nothing, Jas. Nobody would ever be so stupid as to mess with you lot any more.

I tried to ignore what he was sayin an the way sayin it had made his lips an tongue start bleedin again. But I couldn't help noddin. Damn right.

—Why didn't you tell them I didn't say anything, Jas? What's happened to you over the last year? the gora says before havin another coughin an splutterin fit.—You've become like one a those gangsta types you used to hate.

Damn right.

—Why didn't you tell them I didn't say anything?

—OK, Daniel, I go,—swear on your mother's life you din't call us Pakis.

—For fuck's sake, Jas, you know my mother's dead.

—So, swear on your mother's life.

—But Jas, she's dead. You came to the funeral.

I picked up the jacket, turned around an jogged back to the car. Hardjit'd been wise to take it off. He'd worn the jacket during other fights but wanted to be careful with it now cos he'd just had the word 'Desi' sewn onto the back. He'd thought bout havin 'Paki' sewn on but his mum'd never let him wear it an, anyway, nobody round here ever, ever used that word.

FRANCES MOLLOY

FRANCES MOLLOY was born in 1947 in Derry, Northern Ireland. Before her untimely death at age forty-four, Molloy found a small following for brilliantly depicting the absurdity of the Irish "Troubles" in fiction long and short. In this chapter from her picaresque novel *No Mate for the Magpie* (recently adapted into the short play *Odd Habits*), Molloy's naïve narrator Ann exposes the horrendous reality of convent life. Molloy uses Ann's short-lived convent stay to ridicule such venerable conventions as self-flagellation, worldly detachment, custody of the eyes and lips, and marriage to Christ.

From NO MATE FOR THE MAGPIE

(1985)

A toul me ma an' da that they had no need te keep me for a had decided te lave home. They said, ye'll do no such thing, me lady, ye'r too young te be lavin' home, ye'll stay in this house way us till the day an' hour ye get married. A allowed that at that rate of goin' a would be at home for a quare long time because a had no intention of iver gettin' married.

If me ma had of went te any hops hirsel' an' seen the kine of boys that were at them she mightn't have been so keen on talkin' about me marryin'. They were no Beatles them, oh no, they didn't want te hold yer hand or love ye, yeah, yeah, yeah. All they wanted te do was ate big pieces outa the side of yer neck or shove their slevery oul tongues down yer throat till ye were damn near choked, or grope aroun' way their dirty hacked oul han's inside yer knickers when they had ye pasted to the nearest wall without even askin' ye yer name.

A could see that me ma an' da had their plans laid, for me te carry on workin' in the factory till a married wan of these boyos, an' a wanted none of it. A decided then an' there that a might as well do some good in the worl' instead, but a must of been headin' in the wrong direction, for a ended up in a convent.

Wheniver a toul me ma an' da that a wanted te be a nun, me da tried to get me te change me mine be gowlin' an' shoutin' an' sayin' that a would go away te be a bloody nun over hes dead body, me lady. A toul me da that a thought it a cryin' shame that he planned to die so young an' lave me poor ma a lonely widda woman. When a said that me da took a swipe at me an' missed for he wasn't a very good shot.

He kept on gowlin' at me ivery day till the very day the nuns landed at our house te interview me. Then me da got feared that a was maybe goin' te go away after all an' that he would niver see me again so he started te be wile nice te me allthegether instead.

A wheen of weeks before a was due te go inte the convent, a took a wile yearnin' for life an' got it inte me head that if a didn't get te see Brendan Boyer doin' the Hucklebuck just wan time before a went away a would probably die. When a made this announcement te me family they were highly delighted.

The Royal Showband was makin' a tour of the north of Ireland at the time, an' weren't they comin' te our town just two nights before a was due te go away. Me ma an' da took this as a blessin' in disguise an' a fair enough indication of how the lord could be seen te act in strange an' mysterious ways. Me da put himsel' inte debt be buyin' me a gran' new frock, me big brother bought me a pair of red shoes way heels on them seven inches high, an' me ma surpassed hirsel' completely be gettin' me lipstick an' powder te put on me face, a thing she'd forbid me te do in the past.

On the night of the dance when a landed at the hall way me big brother, there were two thousand other people standin' waitin' te get in an' we were nearly kilt in the crush as soon as the doors opened. In the first half of the night, some wee band from the back of beyond come on te play for us, but the two thousand people threw pennies at them an' shouted at them te get aff. (In them days pennies were fairly big things.)

Be the time Brendan Boyer an' the Royal Showband got up on the stage te play, a had managed te fight me way forward te the front of the hall an' get mesel' inte a quare good position te view the Hucklebuck. It was ivery thing a had iver imagined it te be an' a was so delighted that be the time the dance was over a had plucked up courage te go an' ask Brendan Boyer for hes autograph. A toul him that a was goin' away te a convent an' a would niver see him again so he wrote hes name on me arm an' asked me to pray for him. A toul him a would, ivery day, an' a would niver wash me arm again for the rest of me life. Well, a prayed for him ivery day all right but a had to wash me arm a lot sooner than a thought.

Wheniver a got home that night a was ten feet seven inches aff the groun' an' me ma an' da were waitin' up te hear how a had got on. A toul them all about the dance an' showed them the autograph an' me da said a could look forward te a lot of other gran' nights like that wan an' forget all this oul nun business an' enjoy mesel' when a was young. Me ma said that me da was right, an' if a still wanted te be a nun when a was twenty, hir an' me da would be only too willin' te encourage me.

If a could of thought of some fool-proof way of keepin' things as they were at that very minute a would gladly have called the whole thing aff, but a knew that me da was playin' hes trump card an' as soon as a'd respond the only thing he'd have te offer was sendin' me back te the factory so a said te him, da, a'm goin'.

The day a landed at the convent, the first thing the nuns done was sen' me aff way another young girl te get dressed up in the garments. While we were walkin' up the corridor a spoke te hir, just to be civil an' pass the time of day. She niver answered me but she put hir han' te hir lips an' looked real startled. A could of kicked mesel' for openin' me mouth an' a wondered at the unkindness of the other nuns for not warnin' me that the poor girl was mute. A got the shock of me life a wheen of moments later when we got te the tap of the stairs, for didn't she pull me sleeve an' beckon me te folly hir inte a doorway so she could confab way me. It was then a discovered that nuns weren't allowed te talk but it didn't bother me much because a had niver been wile fond of talkin' te nuns anyway.

Wheniver a come down dressed up in the garments me ma burst inte tears at the sight of me because a looked like somethin' no woman could iver have given birth te. Me da was about te give me a big hug but he thought the better of it when he seen the face of the oul Reverent Mother tellin' him that a would have te go te the chapel so he just shook han's way me instead. A took a wile big deep breath an' said nothin' an' made sure not te look at me ma an' da in case they would know what a was thinkin'.

After they went away a was glad that the nuns had this rule of silence because a knew that me voice wouldn't be workin' right. When we come outa the chapel after prayin' for a wheen of hours, we had our supper, a gran' big feed. While we were aten, wan of the young nuns was readin' out loud te us all about how poor St Maria Goretti got hirsel' raped an' brutally murdered an' a allowed that if anythin' in this worl' could be worse than me grannie's banquets, then this was it.

After supper the nuns brought me upstairs where they had a big do arranged te welcome me an' another girl called Una, from Athlone in County Westmeath. Una was twenty-one an' it turned out that she had an identical twin sister who went aff an' left hir te marry some man. The other young nuns sung songs, an' played music, an' recited poems, an' danced for the two of us an' a was delighted till the Reverent Mother turned roun' an' toul me that it was my turn. A thought she was makin' a joke on account of the fact that most people a had met before that time had had a sense of humour so a laughed it aff accordingly.

That was the first mistake a made in the convent. No, it wasn't really, come te think, it was just the first mistake a was aware of at the time. Later on a learned that nuns weren't allowed te cross their legs because it wasn't ladylike.

The nixt mornin' after mass, the mother of novices took me inte hir office an' toul me te kneel on the floor, so a did. Then she started te list aff all the rules of the convent te me. The first wan was custody of the eyes. That meant that a was te learn te be shifty an' niver te look at a body if a was tallkin' te them but te look at the floor instead. Then she toul me the rule a knew about anyway only she called it custody of the lips. That meant that a was not only te be shifty but a was te walk right by people without even botherin' te pass them the time of day.

When she toul me a was always te keep custody of the han's an' niver te touch another nun a allowed that that wouldn't bother me much. The nixt rule was the worst rule of them all. She toul me that a would have te tittle-tattle te the Reverent Mother or hir if a iver seen wan of the other nuns breakin' the rules. A allowed there an' then that a would need te take great pains niver te see what any of the other nuns were doin' but that if perchance a slipped up, a would just have te make do way an oul rule of me ma's—niver go stickin' yer nose inte other people's business.

That mornin' when a'd been at mass a took me period, so as soon as a could get a word in edgeways a asked hir could a have some sanitary towels. She set aff an' landed back a wheen of minutes later way a pile of blood-stained cloths an' handed them te me. A toul hir that a didn't want them because some-body else had been usin' them. Well, she didn't take that very

FRANCES MOLLOY

well atall an' she launched inte me way a new lecture as long
as the day an' the morrow, about learnin' obedience an'
humility an' how self-will hinders the search for perfection an'
holiness an' how a must learn te turn away from all earthly
desires an' give mesel' over completely te god. She said that a
must always bear in mine how great an' manifole were the gifts
that god bestowed on them that loved him.

A allowed that at that rate of goin' these nuns musta loved
god a quare good bit because it appeared te me that the seven
poun' that a had brought them for sanitary protection was a
great an' manifole gift indeed considerin' what they were
sellin'. As if that wasn't bad enough, she then took a whip way
leather thongs that had wee bits of lead fastened te the en's of
them outa hir drawer an' showed it te me an' toul me that it
was called the discipline. She demonstrated how it worked be
beatin' hersel' on the back way it.

Before ye go away te be a nun ye have te go te a doctor te
have yer head examined te see if ye'r mental, an' if ye happen
te be foun' te be mental, the nuns will have nothin' atall te do
way ye. Now it was just as well that a'd had me head looked at
before a went inte the convent because if a hadn't have, a
would of been askin' mesel' questions about me own sanity, for
here was this woman standin' in front of me, flayin' hirsel' way
a whip, an' me kneelin' there watchin' hir doin' it way the
blood runnin' down me thighs.

Wheniver she was finished flayin' hirsel' she handed the
whip te me an' said that it was no longer obligatory te use it but
that if a had a fervent desire te strive after holiness a might fine
it useful an' a could keep it in the locker beside me bed an'
beat mesel' way it ivery night before a went te sleep. She
warned me te be careful not te make any marks on mesel' way
it before the followin' Wednesday when a doctor was comin' te

give Una an' me a thorough physical examination (te see if we were pregnant a suppose).

Well, seein' as it wasn't compulsary te whip mesel', a decided te decline hir kind offer of the whip so a said te hir that a would try te strive after holiness some other way. That didn't please hir very much so she launched inte me way a new lecture an' at the en' of it she give me penance te do in the middle of the refectory when all the other nuns were aten up their supper.

On the followin' Wednesday, Una an' me had te stay in our beds till after the doctor examined us. He examined me first because my bed was nearest te the door, an' low-an'behold didn't he spot the autograph on me arm an' ask me all about it. A toul him how a had been te see the Hucklebuck an' he toul me that hes daughter was a great Brendan Boyer fan an' that even hes wife liked him an' thought that hes voice compared in quality an' range te that of Elvis Presley, an' a agreed.

As soon as the doctor left the dormitory, the mother of novices who had been present at the examination, ordered me te get dressed at once an' go te the Reverent Mother's office. Wheniver a got there, the dressin' down the two of them give me surpassed any dressin' down a had iver had before. They said a was defilin' the holy cloister be houlin' on te worldy desires, an' when a went up the stairs te wash the autograph aff me arm a felt like the greatest sinner iver born even though a knew a shouldn't because a had niver kilt anybody.

Before a was in the convent very long a foun' out that a wasn't te be allowed te do any good in the worl' atall because a would have te spen' the rest of me life gettin' detached an' savin' me soul be imitatin' Christ. Accordin' te this book that was wrote be a Thomas A. Kempis, if ye didn't turn yer back on iverybody in the worl', ye didn't stan' a snowball's chance in hell of iver gettin' inte heaven.

It saddened me somethin' shockin' allthegether when a thought of the fate that lay before me poor ma an' da because they weren't imitatin' Christ, for there was no way that a body could iver imitate Christ an' manage te live in our house at the same time. A knew a was supposed te be detached, but someway a could niver get detached enough te think of livin' happy up in heaven for iver an' iver while me poor ma an' da were burnin' down in hell.

A thought hard of a way te get me da te take te the drink an' learn te walk on water an' a concluded that it might just be possible, but wheniver a reflected on the total futility of tryin' te turn me poor ma back inte a virgin again a give up in despair. But a'm not a wan that despairs for very long about anythin' so a soon started te look for ways outa me dilemma.

The first thing a done then was read Thomas A. Kempis's book a couple more times te see if a could fine any loopholes in it an' a did. Te begin way, for a body that done so much preachin' about humility, he didn't seem te have a lot of it himsel' for he was foriver talkin' on about what god thought about iverythin' like he was privy te the mine of god, or was even god himsel'. A don't know why the superiors were always goin' on about how great he was because if a body reads hes book anyway well atall the only reasonable conclusion they could possibly come te was that the man was a terrible oul fanatic an' cod allthegether, that couldn't put two consecutive words on a page without contradictin' himsel'.

The hardest thing about life in the convent was the lack of human contact. The voice of god was the only thing that we were allowed te hear, an' the voice of god had no human warmth. It was the cold metallic peal of a bell, tellin' us when te rise, when te pray, when te ate, when te study, when te work an' when te go back te bed again. A often wondered what the other nuns thought about it but a wasn't able te ask them. A niver thought very highly of it mesel' though. For me it could niver compensate atall for the gentle caress of me da's voice sayin' te me at twelve a-clock at night, gone te yer bed ye bastard ye or a'll fell ye.

It would have been intolerably borin' in the convent a suppose if it hadn't been for the fact that we were took out for two wee trips ivery year. In May we went te visit a shrine in Knock where Our Lady appeared te the Irish in the nineteenth century an' said nothin' te them atall, on account of the fact that anythin' she might of felt like sayin' would have been exaggerated outa all proportion an' be the en' of six months would have meant somethin' quite different from what she had intended, so she just looked at them instead.

The other annual excursion we made was te a place called Glendalough, in the County of Wicklow, te visit the tomb of wan of Ireland's most revered sons, the Holy Saint Kevin, patron saint of woman-beaters.

Wheniver a was in the convent for six months the nuns toul me that a was te get married te Christ an' that a bishop was te perform the ceremony. The night before the weddin' a had curlin' pins put in me hair an' on the mornin' of the big day all the other nuns started te fuss over me. They dressed me up in a weddin' frock an' put a wreath an' a veil on me head. They got me te stan' way me han's joined thegether an' a wile holy lookin' face on me te have me weddin' photo took.

Una was gettin' married te Christ the same day as me an' a lot of other nuns were makin' vows of wan kine or another so we had te go in a procession te the altar. A had te go up the aisle first because a was the baby nun on account of the fact that a was the youngest girl in the convent. When a got up te the altar the bishop was standin' there waitin' an' he said te me, what is it that ye seek child, in the latin tongue, so a said te him, *mihi absit gloriari, nisi in cruce domini nostri Jesi Christi, per quem mihi mundus crucifixus est et ego mundo,* an' he musta been pleased enough way me answer for he picked up a pair of scissors an' started te cut the hair aff me.

As soon as he had finished hes job of barberin', two nuns come up behine me an' took me weddin' frock aff. Then the bishop put the holy habit on me while the two of us confabbed away in latin. After he was finished marryin' me to Christ, the bishop toul me that a was no longer te be called Ann an' he give me a new name, a real holy-soundin' name that a had niver heard before in all me life. Then he give me a lit candle an' said te me, go show yer light te the worl'.

Because of the importance of the occasion, the nuns wrote a letter te me ma an' da askin' them te be present te see their daughter gettin' married. Wheniver a was leadin' the procession up the aisle a kept proper custody of the eyes as befitted me status as a bride of Christ but nivertheless a couldn't help noticin' that me ma an' da weren't in the chapel. A took te worryin' then that maybe they'd had an accident an' gone over the ditch somewhere in the oul crock of a car that me da was sure te have borrowed for the day. Well, when a turned roun' te show me light te the worl' for the very first time what did a see but me ma an' da sittin' up in the front of the chapel in the seats that had been reserved for them.

A had been practisin' religious decorum ivery day for six months an' a was fairly good at lookin' holy be this time but me face went away an' let me down the very minute a turned roun' be breakin' out of its own accord inte a big beam of a relieved smile at the sight of me ma an' da safe that toul the Reverent Mother that a was still houlin' on tight te worldly concerns.

After all the ceremony was over a went te the refectory way

the other nuns te have the weddin' feast. It was the greatest feed a had iver seen in me life but a didn't know what wan half of the things a was aten were on account of the fact that a wasn't allowed to ask.

A went te the parlour after that te meet me ma an' da an' a was so delighted te see them that a nearly jumped on the two of them the way a had jumped on me da the day me wee sister was born but a didn't for fear the Reverent Mother would give me more penance te do because a was fed up te the teeth way penance already.

Me ma an' da brought me wee sister an' two of me wee brothers way them. Me big brother was invited too but he refused te come, sayin' that if a wanted te bury mesel' alive there was nothin' he could do te stap me but he was damned if he was goin' te look at me doin' it. Me wee sister an' brothers made a quare bad impression on the Reverent Mother. She asked me wee sister if she wanted te be a nun like me an' me wee sister said te hir, naw. Then she said te me wee sister, why do you not want to be a nun, child? an' me wee sister said te hir, because a want te be a wife like me ma.

Me two wee brothers would do nothin' atall but fight an' wrestle on the convent lawn that people weren't even allowed te walk on so me ma had te keep on tryin' te stap them in case they would ruin their good suits. The two of them didn't talk te me atall because they thought a was a nun but they looked at me suspiciously when they thought a didn't notice because of the custody of the eyes that a appeared te be keepin'.

Wheniver the Reverent Mother's back was turned me ma said te me, Ann, a mean sister, ye'v got bigger. A said te me ma, ma, don't call me sister, me name is Ann. Me ma said, god forgiv' ye for showin' such disrespect, of course yer name is sister now, an' a allowed that me ma's menopause musta come back te have another go at hir. Then me ma started te tell me about the great feed of sandwiches that the nuns had give hir an' me da an' the wains. She asked me was a gettin' enough te ate in the convent an' a toul hir that the food was great allthegether but she wouldn't believe me because of the vow of poverty. She nearly drapped down dead wheniver a toul hir about the two glasses of wine a had had way the weddin' feast because she had got me te take the pledge when a was fourteen, niver te touch alcoholic drink in the whole of me life. A had te explain te me ma that things like pledges were nothin' more than worldly concerns an' could have no place in the life of a religious.

Before me ma an' da went away that night me ma took a big wad of notes outa hir han'bag an' toul me that it was money the people of our town had give te me da an' hir te bring te me. A could hardly believe me eyes an' a said te me ma that it was wile big of the people of our town te mine about me after a had been gone such a long time. A said that seein' as the money was mine a would like te see it used te buy me ma a washin' machine. She wouldn't hear of the like an' said that a must give it te the missions. A toul me ma that she WAS the missions an' a tried te pull rank on hir be pointin' out that a was a nun an' knew more about the missions than she done but that didn't work on me ma.

When a tried te give the money te me da he looked aroun' te see if any of the other nuns were lookin' an' they weren't so he give me a big hug an' said, that's my Ann, but he wouldn't take the money either. After that a tried te get me wee brothers an' sister te take it but they just shied away from me way their han's in their pockets. In the en' a had te give all that money te the oul Reverent Mother an' she had no objection te pocketin' it.

Four months after that day the mistress of novices toul me that a was te go te the city te help the directoress of vocations

te do some shoppin'. A was scared stiff when a heard it because
a hadn't been out shoppin' for such a long time but a done
what a was toul an' went away in the big car way blacked out
windows. As soon as we arrived at the shoppin' part of the city,
the directoress, who was drivin' the car, toul me te go te the
post office an' buy wan an' eleven pence worth of stamps. She
put hir han' inte the slit at the side of hir habit an' took out
half-a-crown an' handed it te me. A looked at it way wonder
because a had forgot what a half-crown looked like.

A asked the directoress if she was comin' too but she said
she would stay in the car. It had been ten months since a'd
been out on a busy street so a walked along feelin' kinda
strange, keepin' custody of the eyes as best a could in the way
the nuns had taught me. A was about te go inte the post office
when this wee wain of about four year oul come chargin' roun'
a corner an' bumped straight inte me. A was all delighted
because a hadn't seen such a wee wain in months. A crouched
down on me hunkers an' said te it, hello wain, what's your
name? an' a patted it on the head. The wee wain was lookin' at
me wonderin' what kine of a rare creature a was when its ma
landed on the scene pushin' a pram an' draggin' another wain
of about two year oul be the han'.

She started te apologise for hir wain bumpin' inte me an' a
said that it was all right. Then she spotted me accent an' said te
me, de ye come from the north? an' a said a did. The two of us
went on te confab about wains an' things an' soon a whole
crowd of people had gathered roun' te look at me. There was a
wile lot of pushin' an' jundyin' goin' on an' some oul wan
started shoutin' at all the people goin' by on the street te for
god's sake come quick an' have a look at this lovely wee nun.
Before long, people were takin' out their purses an' tryin' te
give me money te pray for them an' a was standin' there not

knowin' what te do so in the en' a started te pray te St Jude again that the groun' would open up an' swally me, but it didn't.

Wheniver a got back te the convent a was sent straight away te the Reverent Mother's office where a foun' out that the directoress didn't take me out te help way the shoppin' atall. She only brought me out te watch for any signs of worldliness in me an' it seems that she spotted plenty.

PUSH IS THE ONLY NOVEL by acclaimed American poet Sapphire. Born Ramona Lofton in 1950 in Fort Ord, California, she studied dance at City College of New York, taught high school equivalency classes in Harlem, and began writing poetry in the 1980s, reading at the Nuyorican Poets Café among other venues. She published her first poetry collection in 1994, and *Push* in 1996. At once harrowing and uplifting, it tells the story of Precious Jones, who at its outset is expecting her second child by her father, Carl. (The first was Little Mongo, which "is short for Mongoloid Down Sinder, which is what she is.") In this excerpt Precious, who was expelled from middle school simply for being pregnant, attends her first day at the alternative school Each One Teach One. There she meets Miz Rain, the radical educator who changes her life, and the fellow students who become an alternative family for her. Despite the negative educational experiences she recalls in this section, Precious is hungry for knowledge, constantly absorbing new words ("the school gonna give me a stipend, thas money for goin' to school") and creating memorable metaphors of swimming pools and birds.

From PUSH

(1996)

First thing I see when I wake up is picture of Farrakhan's face on the wall. I love him. He is against crack addicts and crackers. Crackers is the cause of everything bad. It why my father ack like he do. He has forgot he is the Original Man! So he fuck me, fuck me, beat me, have a chile by me. When he see I'm pregnant the first time he disappear. I think for years, for a long time I know that much.

After my baby and me come out of the hospital my muver take us down to welfare; say I is mother but just a chile and she taking care of bofe us'es. So really all she did was add my baby to her budget. She already on the 'fare wit' me so she just add my daughter. I could be on the 'fare for myself now, I think. I'm old enuff. I'm 16. But I'm not sure I know how to be on my own. I have to say sometimes I hate my muver. She don't love me. I wonder how she could love Little Mongo (thas my daughter). Mongo sound Spanish don't it? Yeah, thas why I chose it, but what it is is short for Mongoloid Down Sinder, which is what she is; sometimes what I feel I is. I feel so stupid sometimes. So ugly, worth nuffin'. I could just sit here wif my muver everyday wif the shades drawed, watching TV, eat, watch TV, eat. Carl come over fuck us'es. Go from room to room, slap me on my ass when he through, holler WHEEE WHEEE! Call me name Butter Ball Big Mama Two Ton of Fun. I hate hear him talk more than I hate fuck. Sometimes fuck feel good. That confuse me, everything get swimming for me, floating like for days sometimes. I just sit in back classroom, somebody say something I shout on 'em, hit 'em; rest of the time I mine my bizness. I was on my way to graduate from I.S. 146 'n then fuckface Miz Lichenstein mess shit up. I . . . , in my inside world, I am so pretty, like a advertisement girl on commercial, 'n someone ride up here in car, someone look like the son of that guy that got kilt when he was president a long time ago or Tom Cruise—or anybody like that pull up here in a car and I be riding like on TV chile—JeeZUS! It's 8 a.m. o'clock! I know I woketed up at 6 a.m., lord where the time go! I got to get dress for school. I got to be at school by 9 a.m. Today is first day. I been tessed. I been incomed eligible. I got Medicaid card and proof of address. All that shit. I is ready. Ready for school. School something (this *nuthin'*!). School gonna help me get out dis house. I gotta throw some water on my ass and git up. What I'm gonna wear what I'm gonna wear? One thing I do got is clothes, thanks to my muver's charge at Lane Bryant 'n man sell hot shit. Come to building go from door to door, I got your size he call out in hallway I got your size. I got to get dress. I wear my pink stretch pants? I think so, wif my black pesint blouse. I go splash some water on my ass, which mean I wash serious between my legs and underarm. I don't smell like my muver. I *don't*. I ain' got no money for lunch or McDonald's for breakfast. I take piece of ham out frigidare, wrap it in aluminum foil, I'll eat it walking down Lenox, not as good as Egg McMuffin but beat nuffin'. I double back to my room. On top my dresser is notebook. Ol' Cornrows say bring self, pencil, and notebook. I got self, pencil, and notebook. Can I get a witness! I'm outta here!

I always did like school, jus' seem school never did like me. Kinnergarden and first grade I don't talk, they laff at that. Second grade my cherry busted. I don't want to think that now. I look across the street at McDonald's but I ain't got no money so I unwrap ham and take a bite. I'm gonna ask Mama for some money when she get her check, plus the school gonna give me a stipend, thas money for goin' to school. Secon' grade they laffes at HOW I talk. So I stop talking. What for? Secon' thas when the "I'mma joke" start. When I go sit down boyz make fart sounds wif they mouf like it's me fartin'. When I git up they snort snort hog grunt sounds. So I jus' stop getting up. What for? Thas when I start to pee on myself. I just sit there, it's like I paralyze or some shit. I don't move. I *can't* move. Secon' grade teacher HATE me. Oh that woman hate me. I look at myself in the window of the fried chicken joint between 127th and 126th. I look good in my pink stretch pants. Woman at Lane Bryant on one-two-five say no reason big girls can't wear the latest, so I wear it. But boyz still laff me, what could I wear that boyz don't laff? Secon' grade is when I just start to sit there. All day. Other kids run all around. Me, Claireece P. Jones, come in 8:55 a.m., sit down, don't move till the bell ring to go home. I wet myself. Don't know why I don't get up, but I don't. I jus' sit there and pee. Teacher ack all care at first, then scream, then get Principal. Principal call Mama and who else I don't remember. Finally Principal say, Let it be. Be glad thas all the trouble she give you. Focus on the ones who *can* learn, Principal say to teacher. What that mean? Is she one of the ones who can't?

My head hurt. I gotta eat something. It's 8:45 a.m. I gotta be at school at 9 a.m. Ham gone. I ain't got no money. I turn back to chicken place. Walk in cool tell lady, Give me a basket. Chicken look like last night's but people in there buying it ol' or not. Lady ax, Fries? I say, Potato salad. Potato salad in the refrigerator in the back. I know that. Lady turn roun' to go in back, I grab chicken and roll, turn, run out, and cut down one-two-six stuffing chicken in my mouth. "Scarf Big Mama!" this from crack addict standing in front abandoned building. I don't even turn my head—crack addicts is *disgusting*! Give race a bad name, lost in the hells of norf america crack addicts is.

I look at watch, 8:57 a.m.! But shit I'm almost there! Coming around the corner of 126th onto Adam Clayton Powell Jr Blvd. I throws the chicken bones into the trash can on the corner, wipe the grease off my mouth with the roll then stuff rest of roll in my mouf, run across 125th, and I'm there! I'm in the elevator moving up when I realize I left my notebook and pencil in the chicken place! Goddam! And it's 9:05 a.m. not 9:00 a.m. Oh well teacher nigger too. Don't care if she teacher, don't no niggers start on time. The elevator goes Bing! I step out. My class last door on left. My teacher Miz Rain.

I'm walking across the lobby room real real slow. Full of chicken, bread; usually that make me not want to cry remember, but I feel like crying now. My head is like the swimming pool at the Y on one-three-five. Summer full of bodies splashing, most in shallow end; one, two in deep end. Thas how all the time years is swimming in my head. First grade boy say, Pick up your lips Claireece 'fore you trip over them. Call me shoe shine shinola. Second grade I is fat. Thas when fart sounds and pig grunt sounds start. No boyfriend no girlfriends. I stare at the blackboard pretending. I don't know what I'm pretending—that trains ain' riding through my head sometime and that yes, I'm reading along with the class on page 55 of the reader. Early on I realize no one hear the TV set voices growing out black-

board but me, so I try not to answer them. Over in deepest end
of the pool (where you could drown if not for fine lifeguard
look like Bobby Brown) is me sitting in my chair at my desk
and the world turn to whirring sound, everything is noise,
teacher's voice white static. My pee pee open hot stinky down
my thighs sssssss splatter splatter. I wanna die I hate myself
HATE myself. Giggles giggles but I don't move I barely breathe
I just sit. They giggle. I stare straight ahead. They talk me. I
don't say nuffin'.

Seven, he on me almost every night. First it's just in my
mouth. Then it's more more. He is intercoursing me. Say I can
take it. Look you don't even bleed, virgin girls bleed. You not
virgin. I'm *seven.*

I don't realize I've gone from walking real real slow to
standing perfectly still. I'm in the lobby of first day of school
Higher Education Alternative/Each One Teach One just
standing there. I realize this 'cause Miz Rain done peeked her
head out last door on the left and said, "You alright?" I know
who she is 'cause Miss Cornrow with the glasses had done
pointed her out to me after I finish testing and show me my
teacher and classroom.

I make my feet move. I don't say anything. Nothing in my
mouth to say. I move my feet some more. Miz Rain ask me if
I'm in the A.B.E. class. I say yes. She say this is it and go back
inside door. The first thing I see when I step through door is
the windows, where we is is high up, no other buildings in the
way. Sky blue blue. I looks around the room now. Walls painted
lite ugly green. Miz Rain at her desk, her back to me, her face
to the class and the windows. "Class" only about five, six other
people. Miz Teacher turn around say, Have a seat. I stays standing at door. I swallow hard, start to, I think I'm gonna cry. I
look Miz Teacher's long dreadlocky hair, look kinda nice but

look kinda nasty too. My knees is shaking, I'm scared I'm
gonna pee on myself, even though I has not done no shit like
that in years. I don't know how I'm gonna do it, but I am—I
look at the six chairs line up neat in the back of the room. I
gotta get there.

The whole class quiet. Everybody staring at me. God don't let
me cry. I takes in air through my nose, a big big breath, then I
start to walk slow to the back. But something like birds or light
fly through my heart. An' my feet stop. At the first row. An' for
the first time in my life I sits down in the front row (which is
good 'cause I never could see the board from the back).

I ain' got no notebook, no money. My head is big 'lympic
size pool, all the years, all the me's floating around glued
shamed to desks while pee puddles get big near their feet.
Man don't nobody know it but it ain' no joke for me to be
here in this school. I glance above teacher's head at the wall.
Is a picture of small dark lady with face like prune and dress
from the oldern days. I wonder who she is. Teacher sit at desk
marking roll sheet, got on purple dress and running shoes.
She dark, got nice face, big eyes, and hair like I already said.
My muver do not like niggers wear they hair like that! My
muver say Farrakhan OK but he done gone too far. Too far
where I wanna ax. I don't know how *I* feel about people with
hair like that.

The teacher is talking.

"You'll need a notebook like this," she hold up a black 'n
white 79-cent notebook just like what I left in chicken place. As
she talking girl walk in.

"It's nine thirty-seven," teacher say. "Jo Ann you *late.*"

"I had to stop and get something to eat."

"Next time stay where you stop. Starting tomorrow this
door will be locked at nine o'clock!"

"I better be on the side that's in," grumble Jo Ann.

"We agree on that," say teacher, she look Jo Ann in eye. She not scared of Jo Ann. Well gone Miz Rain.

"We got some new people—"

"I found something!" Jo Ann shout.

"I beg your pardon," say teacher but you can see she ain' beggin' nothin', she mad.

"No, I'm sorry Ms Rain"—I see right now Jo Ann is clown—"but I jus' want to say, do anyone need an extra notebook I foun' in the chicken place?"

"It's mine!" I say.

"Git a grip," Jo Ann say.

"I got one." I shocks myself saying that. "I left that book at Arkansas Jr. Fried Chicken on Lenox between one-two-seven and one-two-six this morning."

"Well I'll be a turkey's asshole!" Jo Ann screamed. "Thas where I found it."

I reaches my hand she smile me. Han' me my book, look at my stomach, say, "When you due?"

I say, "Not sure."

She frown, don't say nothing, and go sit a couple seats away from me in the row right behind me.

Miz Rain look pretty bent out of shape then melt, say, "We got more new people than old people today, so let's just go back to day one and git to know each other and figure out what we gonna do here together." I look at her weird. Ain' she spozed to *know* what we gonna do. How we gonna figure anything out. Weze ignerent. We here to learn, leas' I am. God I hope this don't be another . . . another . . . I don't know—another like before, yeah another like the years before.

"Let's try a circle,' teacher say. Damn I just did sit myself down in front row and now we getting in a circle.

"We don't need all those chairs," teacher say waving at Jo Ann who dragging chairs from second row. "Just pull out five or six, however many of us it is, and put 'em in a little circle and then we'll put 'em back in rows after we finish introducing ourselves." She sit herself in one of the chairs and we all do the same (I mean she the teacher 'n all).

"OK," she say, "let's get to know each other a little bit uummm, let's see, how about your name, where you were born, your favorite color, and something you do good and why you're here."

"Huh?" Big red girl snort. Miss Rain go to board and say, "Number one, your name," then she write it, "number two, where you were born," and so on until it all on board:

1. name
2. where you were born
3. favorite color
4. something you do good
5. why you are here today

She sit back down say, "OK, I'll start. My name is Blue Rain—"

"Thas your real name!" This from girl with boy suit on.

"Um hmmm, that's my for real hope to die if I'm lying name."

"Your first name *Blue*?" same girl say.

"Um hmm," Ms Rain say this like she tired of mannish girl.

"Splain that!"

"Well," say Ms Rain real proper. "I don't feel I have to explain my name." She look at girl, girl git message. "Now as I was saying my name is Blue Rain. I was born in California. My favorite color is purple. What do I do good? Ummm, I sing purty good. And I'm here because my girlfriend used to teach here and she was out one day and asked me to substitute for her, then when she quit, they asked me did I want the job. I said yeah and I been here ever since."

I look around the circle, it's six people, not counting me. A big redbone girl, loud bug-out girl who find my notebook at chicken place, Spanish girl with light skin, then this brown-skin Spanish girl, and a girl my color in boy suit, look like some kinda butch.

Big Red talking now, "My name Rhonda Patrice Johnson." Rhonda big, taller than me, light skin but it don't do nuffin' for her. She ugly, got big lips, pig nose, she fat fat and her hair rusty color but short short.

"I was born in Kingston, Jamaica." Ain' that something! She don't talk funny at all like how coconut head peoples do. "My favorite color is blue, I cook good."

"What?" somebody say.

"Name it!" Rhonda shoot back.

"Peas 'n rice!"

"Yeah yeah," like why even mention somethin' so basic.

"Curry goat!"

"Yeah, you name it," Rhonda say. "My mother usta have a restaurant on Seventh Ave before she got sick, she taught me everything. I'm here," she say serious, "to bring my reading up so I could get my G.E.D."

The skinny light-skin Spanish girl speak, "My name is Rita Romero. I was born right here in Harlem. I'm here because I was an addict and dropped out of school and never got my reading and writing together. My favorite color is black." She smile messed up teef. "I guess you could tell that." We could looking at her clothes 'n shoes, all black.

"What you do good?" Rhonda ax.

"Hmm," she say, then in shaky voice real slow, "I'm a good mother, a very good mother."

Brown girl talk. We about the same color but I think thas all we got the same. I is *all* girl. Don't know here.

"My name is Jermaine."

Uh oh! Some kinda freak.

"My favorite color—"

"Tell us where you born first," Rhonda again.

Jermaine give Rhonda a piss on you look. Rhonda cut her eyes at Jermaine like jump bad if you want to. Jermaine say she was born in the Bronx, still live there. Red her favorite color. She a good dancer. She come here 'cause she want to get away from negative influence of the Bronx.

Spanish girl Rita say, "You come to *Harlem* to get away from bad influence?"

Jermaine, which I don't have to tell you is a *boy's* name, say, "It's *who* you know and I know too many people in the Bronx baby."

"How did you find out about the program?" Miz Rain ax.

"A friend."

Miz Rain don't say nothin' else.

Girl foun' my notebook next. "Jo Ann is my name, rap is my game. My color is beige. My ambition is to have my own record layer."

Miz Rain look at her. I wonder myself what is a record layer.

"Where was you born and why you at this school," Rhonda ax. OK, I see Rhonda like to run things.

"I was born in Kings County Hospital. My mother moved us to Harlem when I was nine years old. I'm here to get my G.E.D., then, well I'm already into the music industry. I just need to take care of the education thing so I can move on up."

Next girl speaks. "My name is Consuelo Montenegro." Ooohhh she pretty Spanish girl, coffee-cream color wit long ol' good hair. Red blouse. "Why I'm here, favorite color— what's-alla dat shit?" She look Ms Rain in face, mad.

Miz Rain calm. Rain, nice name for her. Ack like she don't mind cursing, say, "It's just a way of breaking the ice, a way of getting to know each other better, by asking nonthreatening questions that allow you to share yourself with a group without having to reveal more of yourself than might be comfortable." She pause. "You don't have to do it if you don't want to."

"I don't want to," beautiful girl say.

Everybody looking at me now. In circle I see everybody, everybody see me. I wish for back of the class again for a second, then I think never that again, I kill myself first 'fore I let that happen.

"My name Precious Jones. I was born in Harlem. My baby gonna be borned in Harlem. I like what color—yellow, thas fresh. 'N I had a problem at my ol' school so I come here."

"Something you do good," Rhonda say.

"Nuffin'," I say.

"Everybody do something good," Ms Rain say in soft voice. I shake my head, can't think of nuffin'. I'm staring at my shoes.

"One thing," Ms Rain.

"I can cook," I say. I keep my eyes on shoes. I never talk in class before 'cept to cuss teacher or kids if they fuck wif me.

Miz Rain talking about the class. "Periodically we'll be getting into a circle to talk and work but let's put our chairs back in rows for now and move on with our business. Well, first thing, this is a basic reading and writing class, a pre-G.E.D. adult literacy class, a class for beginning readers and writers. This is *not* a G.E.D. class—"

"This not G.E.D.?" Jermaine ax.

"No, it's not. This class is set up to teach students how to read and write," Miz Rain say.

"Shit I know how to read and write, I want to get my G.E.D.," Jo Ann say.

Miz Rain look tired, "Well then this class isn't for you. And I'd appreciate it if you watch your language, this *is* a school."

"Ain' shit to me—"

"Well then go, Jo Ann, why don't you just tip," Miz Rain seem like, you know, well *leave* bitch.

Spanish girl, Rita, say, "Well this here *is* for me. I can't read or write."

Rhonda come in, "I can a little, but I need help."

Jermaine look unsure.

Miz Rain, "If you think you want to be in the G.E.D. class all you have to do is come back to this room at one p.m. for placement testing." Jermaine don't move. Consuelo look to Jermaine but don't say nuffin'. Jo Ann say she be back at one, fuck this shit! She ain' illiterit. Miz Rain look at me. I'm the only one haven't spoken. I wanna say something but don't know how. I'm not use to talkin', how can I say it? I look Miz Rain. She say, "Well Precious, how about you, do you feel you're in the right place?"

I want to tell her what I always wanted to tell someone, that the pages, 'cept for the ones with pictures, look all the same to me; the back row I'm not in today; how I sit in a chair seven years old all day wifout moving. But I'm not seven years old. But I am crying. I look Miz Rain in the face, tears is coming down my eyes, but I'm not sad or embarrass.

"Is I Miz Rain," I axes, "is I in the right place?"

She hand me a tissue, say, "Yes, Precious, yes."

KEN SARO-WIWA is beloved within Nigeria for his popular television series *Basi and Company,* and admired worldwide for the environmental activism that eventually cost him his life. He was born in 1941 in Bori, Rivers State. After graduating from the University of Ibadan, he worked as a teacher, education commissioner, entrepreneur, television producer, playwright, and novelist. In 1990 Saro-Wiwa founded the Movement for the Survival of the Ogoni People (MOSOP) to protest the environmental degradation visited upon his region by Shell and other large oil companies. He was executed, along with eight other MOSOP leaders, in 1996. Saro-Wiwa's novel *Sozaboy* is both a massively successful linguistic experiment (and source of this collection's title) and also an important account of the 1967–70 Nigerian Civil War. This chapter comes at a point when Saro-Wiwa's narrator Mene has been mulling over the advice of his new girlfriend Agnes, his neighbor Zaza, and "the tall man . . . at the Upwine Bar," all of whom had pressured him to enlist in the war. For Mene, their advice prompts an intensely symbolic dream that connects bureaucratic Standard English (or "big big grammar") with the violence he will soon experience firsthand.

From SOZABOY: A NOVEL IN ROTTEN ENGLISH

(1985)

So one afternoon as we were playing football one policeman came and told us that we must go to the church now now. Church from football? With sweat on our bodies? This policeman must be stupid. What is his trouble, anyway? Can policeman confuse himself like this? If it is *kotuma*, somebody will understand. Because after all, *kotuma* is just man with small education, no plenty job, just chopping small small bribe from woman or man in Dukana. But police is big man going on transfer from Lagos to Kano and so on. And he can be promoted too to sarzent, then inspector and so on. So it is not good that he should confuse himself. So, nevertheless, since he say we must go to church, we all begin to go there. Everybody. Are we going to pray in the church, and today is not Sunday? Will this police force us to begin to pray? Ha!

As we entered the church now, not only those who were playing football were inside that church. Everybody in Dukana. Plus Chief Birabee, smiling that idiot foolish smile which he will be smiling whenever he sees soza or police or power. Trouble don come again, oh. Even people who do not go to church are entering this church today. I beg, God, make you no vex for these people, and this nonsense police who is causing all this trouble. So we waited inside the church. People were talking, talking. Because in this Dukana people will always talk. After some time, Chief Birabee with idiot smile looking at policeman begin to shout "Keep quiet all of you, oh! Keep quiet all of you, oh!" Then after some time he will shout again, "Keep quiet all of you, oh. Hei! Why can't you people close your mouth?" The people will keep quiet for small time then after some time they will begin to hala again.

As you see these Dukana people, they are not talking anything good oh. I can see they are all fearing, because once they see police or soza or even *kotuma,* they must begin to fear. Useless people. And when they are fearing like that, they cannot say what is inside their mind. Just smiling idiot foolish smile like that Chief Birabee smile. Myself too, I was not happy as they have called us to church and leaving us there just like that. So after some time one motor begin to come. At first I think that it is my master's motor. But not so. It is small car. And the porson who is inside it come down quickly. He is wearing better cloth, so you can see at once that he is a very important porson. As he walked into the church, the police shouted "All stand". Everybody stood up. The man in fine shirt walked to where Chief Birabee was sitting and shook hand with him. Chief Birabee was smiling that his foolish idiot smile, super. Prouding. Because the man with fine shirt is shaking hand with him in front of the Dukana people.

The man with fine shirt sat down and we all sat down too. Plenty of talking.

"Silence!" shouted the police. "Silence, I say!"

The people cannot understand him. They were laughing because of how he was shouting. Myself too, I was laughing. Then the police came to where I was sitting and used his stick on my head. Everybody kept quiet. I stopped laughing by force. That is how my own things are. Every time trouble. Always. So I kept quiet with several people shouting little shouts inside my head from the policeman's stick's blow. I said to myself, 'trouble don begin'.

The man with fine shirt stood up. And begin to talk in English. Fine fine English. Big big words. Grammar. 'Fantastic. Overwhelming. Generally. In particular and in general'. Haba, God no go vex. But he did not stop there. The big grammar continued. 'Odious. Destruction. Fighting'. I understand that one. 'Henceforth. General mobilisation. All citizens. Able-bodied. Join the military. His Excellency. Powers conferred on us. Volunteers. Conscription'. Big big words. Long long grammar. 'Ten heads. Vandals. Enemy'. Everybody was silent. Everywhere was silent like burial ground. Then they begin to interpret all that long grammar plus big big words in Kana. In short what the man is saying is that all those who can fight will join army.

My heart begin to cut. Plenty. Join army? For what? So I am now a soza. No. No. I cannot be soza. Soza for what? Ehn? I begin to shout, No. No. The man with fine shirt was looking at me. The policeman was coming to me. Is he coming to take me to be soza? The policeman was coming. My heart was cutting, beating like drum. *Tam tum. Tam tum tum.* Then I see that it is not just one policeman but many sozas. Plenty of them with gun pointing at me. My heart was beating. *Tam tum, tam tum tum.* I don't want to be soza. So as I see them coming with their gun, I jumped out of that church and started to run. Then I heard Chief Birabee and the others shouting "Hold am! hold am!" They were shouting from every side. Then the sozas started running after me. Pursuing me. I ran and ran like a dog. Still the sozas pursued me, pointing their gun.

Oh my father wey don die, help me today. Put power inside my body. Make I no tire. I can hear the sozas saying "You are now a soza. You will fight the enemy." Na lie. Na lie. I ran towards the river. The sozas and the police were still following me. Then when I got to the river, I just jumped inside it and begin to swim. All those sozas cannot catch me. They cannot swim like myself. They are afraid of the river.

Then when I reached the other side of the river, I stopped. I went out of the water. My khaki was wet. I sat down on the white sand. No sooner than one thousand sozas appeared behind me, all their guns pointing at my back. God in Heaven. What kain trouble be dis? Immediately I jumped into the river again and begin to swim to the other side. My heart begin to beat drum more than before. *Tam tum tum. Tam tum tum. Tam tum tum.* I was swimming. I am afraid of the sozas. I do not want to join the sozas. Now the sozas do not follow me, they begin to shoot their guns: *Tako, tako. Tako—tako—tako.* Oh, Jesus. You know, I am young boy. I have never do anybody any bad thing since they born me. You know I love my neighbour as myself. Even I am good Samaritan several times. I have not called another man's wife. I have not tief another person money. I do not go juju house. Forgive me my tresspasses. *Tako, tako, tako.* My heart was beating, *tam tum tum. Tam tum tum.* I have not tief another person money. *Toko, tako, tako.* Oh my mother, pray for me, make these sozas no kill me. Let them kill snake, leopard and tiger. All those bad animals who live inside bush. But make them no kill me.

I was swimming all this time, oh. Then I reach the other bank again and I climbed it and got into the bush. The bush catch my leg and wound me for body. My body all full of wound. Blood. The blood of our Lord Jesus Christ. Oh God, help me, I beg you in the name of Jesus. I will do everything you want. I will be good boy from now till kingdom come. The sozas were still following me. Shooting. And I was running like dog.

I run until I get back to the church in Dukana. Now nobody in the church at all. All those people who were there are not there again. Now I look through the window of the church and I see all the sozas, very many of them moving like forest towards the church. They were not shooting again. They were singing very loud:

> *My father don't you worry*
> *My mother don't you worry*
> *If I happen to die in the battle field*
> *Never mind we shall meet again.*

Fear catch me well well as the sozas are moving towards the church. So I ran. From the church. I ran to my mama's house where I used to stay. But when I got there, my mama's house is not standing again. Ah—ah. Where is my mama house? Where have it disappeared to? What have happened to it? And where is my mama?

Then the sozamen began to sing another song:

> *Why do you delay*
> *Come and save the nation*
> *Why do you delay*
> *Come and save the nation*
> *Oh why do you delay*
> *Come and save the nation*
> *There is danger*
> *Why do you delay?*

So now when I hear there is danger my mind come go to Agnes. I am thinking what has happened to her. So I come run to her house. And when I get there I see that her house is not

there too. And she is not here either. So what have happened
to Agnes and her mama? Oh God, what is happening?

Then the sozas began to sing another song:

We are sozas marching for our nation
In the name of Jesus we shall conquer.

The sozas were moving nearer now. And then they begin to
shoot. *Tako, tako, tako.* And still I cannot see Agnes. And I do
not see my mama too. And my mama house and Agnes mama
house are not there. And all the Dukana people have disappeared. Not even one person in the town. Fear cut my heart.
The sozas were moving nearer and their bullet begin to fall
near me. Plenty bullets. I begin to shout "Mama, mama,
mama!" I was shouting like that when I opened my eyes.

Ah, so it is all dream. Very bad dream. Already, day don
begin to break. My mama come to ask me why I am calling her.
I told her that I was dreaming. I told my mama how I dream of
many many sozas singing song and shooting gun and pursuing
me. And I ran away from them and fell into the river and how
they continued to pursue me. And how I return to Dukana and
I cannot find her or her house. And all the people of Dukana
are no longer there.

My mama told me that she too have been dreaming how
aeroplane came to Dukana and dropped big big mortars on
top of the church and how everybody was afraid and running
about and hiding and calling God to help them. And she ran
with them but I was not near her and she started looking for
me but she could not find me.

Well, well, well, this dream and my own are almost identical.
What can it mean? I tell you, I was very confused that morning.
And that day I was turning the dreams for my mind. And I

remembered too what the tall man said at the Upwine Bar. What Agnes said. What Zaza said. What the thick man said about salt and no salt inside the salt of our body. I fear.

And now everyday they were talking more and more about the war. The radio was shouting about it all the time. And they were saying that everybody must be ready for it. Trouble!

NOVELIST AND SHORT STORY WRITER Sam Selvon was born in 1923 in San Fernando, Trinidad. After graduating from Naparima College and serving in the Royal Navy reserves, he moved to London in 1950, where he began to publish poems and short stories. Throughout the 1960s, Selvon chronicled the experience of West Indian immigrants to England, most notably in his novels *The Lonely Londoners* and *Moses Ascending.* Selvon moved to Canada in 1978, and died in 1994 in Port of Spain, Trinidad. *The Housing Lark* is a lighter and lesser-known novel that follows the struggles of Battersby (or Bat) to purchase a house along with some of the hilariously unreliable characters who appear in this excerpt: Alfy, Fitz and his wife Teena, Gallows, Nobby, Poor, and Syl. (The last member of the motley collective is a Jamaican calypso musician named Harry Banjo who has been unjustly imprisoned for an offense of Poor's.) This section relates the country excursion Bat has organized in order to fund-raise for the house. Selvon shows how the Trinidadian crowd—who are continually mistaken for Jamaicans by Anglo onlookers—coalesces around food, drink, and most of all talk. "It don't matter what the topic is," Selvon's narrator comments, "as long as words floating about, verbs, adjectives, nouns, interjections, paraphrase and paradise, the boys don't care."

From **THE HOUSING LARK**

(1965)

Planning to buy a house is one thing, planning to give excursion to Hamdon Court is another. But Battersby was a old hand at this sort of thing. Back home in Trinidad, nearly every weekend Bat chartering a bus and going round by his friends inviting them to excursion in Mayaro, in Los Iros, in Columbus Bay, in Toco and Blanchisseuse. Being as Trinidadians does thirst after fete as pants the hart for crystal streams, he never used to see trouble to get excursionists.

In Brixton, where the most you could do is cruise in the park or go to the cinema, the news spread like wildfire, and this Sunday morning as the driver park the coach just behind the market by Somerleyton Road, it already had people waiting, as if they fraid they come late and the coach go to Hamdon Court and left them behind.

'Let we have some order man, don't scramble so to get in the bus, it have room for everybody.'

Battersby was standing up near the door with the driver, ticking off the members of the party and collecting money as they get in. It look as if the whole of Brixton was going on this excursion to Hamdon Court. Friend invite friend, cousin invite aunt, uncle invite nephew, niece invite godfather, and so this Sunday morning bright and early all of them congregate in this side street behind the railway station. And the girls in all kind of crinoline and crinolette, can can and cotten, bareback and barebreast, and wearing toeless sandals and with ribbons in their hair, and the boys in some hot shirts and light-coloured trousers what they never get a chance to wear since they come to England.

'Let the old folks go in first,' Battersby say.

Mother, father, uncle and other elders go in, carrying the children. Some of the children getting big cuff and slap as they prancing about with too much excitement. Battersby grudge seeing so much children because they was paying half-price. By the time the old people get in, the others start to scramble for end seat and back seat and front seat. Battersby give up trying to keep order. And the food and drink—well, it look like they setting off for an expedition to the North Pole or something. All kind of big iron pot with pilau and pigfoot and dumpling, to mention a few delicacies, and one old lady have a bunch of watercress wrap up in a paper, because she say she don't ever miss her watercress with her Sunday lunch.

Some of the boys high already, as if they been feting all night and just come to sleep in the coach. The only time they showing any life is when a bottle of grog passing around.

While all this pandemonium going on, with people forgetting things and saying to hold back the coach while they run home for a cardigan or a thermos flask, what should happen but Mr Poor appear on the scene in a char-a-banc. Whenever a boat-train coming in, especially, you sure to see one of these vehicles park up outside Victoria or Waterloo, to convey friends and relatives to their destinations in the land of hope and glory. And fellars who possess such means of transportation don't be afraid to make a few quids. In Victoria one night a fellar from Birmingham come down empty, and it look like the people he come to meet didn't turn up, and he start to go around asking if anybody going up to Birmingham, or in transit, five pounds a head? Sure enough by the time he leave Londontown the char-a-banc full up, and he would of made more money if it wasn't for so much luggage the immigrants bring with them.

Well papa, Poor pull up in this big empty char-a-banc just behind the coach, and announce to everybody that he going to Hamdon Court, and that he was prepare to take a dollar a head!

Hear the classic comment from Charlie Victor, to the English thing he bring with him: 'That is one of the typical reasons why they can't get on.'

Bat wasn't so delicate. 'Poor,' he say, 'pull that char-a-banc out of here otherwise I will mutilate you.'

And Poor, pounding the side of the char-a-banc like if he beating somebody: 'Brit'n is a free country! I could do what I want!'

Charlie Victor tell the thing: 'Of course, legally he could get in trouble plying for hire. I do hope things are settled amicably.'

By this time pandemonium not only existing, it reigning. Some people who in the coach already start to come out, saying they want back their money, they prefer to go with Poor. And Bat have his hands spread out barring them, like how sometimes you see the police holding back a crowd.

'Take it easy,' Bat saying, 'nobody getting their money back.' And turning to Poor: 'Poor, you should be in jail! You send poor Harry Banjo to jail when it should have been you!'

'That is true,' a old woman say, and turn back to sit down in the coach.

But though it had a lot of them who feel that Poor was a traitor, still, a dollar is a dollar anyhow you look at it. Besides, Poor did take the char-a-banc to a garage and get it wash down and polish, and it shining in the morning sun, whereas the coach company, being as how they know it was a spade excursion, perhaps, send a old dent-up coach what look like it barely manage to reach Brixton, and would need a lot of encouragement to start.

Poor instigating: 'Look at that coach! You all not frighten to travel in it? Is so you treating OUR PEOPLE Bat? If it can't start I will give you a push!'

The English driver say, 'Get out of it,' and turn to Bat, 'If everybody's here let's go.'

To tell truth, it look like if everybody really there. The coach full up, and it still had people standing up outside.

'Only one coach coming Mr. Battersby?' a woman ask.

'Yes,' Bat say, 'but there's plenty of standing room inside.'

As things turn out, it had more people than the coach could hold, and Bat couldn't stop them from going with Poor. By the time the char-a-banc full up, Poor ready to pull out first and racing the engine to make style. Bat was just getting in to close the door of the coach when a woman push her head out the window and shout across to the char-a-banc: 'That you there Mavis girl? Come over in the coach, man!'

'I can't!' Mavis shout back, 'we going to start!'

'Hold the coach up,' the woman tell Bat, getting up, 'I thought Mavis wasn't coming again. I want to go with she.' And she went over to the other vehicle.

'All right, all right,' Bat say, slamming the door. 'Hold tight. Let's go.'

Poor take off in front with the engine racing, leaving a set of exhaust smoke behind.

By the time the coach pull out from behind the market, like if fete start up right away. Fellars begin beating bottle and spoon and singing calypso, others beating the woodwork and the upholstery to keep time, people as if they just seeing one another for the first time and finding out that they sitting down far apart and wanting to change seat, some children begin to cry and say that they hungry, three bottles of rum start to make rounds as if they ain't have no owner, as if the Aladdin geni produce them for the excursionists! And man, woman and child knocking back liquor, bottles of pop opening up all over the coach, a woman open up a pot of pilau and start dishing out food, and a man give a little boy ONE clout behind his head and the boy start bawling and crying, 'Ma, man, look Pa hit me!' A banjo and two mouth-organ come in sight, a girl say she feeling hot and threatening to take off she blouse, and a mother encouraging her child: 'Go on Elouisa! Say that recitation that the English people teach you in school! Go on, don't play shy.' And she turn to her neighbour and say, 'Just wait, she could really say poultry good, is only shy she playing shy.' The neighbour say, 'Albert not good at poultry, but if you see, him twist! Albert? Where he gone to? ALBERT!" And Elouisa stand up in the gangway biting her finger and looking down and swinging from side to side, like how little girls do when they shy, and my boy Albert, as if he sense a partner, begin to twist in front of she.

And of course, I shouldn't have to tell you that photo take-outer Alfy is in front of the coach trying to balance and control his Zeiss and capture the spirit of the moment on film.

Battersby push his hand out and make contact with a bottle of rum in the air. He cock his head back and pour the rum in a stream in his mouth without his lips touching the bottle. As if his head and his hand catch cramp in that position, and luckily Nobby haul the bottle away.

'Ah,' Bat say, 'I was longing to wet my throat.'

'Wet your throat!' Nobby repeat. 'I thought you was bathing!'

'Anyway,' Bat say, wiping his mouth with his hand, 'praise God we on the way at last. I thought we would never leave the market-place.'

'You should of bust a crank handle in Poor's head,' Fitz say.

Right down in the back of the bus, Charlie Victor sitting sedately with the piece of skin what he bring to the excursion. It have a lot of fellars in town who go about as if they don't want to have anything to do with West Indians. They talk with their English friends about the waves of immigration, and deplore the conditions immigrants live in, and say tut-tut when any of the boys get in trouble. As if they don't want to be known as immigrants themselves, they talk about coming from the South American continent, or the Latin countries, and make it quite clear that they themselves like a race apart from the hustlers and dreamers who come over to Brit'n looking for work. But in truth and in fact, loneliness does bust these fellars arse. They long for old-talk with the boys, they long to reminisce and hear the old dialect, or to go liming in the West End just floating around looking at the things passing by. Charlie Victor in Brixton had a way of making it clear that though the gods will it for him to be one of OUR PEOPLE, he was in a class by himself. Nothing give Charlie greater kicks than to stroll through the market during the day and hear all them housewives call out: 'Morning Mr Victor!' while he nod and give a little smile. This time so he have his eye on all them yam and green banana and pig tail and pig foot what for sale on the stalls, and his mouth watering. If in fact one of the housewives say: 'Mr Victor, why don't you come and eat a food next Sunday please God?' nothing would of please him more. Because the English house what he staying in near the Oval, all he getting there is mash potato and watery cabbage and some thin slice of meat what you could see through, and bags of tea—a big tea-brewing machine like what you see in them cafe always going in the kitchen. My boy looking thin and poorly and off-colour, as it were. He get so Anglicised that he even eating a currant bun and drinking a cup of tea for lunch! So though in fact he fooling himself that he just like any English citizen, loneliness busting his arse every day. That's why when he hear about the excursion he grab the chance to mingle with OUR PEOPLE, to hear the old-talk and to see how in spite of all the miseries and hardships they could still laugh skiff-skiff and have a good time. So he pick up this blue-foot what living in the same house as him, name Maisie, and decide to come.

Hear him as he paying Battersby before going in the coach: 'I heard about your efforts to raise money to buy a house and I must say it is commendable. In fact I thought of patronising the excursion and helping the cause.'

'Every little bit helps,' Bat say, eyeing the thing with Charlie.

'Quite so,' Charlie say. 'Here, have an extra ten bob. And do feel freed to call on me for advice at any time. You know I am in the Housing Business.'

'Too many cooks spoil the soup,' Bat say, watching Maisie backside as the skirt tighten as she going in the coach.

Now, sitting down in the back with the thing, Charlie getting in the mood, and his foot keeping time with the calypsos. When the bottle of rum pass around for the first time, he shake his head, but you could see him watching it like a lost man in a desert who sight a mirage.

'Why ain't you had one?' Maisie say. In point of fact Maisie herself ready to let down her hair, but she waiting for Charlie to make a start.

'They're all putting their mouths to the bottle,' Charlie say disapprovingly.

But when another bottle start up, the temptation was too

great. Charlie swipe it in mid-air, and hold it between his legs and make a quick dab with his handkerchief over the neck. It look like he catch the cramp from Battersby: Maisie had was to pull the bottle away from him to get a drink.

'Let me show you how to kill an empty bottle,' Charlie say.

'It isn't empty yet,' Maisie say.

Charlie take care of that and put the bottle upright on the ground. He light a match and drop it in, and quickly press his hand over the mouth. As the match out and the bottle begin to cloud up, he pull his hand away quick from the bottle and it make a little vhoom! noise.

By the time the coach reach Hamdon Court, you would think the party went out for the day and now coming home to roost in the palace. They finish off three bottle of rum and a crate of beer, and empty bottles rolling all over the floor and clinking. Two pot of peas and rice finish, the children's clothes have chocolate smudge and mineral water stain, and one little girl trip and fall over a pan of stew and splatter it about on all who near. People hiccupping and belging, some of the elders dozing. In point of fact, if all of them did get together and went in the park, or if to say the coach did really break down and they couldn't reach, it won't of made any difference.

Nevertheless, as the coach pull up and they see the char-a-banc waiting, as if the party throw in second gear as they dismount, the men making a beeline for the nearest Gents, and the women dittoing for the Ladies.

'Rmember we leaving at six o'clock,' Battersby shout out. 'The coach going to be waiting in the parking area, and if anybody late that is their lookout.'

Meet Fitz and the family as they hop off. The first picc'n, Willemeena, is the one that trip over the pan of stew, and the splattering make a sort of design on her dress, so it don't look too bad. Her hair plait. How Teena manage to do it is a mystery. But it plait, and it have a blue ribbon on each plait. Next come Henry the First. He have a bruise on his knee, and his clothes all dusty—Teena hitting out the dust and at the same time registering some blows for the slow way he coming out. Then Teena herself, all prim up in a cotton frock with sunflowers. She had a hair-do for the occasion and the hair iron out smooth and shiny.

Teena turn to Jean and Matilda, who stand up waiting for a sort of general dispersal.

'Girl,' she tell them, 'these men! You see how all of them drunk already? That's what I don't like about OUR PEOPLE. We not civilise.'

'I for one hardly touch the rum,' Fitz say, grumbling. 'You stick behind me like a leech!'

'Otherwise you just like them!' she say, pointing to the boys, who was straggling back from the Gents. 'And let me tell you something, I didn't come down here to look after the children. You best hads hold on to them. I am going with Jean and Matilda.'

'Oh God, at least take Willemeena with you,' Fitz beg.

'All right,' Teena concede. 'But you look after Henry, and don't let me catch you behaving like Gallows and them other fellars.'

Gallows was sporting a beer right there on the pavement, after taking off the crown cork with his jaw teeth.

Fitz wait until Teena walk off a little way ahead with Jean and Matilda. Then he give Henry a slap on his bottom and tell him, 'Go on, run after your sister and mother, and cry and say you want to go with them.'

'Ma say to stay with you.'

'Here.' Fitz give him a shilling. 'That's for you and Willy to buy lollipop or ice cream or something. Go on, scoot!'

And Fitz begin to look around desperately for a drink or three or four to catch up with the boys. Alfy haul a flask from his back pocket and give him.

'Well now,' Poor stroll over as the excursionists going in twos and threes and sevens, 'what's happening boys? All you look like if all you mow down about six bottles already.'

Poor dress to kill, as if he trying to make up in some way for the treatment he expect. He have on a brown shirt with black stripes and gold stars, and a sharkskin trousers in light blue, and a pair of two-tone shoes. But all that didn't help, because nobody answer him as they begin to stroll in the grounds of the palace. Sylvester who was keeping his rum in reserve, produce a flask and pass it around as they walking. Everybody had a swig. They skip Poor.

Hear him: 'You all not getting on catholic. What happen, I is a leper or something?'

To see him straggling along, is as if he take the place of Gallows, who was always the one trying hard to buttards. (That's a good word, but you won't find it in the dictionary. It mean like if you out of a game, for instance, and you want to come in, you have to buttards, that is, you pay a small fee and if the other players agree, they allow you to join. It ain't have no word in the English language to mean that, so OUR PEOPLE make it up.)

'What happen Alfy? Nobby? Syl, that is a sharp shirt you wearing boy—you cut it from a sari length? Anybody want a cigarette?' And Poor pull out a pack of twenty and rip off the cellophane as if is an emergency. He pass it over to Syl. Syl take it intact and pass it over to Alfy, Alfy to Nobby, Nobby to Fitz, and so the pack of cigarettes make a rounds with all the boys and escape and reach back to Poor safe and sound.

That incident commemorate the excursion.

'Not even you, Gallows?' Poor ask desperately.

But this time so, old Gallows in glory now that the boys have somebody else to lambast and give tone to. He like a kingpin in the middle of the crowd and only casting some looks of disdain at Poor, and the boys giving him kicks by playing up and treating him as if he win a pools or something.

'All right, all right,' Poor say, and light up one himself. 'Keep to your blasted selves. I have my own rum here.' And he open up a little zipper bag he had with some sandwiches and a bottle of rum. He put the bottle to his head and drink off a quarter without stopping. He cork back the bottle and put it in the bag, and wipe his hand across his mouth.

He did know it was so they would behave. Ever since Harry Banjo went on vacation everybody begin to treat him like if he was a criminal, as if it was his fault. What the arse they expect him to do, they expect him to go to the police and say that the cigarettes don't belong to Harry, that he was just holding them for him? Even Gallows, one day by the market, passing him straight! True he had his head bend down as usual, but still. And Poor pull Gallows up and say, 'What happening Gallows?' And Gallows say, 'I don't want to have anything to do with you, Poor. You send Harry Banjo to jail. Harry was a nice fellar, nicer than you, don't mind he was a Jamaican. The man only in the country a short time and you get him in trouble and save yourself. I low, but you so low you crawling.' Poor pretend he didn't know what the ostracisement was about. 'Oh ho, so that is it! All of you blaming me for what happen to Harry? I must be Harry father! Harry ain't have tongue in he mouth? What you expect me to do?' But Gallows just walk off and leave him. 'A bloody old arse-catcher like you,' Poor call after him. 'The whole set of you is only reformed criminals. Any one of you bastards would of done the same thing.' And when he hear about the excursion, he went and borrow the char-a-banc from a fellar, and only come to try and make ta-la-la and mess up things.

The way he feel now, he wish he did bring a bird with him, at least to keep company. He look around to see if he couldn't spot a thing. Sure enough, birds pelting all about the place in some tight-fitting summer frocks. By and by he drift away from the boys, hoping he could inveigle a thing to walk about the grounds with him at least, if he can't raise a sleeper.

Syl, too, as if he suddenly realise that the palace grounds is a happy hunting ground and stop strolling along suddenly and begin to swivel his head. Suddenly he kiss the cross on the chain around his neck and take off, his eyes staring on some distant object.

'Wait Syl!' Alfy call out, and run after him, being as Syl was the only one with rum at the moment. Alfy take the flask from Syl pocket while he was still walking, Syl didn't even look at him, he just keep his eyes on the horizon lest he lose sight of his selection in all them bevies.

'Once he start eye-gaming,' Nobby say, 'we ain't going to see him for a while.'

'The man come all this way to look for women,' Bat say. 'He would strain his eyes one of these good days.'

'We ain't had a drink for a long time,' Gallows say, as Alfy come back with the flask.

As they stand up to have a drink, they was just by one of the palace bedroom. You could imagine the old Henry standing up there by the window in the morning scratching his belly and looking out, after a night at the banqueting board and a tussle in bed with some fair English damsel. You could imagine the old bastard watching his chicks as they stroll about the gardens, studying which one to behead and which one to make a stroke with. If to say he had all of them there at the same time, you have to wonder how he would call out to them, because he had about three Catherines, two Annes, one Jane, and a lot of other small fry on the side. Hear him to Jane: 'Jane, call Catherine for me.' And Jane: 'Which one you want, a, b, or c?' Or imagine him hailing out himself: 'Catherine!' And three of them looking up wondering which one he going to send to the Tower for a beheading. And suppose old Henry was still alive and he look out the window and see all these swarthy characters walking about in his gardens!

In reality it was Teena who look out the window, just in time to catch Fitz putting the flask to his head, and she shout out in a loud voice: 'All right Mr Fitz! That is what you all doing, eh? Wait till I catch up with you!'

And when Fitz look up startled he see Teena looking out of King Henry window.

'What you doing up there?' he shout.

'I didn't come to Hamdon Court to drink rum and idle,' Teena say, 'I am teaching tthe children some history. But you just wait until I get down there!'

Of course I don't have to tell you that by this time all them Englishers looking on as if they never see two people talking in their lives.

And hear Fitz, high with rum: 'Don't teach the children no wicked things! Henry Eight was a evil character living with ten-twelve women!'

'It don't say so in this book,' Teena say, waving a brochure.

'Never mind the book,' Fitz say, 'he uses to behead them one after the other in the Tower. And in truth this palace ain't even belong to him, was a test name Wosley who build it, and give him as a present—'

'Here here, what's all this?' a attendant come up. 'You can't be shouting like that. Move along now.'

And upstairs in the palace, one of the seven hundred servants what used to hustle for Henry tell Teena she best hads don't shout like that through the window, because Anne of Cleves was catching up on some sleep after a heavy night.

We will catch up on some more historical data in a while, but right now my boy Charlie Victor dying for a drink, wishing he could join the boys, because he know that whatever they doing, is not looking at old armour and furniture and walking from room to room looking at all the paraphanalia that was in vogue in the days of yore. Charlie with the genteel folk admiring the past, but he feeling hungry and thirsty. As for Maisie, she would of prefer to be sky larking with the boys. Funny thing with women, you always feel you want to act as decent as possible, to be on your ps and qs: if people drinking rum and whisky you would get a sherry for she, because that is a lady's drink: if bacchanal and jumping up and revelry going on, you want to keep she aside from all that rough play. And you worrying about the thing, if you should catch a taxi instead of a bus, if you should go to theatre in the West End instead of sporting a coffee in a cafe near the station, if you should take a room in a hotel instead of taking she to some smelly two-be-four room that you sharing with a mate. And all the time, all the women waiting for is a chance to break away and let her hair down. They want to shake and twist and fire hard liquor, and if you only realise it, they ready to make a stroke at the blink of an eye.

So Maisie trudging along with old Charlie, but all the time she studying that if she was with the boys she would be getting high kicks instead of walking about as if she in the cemetery, because them Englishers, from the time they get in a palace or a tower or a art gallery or any kind of exhibition, they behave as if they on holy ground, and you can't even raise a cough. Another thing is, you wouldn't mind breezing in for a half hour on such occasions, but them places and events, you could spend a day and a night and you wouldn't see half the things.

Charlie start to get restless. 'Let's go and see the gardens,' he suggest. 'It's getting near to lunch, anyway.'

'Come on,' Maisie say, as if she was just waiting for the cue, 'let's find the others.'

On the green banks of old father Thames most of the excursionists was scattered, getting ready for lunch.

'What did you bring?' Charlie ask Maisie.

'Well, I have some cucumber and cheese sandwiches, four currant buns, and a Thermos of tea,' Maisie say.

Charlie groan. All around him pot cover flying off and some heavy yam and sweet potato putting in appearance. Leg of ham, leg of lamb, chicken leg and chicken wing and chicken breast. One woman have a big wooden spoon dishing out peas and rice from the biggest pot Maisie ever seen in her life, except for a few she see in the palace, when they visit the kitchen, and she selling a plate for two and six. A lot of people queuing up with paper plates.

'I think I'll have a plate of that,' Charlie say, throwing decorum to the winds. 'You could have all the sandwiches, and the currant buns, and the Thermos of tea.'

'Come over here with we,' Matilda call them, where the usual gang was sitting. 'We have plenty food, man.'

'Thank you,' Charlie say, and take out his handkerchief to spread for Maisie to sit down.

'Fire two,' Bat say, throwing over a bottle.

All this time the boys attacking chicken legs and some thick slice of beef and ham, and a bottle of pepper sauce passing from hand to hand.

'Nobody ain't bring any curry?' Syl looking around from group to group.

'You best hads tackle a pig foot and say the Lord is good,' Jean tell him.

Everybody sharing what they have with the others, because at times like these the spirit of generosity flow.

'Would anybody like a cup of tea?' Maisie ask, feeling guilty with so much food about the place.

'Go on Henry,' Teena say, 'you and Willy have a cup. And don't spill it. Sit down quiet on the grass and drink it, don't go running all over the place like a blue-arse fly. Fitz, you not to drink any more, rum coming out of your ears.'

'I just had a little to wash down some chicken stew,' Fitz say.

'I know. You been washing down after every mouthful.'

One of the highlights of an excursion is eating out in the open, and Alfy busy with his Zeiss, going around taking a photo at a dollar a time. As he look by the river he spot a fellar rowing a boat.

'Who is that Nobby?' he ask. 'Ain't is Gallows?'

'How could it be Gallows?' Nobby ask.

'We left Gallows in the Maze,' Bat say. 'How he get in the river?'

This time Gallows see them and row up close. 'Aye, keep food for me!' he yell.

'Plenty food here,' Jean shout, 'but what you doing in the river?'

'Maybe fish biting,' Matilda say.

'Those bitches left me in the Maze,' Gallows say, coming ashore and handing the boat over to some other excursionists. 'They thought I couldn't get out. I ask a Englisher if he see a party of desperate West Indians anywhere, and he say he see some having a banquet by the river, that it look like if you all slaughter a few animals for the feast. So I say, "Ta mate, if you hungry we will give you a baron of beef." What you have there to eat?'

'Only caveeah and smoke salmon remaining,' Teena say, 'and some patty-the-four-grass.'

'Don't make them kind of joke with me, man,' Gallows say, helping himself to pots all around, 'I am a creole of the first degree.'

Half an hour later, men lay down on the grass rolling. Some pull out their shirts, some belging, some picking their teeth, and a few old fellars catching a snooze. Bat put his head in Matilda lap and looking up at blue skies. If you ever want to hear old-talk no other time better than one like this when men belly full, four crates of beer and eight bottle of rum finish, and a summer sun blazing in the sky. Out of the blue, old-talk does start up. You couldn't, or shouldn't, differentiate between the voices, because men only talking, throwing in a few words here, butting in there, making a comment, arguing a point, stating a view. Nobody care who listen or who talk. Is as if a fire going, and everybody throwing in a piece of fuel now and then to keep it going. It don't matter what you throw in, as long as the fire keep going—wood, coal, peat, horse-shit, kerosene, gasoline, the lot.

'Boy, we should of gone and see the palace. I mean, that's what we come for.'

'I don't mind visiting the cellars. You think we could broach a cask of rum?'

'Not rum man, wines. Wines and hocks and meads and ports and ciders of various vintages. They used to live high in them days.'

'And don't talk about the food. Beef, mutton, veal, lamb, kid, pork, cony, capon, pig.'

'What about deer?'

'You mean venison. Yes; that too, red and fallow deer, not to mention dishes of sea fish and river fish, and all kinds of salads and vegetables and fruits.'

'Boy, they really used to live high in them days in truth. And pheasants and quail, and suchlike delicacies. They used to kill about twelve cow and ten sheep, and roast them whole.'

'Yes, them was great days, with nights of the round table and Richard with the lion heart and them fellars.'

'Don't forget Robin Hood and the Merry Men. And what about the fellar who was watching a spider and make the cakes burn?'

'And a one-eye test, I think was the Battle of Hastings, when he look up in the air and a arrow fall and chook out his eye.'

'That was William the Conqueror.'

'Nelson had one eye too.'

'That was the Battle of Trafalgar.'

'Boy, I feeling sleepy.'

'Ain't it had a film with Charles Laughton as the king, with a big turkey leg in his hand?'

'Charles Laughton was great. That is actor.'

'You know, old Henry just used to lick stroke, and when he tired, throw them in the Tower and say, "Off with the head!"'

'That remind me, none of we studying poor Harry Banjo. Anybody went to see him?'

'I think Gallows went.'

'How he looking Gallows?'

'He say he will kill Poor when he come out.'

'It would be good if we could get that house before he get out, and give him a pleasant surprise.'

'What house.'

'The house. That remind me, Battersby—'

'Look at that thing in the blue dress. Watch how she sitting down in the boat with she legs cock up, you could see right up.'

'I must say you boys surprise me with your historical knowledge. It's a bit mixed up, I think, but it's English history.'

'We don't know any other kind. That's all they used to teach we in school.'

'That's because OUR PEOPLE ain't have no history. But what I wonder is, when we have, you think they going to learn the children that in the English schools?'

'Who say we ain't have history? What about the Carib Indians and Abercomby and Sir Walter Raleigh?'

'Stop fugging around with that camera Alfy. Relax man, relax. Take it easy and enjoy the summer.'

'Boy I wish I was back home now. You don't wish?'

'Yes boy, life too hard over here, you have to live hand to mouth.'

'I wonder how they does treat you in jail.'

'How you mean treat you? Jail is for criminals.'

'Like you.'

'The police evil boy. You read how they exposing them?'

'I feel to piss.'

'Go and find a tree. I just leak against a oak over there.'

'Life funny boy.'

'You telling me.'

'I wonder what o'clock.'

'Syl, why you don't go back to India boy? That is your mother country.'

'Brit'n is my country.'

'Yes Syl, how come you don't wear dhoti and turban?'

'I wonder if I ever get in trouble if the Indian High Commissioner would help me, or if he would send me to the Trinidad office?'

'Man, you don't know if you Indian, negro, white, yellow or blue.'

'All he know is he is.'

'That sound like I dris when I's dri.'

'You see that ad? You see how they fugging up OUR PEOPLE. As if that's the way we speak.'

'Yes, like if you want a nigger for neighbour vote labour.'

'They too evil in this country.'

And so it going on and on, like bees lazily droning in the summer air. It don't matter what the topic is, as long as words floating about, verbs, adjectives, nouns, interjections, paraphrase and paradise, the boys don't care. It like a game, all of them throwing words in the air like a ball, now and then some scandalous laugh making sedate Englishers wonder what the arse them black people talking about, and the boats on the river, every time a boatload pass Syl waving to them, and you could see them white people getting high kicks as they wave back. You could imagine the talk that going on on the boat: 'Look dear, come and see, there's a party of Jamaicans on the bank.' And big excitement on the boat, everybody rushing to the gunnels (is a pity some of them don't break their arse and fall in the Thames) to see. And this time the boys sprawl on the grass, shirt out, socks and shoes off, belts slackened, scratching and yawning and spitting and hawking and breaking wind, and now and then this bacchanal laughter ringing out: some women washing their pots and pans in the river, and the children dashing about like blue-arse flies and you hearing the elders shout: 'WILLEMEENA! COME AWAY FROM THERE!' or 'ALBERT! IF YOU FALL IN THAT RIVER TODAY I LEAVE YOU TO DROWN!'

By and by the girls depart for another tour, this time they say they going to see the grapevine that hundreds of years old, and still bearing. Charlie, having the time of his life with the boys, inveigle Maisie to go along with them, and Poor, who was sitting down under a tree all this time by himself, take off after the girls, hoping he could talk with Maisie and raise a stroke for the night.

They didn't leave Hamdon Court until about eight o'clock the night, because you could imagine the confusion, children get lost, a woman remember she left her best pot by the river, two others dash back to buy mementoes, some fellars in a big argument with a attendant because they leave some empty bottles on the grass and he want to know if they can't read where it say KEEP BRITAIN TIDY, one old fellar holding his belly and balling and saying that he think he have a pennycitis (somebody ask him if he could afford it) and Battersby better get a ambulance for him, Poor discover the two back tyres of the char-a-banc flat and start cussing the boys in general because he don't know which one responsible, and the English driver of the coach threatening to go and leave them all behind and report the matter to the company.

And to crown it all, as they on the way back home eventually, Bat start to pass a hat around for something for the driver. Something for the driver! they ask him, how you mean something for the driver? Yes yes, Bat say, that is the custom, everybody who go on excursions have to sub up to give something for the driver. But he catch them at a bad time, nobody don't want to give a ha'penny, now that the fete finishing they start to find faults with everything, the organisation was bad, they should of had two or three buses, they should of had a guide to conduct them around the palace, somebody lost a wristwatch and the whole coach-load of them was thieves.

When they reach back to Brixton, Bat had was to give the driver a bottle of beer what escape destruction.

'Anyway,' Bat say, 'never mind, next time we go make up for it. I thinking of going further afield. These coaches does go to Scotland and Wales?'

'You don't want a coach mate,' the Englisher say maliciously. 'They should put the lot of you on a banana boat and ship you back to Jamaica.'

SECTION FOUR • "A NEW ENGLISH" • ESSAYS ON VERNACULAR ENGLISH

"A NEW ENGLISH"

ESSAYS ON VERNACULAR ENGLISH

SECTION FOUR • "A NEW ENGLISH" • ESSAYS ON VERNACULAR ENGLISH • SECTION FOUR • "A NEW ENGLISH" • ESSAYS ON VERNACULAR ENGLISH • SECTION FOUR • "A NEW ENGLISH" • SECTION FOUR • ESSAYS ON VERNACULAR ENGLISH • SECTION FOUR • "A NEW ENGLISH" • SECTION FOUR • "A NEW ENGLISH" • ESSAYS ON VERNACULAR ENGLISH • "A NEW ENGLISH" • SECTION FOUR • ESSAYS ON VERNACULAR ENGLISH • SECTION FOUR • "A NEW ENGLISH" • ESSAYS ON VERNACULAR ENGLISH • SECTION FOUR • "A NEW ENGLISH" • ESSAYS ON

SECTION FOUR

"A NEW ENGLISH"

ESSAYS ON VERNACULAR ENGLISH

THE SEVEN ESSAYS in this section provide the intellectual scaffolding that undergirds much of the literature in this collection. Many of the writer-critics included here are primarily concerned with the "New English" of one particular region—Kamau Brathwaite and M. NourbeSe Philip with the West Indies, Chinua Achebe and Gabriel Okara with Africa, and Gloria Anzaldúa and James Baldwin with North America—but all share the tenet that, as Okara puts it, "living languages grow like living things, and English is far from a dead language."

Chronologically, the section begins with Thomas Macaulay's now-infamous lecture on education in India, which was in many ways unintentionally responsible for the literary flowering represented throughout *Rotten English*. From there we jump directly to the anticolonial period and its lively debates over whether and how to appropriate the language that colonialism brought. Many of these writers respond to attacks on two fronts: from those who would protect the "purity" of Standard English (or, in Gloria Anzaldúa's case, both Standard English and Castilian Spanish), and from those, like Obi Wali and Ngũgĩ wa Thiong'o, who would eschew English entirely. To both camps they counter with ample evidence of the elastic and organic quality of language. Their essays continue to underpin the rich literary output of the following decades as poets, novelists, and theorists expand upon and challenge the ideas of Achebe, Baldwin, and the others.

There is a vast amount of valuable scholarly work on the history and methods of vernacular writers, some of which I have included in the Suggestions for Further Reading. Here, however, we hear only from theorists who are also practitioners. Their words can be taken as manifestos of sorts, whose results we may observe elsewhere in *Rotten English*. Notably, despite these writers' accomplishments in vernacular fiction and poetry, the formal conventions of the essay are still strong enough that most of them (with the exception of Anzaldúa and M. NourbeSe Philip, and those two only for selected portions) choose to write in Standard English. The vernacular essay, it appears, is as yet an untapped form.

CHINUA ACHEBE is considered by many to be the progenitor of
the African novel in English, as well as one of its most distinguished practitioners. He was born Albert Chinualumogu
Achebe in 1930 in Ogidi, Nigeria. He attended the University
of Ibadan and the University of London, studied broadcasting
at the British Broadcasting Company, and later worked at the
Nigerian Broadcasting Company. In 1958 he published his
best-known novel, *Things Fall Apart*. Since then he has written
several other novels as well as poetry and essays. In this essay
Achebe uses his own work as well as that of the African writers
Olaudah Equiano, Joseph Kariuki, Christopher Okigbo, and
Amos Tutuola to discuss the creative possibilities of a colonial
tongue. Achebe identifies significant benefits to writing as a
non-native speaker: one is necessarily and implicitly innovative. While acknowledging the problems of writing in English,
Achebe concludes forcefully that "I have been given this language and I intend to use it."

From THE AFRICAN WRITER AND THE ENGLISH LANGUAGE

(1964)

I have indicated somewhat offhandedly that the national literature of Nigeria and of many other countries of Africa is, or will be, written in English. This may sound like a controversial statement, but it isn't. All I have done has been to look at the reality of present-day Africa. This "reality" may change as a result of deliberate, e.g., political, action. If it does, an entirely new situation will arise, and there will be plenty of time to examine it. At present it may be more profitable to look at the scene as it is.

What are the factors which have conspired to place English in the position of national language in many parts of Africa? Quite simply the reason is that these nations were created in the first place by the intervention of the British which, I hasten to add, is not saying that the peoples comprising these nations were invented by the British.

The country which we know as Nigeria today began not so very long ago as the arbitrary creation of the British. It is true, as William Fagg says in his excellent new book, *Nigerian Images,* that this arbitrary action has proved as lucky in terms of African art history as any enterprise of the fortunate Princess of Serendip. And I believe that in political and economic terms too this arbitrary creation called Nigeria holds out great prospects. Yet the fact remains that Nigeria was created by the British—for their own ends. Let us give the devil his due: colonialism in Africa disrupted many things, but it did create big political units where there were small, scattered ones before. Nigeria had hundreds of autonomous communities ranging in size from the vast Fulani Empire founded by Usman dan Fodio in the north to tiny village entities in the east. Today it is one country.

Of course there are areas of Africa where colonialism divided up a single ethnic group among two or even three powers. But on the whole it did bring together many peoples that had hitherto gone their several ways. And it gave them a language with which to talk to one another. If it failed to give them a song, it at least gave them a tongue, for sighing. There are not many countries in Africa today where you could abolish the language of the erstwhile colonial powers and still retain the facility for mutual communication. Therefore those African writers who have chosen to write in English or French are not unpatriotic smart alecks with an eye on the main chance—outside their own countries. They are by-products of the same process that made the new nation-states of Africa.

You can take this argument a stage further to include other countries of Africa. The only reason why we can even talk about African unity is that when we get together we can have a manageable number of languages to talk in—English, French, Arabic.

The other day I had a visit from Joseph Kariuki of Kenya. Although I had read some of his poems and he had read my novels, we had not met before. But it didn't seem to matter. In fact I had met him through his poems, especially through his love poem, "Come Away, My Love," in which he captures in so few words the trials and tensions of an African in love with a white girl in Britain:

> *Come away, my love, from streets*
> *Where unkind eyes divide*
> *And shop windows reflect our difference.*

By contrast, when in 1960 I was traveling in East Africa and went to the home of the late Shabaan Robert, the Swahili poet of Tanganyika, things had been different. We spent some time talking about writing, but there was no real contact. I knew from all accounts that I was talking to an important writer, but of the nature of his work I had no idea. He gave me two books of his poems which I treasure but cannot read—until I have learned Swahili.

And there are scores of languages I would want to learn if it were possible. Where am I to find the time to learn the half dozen or so Nigerian languages, each of which can sustain a literature? I am afraid it cannot be done. These languages will just have to develop as tributaries to feed the one central language enjoying nationwide currency. Today, for good or ill, that language is English. Tomorrow it may be something else, although I very much doubt it.

Those of us who have inherited the English language may not be in a position to appreciate the value of the inheritance. Or we may go on resenting it because it came as part of a package deal which included many other items of doubtful value and the positive atrocity of racial arrogance and prejudice which may yet set the world on fire. But let us not in rejecting the evil throw out the good with it.

Some time last year I was traveling in Brazil meeting Brazilian writers and artists. A number of the writers I spoke to were concerned about the restrictions imposed on them by their use of the Portuguese language. I remember a woman poet saying she had given serious thought to writing in French! And yet their problem is not half as difficult as ours. Portuguese may not have the universal currency of English or French but at least it is the national language of Brazil with her eighty million or so people, to say nothing of the people of Portugal, Angola, Mozambique, etc.

Of Brazilian authors I have only read, in translation, one novel by Jorge Amado, who is not only Brazil's leading novelist but one of the most important writers in the world. From that one novel, *Gabriella*, I was able to glimpse something of the exciting Afro-Latin culture which is the pride of Brazil and is quite unlike any other culture. Jorge Amado is only one of the many writers Brazil has produced. At their national writers' festival there were literally hundreds of them. But the work of the vast majority will be closed to the rest of the world forever, including no doubt the work of some excellent writers. There is certainly a great advantage to writing in a world language.

I think I have said enough to give an indication of my thinking on the importance of the world language which history has forced down our throats. Now let us look at some of the most serious handicaps. And let me say straightaway that one of the most serious handicaps is *not* the one people talk about most often, namely, that it is impossible for anyone ever to use a second language as effectively as his first. This assertion is compounded of half truth and half bogus mystique. Of course, it is true that the vast majority of people are happier with their first language than with any other. But then the majority of people are not writers. We do have enough examples of writers who have performed the feat of writing effectively in a second language. And I am not thinking of the obvious names like Conrad. It would be more germane to our subject to choose African examples.

The first name that comes to my mind is Olauda Equiano, better known as Gustavus Vassa, the African. Equiano was an Ibo, I believe from the village of Iseke in the Orlu division of Eastern Nigeria. He was sold as a slave at a very early age and transported to America. Later he bought his freedom and lived in England. In 1789 he published his life story, a beautifully written document which, among other things, set down for the Europe of his time something of the life and habit of his people in Africa, in an attempt to counteract the lies and slander invented by some Europeans to justify the slave trade.

Coming nearer to our times, we may recall the attempts in the first quarter of this century by West African nationalists to come together and press for a greater say in the management of their own affairs. One of the most eloquent of that band was the Honorable Casely Hayford of the Gold Coast. His presidential address to the National Congress of British West Africa in 1925 was memorable not only for its sound common sense but as a fine example of elegant prose. The governor of Nigeria at the time was compelled to take notice and he did so in characteristic style: he called Hayford's Congress "a self-selected and self-appointed congregation of educated African gentlemen." We may derive some amusement from the fact that British colonial administrators learned very little in the following quarter of a century. But at least they *did* learn in the end—which is more than one can say for some others.

It is when we come to what is commonly called creative literature that most doubt seems to arise. Obi Wali, whose article "Dead End of African Literature" I referred to, has this to say:

> . . . *until these writers and their Western midwives accept the fact that any true African literature must be written in African languages, they would be merely pursuing a dead end, which can only lead to sterility, uncreativity and frustration.*

But far from leading to sterility, the work of many new African writers is full of the most exciting possibilities. Take this from Christopher Okigbo's "Limits."

Suddenly becoming talkative
  like weaverbird
Summoned at offside of
  dream remembered
Between sleep and waking
I hand up my egg-shells
To you of palm grove,
Upon whose bamboo towers hang
Dripping with yesterupwine
A tiger mask and nude spear. . . .

Queen of the damp half light,
I have had my cleansing.
Emigrant with air-borne nose,
  The he-goat-on-heat.

Or take the poem, "Night Rain," in which J. P. Clark captures so well the fear and wonder felt by a child as rain clamors on the thatch roof at night and his mother, walking about in the dark, moves her simple belongings

> *Out of the run of water*
> *That like ants filing out of the wood*
> *Will scatter and gain possession*
> *Of the floor. . . .*

I think that the picture of water spreading on the floor "like ants filing out of the wood" is beautiful. Of course if you had never made fire with faggots, you may miss it. But Clark's inspiration derives from the same source which gave birth to the saying that a man who brings home ant-ridden faggots must be ready for the visit of lizards.

I do not see any signs of sterility anywhere here. What I do see is a new voice coming out of Africa, speaking of African experience in a world-wide language. So my answer to the question *Can an African ever learn English well enough to be able to use it effectively in creative writing?* is certainly yes. If on the other hand you ask: *Can he ever learn to use it like a native speaker?* I should say, I hope not. It is neither necessary nor desirable for him to be able to do so. The price a world language must be prepared to pay is submission to many different kinds of use. The African writer should aim to use English in a way that brings out his message best without altering the language to the extent that its value as a medium of international exchange will be lost. He should aim at fashioning out an English which is at once universal and able to carry his peculiar experience. I have in mind here the writer who has something new, something different to say. The nondescript writer has little to tell us, anyway, so he might as well tell it in conventional language and get it over with. If I may use an extravagant simile, he is like a man offering a small, nondescript routine sacrifice for which a chick, or less, will do. A serious writer must look for an animal whose blood can match the power of his offering.

In this respect Amos Tutola is a natural. A good instinct has turned his apparent limitation in language into a weapon of great strength—a half-strange dialect that serves him perfectly in the evocation of his bizarre world. His last book, and to my mind, his finest, is proof enough that one can make even an imperfectly learned second language do amazing things. In this book, *The Feather Woman of the Jungle,* Tutola's superb storytelling is at last cast in the episodic form which he handles best instead of being painfully stretched on the rack of the novel.

From a natural to a conscious artist: myself, in fact. Allow me to quote a small example from *Arrow of God,* which may give some idea of how I approach the use of English. The Chief Priest in the story is telling one of his sons why it is necessary to send him to church:

> *I want one of my sons to join these people and be my eyes there. If there is nothing in it you will come back. But if there is something there you will bring home my share. The world is like a Mask, dancing. If you want to see it well you do not stand in one place. My spirit tells me that those who do not befriend the white man today will be saying* had we known *tomorrow.*

Now supposing I had put it another way. Like this for instance:

> *I am sending you as my representative among these people—just to be on the safe side in case the new religion develops. One has to move with the times or else one is left behind. I have a hunch that*

those who fail to come to terms with the white man may well regret
their lack of foresight.

The material is the same. But the form of the one is *in char-*
acter and the other is not. It is largely a matter of instinct, but
judgment comes into it too.

You read quite often nowadays of the problems of the
African writer having first to think in his mother tongue and
then to translate what he has thought into English. If it were
such a simple, mechanical process, I would agree that it was
pointless—the kind of eccentric pursuit you might expect to
see in a modern Academy of Lagado; and such a process could
not possibly produce some of the exciting poetry and prose
which is already appearing.

One final point remains for me to make. The real question
is not whether Africans *could* write in English but whether they
ought to. Is it right that a man should abandon his mother
tongue for someone else's? It looks like a dreadful betrayal and
produces a guilty feeling.

But for me there is no other choice. I have been given this
language and I intend to use it. I hope, though, that there
always will be men, like the late Chief Fagunwa, who will
choose to write in their native tongue and insure that our ethnic literature will flourish side by side with the national ones.
For those of us who opt for English, there is much work ahead
and much excitement.

Writing in the London *Observer* recently, James Baldwin
said:

My quarrel with the English language has been that the language
reflected none of my experience. But now I began to see the matter
another way. . . . Perhaps the language was not my own because I

had never attempted to use it, had only learned to imitate it. If this were so, then it might be made to bear the burden of my experience if I could find the stamina to challenge it, and me, to such a test.

I recognize, of course, that Baldwin's problem is not exactly mine, but I feel that the English language will be able to carry the weight of my African experience. But it will have to be a new English, still in full communion with its ancestral home but altered to suit its new African surroundings.

GLORIA ANZALDÚA

IN HER OWN WORDS, Gloria Anzaldúa was a "chicana dyke-feminist, tejana patlache poet, writer, and cultural theorist." She was born in 1942 in the Rio Grande Valley of Texas, USA. She attended Pan-American University and the University of Texas, and taught ages preschool to university. In 1987 Anzaldúa published the groundbreaking work *Borderlands/La Frontera: The New Mestiza,* which used new combinations—of poetry and critical writing, of Spanish and English—to assert the need for a hybrid language that would truly express her experience and that of others on the Tex-Mex border. She also wrote children's books, and edited two seminal collections on the theory and practice of multicultural feminism. Anzaldúa died in 2004. This chapter from *Borderlands* offers overlapping personal and institutional histories of Chicano Spanish. Anzaldúa describes accusations by purists on both sides of the perceived linguistic divide, and counters them by showing how multiplicitous and fluid are the languages that define her.

From BORDERLANDS/LA FRONTERA: THE NEW MESTIZA

(1987)

How to Tame a Wild Tongue

"We're going to have to control your tongue," the dentist says, pulling out all the metal from my mouth. Silver bits plop and tinkle into the basin. My mouth is a motherlode.

The dentist is cleaning out my roots. I get a whiff of the stench when I gasp. "I can't cap that tooth yet, you're still draining," he says.

"We're going to have to do something about your tongue," I hear the anger rising in his voice. My tongue keeps pushing out the wads of cotton, pushing back the drills, the long thin needles. "I've never seen anything as strong or as stubborn," he says. And I think, how do you tame a wild tongue, train it to be quiet, how do you bridle and saddle it? How do you make it lie down?

Who is to say that robbing a people of its language is less violent than war?

—RAY GWYN SMITH

I remember being caught speaking Spanish at recess—that was good for three licks on the knuckles with a sharp ruler. I remember being sent to the corner of the classroom for "talking back" to the Anglo teacher when all I was trying to do was tell her how to pronounce my name. "If you want to be American, speak 'American.' If you don't like it, go back to Mexico where you belong."

"I want you to speak English. *Pa' hallar buen trabajo tienes que saber hablar el ingles bien. Qué vale toda tu educación si todavía hablas ingles con un* 'accent,'" my mother would say, mortified that I spoke English like a Mexican. At Pan American University, I and all Chicano students were required to take two speech classes. Their purpose: to get rid of our accents.

Attacks on one's form of expression with the intent to censor are a violation of the First Amendment. *El Anglo con cara de inocente nos arrancó la lengua.* Wild tongues can't be tamed, they can only be cut out.

Overcoming the Tradition of Silence

Ahogadas, escupimos el oscuro.
Peleando con nuestra propia sombra
el silencio nos sepulta.

En boca cerrada no entran moscas. "Flies don't enter a closed mouth" is a saying I kept hearing when I was a child. *Ser habladora* was to be a gossip and a liar, to talk too much. *Muchachitas bien criadas,* well-bred girls don't answer back. *Es una falta de respeto* to talk back to one's mother or father. I remember one of the sins I'd recite to the priest in the confession box the few times I went to confession: talking back to my mother, *hablar pa' 'tras, repelar. Hocicona, repelona, chismosa,* having a big mouth, questioning, carrying tales are all signs of being *mal criada.* In my culture they are all words that are derogatory if applied to women—I've never heard them applied to men.

. . .

The first time I heard two women, a Puerto Rican and a Cuban, say the word "*nosotras,*" I was shocked. I had not known the word existed. Chicanas use *nosotros* whether we're male or female. We are robbed of our female being by the masculine plural. Language is a male discourse.

[. . .]

Even our own people, other Spanish speakers *nos quieren poner candados en la boca.* They would hold us back with their bag of *reglas de academia.*

Oyé como ladra: el lenguaje de la frontera

Quien tiene boca se equivocal.

—MEXICAN SAYING

"*Pocho,* cultural traitor, you're speaking the oppressor's language by speaking English, you're ruining the Spanish language," I have been accused by various Latinos and Latinas. Chicano Spanish is considered by the purist and by most Latinos deficient, a mutilation of Spanish.

But Chicano Spanish is a border tongue which developed naturally. Change, *evolución, enriquecimiento de palabras nuevas por invención o adopción* have created variants of Chicano Spanish, *un nuevo lenguaje. Un lenguaje que corresponde a un modo de vivir.* Chicano Spanish is not incorrect, it is a living language.

For a people who are neither Spanish nor live in a country in which Spanish is the first language; for a people who live in a country in which English is the reigning tongue but who are not Anglo; for a people who cannot entirely identify with either standard (formal, Castillian) Spanish nor standard English, what recourse is left to them but to create their own language? A language which they can connect their identity to, one capable of communicating the realities and values true to themselves—a language with terms that are neither *español ni ingles,* but both. We speak a patois, a forked tongue, a variation of two languages.

Chicano Spanish sprang out of the Chicanos' need to identify ourselves as a distinct people. We needed a language with which we could communicate with ourselves, a secret language. For some of us, language is a homeland closer than the Southwest—for many Chicanos today live in the Midwest and the East. And because we are a complex, heterogeneous people, we speak many languages. Some of the languages we speak are:

1. Standard English
2. Working class and slang English
3. Standard Spanish
4. Standard Mexican Spanish
5. North Mexican Spanish dialect
6. Chicano Spanish (Texas, New Mexico, Arizona and California have regional variations)
7. Tex-Mex
8. *Pachuco* (called *caló*)

My "home" tongues are the languages I speak with my sister and brothers, with my friends. They are the last five listed, with 6 and 7 being closest to my heart. From school, the media and job situations, I've picked up Standard and working class English. From Mamagrande Locha and from reading Spanish and Mexican literature, I've picked up Standard Spanish and Standard Mexican Spanish. From *los recién llegados,* Mexican immigrants, and *braceros,* I learned the North Mexican dialect. With Mexicans I'll try to speak either Standard Mexican

Spanish or the North Mexican dialect. From my parents and Chicanos living in the Valley, I picked up Chicano Texas Spanish, and I speak it with my mom, younger brother (who married a Mexican and who rarely mixes Spanish with English), aunts and older relatives.

With Chicanas from *Nuevo México* or *Arizona* I will speak Chicano Spanish a little, but often they don't understand what I'm saying. With most California Chicanas I speak entirely in English (unless I forget). When I first moved to San Francisco, I'd rattle off something in Spanish, unintentionally embarrassing them. Often it is only with another Chicana *tejana* that I can talk freely.

Words distorted by English are known as anglicisms or *pochismos*. The *pocho* is an anglicized Mexican or American of Mexican origin who speaks Spanish with an accent characteristic of North Americans and who distorts and reconstructs the language according to the influence of English. Tex-Mex, or Spanglish, comes most naturally to me. I may switch back and forth from English to Spanish in the same sentence or in the same word. With my sister and my brother Nune and with Chicano *tejano* contemporaries I speak in Tex-Mex.

From kids and people my own age I picked up *Pachuco*. *Pachuco* (the language of the zoot suiters) is a language of rebellion, both against Standard Spanish and Standard English. It is a secret language. Adults of the culture and outsiders cannot understand it. It is made up of slang words from both English and Spanish. *Ruca* means girl or woman, *vato* means guy or dude, *chale* means no, *simón* means yes, *churro* is sure, talk is *periquiar, pigionear* means petting, *que gacho* means how nerdy, *ponte águila* means watch out, death is called *la pelona*. Through lack of practice and not having others who can speak it, I've lost most of the *Pachuco* tongue.

Chicano Spanish

Chicanos, after 250 years of Spanish/Anglo colonization, have developed significant differences in the Spanish we speak. We collapse two adjacent vowels into a single syllable and sometimes shift the stress in certain words such as *maíz/maiz, cohete/cuete*. We leave out certain consonants when they appear between vowels: *lado/lao, mojado/mojao*. Chicanos from South Texas pronounce *f* as *j* as in *jue (fue)*. Chicanos use "archaisms," words that are no longer in the Spanish language, words that have been evolved out. We say *semos, truje, haiga, ansina*, and *naiden*. We retain the "archaic" *j*, as in *jalar*, that derives from an earlier *h* (the French *halar* or the Germanic *halon* which was lost to standard Spanish in the 16th century), but which is still found in several regional dialects such as the one spoken in South Texas. (Due to geography, Chicanos from the Valley of South Texas were cut off linguistically from other Spanish speakers. We tend to use words that the Spaniards brought over from Medieval Spain. The majority of the Spanish colonizers in Mexico and the Southwest came from Extremadura—Hernán Cortés was one of them—and Andalucía. Andalucians pronounce *ll* like a *y*, and their *d*'s tend to be absorbed by adjacent vowels: *tirado* becomes *tirao*. They brought *el lenguaje popular, dialectos y regionalismos*.)

Chicanos and other Spanish speakers also shift *ll* to *y* and *z* to *s*. We leave out initial syllables, saying *tar* for *estar, toy* for *estoy, hora* for *ahora* (*cubanos* and *puertorriqueños* also leave out initial letters of some words). We also leave out the final sylla-

ble such as *pa* for *para.* The intervocalic *y,* the *ll* as in *tortilla,
ella, botella,* gets replaced by *tortia* or *tortiya, ea, botea.* We add
an additional syllable at the beginning of certain words: *ato-
car* for *tocar, agastar* for *gastar.* Sometimes we'll say *lavaste las
vacijas,* other times *lavates* (substituting the *ates* verb endings
for the *aste*).

We use Anglicism, words borrowed from English: *bola* from
ball, *carpeta* from carpet, *máchina de lavar* (instead of *lavadora*)
from washing machine. Tex-Mex argot, created by adding a
Spanish sound at the beginning or end of an English word
such as *cookiar* for cook, *watchar* for watch, *parkiar* for park, and
rapiar for rape, is the result of the pressures on Spanish speakers to adapt to English.

We don't use the word *vosotros/as* or its accompanying verb
form. We don't say *claro* (to mean yes), *imagínate,* or *me emo-
ciona,* unless we picked up Spanish from Latinas, out of a book,
or in a classroom. Other Spanish-speaking groups are going
through the same, or similar, development in their Spanish.

Linguistic Terrorism

Deslenguadas. Somos los del español deficiente. *We are your
linguistic nightmare, your linguistic aberration, your linguistic*
mestisaje, *the subject of your* burla. *Because we speak with
tongues of fire we are culturally crucified. Racially, culturally and
linguistically* somos huérfanos—*we speak an orphan tongue.*

Chicanas who grew up speaking Chicano Spanish have
internalized the belief that we speak poor Spanish. It is illegitimate, a bastard language. And because we internalize how our
language has been used against us by the dominant culture, we
use our language differences against each other.

Chicana feminists often skirt around each other with suspicion and hesitation. For the longest time I couldn't figure it out. Then it dawned on me. To be close to another Chicana is like looking into the mirror. We are afraid of what we'll see there. *Pena.* Shame. Low estimation of self. In childhood we are told that our language is wrong. Repeated attacks on our native tongue diminish our sense of self. The attacks continue throughout our lives.

Chicanas feel uncomfortable talking in Spanish to Latinas, afraid of their censure. Their language was not outlawed in their countries. They had a whole lifetime of being immersed in their native tongue; generations, centuries in which Spanish was a first language, taught in school, heard on radio and TV, and read in the newspaper.

If a person, Chicana or Latina, has a low estimation of my native tongue, she also has a low estimation of me. Often with *mexicanas y latinas* we'll speak English as a neutral language. Even among Chicanas we tend to speak English at parties or conferences. Yet, at the same time, we're afraid the other will think we're *agringadas* because we don't speak Chicano Spanish. We oppress each other trying to out-Chicano each other, vying to be the "real" Chicanas, to speak like Chicanos. There is no one Chicano language just as there is no one Chicano experience. A monolingual Chicana whose first language is English or Spanish is just as much a Chicana as one who speaks several variants of Spanish. A Chicana from Michigan or Chicago or Detroit is just as much a Chicana as one from the Southwest. Chicano Spanish is as diverse linguistically as it is regionally.

By the end of this century, Spanish speakers will comprise the biggest minority group in the U.S., a country where students in high schools and colleges are encouraged to take

French classes because French is considered more "cultured." But for a language to remain alive it must be used. By the end of this century English, and not Spanish, will be the mother tongue of most Chicanos and Latinos.

So, if you want to really hurt me, talk badly about my language. Ethnic identity is twin skin to linguistic identity—I am my language. Until can take pride in my language, I cannot take pride in myself. Until I can accept as legitimate Chicano Texas Spanish, Tex-Mex and all the other languages I speak, I cannot accept the legitimacy of myself. Until I am free to write bilingually and to switch codes without having always to translate, while I still have to speak English or Spanish when I would rather speak Spanglish, and as long as I have to accommodate the English speakers rather than having them accommodate me, my tongue will be illegitimate.

I will no longer be made to feel ashamed of existing. I will have my voice: Indian, Spanish, white. I will have my serpent's tongue—my woman's voice, my sexual voice, my poet's voice. I will overcome the tradition of silence.

[. . .]

"Vistas," corridos, y comida: My Native Tongue

In the 1960s, I read my first Chicano novel. It was *City of Night* by John Rechy, a gay Texan, son of a Scottish father and a Mexican mother. For days I walked around in stunned amazement that a Chicano could write and could get published. When I read *I Am Joaquín* I was surprised to see a bilingual book by a Chicano in print. When I saw poetry written in Tex-Mex for the first time, a feeling of pure joy flashed through me. I felt like we really existed as a people. In 1971, when I started teaching High School English to Chicano students, I tried to supplement the required texts with works by Chicanos, only to be reprimanded and forbidden to do so by the principal. He claimed that I was supposed to teach "American" and English literature. At the risk of being fired, I swore my students to secrecy and slipped in Chicano short stories, poems, a play. In graduate school, while working toward a Ph.D., I had to "argue" with one advisor after the other, semester after semester, before I was allowed to make Chicano literature an area of focus.

Even before I read books by Chicanos or Mexicans, it was the Mexican movies I saw at the drive-in—the Thursday night special of $1.00 a carload—that gave me a sense of belonging. "*Vámonos a las vistas,*" my mother would call out and we'd all—grandmother, brothers, sister and cousins—squeeze into the car. We'd wolf down cheese and bologna white bread sandwiches while watching Pedro Infante in melodramatic tearjerkers like *Nosotros los pobres,* the first "real" Mexican movie (that was not an imitation of European movies). I remember seeing *Cuando los hijos se van* and surmising that all Mexican movies played up the love a mother has for her children and what ungrateful sons and daughters suffer when they are not devoted to their mothers. I remember the singing-type "westerns" of Jorge Negrete and Miguel Aceves Mejía. When watching Mexican movies, I felt a sense of homecoming as well as alienation. People who were to amount to something didn't go to Mexican movies, or *bailes* or tune their radios to *bolero,* *rancherita,* and *corrido* music.

The whole time I was growing up, there was *norteño* music, sometimes called North Mexican border music, or Tex-Mex music, or Chicano music, or *cantina* (bar) music. I grew up listening to *conjuntos,* three- or four-piece bands made up of folk musicians playing guitar, *bajo sexto,* drums and button accordion, which Chicanos had borrowed from the German immigrants who had come to Central Texas and Mexico to farm and build breweries. In the Rio Grande Valley, Steve Jordan and Little Joe Hernández were popular, and Flaco Jiménez was the accordion king. The rhythms of Tex-Mex music are those of the polka, also adapted from the Germans, who in turn had borrowed the polka from the Czechs and Bohemians.

I remember the hot, sultry evenings when *corridos*—songs of love and death on the Texas-Mexican borderlands— reverberated out of cheap amplifiers from the local *cantinas* and wafted in through my bedroom window.

Corridos first became widely used along the South Texas/ Mexican border during the early conflict between Chicanos and Anglos. The *corridos* are usually about Mexican heroes who do valiant deeds against the Anglo oppressors. Pancho Villa's song, *"La cucaracha,"* is the most famous one. *Corridos* of John F. Kennedy and his death are still very popular in the Valley. Older Chicanos remember Lydia Mendoza, one of the great border *corrido* singers who was called *la Gloria de Tejas.* Her *"El tango Negro,"* sung during the Great Depression, made her a singer of the people. The everpresent *corridos* narrated one hundred years of border history, bringing news of events as well as entertaining. These folk musicians and folk songs are our chief cultural myth-makers, and they made our hard lives seem bearable.

I grew up feeling ambivalent about our music. Country-western and rock-and-roll had more status. In the '50s and '60s, for the slightly educated and *agringado* Chicanos, there existed a sense of shame at being caught listening to our music. Yet I couldn't stop my feet from thumping to the music, could not stop humming the words, nor hide from myself the exhilaration I felt when I heard it.

There are more subtle ways that we internalize identification, especially in the forms of images and emotions. For me food and certain smells are tied to my identity, to my homeland. Woodsmoke curling up to an immense blue sky; woodsmoke perfuming my grandmother's clothes, her skin. The stench of cow manure and the yellow patches on the ground; the crack of a .22 rifle and the reek of cordite. Homemade white cheese sizzling in a pan, melting inside a folded *tortilla*. My sister Hilda's hot, spicy *menudo, chile colorado* making it deep red, pieces of *panza* and hominy floating on top. My brother Carito barbequing *fajitas* in the backyard. Even now and 3,000 miles away, I can see my mother spicing the ground beef, pork and venison with *chile*. My mouth salivates at the thought of the hot steaming *tamales* I would be eating if I were home.

Si le preguntas a mi mama, "¿Qué eres?"

> *Identity is the essential core of who we are as individuals, the conscious experience of the self inside.*
> —KAUFMAN

Nosotros los Chicanos straddle the borderlands. On one side of us, we are constantly exposed to the Spanish of the Mexicans, on the other side we hear the Anglos' incessant clamoring so that we forget our language. Among ourselves we don't say *nosotros los americanos, o nosotros los españoles, o nosotros los hispanos.* We say *nosotros los mexicanos* (by *mexicanos* we do not mean citizens of Mexico; we do not mean a national identity, but a racial one). We distinguish between *mexicanos del otro lado* and *mexicanos de este lado*. Deep in our hearts we believe that being Mexican has nothing to do with which country one lives in. Being Mexican is a state of soul—not one of mind, not one of citizenship. Neither eagle nor serpent, but both. And like the ocean, neither animal respects borders.

Dime con quien andas y te dire quien eres.
(Tell me who your friends are and I'll tell you who you are.)
—MEXICAN SAYING

Si le preguntas a mi mamá, "¿Qué eres?" te dirá, "Soy mexicana." My brothers and sister say the same. I sometimes will answer *"soy mexicana"* and at others will say *"soy Chicana"* o *"soy tejana."* But I identified as *"Raza"* before I ever identified as *"mexicana"* or *"Chicana."*

As a culture, we call ourselves Spanish when referring to ourselves as a linguistic group and when copping out. It is then that we forget our predominant Indian genes. We are 70–80% Indian. We call ourselves Hispanic or Spanish-American or Latin American or Latin when linking ourselves to other Spanish-speaking peoples of the Western hemisphere and when copping out. We call ourselves Mexican-American to signify we are neither Mexican nor American, but more the noun "American" than the adjective "Mexican" (and when copping out).

Chicanos and other people of color suffer economically for not acculturating. This voluntary (yet forced) alienation makes for psychological conflict, a kind of dual identity—we don't identify with the Anglo-American cultural values and we don't totally identify with the Mexican cultural values. We are a synergy of two cultures with various degrees of Mexicanness or Angloness. I have so internalized the borderland conflict that sometimes I feel like one cancels out the other and we are zero, nothing, no one. *A veces no soy nada ni nadie. Pero basta cuando no lo soy, lo soy.*

When not copping out, when we know we are more than nothing, we call ourselves Mexican, referring to race and ancestry; *mestizo* when affirming both our Indian and Spanish (but we hardly ever own our Black ancestry); Chicano when referring to a politically aware people born and/or raised in the U.S.; *Raza* when referring to Chicanos; *tejanos* when we are Chicanos from Texas.

Chicanos did not know we were a people until 1965 when César Chávez and the farm workers united and *I Am Joaquín* was published and *la Raza Unida* party was formed in Texas. With that recognition, we became a distinct people. Something momentous happened to the Chicano soul—we became aware of our reality and acquired a name and a language (Chicano Spanish) that reflected that reality. Now that we had a name, some of the fragmented pieces began to fall together—who we were, what we were, how we had evolved. We began to get glimpses of what we might eventually become.

Yet the struggle of identities continues, the struggle of borders is our reality still. One day the inner struggle will cease and a true integration take place. In the meantime, *tenémos que hacer la lucha. ¿Quién está protegiendo los ranchos de mi gente? ¿Quién está tratando de cerrar la fisura entre la india y el blanco en nuestra sangre? El Chicano, sí, el Chicano que anda como un ladrón en su propia casa.*

Los Chicanos, how patient we seem, how very patient. There is the quiet of the Indian about us. We know how to survive.

When other races have given up their tongue, we've kept ours. We know what it is to live under the hammer blow of the dominant *norteamericano* culture. But more than we count the blows, we count the days the weeks the years the centuries the eons until the white laws and commerce and customs will rot in the deserts they've created, lie bleached. *Humildes* yet proud, *quietos* yet wild, *nosotros los mexicanos-Chicanos* will walk by the crumbling ashes as we go about our business. Stubborn, persevering, impenetrable as stone, yet possessing a malleability that renders us unbreakable, we, the *mestizas* and *mestizos*, will remain.

AMERICAN NOVELIST and essayist James Baldwin was born in 1924 in New York, and began preaching sermons at his Harlem Pentecostal church at age fourteen. His celebrated first novel, *Go Tell It on the Mountain,* appeared in 1953. In the late 1950s and throughout the 1960s, Baldwin was heavily involved in the American civil rights movement through his writing (especially the essay "The Fire Next Time") and activism. He moved to France in 1970, having lived there intermittently since 1948. After writing several more novels, Baldwin died in 1987. In this influential essay, Baldwin explains the covert connection between power dynamics and designations of "language" and "dialect." Using examples from France, England, and the United States, Baldwin demonstrates how language functions as "a political instrument, means, and proof of power." His insights anticipate the controversy in 1997 over "Ebonics," in which a school funding issue (the Oakland, California, school district sought bilingual funding for students who had not grown up speaking Standard English) misleadingly appeared in the American media as a proposal to teach African American vernacular English in schools. Highlighting the prescience of Baldwin's essay, the Oakland episode perfectly illustrated the complex links among language, education, power, and money.

IF BLACK ENGLISH ISN'T A LANGUAGE, THEN TELL ME, WHAT IS?

(1979)

The argument concerning the use, or the status, or the reality, of black English is rooted in American history and has absolutely nothing to do with the question the argument supposes itself to be posing. The argument has nothing to do with language itself but with the *role* of language. Language, incontestably, reveals the speaker. Language, also, far more dubiously, is meant to define the other—and, in this case, the other is refusing to be defined by a language that has never been able to recognize him.

People evolve a language in order to describe and thus control their circumstances, or in order not to be submerged by a reality that they cannot articulate. (And, if they cannot articulate it, they *are* submerged.) A Frenchman living in Paris speaks a subtly and crucially different language from that of the man living in Marseilles; neither sounds very much like a man living in Quebec; and they would all have great difficulty in apprehending what the man from Guadeloupe, or Martinique, is saying, to say nothing of the man from Senegal—although the "common" language of all these areas is French. But each has paid, and is paying, a different price for this "common" language, in which, as it turns out, they are not saying, and cannot be saying, the same things: They each have very different realities to articulate, or control.

What joins all languages, and all men, is the necessity to confront life, in order, not inconceivably, to outwit death: The price for this is the acceptance, and achievement, of one's temporal identity. So that, for example, though it is not taught in the schools (and this has the potential of becoming a political issue) the south of France still clings to its ancient and musical Provençal, which resists being described as a "dialect." And much of the tension in the Basque countries, and in Wales, is due to the Basque and Welsh determination not to allow their languages to be destroyed. This determination also feeds the flames in Ireland, for among the many indignities the Irish have been forced to undergo at English hands is the English contempt for their language.

It goes without saying, then, that language is also a political instrument, means, and proof of power. It is the most vivid and crucial key to identity: It reveals the private identity, and connects one with, or divorces one from, the larger, public, or communal identity. There have been, and are, times, and places, when to speak a certain language could be dangerous, even fatal. Or, one may speak the same language, but in such a way that one's antecedents are revealed, or (one hopes) hidden. This is true in France, and is absolutely true in England: The range (and reign) of accents on that damp little island make England coherent for the English and totally incomprehensible for everyone else. To open your mouth in England is (if I may use black English) to "put your business in the street": You have confessed your parents, your youth, your school, your salary, your self-esteem, and, alas, your future.

Now, I do not know what white Americans would sound like if there had never been any black people in the United States, but they would not sound the way they sound. *Jazz*, for example, is a very specific sexual term, as in *jazz me, baby*, but white people purified it into the Jazz Age. *Sock it to me,* which means, roughly, the same thing, has been adopted by Nathaniel Hawthorne's descendants with no qualms or hesitations at all, along with *let it all hang out* and *right on! Beat to his socks,* which was once the black's most total and despairing image of poverty, was transformed into a thing called the Beat Generation, which phenomenon was, largely, composed of *uptight,* middle-class white people, imitating poverty, trying to *get down,* to get *with it,* doing their *thing,* doing their despairing best to be *funky,* which we, the blacks, never dreamed of doing—we *were* funky, baby, like *funk* was going out of style.

Now, no one can eat his cake, and have it, too, and it is late in the day to attempt to penalize black people for having created a language that permits the nation its only glimpse of reality, a language without which the nation would be even more *whipped* than it is.

I say that the present skirmish is rooted in American history, and it is. Black English is the creation of the black diaspora. Blacks came to the United States chained to each other, but from different tribes: Neither could speak the other's language. If two black people, at that bitter hour of the world's history, had been able to speak to each other, the institution of chattel slavery could never have lasted as long as it did. Subsequently, the slave was given, under the eye, and the gun, of his master, Congo Square, and the Bible—or in other words, and under these conditions, the slave began the formation of the black church, and it is within this unprecedented tabernacle that black English began to be formed. This was not, merely, as in the European example, the adoption of a foreign tongue, but an alchemy that transformed ancient elements into a new language: *A language comes into existence by means of brutal necessity, and the rules of the language are dictated by what the language must convey.*

There was a moment, in time, and in this place, when my brother, or my mother, or my father, or my sister, had to convey to me, for example, the danger in which I was standing from the white man standing just behind me, and to convey this with a speed, and in a language, that the white man could not possibly understand, and that, indeed, he cannot understand, until today. He cannot afford to understand it. This understanding would reveal to him too much about himself, and smash that mirror before which he has been frozen for so long.

Now, if this passion, this skill, this (to quote Toni Morrison) "sheer intelligence," this incredible music, the mighty achievement of having brought a people utterly unknown to, or despised by "history"—to have brought this people to their present, troubled, troubling, and unassailable and unanswerable place—if this absolutely unprecedented journey does not indicate that black English is a language, I am curious to know what definition of language is to be trusted.

A people at the center of the Western world, and in the midst of so hostile a population, has not endured and transcended by means of what is patronizingly called a "dialect." We, the blacks, are in trouble, certainly, but we are not doomed, and we are not inarticulate because we are not compelled to defend a morality that we know to be a lie.

The brutal truth is that the bulk of white people in America never had any interest in educating black people, except as this could serve white purposes. It is not the black child's language that is in question, it is not his language that is despised: It is his experience. A child cannot be taught by anyone who despises him, and a child cannot afford to be fooled. A child cannot be taught by anyone whose demand, essentially, is that the child repudiate his experience, and all that gives him sustenance, and enter a limbo in which he will no longer be black, and in which he knows that he can never become white. Black people have lost too many black children that way.

And, after all, finally, in a country with standards so untrustworthy, a country that makes heroes of so many criminal mediocrities, a country unable to face why so many of the nonwhite are in prison, or on the needle, or standing, futureless, in the streets—it may very well be that both the child, and his elder, have concluded that they have nothing whatever to learn from the people of a country that has managed to learn so little.

BARBADIAN POET Kamau Brathwaite (see biography in Section One) delivered this lecture at a 1979 conference entitled "Opening Up the Canon." Elaborating on a presentation by the exiled South African poet and activist Dennis Brutus, Brathwaite draws a parallel between South Africa's "prism of languages" and that of the Caribbean. Brathwaite's primary focus, though, is what he calls "nation language," an underground language developed over time by slaves, calypsonians, storytellers, and poets. Using examples from contemporary West Indian poetry, he carefully outlines and illustrates its main characteristics: orality; dactylic meter (as opposed to pentameter); and heavy audience participation. Central to Brathwaite's lecture is the contrast between "the imported alien experience of the snowfall" and "the power of the hurricane."

From HISTORY OF THE VOICE:
THE DEVELOPMENT OF NATION LANGUAGE
IN ANGLOPHONE CARIBBEAN POETRY

(1984)

We in the Caribbean have a similar kind of plurality [to that of South Africa]: we have English, which is the imposed language on much of the archipelago. It is an imperial language, as are French, Dutch and Spanish. We also have what we call creole English, which is a mixture of English and an adaptation that English took in the new environment of the Caribbean when it became mixed with the other imported languages. We have also what is called *nation language*, which is the kind of English spoken by the people who were brought to the Caribbean, not the official English now, but the language of slaves and labourers, the servants who were brought in by the conquistadors. Finally, we have the remnants of ancestral languages still persisting in the Caribbean. There is Amerindian, which is active in certain parts of Central America but not in the Caribbean because the Amerindians here are destroyed. We have Hindi, spoken by some of the more traditional East Indians who live in the Caribbean, and there are also varieties of Chinese. And, miraculously, there are survivals of African languages still persisting in the Caribbean. So we have that spectrum—that prism—of languages similar to the kind of structure that Dennis [Brutus] described for South Africa. Now, I have to give you some kind of background to the development of these languages, the historical development of this plurality, because I can't take it for granted that you know and understand the history of the Caribbean.

The Caribbean is a set of islands stretching out from Florida in a mighty curve. You must know of the Caribbean at least from television, at least now with hurricane David coming right into it. The islands stretch out on an arc of some two thousand miles from Florida through the Atlantic to the South American coast, and they were originally inhabited by Amerindian people: Taino, Siboney, Carib, Arawak. In 1492 Columbus 'discovered' (as it is said) the Caribbean, and with that discovery came the intrusion of European culture. We had Europe 'nationalizing' itself into Spanish, French, English and Dutch so that people had to start speaking (and *thinking*) four metropolitan languages rather than possibly a single native language. Then with the destruction of the Amerindians, which took place within 30 years of Columbus' discovery (one million dead a year) it was necessary for the Europeans to import new labour bodies into the area. And the most convenient form of labour was the labour on the edge of the *slave* trade winds, the labour on the edge of the hurricane, the labour on the ledge of Africa. And so Ashanti, Congo, Yoruba, all that mighty coast of western Africa was imported into the Caribbean. And we had the arrival in our area of a new language structure. It consisted of many languages but basically they had a common semantic and stylistic form. What these languages had to do, however, was to submerge themselves, because officially the conquering peoples—the Spaniards, the English, the French, and the Dutch—insisted that the language of public discourse and conversation, or obedience, command and conception should be English, French, Spanish or Dutch. They did not wish to hear people speaking Ashanti or any of the Congolese languages. So there was a submergence of this important language. Its status became one of inferiority. Similarly, its speakers were slaves. They were conceived of as inferiors—non-human, in fact. But this very submergence served an interesting interculturative purpose, because although people continued to speak English as it was spoken in Elizabethan times and on through the Romantic and Victorian ages, that English was, nonetheless, still being influenced by the underground language, the submerged language that the slaves had brought. And that underground language was itself constantly transforming itself into new forms. It was moving from a purely African form to a form which was African but which was adapted to the new environment and adapted to the cultural imperative of the European languages. And it was influencing the way in which the English, French, Dutch and Spaniards spoke their own languages. So there was a very complex process taking place, which is now beginning to surface in our literature.

Now, as in South Africa (and any area of cultural imperialism for that matter), the educational system of the Caribbean did not recognize the presence of these various languages. What our educational system did was to recognize and maintain the language of the conquistador—the language of the planter, the language of the official, the language of the Anglican preacher. It insisted that not only would English be spoken in the anglophone Caribbean, but that the educational system would carry the contours of an English heritage. Hence, as Dennis said, Shakespeare, George Eliot, Jane Austen—British literature and literary forms, the models which had very little to do, really, with the environment and the reality of non-Europe— were dominant in the Caribbean educational system. It was a very surprising situation. People were forced to learn things which had no relevance to themselves. Paradoxically, in the Caribbean (as in many other 'cultural disaster' areas), the people educated in this system came to know more, even today, about English kings and queens than they do about our own national heroes, our own slave rebels, the people who helped to build and to destroy our society. We are more excited by their literary models, by the concepts of, say, Sherwood Forest and Robin Hood than we are by Nanny of the Maroons, a name some of us didn't even known until a few years ago. And in terms of what we write, our perceptual models, we are more conscious (in terms of sensibility) of the falling of snow, for instance—the models are all there for the falling of the snow—than of the force of the hurricanes which take place every year. In other words, we haven't got the syllables, the syllabic intelligence, to describe the hurricane, which is our own experience, whereas we can describe the imported alien experience of the snowfall. It is that kind of situation that we are in.

The day the first snow fell I floated to my birth
of feathers falling by my window; touched earth
and melted, touched again and left a little touch of light
and everywhere we touched till earth was white.

This is why there were (are?) Caribbean children who, instead of writing in their 'creole' essays 'the snow was falling on the playing fields of Shropshire' (which is what our children literally were writing until a few years ago, below drawings they made of white snowfields and the corn-haired people who inhabited such a landscape), wrote: '*the snow was falling on the canefields*': trying to have both cultures at the same time.
What is even more important, as we develop this business of

emergent language in the Caribbean, is the actual rhythm and the syllables, the very software, in a way, of the language. What English has given us as a model for poetry, and to a lesser extent prose (but poetry is the basic tool here), is the pentameter: 'the cúrfew tólls the knéll of párting dáy'. There have, of course, been attempts to break it. And there were other dominant forms like, for example, *Beowulf* (c. 750), *The Seafarer* and what Langland (?1332–?1400) had produced:

> *For trewthe telleth that loue is trisacle of heven;*
> *May no synne be on him sene that useth that spise,*
> *And alle his werkes he wrougte with loue as him liste*

Or, from *Piers the Plowman* (which does not make it into *Palgrave's Golden Treasury* which we all had to 'do' at school) the haunting prologue:

> *In a somer seson whan soft was the sonne*
> *I shope me into shroudes as I a shepe were*

Which has recently inspired Derek Walcott with his first major nation language effort:

> *In idle August, while the sea soft,*
> *and leaves of brown islands stick to the rim*
> *of this Caribbean, I blow out the light*
> *by the dreamless face of Maria Concepcion*
> *to ship as a seaman on the schooner* Flight.

But by the time we reach Chaucer (1345–1400) the pentameter prevails. Over in the New World, the Americans—Walt Whitman—tried to bridge or to break the pentameter through a cosmic movement, a large movement of sound. Cummings tried to fragment it. And Marianne Moore attacked it with syllabics. But basically the pentameter remained, and it carries with it a certain kind of experience, which is not the experience of a hurricane. The hurricane does not roar in pentameters. And that's the problem: how do you get a rhythm which approximates the *natural* experience, the *environmental* experience?

[. . .]

It is *nation language* in the Caribbean that, in fact, largely ignores the pentameter. Nation language is the language which is influenced very strongly by the African model, the African aspect of our New World/Caribbean heritage. English it may be in terms of some of its lexical features. But in its contours, its rhythm and timbre, its sound explosions, it is not English, even though the words, as you hear them, might be English to a greater or lesser degree. And this brings us back to the question that some of you raised yesterday: can English be a revolutionary language? And the lovely answer that came back was: *it is not English that is the agent. It is not language, but people, who make revolutions.*

I think, however, that language does really have a role to play here, certainly in the Caribbean. But it is an English which is not the standard, imported, educated English, but that of the submerged, surrealist experience and sensibility, which has always been there and which is now increasingly coming to the surface and influencing the perception of contemporary Caribbean people. It is what I call, as I say, *nation language*. I use the term in contrast to *dialect*. The word 'dialect' has been bandied about for a long time, and it carries very pejorative overtones. Dialect is thought of as 'bad English'. Dialect is 'inferior English'. Dialect is the language used when you want

to make fun of someone. Caricature speaks in dialect. Dialect
has a long history coming from the plantation where people's
dignity is distorted through their language and the descriptions
which the dialect gave to them. Nation language, on the other
hand, is the *submerged* area of that dialect which is more closely
allied to the African aspect of experience in the Caribbean. It
may be in English: but often it is in an English which is like a
howl, or a shout or a machine-gun or the wind or a wave. It is
also like the blues. And sometimes it is English and African at
the same time. I am going to give you some examples. But I
should tell you that the reason I have to talk so much is that there
has been very little written on this subject. I bring to you the
notion of nation language but I can refer you to very little literature, to very few resources. I cannot really refer you to what you
call an 'Establishment'. I cannot really refer you to Authorities
because there aren't any. One of our urgent tasks now is to try
to create our own Authorities. But I will give you a few ideas of
what people have tried to do.

The forerunner of all this was of course Dante Alighieri
who at the beginning of the fourteenth century argued, in *De
vulgari eloquentia* (1304), for the recognition of the (his own)
Tuscan vernacular as the nation language to replace Latin as
the most natural, complete and accessible means of verbal
expression. And the movement was in fact successful throughout Europe with the establishment of national languages and
literatures. But these very successful national languages then
proceeded to ignore local European colonials such as Basque
and Gaelic, for instance, and suppressed overseas colonials
wherever they were heard. And it was not until Burns in the
18th century and Rothenberg, Trask, Vansina, Tedlock, Waley,
Walton, Whallon, Jahn, Jones, Whitely, Beckwith, Herskovits,
and Ruth Finnegan, among many others in this century, that

we have returned, at least, to the *notion* of oral literature. Although I don't need to remind you that oral literature is our oldest form of literature and that it continues richly throughout the world today. In the Caribbean, our novelists have always been conscious of these native resources, but the critics and academics have, as is kinda often the case, lagged far behind.

[. . .]

I'd like to describe for you some of the characteristics of our nation language. First of all, it is from, as I've said, an oral tradition. The poetry, the culture itself, exists not in a dictionary but in the tradition of the spoken word. It is based as much on sound as it is on song. That is to say, the noise that it makes is part of the meaning, and if you ignore the noise (or what you *think* of as noise, shall I say) then you lose part of the meaning. When it is written, you lose the sound or the noise, and therefore you lose part of the meaning. Which is, again, why I have to have a tape recorder for this presentation. I want you to get the sound of it, rather than the sight of it.

In order to break down the pentameter, we discovered an ancient form which was always there, the calypso. This is a form that I think nearly everyone knows about. It does not employ the iambic pentameter. It employs dactyls. It therefore mandates the use of the tongue in a certain way, the use of sound in a certain way. It is a model that we are moving naturally towards now. Compare

(IP) To be or not to be, that is the question
(Kaiso) The stone had skidded arc'd and bloomed into islands
   Cuba San Domingo
Jamaica Puerto Rico

But not only is there a difference in syllabic or stress pattern, there is an important difference in shape of intonation. In the Shakespeare (IP above), the voice travels in a single forward plane towards the horizon of its end. In the *kaiso,* after the skimming movement of the first line, we have a distinct variation. The voice dips and deepens to describe an intervallic pattern. And then there are more ritual forms like *kumina,* like *shango,* the religious forms, which I won't have time to go into here, but which begin to disclose the complexity that is possible with nation language.

The other thing about nation language is that it is part of what may be called *total expression,* a notion which is not unfamiliar to you because you are coming back to that kind of thing now. Reading is an isolated, individualistic expression. The oral tradition on the other hand demands not only the griot but the audience to complete the community: the noise and sounds that the maker makes are responded to by the audience and are returned to him. Hence we have the creation of a continuum where meaning truly resides. And this *total expression* comes about because people be in the open air, because people live in conditions of poverty ('unhoused') because they come from a historical experience where they had to rely on their very *breath* rather than on paraphernalia like books and museums and machines. They had to depend on *immanence,* the power within themselves, rather than the technology outside themselves.

[. . .]

Today, we have a very confident movement of nation language. In fact, it is inconceivable that any Caribbean poet writing today is not going to be influenced by this submerged/emerging culture. And it is obvious now to most Caribbean writers, I would say, except perhaps some of the most 'exiled' (and there are less and less of them!) that one has to communicate with the audience. No one is going to assert that a poet cannot live in his ivory tower, or that a poet cannot be an 'individual'—all that we have been through already. But the point is that for the needs of the kind of emerging society that I am defending— for the people who have to recite 'The boy/stood on/the burn/ing deck' for so long, who are unable to express the power of the hurricane in the way that they write words—at least, our poets, today, are recognizing that it is essential that they use the resources which have always been there, but which have been denied to them—and which they have sometimes themselves denied.

THE SCHOLAR AND CIVIL SERVANT Thomas Babington Macaulay was born in 1800 in Leicestershire, England. He attended Trinity College, Cambridge, and became a member of Parliament in 1830. From 1834 to 1838 he served on the supreme council of the East India Company. After returning to England, he held the positions of secretary of war and paymaster general, while at the same time writing a five-volume history of England, the last volume of which appeared after his death in 1859. In many ways, his "Minute on Indian Education" and the policies it advocated inadvertently brought about the linguistic innovations *Rotten English* celebrates. Macaulay recommended English-medium instruction for India with the justification that "the dialects commonly spoken among the natives of this part of India, contain neither literary nor scientific information, and are, moreover, so poor and rude that, until they are enriched from some other quarter, it will not be easy to translate any valuable work into them." When that policy later reverberated throughout the British Empire, its outcome of a reinvented English would have been thoroughly unexpected—and one imagines fairly unpalatable—to its originator.

From MINUTE ON INDIAN EDUCATION

(1835)

W̲e now come to the gist of the matter. We have a fund to be employed as Government shall direct for the intellectual improvement of the people of this country. The simple question is, what is the most useful way of employing it?

All parties seem to be agreed on one point, that the dialects commonly spoken among the natives of this part of India, contain neither literary nor scientific information, and are, moreover, so poor and rude that, until they are enriched from some other quarter, it will not be easy to translate any valuable work into them. It seems to be admitted on all sides, that the intellectual improvement of those classes of the people who have the means of pursuing higher studies can at present be effected only by means of some language not vernacular amongst them.

What then shall that language be? One-half of the Committee maintain that it should be the English. The other half strongly recommend the Arabic and Sanskrit. The whole question seems to me to be, which language is the best worth knowing?

I have no knowledge of either Sanskrit or Arabic. But I have done what I could to form a correct estimate of their value. I have read translations of the most celebrated Arabic and Sanskrit works. I have conversed both here and at home with men distinguished by their proficiency in the Eastern tongues. I am quite ready to take the Oriental learning at the valuation of the Orientalists themselves. I have never found one among them who could deny that a single shelf of a good European library was worth the whole native literature of India and Arabia. The intrinsic superiority of the Western literature is, indeed, fully admitted by those members of the Committee who support the Oriental plan of education.

It will hardly be disputed, I suppose, that the department of literature in which the Eastern writers stand highest is poetry. And I certainly never met with any Orientalist who ventured to maintain that the Arabic and Sanskrit poetry could be compared to that of the great European nations. But when we pass from works of imagination to works in which facts are recorded, and general principles investigated, the superiority of the Europeans becomes absolutely immeasurable. It is, I believe, no exaggeration to say, that all the historical information which has been collected from all the books written in the Sanskrit language is less valuable than what may be found in the most paltry abridgements used at preparatory schools in England. In every branch of physical or moral philosophy, the relative position of the two nations is nearly the same.

How, then, stands the case? We have to educate a people who cannot at present be educated by means of their mother-tongue. We must teach them some foreign language. The claims of our own language it is hardly necessary to recapitulate. It stands preeminent even among the languages of the West. It abounds with works of imagination not inferior to the noblest which Greece has bequeathed to us; with models of every species of eloquence; with historical compositions, which, considered merely as narratives, have seldom been surpassed, and which, considered as vehicles of ethical and political instruction, have never been equaled; with just and lively representations of human life and human nature; with the most profound speculations on metaphysics, morals, government, jurisprudence, and trade; with full and correct information respecting every experimental science which tends to preserve the health, to increase the comfort, or to expand the intellect of man. Whoever knows that language has ready access to all the vast intellectual wealth, which all the wisest nations of the earth have created and hoarded in the course of ninety generations. It may safely be said, that the literature now extant in that language is of far greater value than all the literature which three hundred years ago was extant in all the languages of the world together. Nor is this all. In India, English is the language spoken by the ruling class. It is spoken by the higher class of natives at the seats of Government. It is likely to become the language of commerce throughout the seas of the East. It is the language of two great European communities which are rising, the one in the south of Africa, the other in Australasia; communities which are every year becoming more important, and more closely connected with our Indian empire. Whether we look at the intrinsic value of our literature, or at the particular situation of this country, we shall see the strongest reason to think that, of all foreign tongues, the English tongue is that which would be the most useful to our native subjects.

The question now before us is simply whether, when it is in our power to teach this language, we shall teach languages in which, by universal confession, there are no books on any subject which deserve to be compared to our own; whether, when we can teach European science, we shall teach systems which, by universal confession, whenever they differ from those of Europe, differ for the worse; and whether, when we can patronize sound Philosophy and true History, we shall countenance, at the public expense, medical doctrines, which would disgrace an English farrier, Astronomy, which would move laughter in girls at an English boarding school, History, abounding with kings thirty feet high, and reigns thirty thousand years long, and Geography, made up of seas of treacle and seas of butter.

We are not without experience to guide us. History furnishes several analogous cases, and they all teach the same lesson. There are in modern times, to go no further, two memorable instances of a great impulse given to the mind of a whole society, —of prejudices overthrown,—of knowledge diffused,—of taste purified,—of arts and sciences planted in countries which had recently been ignorant and barbarous.

The first instance to which I refer, is the great revival of letters among the Western nations at the close of the fifteenth and the beginning of the sixteenth century. At that time almost every thing that was worth reading was contained in the writings of the ancient Greeks and Romans. Had our ancestors acted as the Committee of Public Instruction has hitherto acted; had they neglected the language of Cicero and Tacitus; had they confined their attention to the old dialects of our own island; had they printed nothing and taught nothing at the universities but Chronicles in Anglo-Saxon, and Romances in Norman-French, would England have been what she now is? What the Greek and Latin were to the contemporaries of More and Ascham our tongue is to the people of India. The literature of England is now more valuable than that of classical antiquity. I doubt whether the Sanskrit literature be as valuable as that of our Saxon and Norman progenitors. In some departments,—in History, for example,—I am certain that it is much less so.

It is impossible for us, with our limited means, to attempt to educate the body of the people. We must at present do our best to form a class who may be interpreters between us and the millions whom we govern; a class of persons, Indian in blood and colour, but English in taste, in opinions, in morals, and in intellect. To that class we may leave it to refine the vernacular dialects of the country, to enrich those dialects with terms of science borrowed from the Western nomenclature, and to render them by degrees fit vehicles for conveying knowledge to the great mass of the population.

GABRIEL OKARA

THE POET AND NOVELIST Gabriel Okara was born in Bumoundi, Nigeria, in 1921. His novel *The Voice* is considered one of the major works of Anglophone African literature. In this brief essay Okara explains how he adapted Ijaw and Igbo expressions into that novel.

(1963)

Trying to express ideas even in one's own language is difficult because what is said or written is not exactly what one had in mind. Between the birth of the idea and its translation into words, something is lost. The process of expression is even more difficult in the second language of one's own cultural group. I speak not of merely expressing general ideas, but of communicating an idea to the reader in the absolute or near absolute state in which it was conceived. Here, you see I am already groping for words to make you understand what I really mean as an African.

"Once an African, always an African: it will show in whatever you write" says one school of thought. This implies that there is no need for an African writer to exert a conscious effort to make his writing African through the use of words or the construction of sentences. Equally it seems to say that the turns of phrase, the nuances and the imagery which abound in African languages, thinking, and culture are not worth letting the world know about.

As a writer who believes in the utilization of African ideas, African philosophy and African folk-lore and imagery to the fullest extent possible, I am of the opinion that the only way to use them effectively is to translate them almost literally from the African language native to the writer into whatever European language he is using as his medium of expression. I have endeavoured in my words to keep as close as possible to the vernacular expression. For, from a word, a group of words, a sentence and even a name in any African language, one can glean the social norms, attitudes and values of a people.

In order to capture the vivid images of African speech, I had to eschew the habit of expressing my thoughts first in English. It was difficult at first, but I had to learn I had to study each Ijaw expression I used and to discover the probable situation in which it was used in order to bring out the nearest meaning in English. I found it a fascinating exercise.

Some words and expressions are still relevant to the present day life of the world, while others are rooted in the legends and tales of a far-gone day. Take the expression "he is timid" for example. The equivalent in Ijaw is "he has no chest" or "he has no shadow". Now a person without a chest in the physical sense can only mean a human that does not exist. The idea becomes clearer in the second translation. A person who does not cast a shadow of course does not exist. All this means is that a timid person is not fit to live. Here, perhaps, we are hearing the echoes of the battles in those days when the strong and the brave lived. But is this not true of the world today?

In parting with a friend at night a true Ijaw would say, "May we live to see ourselves tomorrow". This again is reminiscent of the days when one went about with the danger of death from wild beasts or hostile animals dogging one's steps. But has the world we live in changed so much? On the other hand, how could an Ijaw born and bred in England, France or the United States write, "May we live to see ourselves" instead of "Goodnight"? And if he wrote "Goodnight", would he be expressing an Ijaw thought? Is it only the colour of one's skin that makes one an African?

In the Ibo language they say something like, "May dawn come", or "May it dawn". Once again it is a wish or a prayer. Isn't the grave sometimes likened to an endless night and is it not only the dead that go to the grave? The Ibos sometimes lighten this somber thought with the expression, "you sleep like a rat while I sleep like a lizard". Because it is thought that rats never sleep, while lizards are heavy sleepers, this never fails to produce peals of laughter.

Why should I not use the poetic and beautiful, "May we live to see ourselves tomorrow" or, "May it dawn", instead of "Goodnight"? If I were writing a dialogue between two friends, one about to leave after visiting the other night, I would do it this way:

> *"Are you getting up now?"* said Otutu as he saw his friend *heaving himself up with his two hands gripping the arms of the chair he was sitting on.*
>
> *"Yes I am about walking now. The night has gone far",* Beni his *friend said, for he was a very fat man.*
>
> *"May we live to see ourselves tomorrow",* his friend also said *and walked panting into the night.*

What emerges from the examples I have given is that a writer can use the idioms of his own language in a way that is understandable in English. If he uses their English equivalents, he would not be expressing African ideas and thoughts, but English ones.

Some may regard this way of writing in English as a desecration of the language. This is of course not true. Living language grows like living things, and English is far from a dead language. There are American, West Indian, Australian, Canadian and New Zealand versions of English. All of them add life and vigour to the language while reflecting their own respective cultures. Why shouldn't there be a Nigerian or West African English which we can use to express our own ideas, thinking and philosophy in our own way?

IN THE AFTERWORD to her experimental poetry collection *She Tries Her Tongue, Her Silence Softly Speaks,* M. NourbeSe Philip (see biography in Section One) meditates on how few models of Caribbean writers were available to her as she grew up in Tobago. Despite that absence, Philip managed gradually to develop her own writerly self, largely by coming to understand how over generations African-diasporic slaves created a "language of the people. Language for the people. Language by the people, honed and fashioned through a particular history of empire and savagery."

THE ABSENCE OF WRITING OR HOW I ALMOST BECAME A SPY

(1993)

I wasn't hard-backed but I definitely wasn't no spring chicken when I started to write—as a way of living my life I mean, although like a lot of women I had been doing it on the quiet quiet filling up all kinds of notebooks with poems, thinkings—deep and not so deep—curses and blessings.

The last thing I expected to end up doing was writing, and when I upsed and left a safe and decent profession—second oldest in the world, they say—for writing, I was the most surprised person. Is in those growing up years as a child in Trinidad and Tobago that you will find the how, why and wherefore of this take-me-by-surprise change.

If someone had asked me when I was growing up to tell them what pictures came to mind when I heard the word 'writer' I would have said nothing. What I wanted to be most of all was a spy, and after reading about spies in World War II, spying was much more real to me than writing. After all there was an Empire and we, its loyal subjects, had to defend it. Black and brown middle class people—my family, short on money but long on respectability, belonged to this class—wanted their children to get 'good jobs' and, better yet, go into the professions. Massa day was done and dreams were running high high—my son the doctor! Education was open to everyone, girl and boy alike—my daughter the lawyer! And if your son or daughter didn't manage to get that far, there was always nursing, teaching or accounting. Failing that there was always the civil service.

Some people might say that this was normal since the writers we had heard about—all white—had usually starved and you couldn't say this about doctors or lawyers. Education was going to be the salvation of the black middle classes—so we believed—and a profession was the best proof that you had put servitude behind you, and were becoming more like the upper classes. Writing was no help in this at all.

In high school I was learning and learning about many things—English literature, French history, American history and finally in my fifth year, West Indian history—poor-ass cousin to English history and the name V. S. Naipaul was there somewhere. V. S. Naipaul, writer. It was a sister of his who taught me in high school who first mentioned him to us, her students. But V. S. Naipaul was Indian and, in the context of Trinidad at that time, in the eyes of the blacks, this was a strike against him. V. S. Naipaul the writer we didn't understand or care to understand. Maybe, without knowing it, we were already understanding how he was going to use us in his writing life.

Books for so! I wasn't no stranger to them—they were all around since my father was a headmaster and living in the city meant I could get to the library easily. Books for so! rows and rows of them at the library as greedy-belly I read my way through Dostoevsky, Moravia, Shakespeare, Dickens. Books for so! Other people were writing them. I was reading them.

I wasn't different from any of the twenty or so girls in my sixth-form class. None of them were looking to writing as a career, or even thinking the thought as a possibility. Profession, vocation, career—we all knew those words; we, the black and brown middle classes, scholarship girls whom our teachers were exhorting to be the cream of society, the white salt of the earth. Profession, vocation, career—anything but writer.

Some people are born writing, some achieve writing and some have writing thrust upon them. My belonging is to the last group, coming slowly to accept the blessing and yoke that is writing, and with so doing I have come upon an understanding of language—good-english-bad-english english, Queenglish and Kinglish—the anguish that is english in colonial societies. The remembering—the revolutionary language of 'massa day done'—change fomenting not in the language of rulers, but in the language of the people.

Only when we understand language and its role in a colonial society can we understand the role of writing and the writer in such a society; only then, perhaps, can we understand why writing was not and still, to a large degree, is not recognized as a career, profession, or way of be-ing in the Caribbean and even among Caribbean people resident in Canada.

What follows is my attempt to analyse and understand the role of language and the word from the perspective of a writer resident in a society which is still very much colonial—Canada; a writer whose recent history is colonial and continues to cast very long shadows.

Fundamental to any art form is the image, whether it be the physical image as created by the dancer and choreographer, the musical image of the composer and musician, the visual image of the plastic artist or the verbal image, often metaphorical, of the writer and poet. (For the purposes of this essay I will be confining myself for the most part to the concept of image as it relates to the writer.) While, however, it may be quite easy to see the role of image as it relates to the visual artist, it may be less easy to do so with respect to the writer. The word 'image' is being used here to convey what can only be described as the irreducible essence—the i-mage—of creative writing; it can be likened to the DNA molecules at the heart of all life. The process of giving tangible form to this i-mage may be called i-maging, or the i-magination. Use of unconventional orthography, 'i-mage' in this instance, does not only represent the increasingly conventional deconstruction of certain words, but draws on the Rastafarian practice of privileging the 'I' in many words.[1] 'I-mage' rather than 'image' is, in fact, a closer approximation of the concept under discussion in this essay. In her attempt to translate the i-mage into meaning and non-meaning, the writer has access to a variety of verbal techniques and methods—comparison, simile, metaphor, metonymy, symbol, rhyme, allegory, fable, myth—all of which aid her in this process. Whatever the name given to the technique or form, the function remains the same—that of enabling the artist to translate the i-mage into meaningful language for her audience.

The power and threat of the artist, poet or writer lies in this ability to create new i-mages, i-mages that speak to the essential being of the people among whom and for whom the artist creates. If allowed free expression, these i-mages succeed in altering the way a society perceives itself and, eventually, its collective consciousness. For this process to happen, however, a society needs the autonomous i-mage-maker for whom the i-mage and the language of any art form become what they should be—a well-balanced equation.

When, in the early 1900s, Picasso and his fellow artists entered their so-called 'primitive stage' they employed what had traditionally been an African aesthetic of art and sculpture and succeeded in permanently altering the sensibilities of the West toward this aesthetic. In the wake of European colonial penetration of Africa and Oceania the entire art world was, in fact, revolutionized and the modernist art movement was

born. These changes did not necessarily increase the understanding or tolerance of the West for Africans and Africa, but
people began to perceive differently.

I-mages that comprised the African aesthetic had previously
been thought to be primitive, naive, and ugly, and consequently had been dismissed not only by white Westerners, but
by the Africans themselves living outside Africa—so far were
Africans themselves removed from their power to create, control and even understand their own i-mages. The societies in
which these New World Africans lived—North and South
America, England, the Caribbean—lacked that needed matrix
in which the autonomous i-mage-maker could flourish. The
only exception to this is to be found in musical traditions,
where despite the hostility of these predominantly white societies, the African i-mage-maker in musical art forms was successful in producing authentic art which has also permanently
influenced Western music.

Caribbean society has been a colonial society for a much
longer time than not, and the role of the i-mage, i-mage-
making, and i-mage control are significant. The societies that
comprise the Caribbean identity may be identified by:

   (a) a significant lack of autonomy in the creation and dis-
       semination of i-mages;
   (b) opposition by the ruling classes both at home and
       abroad to the creation of i-mages that challenge their i-
       mage making powers and the status quo;
   (c) restricting of indigenously created i-mages to marginal
       groups, e.g. reggae and calypso.

While changes like independence have improved some of
these circumstances both within the Caribbean and within
Caribbean societies in the large metropolitan centers overseas,

these factors continue to affect the artist and particularly the writer. The tradition of writing for the Caribbean and Caribbean people is a brief one, and briefer still is the Afro-centric tradition in that writing.

I argued above that at the heart of all creative writing is the i-mage; the tangible presentation of this is the word, or word symbol as I prefer to describe it. The success of the execution of this i-mage, be it poetical or in the extended metaphor of the novel, depends to a large degree on the essential tension between the i-mage and word or words giving voice to the i-mage. Tension is created by the interplay of i-mage and word—i-mage creating word, word giving rise to further i-mage and so on. This process is founded upon familiarity with word and i-mage, 'familiarity' being used here in the sense of being kin to, a part of, related to. What is assumed here, but probably should not be, is also a growing familiarity with be-ing and how it relates to the outer world.

If this process is as it should be, then the autonomous i-mage-maker serves the function of continually enriching the language by enlarging the source of i-mages—in particular, metaphorical i-mage. If we accept that living language continually encapsulates, reflects and refines the entire experiential life and world view of the tribe, the race and consequently of society at large; and if we accept that the poet, the story-teller, the singer or balladeer (through their words) express this process in their work, then we must accept that this process becomes one way in which a society continually accepts, integrates and transcends its experiences, positive or negative. For it is through those activities—poetry, story-telling and writing—that the tribe's experiences are converted and transformed to i-mage and to word almost simultaneously, and from word back to i-mage again. So metaphorical life takes place, so the language becomes richer, the store of metaphor, myth and fable enlarged, and the experience transcended not by exclusion and alienation, but by inclusion in the linguistic psyche, the racial and generic memory of the group.

The progenitors of Caribbean society as it exists today created a situation such that the equation between i-mage and word was destroyed for the African. The African could still think and i-mage, she could still conceive of what was happening to her. But in stripping her of her language, in denying the voice power to make and, simultaneously, to express the i-mage—in denying the voice expression, in fact—the ability and power to use the voice was effectively stymied. We could go further and argue that with the withering of the word in the New World, not only did the i-mage die, but also the capacity to create in one's own i-mage. The bridge that language creates, the crossover from i-mage to expression was destroyed, if only temporarily. Furthermore, alien and negative European languages would replace those African languages recently removed and, irony of all ironies, when the word/i-mage equation was attempted again, this process would take place through a language that was not only experientially foreign, but also etymologically hostile and expressive of the non-being of the African. To speak another language is to enter another consciousness. Africans in the New World were compelled to enter another consciousness, that of their masters, while simultaneously being excluded from their own. While similar prohibitions extended to music and various times, language was one of the most important sites of struggle between the Old World and the New World. The outcome of this struggle was the almost absolute destruction and obliteration of African languages. Together with the accompanying act of renaming by the European, this was one of the most devastating and successful acts of aggression carried out by one people against another. African musical art forms probably owe their survival and persistence to the fact that they were essentially non-verbal.

Once the i-mage making power of the African had been removed or damaged by denial of language and speech, the African was then forced back upon the raw experience without the linguistic resources to integrate and eventually transcend it. The resulting situation became one in which the African was decontextualised, except in so far as her actions generated profits for the owners. The language within which that decontextualisation flourished was in itself and *at best* a decontextualised one for the African. At worst the language would serve to destroy. Language, therefore, succeeded in pushing the African further away from the expression of her experience and, consequently, the meaning of it.

The African in the Caribbean could move away from the experience of slavery in time; she could even acquire some perspective upon it, but the experience, having never been reclaimed and integrated metaphorically through the language and so within the psyche, could never be transcended. To reclaim and integrate the experience required autonomous i-mage makers and therefore a language with the emotional, linguistic, and historical resources capable of giving voice to the particular i-mages arising out of the experience. In summing up his efforts to augment the English language in the sixteenth century, Sir Thomas Elyot wrote, "I intended to augment our Englyshe tonge, whereby men should as well expresse more abundantly the thynge that they conceyved in theyr harts (wherefore language was ordeyned) hauynge wordes apte for the pourpose." That the African needed to express "more abundantly the thynge . . . they conceyved in theyr harts" is undisputed; that the English language lacked "wordes apte for the pourpose" cannot be denied. Over and above her primary function as a chattel and unit of production, the English language merely served to articulate the non-being of the African. The purpose for which language was ordained would remain unfulfilled. I would argue further that it is impossible for any language that inherently denies the essential humanity of any group or people to be truly capable of giving voice to the i-mages of experiences of that group without tremendous and fundamental changes within the language itself. In the instant case, however, since there was no possible expression of the New World experience within any African language, the i-maging could only be expressed through the English language.

Essentially, therefore, what the African would do is use a foreign language expressive of an alien experiential life—a language comprised of word symbols that even then had affirmed negative i-mages about her, and one which was but a reflection of the experience of the European ethnocentric world view. This would, eventually, become her only language, her only tool to create and express i-mages about herself, and her life experiences, past, present and future. The paradox at the heart of the acquisition of this language is that the African learned both to speak and to be dumb at the same time, to give voice to the experience and i-mage, yet remain silent. That silence has had profound effect upon the English-speaking African Caribbean artist working in the medium of words.

Speech, voice, language, and word—all are ways of being in the world, and the artist working with the i-mage and giving voice to it is being in the world. The only way the African artist could be in this world, that is the New World, was to give voice to this split i-mage of voiced silence. Ways to transcend that contradiction had to and still have to be developed, for that silence continues to shroud the experience, the i-mage and so the word. As the poet, Cecilia Bustamente, writes in *The Poet and Her Text*:

> . . . *within this radius (of language) she discovers that having adapted herself as a vehicle of communication for historical and cultural moments between a dominant culture and a dominated one, language is becoming one more tool of subordination, replacement, pressure and distortion. Its potential is unexpressed, a proof that it suffers from margination of the dominated, or rather—the threat of being unable to internalize her own culture which has been violated. In order to express this reality, the social function of language fosters either its communicative values or silence [my emphasis]. Reflecting a similar stress it detects the multiple structures of violence, its authenticity is tested in the confusion of recognition in the tense structures of violation and domination that, whether paradoxical or contrary, are always obstructive . . . This is the dilemma of the dominated: to disappear or change at the prices of their lives.*

Concerning literature and the Caribbean, C. L. R. James has written that "language for us is not a distillation of our past."[2] If by 'language' is meant Queen's or King's English as we know it, this statement is true, because that language, for all the reasons given above, can never be a distillation of our past. But what the ordinary African, the African on the Papine bus, or the Port-of-Spain route taxi, or the Toronto subway, produced from the only linguistic behaviour allowed her—that is, functionality (at its barest level) in the English language—is truly and surely a distillation of her past. It may not be the clearest distillation, but it remains a distillation all the same.

In the vortex of New World slavery, the African forged new and different words, developed strategies to impress her experience on the language. The formal standard language was subverted, turned upside down, inside out, and even sometimes erased. Nouns became strangers to verbs and vice versa; tonal accentuation took the place of several words at a time; rhythms held sway. Many of these 'techniques' are rooted in African languages; their collective impact on the English language would result in the latter being, at times, unrecognizable as English. Bad English. Broken English. Patois. Dialect. These words are for the most part negative descriptions of the linguistic result of the African attempting to leave her impress on the language. That language now bears the living linguistic legacy of a people trying and succeeding in giving voice to their experience in the best and sometimes the only way possible. The havoc that the African wreaked upon the English language is, in fact, the metaphorical equivalent of the havoc that coming to the New World represented for the African. Language then becomes more than a distillation, it is the truest representation, the mirror i-mage of the experience.

Language of the people. Language for the people. Language by the people, honed and fashioned through a particular history of empire and savagery. A language also nurtured and cherished on the streets of Port-of-Spain, San Fernando, Boissiere Village and Sangre Grande in the look she dey and leh we go, in the mouths of the calypsonians, Jean and Dinah, Rosita and Clementina, Mama look a boo boo, the cuss buds, the limers, the hos (whores), the jackabats, and the market women. These are the custodians and lovers of this strange wonderful you tink it easy jive ass kickass massa day done Chagaramus is we own ole mass pretty mass pansweet language. A more accurate description of this language would be to call it a demotic variant of English. The Caribbean demotic. The excitement for me as a writer comes in the confrontation between the formal and the demotic within the text itself.

In the absence of any other language by which the past may be repossessed, reclaimed and its most painful aspects transcended, English in its broadest spectrum must be made to do the job. To say that the experience can only be expressed in standard English (if there is any such thing) or only in the Caribbean demotic (there *is* such a thing) is, in fact, to limit the experience for the African artist working in the Caribbean demotic. It is *in the continuum of expression* from standard to Caribbean English that the veracity of the experience lies.

One can never be less than self-conscious as an African Caribbean writer working in any of the demotic variants of English, whether the demotic variant be a form of standard English or Caribbean English. And for the writer from the Caribbean, language must always present a dilemma. At its most simple, the dilemma can be resolved to an either/or dichotomy: either one writes in a demotic variant of English, or one writes in straight English. Choice of one or the other in this scenario is often seen as a political choice and much bad writing takes place on either side of the divide in the name of linguistic validity. It is not sufficient, however, to write only in dialect, for too often that remains a parallel and closed experience, although a part of the same language. Neither is it sufficient to write only in what we have come to call standard English. The language as we know it has to be dislocated and acted upon—even destroyed—so that it begins to serve our purposes. It is our only language, and while it is our mother tongue, ours is also a father tongue. Some writers—Derek Walcott and Wilson Harris immediately come to mind—have publicly acknowledged their gratitude for the 'blessing' conferred on them by the imposition of the English language and have, in fact, refused to acknowledge that there even exists a dilemma; others like Earl Lovelace have taken up the challenge that the anguish that is English presents for all African Caribbean people.

The issue is, however, more complex than the either/or dichotomy suggests. The place African Caribbean writers occupy is one that is unique, and one that forces the writer to operate in a language that was used to brutalize and diminish Africans so that they would come to a profound belief in their own lack of humanity. No language can accomplish this—and to a large degree English did—without itself being profoundly affected, without itself being tainted. The challenge, therefore, facing the African Caribbean writer who is at all sensitive to language and to the issues that language generates, is to use the language in such a way that the historical realities are not erased or obliterated, so that English is revealed as the tainted tongue it truly is. Only in so doing will English be redeemed.

Subversion of the language has already taken place. It began when the African in the New World through alchemical (al kimiya, the art of the black and Egypt) practices succeeded in transforming the leavings and detritus of a language and infused it with her own remembered linguistic traditions. Much more must now be attempted. If we accept the earlier premises, that at the heart of the language lies the i-mage, metaphorical or otherwise, and that to the artist falls the task of articulating and presenting this image to the people, then the attack must be made at the only place where any true change is ever possible: at the heart of the language—the i-mage and the simultaneous naming of it. The African artist in the Caribbean and in the New World must create in, give voice to and control her own i-mages. This is essential for any group, person, or people, but more so for the African in the New World, since in one sense, our coming upon ourselves, our revelation to ourselves in the New World was simultaneous with a negative re-presentation of ourselves to ourselves, by a hostile imperialistic power, and articulated in a language endemically and etymologically hostile to our very existence. In a very real sense, it can be argued that for the African in the New World learning the English language was simultaneous with learning of her non-being, her lack of wholeness.

The experience of the African in the Caribbean and the New World is now, however, as much part of the English collective experience as England is part, for better or worse, of the African experience (in the same manner, for instance, that Germany will always be a part of the Jewish collective experience and vice versa). That experience expressed in the language—a language that is shared yet experientially different for both groups—has been and continues to be denied, hence terms like broken or bad English, or good English, all of which serve to alienate the speaker even further from her experience. If the language is to continue to do what language must do; if it is to name and give voice to the i-mage and the experience behind that i-mage—the thing we conceive in our hearts—and so house the being, then the experience must be incorporated in the language and the language must begin to serve the re-creation of those i-mages.

There are certain historical and sociological, not to mention etymological, reasons why when we hear certain words and phrases, such as 'thick lips' or 'kinky hair', the accompanying images are predominantly negative; such expressions connote far more than they denote. From whose perspective are the lips of the African thick or her hair kinky? Certainly not from the African's perspective. How then does the writer describe the Caribbean descendants of West Africans so as not to connote the negativity implied in descriptions such as 'thick lips'?

Journal entry Dec. 11, 1986 (Testimony stoops to Mother Tongue)
I want to write about kinky hair and flat noses—maybe I should be writing about the language that *kinked* the hair and *flattened* noses, *made* jaws prognathous . . .

This was how I tried to meet this particular challenge in a particular poem; it is but a small example of the challenge facing the African Caribbean writer who is interested in making English her home. The challenge is to re-create the images behind these words so that the words are being used newly.

The African in the Caribbean and the New World is as much entitled to call the English language her own, as the Englishman in his castle. However, just as we have had to make that i-mage our own, so too must he be made to acquire our i-mages, since we are both heirs to a common language, albeit to different linguistic experiences. Our experiences have touched, in both negative and positive ways, and we remain forever sensitive to each other through the language.

For too long, however, we have been verbal or linguistic squatters, possessing adversely what is truly ours. If possession is, in fact, nine-tenths of the law, then the one-tenth that remains is the legitimisation process. It is probably the hardest part, this reclaiming of our image-making power in what has been for a long time a foreign language. It must be done.

It is, perhaps, ironic that New World Africans, descendants of cultures and societies where the word and the act of naming was

the focal point and fulcrum of societal forces,[3] should find themselves in a situation where the word, their word and the power to
name was denied them. Traditionally, for instance, in many West
African societies, until named, a child did not even acquire a rec-
ognizable and discernible human identity. In the New World
after the destruction of the native peoples, Africans would be
renamed with the name of the stranger. If what the artist does is
create in her own i-mage and *give name* to that i-mage, then what
the African artist from the Caribbean and the New World must
do is create in, while giving name to, her own i-mage—and in so
doing eventually heal the word wounded by the dislocation
and imbalance of the word/i-mage equation. This can only be
done by consciously restructuring, reshaping and, if necessary,
destroying the language. When that equation is balanced and
unity of word and i-mage is once again present, then and only
then will we have made the language our own.

This is not a conclusion

What happens when you are excluded from the fullness and
wholeness of language?

What happens when only one aspect of a language is allowed
you—as woman?
—as Black?

What happens when the language of ideas is completely
removed and nothing is given to replace it?

Surely thought requires language—how can you, without
language, think or conceptualize?

What happens to a language that is withheld or only used in
a particular way with its users—does it become dissociated?
—one level business

—one level orders, commands, abuses, brutality
—one level education to a specific purpose and level

What of celebration?
What of love?
What of trust between individuals?

There can be no conclusion to the issues raised in this essay since language is always and continually changing—a fluid phenomenon. One version of this paper was published many years ago in the journal *Fireweed* (1983), and at that time I called this section Postscript and wrote that it was "not a conclusion because the issues raised here are still very much undecided." The questions I raised then were "how does one begin to destroy a language? How does one replace the image behind the word?" I replied then that those questions remained unanswered and would "probably remain so for a long time." I am now struck at how prescient I was in that original article about many of the issues I was to deal with in my writing subsequent to the writing of the paper. The Absence of Writing could be seen as something of a blueprint for my poetic and writing life.

Have I answered those questions, or do they still remain unanswered? I believe I have come closer to answering them than I did six years ago. The manuscript, *She Tries Her Tongue*, has taken me a long way towards the goal of decentring the language. This is not the same thing as destroying a language which is a far harder thing to do. Also, destruction connotes great sturm und drang when, in fact, what works just as well at

times is a more subtle but equally profound approach. For
instance in the poem, 'Discourse on the Logic of Language',
the issue that I raised in the earlier Postscript—that of father
tongue vis-à-vis a mother tongue, some sort of balance is
achieved despite the anguish of English, and despite the fact
that English is both a mother tongue and a father tongue. In
the accompanying journal I kept as I worked on *She Tries Her
Tongue* I write as follows:

> *I am laying claim to two heritages—one very accessible, the other
> hidden. The apparent accessibility of European culture is danger-
> ous and misleading especially what has been allowed to surface
> and become de rigueur. To get anything of value out of it, one has
> to mine very, very deeply and only after that does one begin to see
> the connections and linkages with other cultures. The other
> wisdoms—African wisdom needs hunches, gut feelings and a lot of
> flying by the seat of the pants, free falls only to be caught at the last
> minute. It calls for a lot more hunting out of the facts before one can
> even get to the essence, because in almost exact reversal with
> European culture not much has been allowed to surface—am
> almost tempted to say that one can for that reason trust that infor-
> mation more.*

I must add now that lack of information bears directly on
one's ability to make i-mages.

The linguistic rape and subsequent forced marriage between
African and English tongues has resulted in a language capable
of great rhythms and musicality; one that is and is not English,
and one which is among the most vital in the English-speaking
world today. The continuing challenge for me as a writer/
poet is to find some deeper patterning—a deep structure, as
Chomsky puts it—of my language, the Caribbean demotic. The

challenge is to find the literary form of the demotic language. As James Baldwin has written, "Negro speech is not a question of dropping s's or n's or g's but a question of the beat."[4] At present the greatest strength of the Caribbean demotic lies in its oratorical energies which do not necessarily translate to the page easily. Just as the language that English people write is not necessarily or often that which is spoken by them, so too what is spoken in the streets of Trinidad, or by some Caribbean people in Toronto, is not always going to be the best way of expressing it on the page. To keep the deep structure, the movement, the kinetic energy, the tone and pitch, the slides and glissandos of the demotic within a tradition that is primarily page-bound—that is the challenge.

In the former Postscript, I wrote that it was "perhaps, ironic that a critique of the use and role of English in a particularly brutal, historical context should be written in standard English, but that in itself throws into sharp relief the dilemma described above." I was not completely satisfied with my argument then that the dilemma as to what language was appropriate was answered by my argument that the English language in its complete range belonged to us, and whatever mode best suited our needs should be used. In fact, the problem was that the piece itself did not, as I now believe it ought to, reflect that range that I spoke of. Unlike the former piece, the opening paragraphs of the present piece, explaining the absence of writing in my early life, are written closer to the Caribbean demotic than to standard English. Could or ought I to have continued the entire piece in this style? Perhaps, but I do believe that the present piece is a far truer reflection of how I function linguistically than the original one.

While I continue to write in my father tongue, I continue the quest I identified in 1983 to discover my mother tongue,

trying to engender by some alchemical practice a metamor-
phosis within the language from father tongue to mother
tongue. Will I recognize this tongue when I find it, or is it rather
a matter of developing it rather than finding it? Whatever
metaphorical i-mages one uses—discovery or development—the
issue of recognition is an important one, since implied within the
word itself is the meaning, the i-mage of knowing again.

There was a profound eruption of the body into the text of
She Tries Her Tongue. This represents a significant development
for me as a poet. The manuscript has become a blaze along a
poetic path. In the New World, the female African body
became the site of exploitation and profoundly anti-human
demands—forced reproduction along with subsequent force-
ful abduction and sale of children. Furthermore, while the
possibility of rape remains the amorphous threat it is, the
female body continues to be severely circumscribed in its inter-
action with the physical surrounding space and place. How
then does this affect the making of poetry, the making of
words, the making of i-mages if poetry, as I happen to believe,
"begins in the body and ends in the body"?[5] *She Tries Her
Tongue* is the first blaze along the path to understanding and
resolving this particular conundrum.

I continue, as I did in the former Postscript, to see the issue
as being one of power, and so control. I still, as I did then, fear
being reductionist, but writing does entail control in many
areas—control of the word, control of the i-mage, control of
information which helps in the process of i-mage-making and,
equally important, control in the production of the final product. By the time the manuscript *She Tries Her Tongue* comes into
print it will be almost two years and many, many rejections
after its completion, despite its winning the *Casa de las Americas*
prize in 1988. As a female and a black living in a colonial soci-

ety of Trinidad and Tobago, control was absent in each of these areas, hence the absence of writing, especially creative writing, and hence the lack of recognition of writing as a possible vocation or profession. As a female and a black presently living in a society that is, in many respects, still colonial (I refer here to Canada's relationship with the United States of America), and a society which is politely but vehemently racist, while I may have gained some control of my word and its i-mage-making capacities, control of information and production is still problematic.

For the many like me, black and female, it is imperative that our writing begin to re-create our histories and our myths, as well as integrate that most painful of experiences—loss of our history and our word. The reacquisition of power to create in one's own i-mage and to create one's own i-mage is vital to this process; it reaffirms for us that which we have always known, even in those most darkest of times which are still with us, when everything conspired to prove otherwise—that we belong most certainly to the race of humans.

END NOTES

1. Readers interested in exploring Rastafarian language further are referred to the works of the Jamaican writer Valma Pollard.
2. C. L. R. James, "The Artist in the Caribbean," in *The Future in the Present* (Westport: Lawrence & Co., 1977), p. 184.
3. Janheinz Jahn, *Muntu* (New York: Grove Press inc., 1961), p. 125.
4. *Conversations with James Baldwin,* Edited by Fred L. Standley and Louis H. Pratt (Jackson: University Press of Mississippi, 1989).
5. Burnshaw, Stanley, *The Seamless Web* (New York: George Braziller Inc., 1970).

AMY TAN

AMY TAN IS BEST KNOWN for *The Joy Luck Club,* an elegantly patchworked collection of stories on four Chinese immigrant women and their American-born daughters. Tan was born in Oakland, California, in 1952, and grew up in California and Switzerland. She studied at San José State University and worked as a speech therapist and business writer before she began writing short stories. In addition to *The Joy Luck Club,* she has written children's books, essays, and novels. In this essay Tan describes the circuitous path by which she came to fiction, and to the particular voices perfected in that fiction.

MOTHER TONGUE

(1990)

I am not a scholar of English or literature. I cannot give you much more than personal opinions on the English language and its variations in this country or others.

I am a writer. And by that definition, I am someone who has always loved language. I am fascinated by language in daily life. I spend a great deal of my time thinking about the power of language—the way it can evoke an emotion, a visual image, a complex idea, or a simple truth. Language is the tool of my trade. And I use them all—all the Englishes I grew up with.

Recently, I was made keenly aware of the different Englishes I do use. I was giving a talk to a large group of people, the same talk I had already given to half a dozen other groups. The nature of the talk was about my writing, my life, and my book, *The Joy Luck Club*. The talk was going along well enough, until I remembered one major difference that made the whole talk sound wrong. My mother was in the room. And it was perhaps the first time she had heard me give a lengthy speech, using the kind of English I have never used with her. I was saying things like, "The intersection of memory upon imagination" and "There is an aspect of my fiction that relates to thus-and-thus"—a speech filled with carefully wrought grammatical phrases, burdened, it suddenly seemed to me, with nominalized forms, past perfect tenses, conditional phrases, all the forms of standard English that I had learned in school and through books, the forms of English I did not use at home with my mother.

Just last week, I was walking down the street with my mother, and I again found myself conscious of the English I was using, the English I do use with her. We were talking about the price of new and used furniture and I heard myself saying this: "Not waste money that way." My husband was with us as well, and he didn't notice any switch in my English. And then I realized why. It's because over the twenty years we've been together I've often used that same kind of English with him, and sometimes he even uses it with me. It has become our language of intimacy, a different sort of English that relates to family talk, the language I grew up with.

So you'll have some idea of what this family talk I heard sounds like, I'll quote what my mother said during a recent conversation which I videotaped and then transcribed. During this conversation, my mother was talking about a political gangster in Shanghai who had the same last name as her family's, Du, and how the gangster in his early years wanted to be adopted by her family, which was rich by comparison. Later, the gangster became more powerful, far richer than my mother's family, and one day showed up at my mother's wedding to pay his respects. Here's what she said in part: "Du Yusong having business like fruit stand. Like off the street kind. He is Du like Du Zong—but not Tsung-ming Island people. The local people call putong, the river east side, he belong to that side local people. That man want to ask Du Zong father take him in like become own family. Du Zong father wasn't look down on him, but didn't take seriously, until that man big like become a mafia. Now important person, very hard to inviting him. Chinese way, came only to show respect, don't stay for dinner. Respect for making big celebration, he shows up. Mean gives lots of respect. Chinese custom. Chinese social life that way. If too important won't have to stay too long. He come to my wedding. I didn't see, I heard it. I gone to boy's side, they have YMCA dinner. Chinese age I was nineteen."

You should know that my mother's expressive command of English belies how much she actually understands. She reads the *Forbes* report, listens to *Wall Street Week*, converses daily with her stockbroker, reads all of Shirley MacLaine's books with ease—all kinds of things I can't begin to understand. Yet some of my friends tell me they understand 50 percent of what my mother says. Some say they understand 80 to 90 percent. Some say they understand none of it, as if she were speaking pure Chinese. But to me, my mother's English is perfectly clear, perfectly natural. It's my mother tongue. Her language, as I hear it, is vivid, direct, full of observation and imagery. That was the language that helped shape the way I saw things, expressed things, made sense of the world.

Lately, I've been giving more thought to the kind of English my mother speaks. Like others, I have described it to people as "broken" or "fractured" English. But I wince when I say that. It has always bothered me that I can think of no way to describe it other than "broken," as if it were damaged and needed to be fixed, as if it lacked a certain wholeness and soundness. I've heard other terms used, "limited English," for example. But they seem just as bad, as if everything is limited, including people's perceptions of the limited English speaker.

I know this for a fact, because when I was growing up, my mother's "limited" English limited my perception of her. I was ashamed of her English. I believed that her English reflected the quality of what she had to say. That is, because she expressed them imperfectly her thoughts were imperfect. And

I had plenty of empirical evidence to support me: the fact that people in department stores, at banks, and at restaurants did not take her seriously, did not give her good service, pretended not to understand her, or even acted as if they did not hear her.

My mother has long realized the limitations of her English as well. When I was fifteen, she used to have me call people on the phone to pretend I was she. In this guise, I was forced to ask for information or even to complain and yell at people who had been rude to her. One time it was a call to her stockbroker in New York. She had cashed out her small portfolio and it just so happened we were going to go to New York the next week, our very first trip outside California. I had to get on the phone and say in an adolescent voice that was not very convincing, "This is Mrs. Tan."

And my mother was standing in the back whispering loudly, "Why he don't send me check, already two weeks late. So mad he lie to me, losing me money."

And then I said in perfect English, "Yes, I'm getting rather concerned. You had agreed to send the check two weeks ago, but it hasn't arrived."

Then she began to talk more loudly. "What he want, I come to New York tell him front of his boss, you cheating me?" And I was trying to calm her down, make her be quiet, while telling the stockbroker, "I can't tolerate any more excuses. If I don't receive the check immediately, I am going to have to speak to your manager when I'm in New York next week." And sure enough, the following week there we were in front of this astonished stockbroker, and I was sitting there red-faced and quiet, and my mother, the real Mrs. Tan, was shouting at his boss in her impeccable broken English.

We used a similar routine just five days ago, for a situation that was far less humorous. My mother had gone to the hospital for an appointment, to find out about a benign brain tumor a CAT scan had revealed a month ago. She said she had spoken very good English, her best English, no mistakes. Still, she said, the hospital did not apologize when they said they had lost the CAT scan and she had come for nothing. She said they did not seem to have any sympathy when she told them she was anxious to know the exact diagnosis, since her husband and son had both died of brain tumors. She said they would not give her any more information until the next time and she would have to make another appointment for that. So she said she would not leave until the doctor called her daughter. She wouldn't budge. And when the doctor finally called her daughter, me, who spoke in perfect English—lo and behold—we had assurances the CAT scan would be found, promises that a conference call on Monday would be held, and apologies for any suffering my mother had gone through for a most regrettable mistake.

I think my mother's English almost had an effect on limiting my possibilities in life as well. Sociologists and linguists probably will tell you that a person's developing language skills are more influenced by peers. But I do think that the language spoken in the family, especially in immigrant families which are more insular, plays a large role in shaping the language of the child. And I believe that it affected my results on achievement tests, I.Q. tests, and the SAT. While my English skills were never judged as poor, compared to math, English could not be considered my strong suit. In grade school I did moderately well, getting perhaps B's, sometimes B-pluses, in English and scoring perhaps in the sixtieth or seventieth percentile on achievement tests. But those scores were not good enough to override the opinion that my true abilities lay in math and science, because in those areas I achieved A's and scored in the ninetieth percentile or higher.

This was understandable. Math is precise; there is only one correct answer. Whereas, for me at least, the answers on English tests were always a judgment call, a matter of opinion and personal experience. Those tests were constructed around items like fill-in-the-blank sentence completion, such as, "Even though Tom was, Mary thought he was———." And the correct answer always seemed to be the most bland combinations of thoughts, for example, "Even though Tom was shy, Mary thought he was charming": with the grammatical structure "even though" limiting the correct answer to some sort of semantic opposites, so you wouldn't get answers like, "Even though Tom was foolish, Mary thought he was ridiculous." Well, according to my mother, there were very few limitations as to what Tom could have been and what Mary might have thought of him. So I never did well on tests like that.

The same was true with word analogies, pairs of words in which you were supposed to find some sort of logical, semantic relationship—for example, "Sunset is to nightfall as ——— is to ———." And here you would be presented with a list of four possible pairs, one of which showed the same kind of relationship: red is to stoplight, bus is to arrival, chills is to fever, yawn is to boring: Well, I could never think that way. I knew what the tests were asking, but I could not block out of my mind the images already created by the first pair, "sunset is to nightfall"—and I would see a burst of colors against a darkening sky, the moon rising, the lowering of a curtain of stars. And all the other pairs of words—red, bus, stoplight, boring—just threw up a mass of confusing images, making it impossible for me to sort out something as logical as saying: "A sunset precedes nightfall" is the same as "a chill precedes a fever." The only way I would have gotten that answer right would have been to imagine an associative situation, for example, my being disobedient and staying out past sunset, catching a chill at night, which turns into feverish pneumonia as punishment, which indeed did happen to me.

I have been thinking about all this lately, about my mother's English, about achievement tests. Because lately I've been asked, as a writer, why there are not more Asian Americans represented in American literature. Why are there few Asian Americans enrolled in creative writing programs? Why do so many Chinese students go into engineering! Well, these are broad sociological questions I can't begin to answer. But I have noticed in surveys—in fact, just last week—that Asian students, as a whole, always do significantly better on math achievement tests than in English. And this makes me think that there are other Asian-American students whose English spoken in the home might also be described as "broken" or "limited." And perhaps they also have teachers who are steering them away from writing and into math and science, which is what happened to me.

Fortunately, I happen to be rebellious in nature and enjoy the challenge of disproving assumptions made about me. I became an English major my first year in college, after being enrolled as pre-med. I started writing nonfiction as a freelancer the week after I was told by my former boss that writing was my worst skill and I should hone my talents toward account management.

But it wasn't until 1985 that I finally began to write fiction. And at first I wrote using what I thought to be wittily crafted sentences, sentences that would finally prove I had mastery over the English language. Here's an example from the first draft of a story that later made its way into *The Joy Luck Club,* but without this line: "That was my mental quandary in its nascent state." A terrible line, which I can barely pronounce.

Fortunately, for reasons I won't get into today, I later decided I should envision a reader for the stories I would write. And the reader I decided upon was my mother, because these were stories about mothers. So with this reader in mind—and in fact she did read my early drafts—I began to write stories using all the Englishes I grew up with: the English I spoke to my mother, which for lack of a better term might be described as "simple"; the English she used with me, which for lack of a better term might be described as "broken"; my translation of her Chinese, which could certainly be described as "watered down"; and what I imagined to be her translation of her Chinese if she could speak in perfect English, her internal language, and for that I sought to preserve the essence, but neither an English nor a Chinese structure. I wanted to capture what language ability tests can never reveal: her intent, her passion, her imagery, the rhythms of her speech and the nature of her thoughts.

Apart from what any critic had to say about my writing, I knew I had succeeded where it counted when my mother finished reading my book and gave me her verdict: "So easy to read."

GLOSSARY

GLOSSARIES are a source of some contention in the world of postcolonial and "minority" literature. Some authors refuse to allow their work to appear with any kind of explanatory notes. Others, notably Raja Rao in *Kanthapura* and Zora Neale Hurston in "Story in Harlem Slang" (included in Section Two), go so far as to provide their own glossaries. Notes and glosses assist with clarity and accessibility, but they can also disrupt the organic flow that writers work so hard to achieve. For better or for worse, they absolve the reader of some of the labor of immersing oneself in an unfamiliar and potentially difficult idiom. As Rohinton Mistry notes, a glossary can be "condescending" since "it underestimates the reader's ability to comprehend through context."

This glossary, therefore, represents a compromise between condescension and clarity. It provides explanations only for those words that are critical for comprehension of the piece and are also very local or now archaic. My aim is to follow authors' instincts regarding how much effort to ask of their readers. Vernacular writers demand immersion; most of them want and intend for us to understand their writing, no matter how forbidding it may initially appear. Sam Selvon, for example, helpfully provides an internal gloss of "buttards," noting with pride the newness and specificity of the word. On the other hand, difficulty or even incomprehension are sometimes part of the point. Tom Leonard uses the daunting appearance of his verse to deter an audience he would not want. In the poem "Good Style," he mockingly asks an imagined reader, "helluva hard tay read theez init," and further declares, "if yi canny unnirston thim jiss clear aff then / gawn / get tay fuck ootma road." Gloria Anzaldúa gives internal translations in places; but elsewhere her aim is to reproduce for non-Spanish speakers the same frustration she often felt in an English-only environment.

Reading any piece of literature, we effectively enter into a covenant wherein we work hard to decode a lexicon that may be unfamiliar to us. With the warning that "I know you feel strange doing it," one of my students advised her classmates to approach vernacular literature by reading it out loud. She was speaking in particular of Irvine Welsh's stories, but the same guidance applies to any of the more phonetic writers like Charles Chesnutt, Paul Laurence Dunbar, and Tom Leonard. There are also many Internet-based resources available, from Spanish-English dictionaries, to slang discussion boards, to glossaries specific to the work of Robert Burns.

No matter how difficult a new writer initially appears, the decoding becomes much easier after a few pages. If, as readers, we enter as fully as possible into a new idiom, we quickly gain fluency. As Brathwaite describes in the excerpt included in Section Four, these are works that rely upon their listeners: as opposed to the "isolated, individualistic experience" of reading a standard text, "the oral tradition on the other hand demands not only the griot but also the audience to complete the community. . . . Hence we have the creation of a continuum where meaning truly resides." In assuming the existence of a perfect audience, vernacular writers in effect create that audience, even if they must educate it to become the audience they need. To quote Mutabaruka, "dis poem has no poet"; in other words, vernacular literature is a communal undertaking.

GLORIA ANZALDÚA, "How to Tame a Wild Tongue"

agringado: Americanized (gringo-ized)
bailes: dances
burla: joke
deslenguadas: rude, course, foulmouthed girls or women
el Anglo con cara de inocente nos arrancó la lengua: the innocent-faced Anglo seized our tongue
los recién llegados: recent arrivals (male or female)
mal criada: spoiled, ill-bred (in this form, female only)
mestisaje: ethnic or cultural mixture
pocho: an Americanized Mexican
reglas de academia: academic rules
somos huérfanos: we are orphans (male or female)

LOUISE BENNETT, "Bans O'Killing"

bans o': a lot of

KAMAU BRATHWAITE, "Wings of a Dove"

pickney: child

ROBERT BURNS, "Auld Lang Syne," "Highland Mary," and "Bonnie Lesley"

aye: ever
birk: birch
braes: banks, slopes, or hills
braid: broad
burn: small river
drumlie: muddy, troubled

fit: foot; footstep
gowans: wild daisies
gude-willie: goodwill
pint stowp: two-quart measure
pou'd: pulled
scaith: harm
syne: since (auld lang syne: since long ago)
waught: draft; drink

PETER CAREY, *True History of the Kelly Gang*

proddies: Protestants

CHARLES CHESNUTT, "Po' Sandy"

cunjuh 'oman: sorceress (conjure woman)
goopher: magic, spell
ha'nts: ghosts (haunts)
kyars: carries
Mars: Master

JUNOT DÍAZ, "The Brief Wondrous Life of Oscar Wao"

abuela: grandmother
asqueroso: disgusting, repulsive
batey: sugar mill
bochinche: commotion
bracero: laborer
chacabana: embroidered dress shirt
gaijin: Japanese word for a non-Japanese person
gordo: fat boy or man (gordo asqueroso: disgusting fat boy)
guagua: bus
guapas: beauties
pariguayo: loser
puta: whore

quisqueyanos: Dominicans
sinvergüencería: shamelessness
tío: uncle
trigueña: olive-skinned
vergüenza: shame
yaniqueques: crunchy fried tortillas

ALAN DUFF, *Once Were Warriors*

fulla: guy (fellow)
Pakeha: New Zealander of European descent

JOHN KASAIPWALOVA, "Betel Nut Is Bad Magic for Airplanes"

Bomana: a large prison near Port Moresby, Papua New Guinea
dimdim: white person
kalabus: prison
kanaka: native Pacific Islander
maski: forget about
P.K: alternative brand name for Wrigley's chewing gum
Strine: Australian

PAUL KEENS-DOUGLAS, "Wukhand"

mareno: a men's sleeveless T-shirt or undershirt
marga: skinny

R. ZAMORA LINMARK, *Rolling the R's*

hapa: Hawaiian word for partial, usually used as shorthand for "hapa haole," or "part white," to designate a person of mixed East Asian and European descent

GAUTAM MALKANI, *Londonstani*

bhanchod: fucker
desi: South Asian

gora: white man or boy
kara: steel bracelet worn by observant Sikhs
khota: ass
pehndu: fool
sala kuta: bastard dog

MARY McCABE, "Comin Back Ower the Border"

biggins: buildings
cleugh: rocky gorge or chasm
corry: mountain hollow
gurlie: stormy, threatening, bleak
keek: peep
kintra: country
mochie: misty
roon: round
shilpit: thin
smirr: drizzle
snell: keen, bitter, sharp
straucht: stretched
yird: ground

CLAUDE McKAY, "Quashie to Buccra"

buccra: white man
cowitch: a medicinal bean that grows on a thick vine
quashie: black man
quattiewut: a quarter-penny worth
shamar: mimosa plant

KEN SARO-WIWA, *Sozaboy: A Novel in Rotten English*

don: done (i.e., already did, as in "my father wey don die")
kotuma: court bailiff, or other low-level civil servant

soza: soldier
wey: who

MARK TWAIN, "A True Story, Repeated Word for Word as I Heard It"

kurtchy: curtsy

SUGGESTIONS FOR FURTHER READING

I. FICTION, POETRY, MEMOIR, DRAMA

Algarín, Miguel, Nicole Blackman, and Bob Holman, eds. *Aloud: Voices from the Nuyorican Poets Café*. New York: Owl Press, 1994.

Anzaldúa, Gloria. *Borderlands/La Frontera: The New Mestiza*. San Francisco: Aunt Lute Books, 1987.

Bambara, Toni Cade. *Gorilla, My Love*. New York: Random House, 1972.

Bancil, Parv. *Crazyhorse*. London and Boston: Faber and Faber, 1997.

———. *Made in England* (play produced in 1998); *Bollywood or Bust Innit* (play produced in 1999).

Baraka, Amiri. *Transbluesency: The Selected Poetry of Amiri Baraka/Leroi Jones, 1961–1995*. New York: Marsilio Publishers, 1995.

Bennett, Louise. *Jamaica Labrish*. Kingston, Jamaica: Sangster's Book Stores, 1966.

———. *Selected Poems*. Edited by Mervyn Morris. Kingston, Jamaica: Sangster's Book Stores, 1982.

Brathwaite, Kamau. *The Arrivants: A New World Trilogy*. London: Oxford University Press, 1973.

———. *Black + Blues*. Havana: Casa de las Americas, 1976.

———. *Trench Town Rock*. Providence, R.I.: Lost Roads Publishers, 1994.

Brooks, Gwendolyn. *Selected Poems*. New York: Harper & Row, 1963.

Burgess, Anthony. *A Clockwork Orange*. London: Heinemann, 1962.

Burnett, Paula, ed. *The Penguin Book of Caribbean Verse*. London: Penguin, 1986.

Burns, Robert. *Poems, Chiefly in the Scottish Dialect*. Kilmarnock, Scotland: John Wilson, 1786.

Cable, George Washington. *The Grandissimes: A Story of Creole Life*. New York: Scribner's, 1880.

Chesnutt, Charles. *The Conjure Woman and Other Conjure Tales*. Boston: Houghton Mifflin, 1899.

Cruz, Victor Hernández. *Maraca: New and Selected Poems, 1965–2000*. Minneapolis, Minn.: Coffee House Press, 2001.

Desani, G. V. *All About H. Hatterr*. 1948; New York: Farrar, Straus and Giroux, 1970.

Díaz, Junot. *Drown*. New York: Riverhead Books, 1996.

Doyle, Roddy. *The Commitments*. Dublin: King Farouk, 1987.

———. *The Van*. London: Secker & Warburg, 1991.

———. *Paddy Clark Ha Ha Ha*. London: Secker & Warburg, 1993.

Duff, Alan. *One Night Out Stealing*. Auckland, New Zealand: Tandem, 1992.

———. *What Becomes of the Broken Hearted?* London: Vintage, 1997.

Dunbar, Paul Laurence. *Lyrics of Lowly Life*. New York: Dodd, Mead, 1896.

Dunne, Finley Peter. *Mr. Dooley in Peace and in War*. Boston: Small, Maynard, 1898.

———. *Mr. Dooley's Philosophy*. New York: R. H. Russell, 1900.

———. *Dissertations by Mr. Dooley*. New York: Harper's, 1902.

Fusco, Coco. *English Is Broken Here.* New York: New Press, 1995.

Grace, Patricia. *The Dream Sleepers.* Auckland, New Zealand: Longman Paul, 1980.

———. *Selected Stories.* New York: Penguin Books, 1991.

Harris, Joel Chandler. *Uncle Remus: His Songs and Sayings.* New York: D. Appleton, 1881.

Harrison, Tony. *V. and Other Poems.* New York: Farrar, Straus and Giroux, 1991.

Headley, Victor. *Yardie.* New York: Atlantic Monthly Press, 1993.

Heaney, Seamus. *An Open Letter.* Dublin: Field Day, 1983.

Hughes, Langston. *Simple's Uncle Sam.* New York: Hill & Wang, 1965.

———. *The Collected Poems of Langston Hughes.* New York: Knopf, 1994.

Hurston, Zora Neale. *Mules and Men.* 1935; New York: Perennial Library, 1990.

———. *Their Eyes Were Watching God.* 1937; New York: Perennial Library, 1990.

———. *The Complete Stories.* New York: HarperCollins, 1995.

Iceberg Slim. *Pimp: The Story of My Life.* Los Angeles: Holloway House, 1969.

———. *Mama Black Widow.* Los Angeles: Holloway House, 1969.

Johnson, Dana. *Break Any Woman Down.* New York: Anchor Books, 2001.

Johnson, Linton Kwesi. *Dread Beat An' Blood.* London: Bogle-L'Ouverture, 1975.

———. *Inglan Is a Bitch.* London: Race Today, 1980.

Keens-Douglas, Paul. *Tim Tim.* Port of Spain, Trinidad: Keensdee Productions, 1976.

———. *Tell Me Again.* Port of Spain, Trinidad: Keensdee Productions, 1979.

Kelman, James. *How Late It Was, How Late.* London: Secker & Warburg, 1994.

———. *You Have to Be Careful in the Land of the Free.* London: Hamish Hamilton, 2004.

Kipling, Rudyard. *Barrack-Room Ballads.* London: Methuen, 1892.

Komunyakaa, Yusef. *Neon Vernacular.* Middletown, Conn.: Wesleyan University Press, 1993.

Kotzwinkle, William. *The Fan Man.* New York: Harmony Books, 1974.

Laviera, Tato. *AmeRícan.* Houston, Tex.: Arte Público Press, 1985.

———. *Enclave.* Houston, Tex.: Arte Público Press, 1985.

———. *La Carreta Made a U-Turn.* Houston, Tex.: Arte Público Press, 1992.

Leonard, Tom. *Intimate Voices.* Newcastle upon Tyne: Galloping Dog Press, 1984.

Linmark, R. Zamora. *Prime Time Apparitions.* New York: Hanging Loose Press, 2003.

Lovelace, Earl. *The Dragon Can't Dance.* London: Andre Deutsch, 1979.

———. *The Wine of Astonishment.* London: Andre Deutsch, 1982.

———. *Jestina's Calypso and Other Plays.* London: Heinemann, 1984.

MacDiarmid, Hugh. *Selected Poems.* Manchester: Carcanet Press, 1992.

McCabe, Patrick. *The Butcher Boy.* London: Pan Books, 1992.

McCourt, Frank. *Angela's Ashes.* New York: Scribner, 1996.

McKay, Claude. *Songs of Jamaica* (1912) and *Constab Badlands* (1912). Reprinted together as *The Dialect Poetry of Claude McKay.* Salem, N.H.: Ayer, 1987.

Medina, Tony, and Louis Reyes Rivera, eds. *Bum Rush the Stage: A Def Poetry Jam.* New York: Three Rivers Press, 2001.

Mighty Sparrow. *One Hundred and Twenty Calypsos to Remember.* Sound recording. Port of Spain, Trinidad: National Recording Co., 1963.

Montoya, José. *In Formation: 20 Years of Joda.* San Jose, Calif.: Chusma House Publications, 1992.

Mootoo, Shani. *Out on Main Street.* Vancouver: Press Gang Publishers, 1993.

Okara, Gabriel. *The Voice.* London: Andre Deutsch, 1964.

Parks, Suzan-Lori. *Topdog/Underdog.* New York: Theatre Communications Group, 2001.

————. *The Red Letter Plays.* New York: Theatre Communications Group, 2001.

————. *Getting Mother's Body: A Novel.* New York: Random House, 2003.

Persaud, Sasenarine. *Canada Geese and Apple Chatney.* Toronto: TSAR, 1998.

Philip, M. NourbeSe. *She Tries Her Tongue, Her Silence Softly Breaks.* Charlottetown, Prince Edward Island: Ragweed Press, 1988.

Pierre, DBC. *Vernon God Little.* London: Faber and Faber, 2003.

Rao, Raja. *Kanthapura.* London: George Allen & Unwin, 1938.

Reed, Ishmael. *Yellow Back Radio Broke-Down.* Garden City, N.Y.: Doubleday, 1969.

————. *The Last Days of Louisiana Red.* New York: Random House, 1974.

————. *New and Collected Poems.* New York: Atheneum, 1988.

Rushdie, Salman, ed. *Mirrorwork: Fifty Years of Indian Writing in English.* New York: Henry Holt, 1997.

Sanchez, Sonia. *Shake Loose My Skin.* Boston: Beacon Press, 1999.

Saro-Wiwa, Ken. *A Forest of Flowers*. 1986; Harlow, Essex, England: Longman, 1995.

Selvon, Samuel. *The Lonely Londoners*. New York: St. Martin's Press, 1956.

———. *Moses Ascending*. 1975; London: Heinemann, 1984.

Soyinka, Wole. *The Road*. London and Ibadan, Nigeria: Oxford University Press, 1965.

———. *The Jero Plays*. London: Methuen, 1973.

Stein, Gertrude. *Three Lives*. 1909; New York: Penguin, 1990.

Swift, Jonathan. *A Dialogue in Hibernian Stile Between A and B, and Irish Eloquence*. Monkstown, Ireland: Cadenus Press, 1977.

Thomas, Piri. *Down These Mean Streets*. New York: Knopf, 1967.

———. *Seven Long Times*. Houston, Tex.: Arte Público Press, 1995.

Tutuola, Amos. *The Palm-Wine Drinkard*. London: Faber & Faber, 1952; New York: Grove Press, 1994.

Twain, Mark. *The Adventures of Huckleberry Finn*. 1884; New York: W. W. Norton, 1977.

Walcott, Derek. *Collected Poems, 1948–1984*. New York: Farrar, Straus and Giroux, 1986.

Walker, Alice. *The Color Purple*. 1982; Orlando, Fla.: Harcourt Brace Jovanovitch, 2003.

Welsh, Irvine. *Trainspotting*. New York: W. W. Norton, 1993.

———. *Marabou Stork Nightmares: A Novel*. New York: W. W. Norton, 1995.

———. *Filth: A Novel*. New York: W. W. Norton, 1998.

———. *Glue*. New York: W. W. Norton, 2001.

———. *Porno*. New York: W. W. Norton, 2002.

White, Tony. *Foxy-T*. London: Faber & Faber, 2003.

Williams, Saul. *The Dead Emcee Scrolls: The Lost Teachings of Hip-Hop*. New York: MTV, 2006.

II. HISTORY AND CRITICISM

Achebe, Chinua. *Morning Yet on Creation Day*. London: Heinemann, 1975.

Arac, Jonathan. *Huckleberry Finn as Idol and Target: The Functions of Criticism in Our Time*. Madison: University of Wisconsin Press, 1997.

Ashcroft, Bill, Gareth Griffiths, and Helen Tiffin. *The Empire Writes Back: Theory and Practice in Post-Colonial Literature*. London: Routledge, 1989.

Bailey, Richard W. *Images of English: A Cultural History of the Language*. Ann Arbor: University of Michigan Press, 1991.

Baker, Houston A., Jr. *Blues, Ideology, and Afro-American Literature: A Vernacular Theory*. Chicago: University of Chicago Press, 1984.

Bhabha, Homi K. *Nation and Narration*. London: Routledge, 1990.

Brathwaite, Kamau. *History of the Voice: The Development of Nation Language in Anglophone Caribbean Poetry*. London and Port of Spain, Trinidad: New Beacon Books, 1984.

Ch'ien, Evelyn Nien-Ming. *Weird English*. Cambridge: Harvard University Press, 2004.

Crowley, Tony. *Standard English and the Politics of Language*. Urbana: University of Illinois Press, 1989.

Dillard, J. L. *Black English: Its History and Usage in the United States*. New York: Random House, 1972.

———. *American Talk: Where Our Words Came From*. New York: Random House, 1976.

Fishkin, Shelley Fisher. *Was Huck Black? Mark Twain and African-American Voices*. New York: Oxford University Press, 1993.

Greenblatt, Stephen. *Learning to Curse: Essays on Early Modern Culture*. New York: Routledge, 1990.

Jones, Gavin. *Strange Talk: The Politics of Dialect Literature in Gilded Age America.* Berkeley: University of California Press, 1999.

Jones, Gayl. *Liberating Voices: Oral Tradition in African American Literature.* Harmondsworth, England: Penguin, 1992.

Kachru, Braj. *The Other Tongue: English Across Cultures.* Urbana: University of Illinois Press, 1982.

———. *The Alchemy of English: The Spread, Functions, and Models of Non-native Englishes.* Oxford: Pergamon Press, 1986.

Lamming, George. *The Pleasures of Exile.* London: Michael Joseph, 1960.

Mannoni, Octave. *Prospero and Caliban: The Psychology of Colonization.* 1950; Ann Arbor: University of Michigan Press, 1991.

Mencken, H. L. *The American Language: An Inquiry into the Development of English in the United States.* New York: Knopf, 1936.

Nero, Shondel, ed. *Dialects, Englishes, Creoles, and Education.* Mahwah, N. J.: Lawrence Erlbaum Associates, 2006.

Ngũgĩ wa Thiong'o. *Decolonizing the Mind.* London: James Curry, 1981.

North, Michael. *The Dialect of Modernism: Race, Language, and Twentieth-Century Literature.* New York: Oxford University Press, 1994.

Paulin, Tom. *A New Look at the Language Question.* Dublin: Field Day, 1983.

Platt, John, Heidi Weber, and Ho Mian Lian. *The New Englishes.* London: Routledge, 1984.

Rushdie, Salman. *Imaginary Homelands: Essays and Criticism, 1981–1991.* New York: Viking, 1991.

Said, Edward. *Culture and Imperialism.* New York: Knopf, 1993.

Soyinka, Wole. *Art, Dialogue & Outrage: Essays on Literature and Culture.* Ibadan, Nigeria: New Horn Press, 1988.

Viswanathan, Gauri. *Masks of Conquest: Literary Study and British Rule in India.* New York: Columbia University Press, 1989.

Walder, Dennis. *Postcolonial Literatures in English: History, Language, Theory.* Oxford: Blackwell, 1998.

Young, Robert J. C. *Colonial Desire: Hybridity in Theory, Culture and Race.* London: Routledge, 1995.

Yule, Colonel Henry, and A. C. Burnell. *Hobson-Jobson: A Glossary of Colloquial Anglo-Indian Words and Phrases, and of Kindred Terms, Etymological, Historical, Geographical and Discursive.* 1886; London: Routledge, 1985.

Zabus, Chantal. *The African Palimpsest: Indigenization of Language in the West African Europhone Novel.* Amsterdam: Rodopi, 1991.

ACKNOWLEDGMENTS

THIS COLLECTION began its life as an undergraduate course at St. John's University. For that reason I would like first to thank the SJU English Department, especially Steve Sicari and Derek Owen, for encouraging me to teach this unusual class. The adventurous and insightful students of English 3690 contributed greatly to my understanding of vernacular literature. In particular, Saonjie Hamilton led me to Paul Keens-Douglas's poem "Wukhand," Claudia Navarrete offered valuable advice on how to read some selections, and Jenn Lebowitz reflected thoughtfully on her encounter with the literature. It was Jonathan Arac's book *Huckleberry Finn as Idol and Target: The Functions of Criticism in Our Time* that gave me the initial idea for a course based around creolized Englishes in a comparative context. For suggestions on writers to include in both the course and the resulting anthology, I am indebted to Tanya Agathocleous, Chaya Bhuvaneswar, Amanda Bower, Tisa Bryant, Kirsten Cole, Michael Cooper, Michael Malouf, Josh Miller, Marisa Parham, Lisa Outar, Lily Shapiro, Abby Sider, Michael Siff, H. Anna Suh, Robin Varghese, Wendy Walters, Susan Wilk, Monty Worth, and beyond all others Jolisa Gracewood, my unofficial coeditor, who introduced me to many of the selections, carefully edited my writing, and shared my enthusiasm for the project. Arthur Sherman of the St. John's University library helpfully ordered many of the books, and the Brooklyn Public Library shuttled others to my local branch. It was through the advice and guidance of Sarah Piel and Inkwell Management's Lori Andiman, Michael Carlisle, and Andrew Levine that *Rotten English* landed in the capable hands of Morgen Van Vorst and Amy Cherry at Norton. Jahan Ramazani kindly advised on many aspects of the anthology's organization. Fred Courtright of the Permissions Company patiently and competently marshaled a complicated transcontinental permissions process. Amy Robbins thoughtfully and meticulously copyedited the manuscript. Orin Herskowitz commented on the introduction, served as a test audience for some selections (along with Lily Shapiro and my English 3690 students), scanned, faxed, and assisted in innumerable other ways. Julie Diamond provided general support and encouragement throughout. The memory of Eqbal Ahmad continues to inspire. Finally, as a working parent I would also like to thank the people who kept my children safe and happy while I researched, taught, and wrote: Carrie Lynch, Mark-Joshua Kortlucke-Ortega, and the staff of P.S. 261 and the Montessori Day School of Brooklyn.

CREDITS